'The Swoop'
by John Clark.

This edition published 2020.

John Clark asserts his rights to be identified as the author of
this work under European Law and International
Conventions.

'The Swoop", Volume 3 of 'The Moses Hoffman Trilogy' is a
work of fiction and any resemblance to characters living or
dead are purely coincidental, except for references to people
who are clearly in the public domain.

Bibliografische Information der Deutschen
Nationalbibliothek:
Die Deutsche Nationalbibliothek verzeichnet diese
Pubikation in der Deutschen Nationalbibliografie,
detaillierte bibliografische Daten sind im Internet über
dnb.dnb.de abrufbar.

Copyright: John Clark, 2008 & 2020.

Herstellung und Verlag: BoD -Books on Demand,
Norderstedt.
This edition printed and distributed by BoD, Germany.

A BERLIN PICTURE COMPANY PUBLICATION.

ISBN: 978 3750413689

"THE SWOOP"

by

John Clark

The Moses Hoffman Trilogy
Volume 3

A BERLIN PICTURE COMPANY PUBLICATION
2020

CHAPTER 1.

A quiet day in tranquil surroundings.
No wind, no rain.
Mild and sunny, midway between solstice and equinox.
Nothing much is happening, so Amanda settles down to read.
She is content and the myrtles are flourishing.
The year is going well and summer is coming to the green hills of Arizona. The Mimosa is blooming in the kitchen. In the fridge, there are three red peppers, a tin of tomato concentrate, two bars of chocolate, butter, a bundle of fresh pondweed and three duck eggs. She decides she'll go to a restaurant that night, unwraps one of the bars of chocolate.
She starts reading as she nibbles.
"The Great British Crash[1] was christened 'The Swoop' after a weekend-long meeting of Ministers with branding advisor Jim Tewkesbury[2], whose team packaged the whole phenomenon with a set of proposals slammed together in less than three weeks, then managed to sell it to an uncomplaining electorate

---

1 There is some uncertainty as to the exact year following the solar calendar revision. Subsequently, it was concluded that the whole crisis had been provoked by the misguided assumption that risk could be sold as an asset via the so-called derivatives market, a concept initiated in Chicago.
2 James Helen Tewkesbury, the official biography in seven volumes is available on "pedia".

with extraordinary success."
Amanda adds a question mark of her own, then carries on reading.
The policies met with almost universal approval. The summer had been dry and hot. People were thirsting for something to cheer about, after the England cricket team's shock defeat in their first ever test match against the Netherlands.[3]
Mortgage debt, bought up by the Ministry of Finance for ten cents in the Euro, was decreed a 'heritage investment in the future'. They would give the Ministry a twist on its old name, calling it the 'National Treasury' to succour a sense of well-being, as government debt was replaced by the 'wealth of housing equity', only one of Tewkesbury's neat turns of phrase. Parity with the Euro enabled Ministers to ditch the Pound Sterling, with swiftly minted Euro-Pound coins quickly entering circulation. A clever bit of sidestepping by the European Central Bank President saw the term lira re-introduced in Turkey and Italy, reviving the once proud 'pound' sign outside the UK. In a single deft afternoon of administrative finesse, she enabled all Europe to benefit from the long history of a currency created in Ancient Rome and hammered into shape by the mints of Anglo-Saxon England. Tewkesbury is also credited with the nickname 'puro', which advertisers hooked onto with alacrity.
'The Swoop' was a sound money policy that sounded good.

This all helped the British to salvage their lost pride, without improving their demonstrably slender understanding of arithmetic. Considering the scale of their losses, pride was hardly on anyone's agenda anyway and very few people wanted to calculate the true extent of their impoverishment. The warning signs had been there for all to see as early as 2007.[4] '

---

3 Van der Valk's double century for Holland and her hat-tricks in England's second innings sealed the victory.
4 In London, the Bank of England's executive director for

Amanda skips the next section, which was quoted in every book of english history written in the last two hundred and fifty years, vilifying Eric Selby in a way that had once been reserved for Guy Fawkes.[5] Then she reads the introduction to volume 2, which is where she expects to spend most of her time compiling a basic guide to the Swoop for herself.
Her attention is momentarily distracted by a group of drunks who rush past on their way to an ice-hockey match.
They are soon gone.
All is calm.
The dull green acacias regain their pinkish hue and rock gently from side to side as Amanda reads line by line.

'The financial sector shed staff in their foreign currency departments as the need for meaningless transactions diminished, but that was a side issue. Calls for sympathy strikes in solidarity with the redundant bankers fell on deaf ears, as Tewkesbury had predicted in his notorious private letter to the Prime Minister[6] , which became known as the Titanic Note, 'no more lifeboats for sinking financial ships'. He had caught the mood of the moment. Financial services soon became pariah professions[7], 'sub-prime', in the jargon of the moment, as the

---

financial markets, Paul Tucker, gave a speech in which he said there was a real risk that there could be a 'feedback loop' between the financial markets and real economy that would result in a downward spiral." The Guardian, December 2007
see also: "Northern Blob a Study in Competence" Tewkesbury, J.H., Fabian Society Pamphlet, 2014
5 See Appendix C.
6 Edward Smith, Founding Leader of the Contrivative Party.
7 The worship of central bankers over the past decade has been shown for what it was, a mere shift of blind faith from one group of fallible tunnel-visionaries to another. They have proved no better defenders of the public interest than

entire sector was blamed for undermining the economy with false promises of prosperity and systemic pilfering. This wasn't Greece. Britain would never settle for austerity.[8]

"No-one really cares what money is called, just so long as everyone agrees that 1 is 1 in the accounting programmes," the pragmatic ECB President had boldly asserted during an impromptu press conference from her office in Prague.[9]
A collective sense of relief swept throughout the land. House price madness was over.'
One of the fastest readers in the department, Amanda then turns to a series of documents prepared by the Court of Inquiry, who had investigated Tewkesbury's relationship with Eric Selby. The Court of Inquiry had taken five years to turn up precisely nothing by way of new evidence. She is sceptical. It feels good. Something will come of her efforts, she is sure.
 She reads more.
 'The Swoop' was most remarkable for seeing in a new era of productive prosperity, whose benefits lasted well into the middle decades of the twenty first century and brought Tewkesbury the Nobel Prize for Marketing[10] in 2035, shortly

---

their forebears during the great crash of 1929. The sickening spectacle of those responsible walking off with millions of pounds of other people's money in bonuses has rightly put bankers akin to mafia racketeers in public esteem. Simon Jenkins, The Times, London, May 2008.
8 Determinist economists have long maintained that the ever increasing price of oil was also partly to blame. see: Blither, T., The Real World, 2120 Pergament Press, Goolong, New South Wales.
9 ECB – European Central Bank – a financial bureaucracy.
10 Previously known as the Nobel Prize for Economics, the award was renamed following the Morgan Commission's conclusion that economies and markets follow economic theory in the same way that sales respond to advertising and

before he was lost at sea on the ill-fated maiden voyage of the Royal Yacht Britannia. A couple of years short of retirement, this energetic 67 year old, this darling of the British Left, the man who had coined the term 'social democratist' as part of the Swoop campaign, seemed destined for another term as Secretary General of SemInt, the Semantic League of Interaction. Instead, he was dead and there were ten thousand suspects on the police list of potential assassins, ranging from deluded dentists to little old ladies who believed in nest-eggs.

This was why 89% of Britains polled believed that he had been murdered. They were proved right, not only by successive network belief tests, but also by the trial and conviction of Eric Selby[11] and other members of the infamous 'Legacy Gang'.

A set of alarms distract Amanda from her reading, turning the acacias blue, but they are quickly reset and she can continue. She ought to feel hungry, but the feeling soon passes. She has the uncomfortable feeling that her colleagues are massing in expectation of some breakthrough that she doesn't expect to happen. Sometimes research brings unexpected stress. Amanda just carries on reading.

With the business in property loans at an end, intangible trades and loss of goodwill forced the British Banks to amalgamate into three small associations, the Direct Debit Group, whose cards were the only ones now accepted by cash

---

marketing campaigns. The 'theories' of economics were all found to be completely worthless. Only their value as marketing tools could be verified, hence the change of name, which was initiated in 2027. see: pedia.

11 Selby, E – UKM/AEP1624/534FGQA Readers are warned that unauthorised biographies and hagiographies are not to be relied upon.

machines, Rump Asset Management, better known as RAM[12], rent collectors from the semi-detached suburban poor and London Repo [13], whose tough guy bailiffs became familiar figures at motorway interchanges and supermarket car parks, intercepting cars for roadside auction. While European bus operators offered tours for Romanians and Bulgarians on the lookout for second hand cars, Britain's debtors suddenly took a liking to public transport and left their Audis and BMWs at home, or rented garage space with their dwindling pool of prosperous friends. The road building programme was declared redundant and motorway building work ground to halt. The reduction in CO2 output set an example that almost saved the planet.

Young Eric Selby not only saw his career prospects diminish, but the familiar surroundings of his suburban childhood were erased in a matter of weeks.[14] Visiting his parents in their new home became a torment, with Fiona clicking away at her needles and his father escaping to the pub whenever he could. Hardly surprising then, that Eric turned first to crime and finally to murder, but before considering that epic tale of plunder, we need to understand his career as one of a new breed of politician, committed to the elimination of waste and the elision of fiscal risk.

The next footnote, a general proviso attached to all historic documents, makes Amanda smile.

---

12 RAM was subsequently renamed as Royal Asset Management in 2022, following the Tewkesbury Commission's recommendations.

13 London Repo is currently a section of the Cosmopolitan Police Economics Division.

14 Crime in Context – the collapse of family structures and triggering criminal behaviour – a compendium, Schroeder G & Fischer J (Eds), Bushlands Press, Texas, 2040.

THE SWOOP

This report harks back to an era before the empathic miasma replaced archaic networking and reflects the curiously extreme forms of individuality prevalent in this early modern society, when concepts of ideology, sexual orientation and net individual worth were accorded great note.

She stops reading.

Her specialism as a historian sets her aside the mainstream. Amanda tracks the archives for surviving websites and is able to read half a dozen forms of code, the antique html and its successor xml, which still provides a Rosetta stone key to lost early languages. This was all stuff defined before the era of quantum nets and the global hologram that sustains the Miasma. After half a dozen courses in metadata structures, a couple of years ago, she had been given a permit allowing to look at the archive as a preferred researcher. She has even ventured into paper-based documentation, though she finds this curiously long winded form of communication hard to evaluate. People seemed to have written all kinds of classes of documentation, from short notations of objects they desired, the so-called 'shopping lists', to declarations of affection referred to as 'love letters' and even purported to express their wishes following their deaths, creepy to read and scary to appreciate, documents known as a 'last will and testament', as if there was going to be a very last moment at sometime in their lives.

Professor Josephson had warned her away from this necromancy, with its predictions of who would acquire what, when the subject demised. She knew that demise was inappropriate for subjects like herself and had been warned not to torment herself with questions of mortality. "Get tangled up with that and you'll catch religion," he cautioned her gently.

No matter, she really needed Selinsky to come back from holiday before tackling any more of the printed stuff.

Amanda herself had been created as part of the 37th Framework Programme of the European Union Information Society Programme[15] following the 'General Agreement on People and Characters'[16] that is probably the Balaban Islanders'[17] greatest collective contribution to human knowledge, the 'Pure Thought' Programme. Devised following their discovery of 'separation', the programme enables the isolation of higher mental functions from bodily co-ordination and basic instincts without disturbing the equilibrium of character attributes and sensation, 'Pure Thought' has been accepted as the pinnacle of 'knowledge based societies'. Thankfully, Amanda is fully committed to the 'Global Governance Directive'.[18] and its Code of Ethics, with none of the soft edges that marred the first generation characters (see deletions[19]).

She has become one of the fondest personas in the Miasma and has regularly risen to the top million, though she normally hovers between 2,3 and 2,5 of the permitted 12million characters who have been accorded free will and full electoral enfranchisement.

At the last election, after a great deal of consideration, Amanda voted for the government to be re-elected.

The Balaban Islanders had been extraordinarily perceptive when they proposed the 12 million limit. With the global population reaching the marginal 15billion level, they had recognised that human decision making seems to work best in communities with a population between 3 and 15 million. Beyond that figure, either a 'strong man' with dictatorial

---

15 www.cordis.lu
16 The rubric of the accord can be found as Appendix 1.
17 A mid-Atlantic equatorial archipelago
18 The Directive is ubiquitous.
19 Deletions – access denied.

tendencies emerges, or the body politic atrophies, or both.[20] They also recognised the temperamental patterns that ensured that about 1,000 users per character would provide coherence, that dose of common sense everyone seeks in their leaders. This meant that 'indirect democracy' proved very effective, with everyone enjoying the potential of level 2 enfranchisement to express their wishes and assert whatever influence they could via proportional representation. Centuries of party politics had demonstrated that common sense is a elusive and transitory quality, effectively effaced by universal suffrage.

Now, everyone has been given a voice, if not a vote.

As expected when the Miasma was introduced, about 70% of characters are non-functional, providing a playground for sports fans and hedonists, gardeners and other obsessives. Julian Beckham and Marge Potter were the pinnacle of this strange pyramid of personal pleasure, each attracting twenty or thirty million simultaneous users, who refine and wallow in football skills and sexual adventures of remarkable authenticity. Anyone who claims never to have enjoyed these characters is lying. The stats reveal that every adult on earth has logged in to both Julian and Marge with dogged regularity from adolescence on.

The Balaban Islanders were even credited with inventing the hives, where any-one can subsist in a framework of simple stimulation, pleasure, pain, erotic ecstasy, gluttony, or endless sleep. The hive zone entraps 30% of the global population for at least 40% of their lives, people affectionately known as the Pratchet, or sometimes Web-2 personalities. There was something unexplained about the precise attribution, but since the Balaban Islanders[21] were happy to claim credit for anything,

---

20 Stalin & Rice, "Comparative Intolerance", Balaban Books, 2031. see also Italy (anach).
21 The Balaban Islands will be officially submerged in 2350, the inhabitants resettled and their resources transferred to the Miasma Licensing Agency . All shipping

no-one else bothered to come forward to take responsibility for this rather demeaning initiative.

Midway in the hierarchy is the Temple, respectfully according the sensibilities of prayer and meditation a status somewhat higher than the hives, though there has been a continuing controversy whether 'spiritual well-being', which turned out to be a booming general buzz of baby-like stimulation, should really be consigned as a 'hive' option for the religiously deluded. Much to the modest pride of Buddhist monks everywhere, 'Om' has become the most commonly used word of all humanity, while Catholics were globally appeased, as the most popular named character in Templar affairs is simply known as 'The Pope'.[22] The Vatican had also held out for a 35% cut of revenue from all religious subscriptions, which made them the 17th richest organisation on the planet.[23]

has been warned.

22 The Trans-Denominational Synod of 2044 instructed Christians everywhere to assume the meditational Om was in reality a decayed version of the anglo-saxon exclamation "Oh Mother", itself an abbreviation of a Marian cult chant which entered the liturgy following the Conference of Australasian Bishops in 2033.

23 Interim financial rankings by Standard Economics:
i) Standard Economics
ii) Guzzle Inc.
iii) Porn Proof Pleasure GmbH
iv) The Quantification Corporation
v) Emotional Liability Ltd.
vi) FIFA
vii) The American Food and Drug Administration (Beijing) S.A.
viii) Associated Porn (private equity)
ix) Hive Huddle Maintenance.
x) Billinda & Sons.
xi) Mr Fred Q. Smithson
xii) Tewkesbury Investments.

The Balabans were clever enough to recognise the limits of talent, enthusiasm and determination. Despite the gradually increase in population, the world has never spawned more than 7,000 Universities, each with around 500 competent professors within their much larger academic bodies, covering everything from high energy physics to archaeology. There have never been more than two per cent of the population with a useful commitment to politics, either at local, or regional level, with about the same proportion of good managers and administrators in industry and the public sector. Of course, the do-gooders, activists, gossips and busy-bodies created a useful bridge between the decision makers and the host of people to whom they are responsible.

When the Miasmatic Present was adopted,[24] named characters were originally based on the membership of learned societies and associations, who were each accorded a provisional batch of identities. There had been surprisingly little bickering over names. The French took Diderot, Chauvin and Deneuve.[25] The Caribbean were happy with Fidel, Bob, Viv and Toussaint. The Germans had a long discussion over Max Planck as there were already over 70 research institutes bearing his name, but

---

xiii) Global Canalisation and Concrete.
xiv) Dreamtime Deliveries Pty.
xv) Miasma Patents A
xvi) Power Unlimited (Political)
xvii) Miasma Licencing Agency.
xviii) Power Unlimited (Energy)
xix) The Correction Facility
xx) Vatican
These recent figures reveal the Vatican has fallen three places in the rankings since this text was last revised at 03.00hrs.
24 Global Democracy - Edict 1 of the Founding Council
25 France also retains the use of Thomson generating codecs.

eventually found enough other worthies, like Marlene and Wolfgang to cover the gaps. The British were delighted to hang on to Newton, Faraday and Watt, with Thatcher, Ballard, Dougan and Bevan following soon after.

The Americans had real identity problems and ditched Smithson for Edison, because at least they thought they knew who Edison was and it avoided confusion with Fred Q. Smithson the well-known entrepreneur and social benefactor.[26]

Envious of the Israeli's wealth of biblical names, the whole theological community was eventually placated by their generosity and a long list of old testament prophets were soon in virtual existence through the revivalist movement.[27]

Only the use of alter egos raised significant ethical problems, apart from French objections to the use of Chinese as the main stem language for translation, but a working group to monitor dualities was set up under Laing, after Freud's resignation and little more was heard on the issue after the working committee chose to resolve a series of linguistic questions, before publishing any further reports.

The fundamental mechanism of consortia building had been developed by the European Union[28], as a way of ensuring conformist research projects, but it had a smoothing effect on political decision making that encouraged a set of attitudes that would leave the status quo unchallenged. Egoism was at bay

26 The decision to use historic characters for naming purposes had two goals, to enable immediate character recognition for users and to avoid the confusion of names deriving from the archaic avatar communities. Although rejected by the USA as a national champion, Smithson was later to achieve his own position of prominence.

27 The State of Israel was considerably smaller before the capital was relocated to Rome in 2070.

28 The European Union - A Fundamentalist Neo-Christian Capitalist Non-Aggression Pact, (see also " Corruption", Tewkesbury 2013).

and its temperamental enthusiasts were quickly marginalised. They became a significant source of unbridled resentment, which, to this day, remain one of the principal threats to successful governance.

After a dedicated afternoon reading, Amanda goes onto the balcony to watch the sunset
Smoke curls from a distant factory chimney.
A grey heron sneezes.
A crow sings.
A fox cub yelps.
A beaver lies lazy in the river.
Then a kingfisher flashes blue as it flies downstream.
The Caucasian Wing Nut Trees are shedding strings of seeds.
Rainclouds are gathering on the horizon as the sun breaks through to create a marvellous spectacle of evening pinks and blues.
There's an ominous roll of distant thunder.
Amanda catches sight of her reflection, dark hair, slender as a Burmese heroine, her light brown eyes shimmering with gold, in the glow of the setting sun. She is beautiful, talented and irresistible, she concludes. It is time to head for the 'history room', her favourite place, where she'll run into friends and colleagues. It isn't so much a space, she tells herself, as a state of mind.

CHAPTER 2

Joe Smather greets Amanda with his usual amiable allusions to her physical attractiveness, 'hmmm, nice ass', (he pays the fine) and receives an affectionate grin in return, 'your's too', before they settle down to work.

For him, she is like the perfect student, gorgeous, gamine, receptive, attentive and intelligent. He could flirt, but knows nothing would ever come of it and enjoys his place as father figure to her curiosity, rather than the wicked uncle of her underwear. Amanda treats Joe the way she treats all men – he is biological, she is a digital entity. Until something very special indeed happens, their interaction is informatic and will stay that way. No need to make a fuss, she'd told him more than once, that's just the way it is, you bio, me digital, get used to it. Nowadays, the majority prefer things that way. You'd have to be a hyper-sensitive to recognise the difference were it not for the formality of initial handshakes between systems.

"I'm still worried about my brother," he confides, as they began to sift the files.

"Well, the life of a free-rover was his own choice," she answers blandly, wondering why Joe has chosen a pink cotton pullover for the meeting. "I admire his resolve. It must be strange having the Miasma blocked for so many weeks at a time."

"Oh, we get to interact once every couple of months," Joe says defensively, "which is a damned sight more than most families manage even when they're permanent."

"I know, it surprises me how little of real value emerges between family members." Amanda can be very digital when it suits her. She isn't 'supposed' to be able to appreciate the rich subtleties of human relationships, which is just more official garbage in Joe's opinion. Amanda has a very highly developed sense of what Joe calls feminine intuition.

"We always assume historically that family integration was higher, but I'm not so sure. Anyway, Bill seems to have wandered further off the beaten track. Further away than ever. I haven't heard from him for three months."

"You could run a deep trawl," she suggests indifferently.

Joe pauses before replying. "I could, but he would get to know I'm looking for him and he gets upset if he thinks I'm prying."

"He's probably found a new girlfriend," says Amanda with a cheerful grin.

"You think so? It's always a possibility, I suppose."

"Well, that was what seemed to be the case last time, no suppose about it."

"Yes, but we can't always trust what 'seems to be the case', unless it really is the case."

"Hang on Joe, I think Lisa's coming," Amanda interrupts, thinking Joe is being a little too earnest about his brother's whereabouts.

"Oh good," he says, grinning. "Then we should have a chance to catch up on Selby's first weeks during the Swoop."

Lisa comes in with a broad smile, strokes the acacias affectionately, turns to Amanda and Joe, hugs them both, takes a seat at the end of the table, then floods them with information. She is tall and freckled, with an Aleutian sense of humour. "I think I've got to the bottom of that, as far as it is reasonable to go. What do you think, Amanda?" Lisa can be disconcertingly digital for a living breathing young woman with enviable genetic credentials and full biological status. She'll turn out to be a manager, that one, if she's not careful. Selinsky, the anally retentive archi-bore had said that.

Amanda swiftly surveys the information, sifts out the speculative elements and returns a much truncated version to their thought patterns.

"I knew you'd do that," Lisa complains. "You've set the whole issue of how he met Braunovsky on one side."

"That's my job," replies Amanda. "It was just a first sift, would you like me to leave it in for now?"

Joe has second thoughts before suggesting they run the sequence with Lisa's conjectures included. "We probably have enough time before the others get here."

"Is that OK, Lisa?" asks Amanda.

"Sure, let's go," she says brightly, "it'll save us arguing with Robert till later."

"Right," Joe confirms. "I think we can all agree that Robert would insist we run a reality check before following up on this and I frankly don't have either the time, or the inclination. I mean, God knows, 'reality', who cares?"

They all laugh at the oldest Miasmatic joke of all.

"Who needs all this network shit anyway?" says Joe.

Having reached consensus, Amanda undoes the pause and lets the sequence flow. The experience begins with a simple warning that the material is a personalised version of events and they sit back to see what will happen. As it starts, Amanda gives a little gasp of surprise. "Oh Lisa, this is really good work, it feels so authentic."

Joe and Lisa find themselves standing in the queue for tickets at the Tate Modern[29] on London's Bankside. Lisa's long blonde

---

29 The Tate Modern was located in the former Bankside Power Station, a compelling example of Tewkesbury's observation that the British tended to tack new distractions

hair sparkles with a dozen highlights and her healthy skin is in marked contrast to the puffy complexions of the school-teachers standing in front of her. Joe catches sight of a face reflected in the glass ticket booth and realises he has those swarthy good looks Englishwomen admire and despise with equal enthusiasm. 'Hairy brute,' says the husband to himself. 'Fancy him,' thinks the wife. 'I'll do you, so long as you have a shave first, or rough around a three day beard.'

So that is what Lisa wants, Joe tells himself, sneaking another glance at his reflection.

Eric Selby is standing some five places behind them.

Joe feels a trickle of excitement run along his spine. He is only a few feet away from one of the most notorious figures of the early modern era.

This is history and this is the thrill of being a reconstructionist historian. There is Eric Selby, a slight figure, an amiable, pale looking young man with glasses. No-one had ever implied he was exceptional. Wearing a brown leather jacket and a pair of old jeans, he looks stressed, but so does everyone in London. Podgy figures and bad skin, the clinical impact of a culture that made intimate links between hard work, lies and greed, then compounds the issue with commuting, lack of sleep and wearing badly made shoes and suits for the office. Selby hasn't taken any notice of Joe. He seems to be eyeing up Lisa, until Amanda catches his attention.

Amanda is less than pleased. "Is this your idea of a joke?", she mutters from her place behind the glass of the ticket booth. "Hmmm, that will be forty eight pounds, two adults, or would you like 'day passes', they're only, er, sixty for both of you."

"Wait a moment," says Joe, reaching into his jacket pocket to retrieve a press pass. "I think you should let us in free with one of these."

"Amanda?" says Lisa in a controlling tone, "if Selby pays by

---

into old buildings.

bank card, could you please note the account number and the transaction code?"

Amanda rolls her eyes, scowls and tugs at a strand of hair that has come loose and flopped over her forehead. She never misses such obvious details as that!

Eric was known to have fifteen bank accounts and to use thirty-two credit cards[30], eighteen of which had reached their limit. Another eleven were used to maintain the minimum payments on the first eighteen and one was new, having arrived in the post three days after he had bought the weekly shop at a supermarket in Haringey. A shop assistant had asked if he needed more money and Eric had found it hard to say no, so he now had a rather pretty purple card claiming to come from the Commercial Bank of Rotherford of which there are no surviving records.

Amanda hands them the tickets, scowls and turns her attention to the next visitors. After them, it will be Selby's turn.

Lisa takes Joe by the hand and leads him into the gargantuan gallery. "He'll never suspect he's being followed by people who were ahead of him in the queue."

"He probably has no idea that anyone should be interested in him at this stage," Joe reminds her. "And the shock of discovering what we know about him would be traumatic. He was staring at you the way young guys do."

Lisa laughs. "I wonder how many of these visitors are observers like us? Do you think the queue will get longer and longer once people pick up on our findings?"

"All gallery and no art," says Joe, as they enter the cavernous main hall of the former power station. "A bit pompous really. Very Londony in its way. Makes you feel sad for the paintings they've entombed, especially the ones that were intended to be left leaning against a studio wall, or were destined for a friend's bedroom."

"This was an era of suppressed personalities. Everyone was too

---

30 A system of money lending at high rates of interest.

worried about money to be themselves, so they behaved according to more or less fashionable assumptions about how people should go about things. It was all a symptom of trivialisation. Let's go find the bar."

"Is this the spot where the young lawyer killed himself?"

"Yes, one of the places Eric will want to see."

"He jumped from up there, as high as he could get and, er, then he landed about here."

Lisa points at a repainted patch on the concrete floor. She wonders whether to call for a reconstruction of the event, but decides against.

"Sad."

"Very, but one of London's best known urban legends. The overworked victim of rampant careerism."

Joe shudders, "I'd rather be alive than be a legend."

"OK, look, he's going into the café," Lisa whispers as Eric walks past them, his shoes making an unusual, but nevertheless irritating squeaking noise on the over polished floor.

"I wonder who he's going to meet?"

"You should know that. Didn't you check your homework? I'm sure I told you. According to 'All Known History', the sister, they had a serious discussion that may have changed history, but you know how things get exaggerated. Anyway, they were supposed to have been particularly close."

"What's she like?" Joe asks, wondering whether his memory is playing tricks on him.

"Small, fat and venomous, according to Smithson," says Lisa.

"That's what I've always thought. Well, either they were wrong about the girl, or Smithson was wrong, or some-one is playing a joke on us. Small and fat is oh so very very seriously wrong."

"Is that some-one playing the joke called Amanda by any chance?"

"She has the key to 'all known history'."

There's a sudden flash, "NO".

"Wait till we get back. Amanda's not allowed to meddle with the data. Not to that extent. She can smooth a bit but its supposed to be cosmetic so the enactment feels genuine, not a kind of character rewrite. I mean, this girl, she's gorgeous and well, incredible, not small and fat. It makes you wonder what else is not quite as it first seems."[31]

They buy something to drink that looks like a turquoise printing error with straws and go to the table next to Eric's. He's talking excitedly to the tall skinny woman who is in her late thirties, an exotic beauty with dark hair, flashing eyes and perfect coffee coloured skin.

"She looks like one of your fantasies, Joe."

"Squat she isn't and she isn't one of my fantasies, not yet, but who the hell can she be? I've seen photos of sister Jessica. Smithson was right. This is some-one else."

"Nice pullover."

Joe splutters. "Flatters her figure. Nice? She's er stunning."

The pearly grey sleeveless sweater with a high collar was almost fashionable that season, but only suited slim women, so they hadn't sold as well in England as they had in Italy. It is not for nothing that the phrase 'bella figura' has no equivalent in english.

Then Joe tries to overhear their conversation using the directional microphone in his fountain pen.

"And she has an unusual accent, archaic, a bit of a lilt, yet it sounds like a version of British english. Its not Australian, nor Argentinian."

"They have already begun plans to make the Swoop permanent," the woman tells Eric. "We'll all be strapped for cash, all the time, forever and a day, but they intend to make life less expensive. Clever mix. It's outrageous, robbery with appeasement."

---

31 The security system for 'All Known History' has Level 12 approval.

"I don't understand. What do you mean, Mona?"

Mona – Now they know. Joe checks the name and discovers it was originally Scottish. He placed the accent, a town called Aberdeen, which he knows nowadays is a small fishing village on the Caledonian mainland, but had a long and prosperous history as a centre for old oil. He logs her as Mona from Aberdeen. Physical details and analytics to follow.

There's a slight sway to her voice that Joe enjoys. Actually he's entranced. She's captivating. He's predictable. Lisa is unimpressed.

"Your friend Mr. Tewkesbury," Mona says pleasantly, "is proposing a new form of housing finance, permanent leasehold. They are going to appropriate the land, then rent it out on leases to the people who use it. They will pay next to nothing. he's calling it the 'Peppercorn Plan'. A plot of land big enough for a house and a garden will costs only fifty a year. All people will have to pay towards their homes will be the construction costs. They've pitched it so low that farmers will no longer be tempted to sell land for development. The packaging is to be presented as a plan to save the countryside. It will also ensure young farmers can acquire small-holdings when they leave college for intensive green food production."

"Hell-fire and damnation," Selby exclaims, with tears in his eyes.

"What?"

"That is all I have left. They've screwed my career. Now, Dad has had to sell up in Rickmansworth, all I have is the land in Yorkshire. Grandpa divided it equally between Jessica and me. 600 acres each, well above sea level, but south of the promised ice-line, not far from Bawtry, near the airport. It will be used for building one day, when the sea level rise forces them to abandon Hull and Goole. Grandpa already has the development rights in place. That's the plan. He thinks it will be lakeside in the near future. It won't be worth a penny if this goes through.

How long do we have before their plans are made public?"

"Probably about three months, but maybe less. They need to get the legislation through Parliament, so they won't tell the press for a few weeks, unless someone leaks. The details are hellish and there will be almighty protests, except from the poor, but they don't matter, do they? Be good, my darling I have to get back to work. I'll see you tonight, my place, midnight, Oh, and don't bother showing up if you're drunk."

"Why midnight? We could meet up for dinner."

"Not tonight, darling. I'm seeing some people."

"Not my sort?"

"Eric, they are business, you are pleasure, enjoy, please me, and don't be late." She smiles to reveal a broad expanse of healthy teeth, then she dashes away.

"So he's got himself a girlfriend," says Lisa, pretending she hasn't notice the way Joe is disconcerted.

"Good for him, I wonder who she is? Mona from Aberdeen, born probably between 1970 and 1980. She doesn't look very Scottish, more Caribbean than North Sea. I didn't get a pingback when I tagged her name."

"Maybe her Mum and Dad were from Jamaica. We can trace her, or should we try to stick with him and find out more?"

"What time is it?"

"Four thirty."

"Seven and a half hours before midnight."

"Amanda will be furious, Johnson too."

"I don't care about Johnson. Can we fast forward?"

"But you do care about Amanda."

"You know I do. There's every justification to keep going. This Mona could be a major new figure in the whole field of Selby studies."

"And she's tasty, they'll love her in replication."

"I don't hold with the use of historical figures as fantasy models."

26

"Lisa, all these people have been dead for over a century, longer. Hey, here comes the sister. Oh, my God, she's unmistakable, the venomous little bitch herself."

"Oh, another of Johnson's clichés. The loathsome cowgirl."

"What are you trying to say?"

"Well, the other woman has been overlooked, so all the opprobrium fell on the sister. People have been trying to save time, pitching in on the bookmarks for this meeting, starting where the tag begins for Jessica's entrance, without bothering to track back a little to find out what happened just before, or if they did, not realising that the woman might be important. Penny pinching historians, none of them wanting to do the in depth research and pay for the extra half hour. Amazing."

"Just listen for once, will you? Eric seems to be telling her his news."

"Jess," Eric gasps, "we've got to move really fast and sell the land."

"Don't be silly, the values will recover before we need to sell."

"No. We've got to sell right away."

"Why Eric, why? Eric, have you been drinking?"

"There's a plan to collapse land values."

"What?"

"There will be a proposal soon."

Eric takes one of the café serviettes and scribbles something on it, then pushes it towards Jessica for her to read.

"Then it's probably true."

"Tewkesbury again, I'm sure, I can even follow the logic as far as it goes."

"I loathe these fucking people," says Jessica. "I mean, what was Thatcher's dream, a property owning democracy, that's what she wanted and that's what Britain is thanks to her and Blair. It works. That's what it always should have been, at least for the last three hundred years, since the civil war. They debated it then, in the seventeenth century, OlliCrom and that lot. Everyone who has an interest in a society should have a say and the people who have an interest in society are everyone who owns something. If you don't own anything you can fuck off. It's that simple. Owners have an interest, so they get to vote. A property owning democracy. You don't meddle with the definition, you give more people a chance to become owners. Then they are stakeholders and should have their say. Because they have a real interest in society, not just spongers and hangers-on, they will use their votes wisely. Actually, I wish they'd tried that in Iraq, they might have had more chance."

"Alec really enjoyed Iraq."

"Our dear cousin is a religious psychopath, even you know that, on top of which, the Army threw him out after that business in Basra. People do try to blame him for the Syria stuff, but I don't see that actually."

"You can fool some of the people all of the time and all of the people some of the time and by 'some of the time', I mean an election year. I'm sure that was Tewkesbury."

"Renew Labour, sounds catchy, the promise of all round improvements."

"When is the next election due?"

"Still three and a half years, if they last that long."

"Fooling around now, to be ready in time for the next election."

"Stop fooling me Eric and explain what Tewksy wants us to think."

"The cost of credit has gone through the roof and house prices have collapsed, so no-one can afford to sell, because of the losses, or buy because of the interest and the down payments. Stagnation and frustration, an economic crunch, just like the Americans. The low interest rate ploy didn't work, it just pushed everyone into austerity."

"We know that. Come on Eric, better please."

"Land values are the key. They can't build cheap new homes on expensive land, because they will still be unaffordable. So they have to collapse the price of land as well. Then they are going to introduce a scheme for people to buy new homes with prices based on the building costs."

"How much does it cost to build a house."

"You can do something nice for about sixty thousand."

"Is that all? You can't even buy a garage for that kind of money."

"Spread the costs over twenty years, that's about three thousand a year plus interest. Even at 12%, you can give people a home to buy for less than a thousand a month. Bring interest right down and you could bundle the whole thing for a hundred a week, which is less than most students pay for a room. Set that as the benchmark and the value of nearly all existing homes will stay under a hundred thousand, unless you have some sort of pompous mansion in Putney. The value is defined by the costs. A modest flat would cost next to nothing, which is all they are anyway. The only thing that's stopping it is the price of land. So, that's what Tewkesbury is going to do, collapse the price of land. Large parts of the insurance industry will begin to fold as well, which he says serves them right."

"It's dispossession."

"Not at all. Everyone can stay where they are, no problem, they just won't be the owners if they take up his offer, not officially. They'll swap the debts on their house for a long term lease that costs next to nothing. That way they won't have to sell up and downsize and their children can inherit the rights to the family home. Tewkesbury says that if you were born in London you should be able to live in London. Catchy proposition, isn't it. The housing thing isn't going to go away, apart from the bits that flood from global warming, or get crunched under a glacier."

"It won't be the first time."

"Forcing people to give up ownership. It's never happened here before."

"Yes it has, Sixteenth century, they dispossessed a lot of Catholics."

"Really?"

"Go to Church on Sunday," Jessica explains, "or pay a whopping fine, that's how it worked. Naturally, the recusants thought there would be hell to pay if they worshipped with the Anglicans. Pay the fine, or go to goal. Sell your land to pay the fine. For a good Roman Catholic the consequences of attending the English Church on Sunday was to face the threat of excommunication and eternal damnation via Rome, so the devout ones sold their homes and farms to the highest bidder and hoped for the best. The bidder would usually turn out to be someone with close links to the government. Shakespeare's[32] Dad got trapped that way."

Joe leans across to Lisa and whispers, "She knows more about early Britain than I do".

"Of course she does, she lived a long time ago and was a student there," Lisa reminds him.

"You think she read all the books?"

"Almost certainly, they taught everyone to read back then."

"Extraordinary."

"People put a lot of faith in books."

"Like the Bible and Koran?"

"Nah, twit, they trusted books. They trusted in the printed word and thought literacy was something wonderful. They even had public libraries, where anyone could go just to read things."

"But you couldn't tell what the author was thinking."

"That was the trick, you had to be pretty bright to work things out. Simple folk just settled for stories."

"They always have done."

"Look they're leaving."

---

32 Shakespeare, William – an english dramatist and poet, whose identity has now been confirmed as a 'character' in perpetuity.

"Do you think he'll lead us to Mona the skinny chick?"

"Don't show your age, Joe, she's a scrawny old hen in his eyes."

Joe doesn't seem convinced, "I wouldn't say exactly scrawny, more elegant and languidly flexible."

"Keep you fantasies to yourself please Joe," says Lisa tartly.

"Really Lisa, we're in reconstruction," Joe protest, "Anyway, she seems to be expecting him to play the cockerel."

Eric and Jessica are about to leave the gallery, but just as Joe and Lisa start to follow, to their annoyance, Amanda breaks in.

"Sorry guys, there's a discontinuity, you can't get closer now." She gives them a pert little smile, which she's been practising while doing her stint selling tickets, "We do have a general impression of London, if you'd like to continue, but no-one has ever caught sight of Eric. You need some more groundwork before it will make sense to proceed, I think we should discuss it in the Group, don't you? And Johnson is on his way. He'll want to hear all about this."

Joe and Lisa give one another a regretful look and agree to break off, and they are gently relocated by the Miasma.

Reconstructionism is not quite perfect and reconstructionists not always harmonious.

Should that be a surprise among historians?

"Hi Amanda, hi Lisa, hi Joe," Robert Johnson greets them as he arrives, "I got the message about your trip, exciting stuff, what did you find?"

"It was great to be where it all started, " Lisa said politely.

"Yes, I recall Eric and Jessica's conversation of course. I even have the transcript somewhere. You are lucky to have been there live."

He smiles and Amanda notes the glint of superiority reflected in his titanium framed spectacles.

"I'm surprised you haven't been there yourself," says Joe.
"I use my credits for more off-beat stuff. But it's great you went there. Two big factors people overlook when they take a look at early twenty-one England are essentially peculiar to Britain and both have their roots in the twentieth. I mean, we all know about the greed and the superficiality, taken as read, but we miss the bossiness of people at work, I can give you examples. People were expected to be 'on message' and talked about their bosses as 'control freaks'. There was a culture of pushiness, with people driven by managers of extreme determination, real furies, bi-polar, manic depressive managers. Very unhealthy, one of the seeds of trivialism. People took one look at who they were working for and retreated towards the infantile. Then, when we look at the property crash, it's easy to overlook something that started two, or three decades earlier, that strange business of dividing up houses that were intended for single families into lots and lots of small apartments, so two or three times as many people ended up living and paying to live under the same roof, but all of them assumed that it was theirs. How people blinded themselves to that kind of travesty is a mystery to me. Most of the buildings had been put up a hundred years before as modest family housing. A strange trick. They tried to make these old houses more habitable, and a weird culture of home improvement took root. On the one hand, speculators could sell off the apartments for more than the houses were worth as single homes, on the other, people were happy to be able to live closer to their work in the city centres, so they were willing to pay up.
    Children just got caught in the debris. People started going crazy adding things on to these shoddy buildings, extra bathrooms, kitchens, garages, winter gardens, decking, you name it. Really, they were just bolting new technology onto old frames, so it rarely worked. Then they started doing more and more, rebuilding places from the inside out, burrowing

underneath to create deep cellars for all kinds of purposes. Tewkesbury twigged that it would be much better to build anew instead of messing about with these nineteenth century places. He also realised that the only way to make a new start was to put a shock in the system and that is what he did. Rising sea levels helped[33], but it was his idea. The London Lakes Scheme[34] proved him right. Eric was one of the unlucky minority who lost out. There weren't many losers, but our friend Eric was certainly one of them. Sorry, got to leave you, meeting, great, soon..."

He's gone, even before the echoes of his voice have died away. Then, just as abruptly, he pops back in for a parting shot. Even Amanda quivers, as the other two jump with surprise, "For fucks sake Johnson!"

"Amanda!"

"Yeah, forgot, piece of advice," Johnson gabbles. "Just keep an eye on the niggles in his life, follow the niggles, that's it. Busy, busy, busy."

Then a click and he is absent.

"Fuck you! Asshole."

"Amanda!"

---

33 The general rise in sea levels of 30metres between the years 2000 and 2100 was amplified around the British coastline by the unusually high tidal range.

34 London Lakes were themselves lost as sea levels rose due to climate change and the world's land area was approximately 1% greater in the Pre-Miasma. Population density was 200 persons per square kilometre, rather than the miasmatic optimum of 1000, (100 square metres of land per capita, which is 33.3 metres^2). The land issue has been resolved by tiering, which ensures a natural cover of vegetation over all new structures and buildings constructed with a minimum of 5 subterranean cellar levels to each floor above ground. The world's deepest structure at Heathrow now belongs to Dreamland Deliveries.

"You shouldn't talk like that about someone," Joe remonstrates, for forms sake as much as annoyance.

"You know what I mean," replies Amanda, as the acacias vibrate with alarm.

"But we also know, that three months later, they created the British Land Bank, offering to wipe out their debt, then buy people out for 15% of the market value of their property with no legal fees and a free ten-year insurance policy with Palace Yard Assurance. Almost every home owner in the country took up on the offer and used it to pay off their credit cards. Quick fix. What they were really doing was to undermine the Banks' capital base. Without new investors, and who was likely to pose as a new investor in such times, the banks had no choice but to fold themselves into RAM!"

"Tewkesbury had his own agenda and his own share of genius."

"Old money to no money," Joe continues. "A revolution of their own making. Inside 5 years the country was more or less free of debt and mortgage costs no longer deterred the younger generation from setting up home. It was a fresh start, root and branch reform. There was lots of romance, lots of sex and lots of lovely babies. You have to give it to Tewkesbury, he had incredible luck. I'm amazed he got away with it. It took balls. So why did Eric end up murdering him nearly a quarter of a century later?"

"What was their slogan at that election, 'Last time we cured you of smoking, this time we'll cure you of debt'?"

"Tewkesbury broke every rule in the book, but he understood that money was just a symbol, an intangible symbol of exchange. If you look at a house one day and say its worth half a million, then you look at it the next day and say its worth forty thousand, the house hasn't changed. It's still somewhere for people to eat and sleep, cook dinner, make babies, bring up kids. It will still need the roof repairing sooner of later. That was the message they got through via movies and tv series.

Even if it isn't worth a thing, it will be here tomorrow and you can live in it."

"I don't understand why business wasn't hit."

"Another of Tewkesbury's perceptions. He understood how the gradual reduction in asset values as they are written down on the books meant that the value of businesses and industry is calculated in a completely different way to the valuation of private property. In business, it is assumed that the value of assets diminish, machines wear out, technology becomes outdated, buildings need to be repaired and rebuilt. Capital gets used up, that's the rule. It's quite possible to have a factory full of machines that are officially worth nothing, but they're working away and churning stuff out all the same. With property, people thought that a ruinous dump would be worth more from year to year. Opposites, but it doesn't matter."

Joe can see the others don't like what they're hearing, "Tewkesbury knew that economics is largely a matter of psychology, like the old story of grandfather's hammer, which had only had two new heads and three new shafts in a hundred years and was as good as it had ever been. No-one ever describes their home as fifteen cubic metres of reinforced concrete, forty-five metres of plastic tubes, a couple of trenches, a hundred metres of cable, a few hundred roof tiles and thirty lengths of timber, with eleven windows and nine doors, subdivided by a hundred odd square metres of plasterboard that required a thousand hours of labour to build. No, they say they have a charming modern cottage in a secluded setting on the outskirts of Liverpool. Well, not Liverpool, any more, of course, but Blackburn, or Bolton, or another of those heritage places."[35]

---

35 By 2180, the general rise in sea levels had encroached on the British cities of Leith, Hull, London, Southampton, Plymouth, Bristol, Cardiff, Liverpool and Glasgow. The Dutch barrier reef had protected Amsterdam, Rotterdam and Antwerp, however Bremerhaven had suffered 80%

"Joe," says Lisa firmly, "I have to go".
He was telling her things she already knew, but she wasn't going to tell him that.

---

destruction, while the ice scoured settlements to the north.

CHAPTER 3

Amanda only takes about 5% of her visitors seriously. The rest are either students, or browsers, people with a sudden enthusiasm sparked by some news item, or popular entertainment. She also has surges when anniversaries come around. As a founder member of the 'Symbols are Not Society Association', and a rather abrasive member at that, Amanda is wary of newcomers. Luckily, when Lisa and Joe left there were only two other regulars to cater for and she had the chance to talk to her mentor, Quentin Smithson.[36]

He is politely interested without being fascinated, but suggests she lets Lisa and Joe continue their glide-throughs of the Eric Selby archive to see if they can pick up a trail to the late-night rendezvous.

"If you can find the address, then this woman's identity should be fairly easy to track down. How many Monas were born in Scotland in the 1970's? Can't be that many, can it? Do you think she could be one of Tewkesbury's people?"

"I doubt it," replies Amanda. "They've all been researched to death. There's no dark lady in his sonnets."

"Pity. I could do with a new dark lady."

"You mean you've had one before, dear Quentin?"

"Oh, I have a collection at home," says Smithson, hoping to make light of his admission.

----

36 Mr. Fred Q. Smithson – see note 20.

Amanda laughs, "Damn, the Alaskans are down again. I wanted to keep an eye on Lisa."

"Is she interesting?"

"Yes, but not your type. Firstly she's genuinely female."

"Are you sure?"

"Yes"

"And secondly?"

"She's too nice for someone like you."

"You're a hard Mistress, Amanda."

Amanda's pleasure centres glow. "And you are very very greedy."

"I am, I am," cackles Quentin, "When my mind is up to it! Send me the reports darling, and I'll go over them tonight."

"Oh, the Alaskans are up, see you later."

Amanda envies anyone who has managed to get a place in Alaska. The tranquil blue sea, warm enough to bathe in all the year round, thanks to the Columbia current, yet with midsummer nights when the sun never sets. They had all the luck with climate change and the chance to seed the once barren landscape with only the choicest species of plant and animal. Lisa's house in Summit Valley is set on a hillside with drinking-water tapped from a mountain spring and a second source deep underground bringing thermal energy to the surface from one of the 57 volcanoes on the Aleutian Islands. The green plexiglass weed tank in her yard absorbs 200 personal units of CO_2 and the credits are enough for Lisa to follow any whim she pleases. The lungs of the earth.

Alaska has replaced the Amazon Basin as a symbol of abundance. The acacia trees in her yard are taller than the house. Silence is only broken by the rustle of the wind in the trees and the occasional yelp from Lisa's sheep as they wander across the hillside.

The bonds of friendship between Amanda and Lisa are probably as deep as possible for a Category 7 AI entity and a young woman. Their affection is as close to love as either dares admit and far richer than either of them had previously found with the 'men in their lives'.

"Hi, it's me, Amanda," she whispers in Lisa's ear.

Lisa's voice drops a register as she whispers a husky reply, "I've missed you."

A kind of a pair after five years of friendship, Lisa and Amanda try to meet up in private a couple of times a month, away from the attentions of the other historians. They talk about Joe, as usual, how he never seems to notice their affection.

"There's a simple enough explanation."

"I know. I think he's in love with someone we haven't met. He's not even flirty with anyone else. I did try," says Amanda, "I gave him a chance, but it wasn't, you know...it would never work."

"Poor romance."

"I did my best, but nothing there. I don't know who she is."

"Anyway he's too worried about his little brother Bill," Lisa says.

"Never mind him," says Amanda, as she runs her tongue down Lisa's spine.

"Wait a minute, I'm still pumping gas."

Lisa is sweating pleasantly, but continues to tread steadily on the pedals of her exercise bike and the little pumps gush a jet of coolant that freezes a white coat of oxygen, nitrogen and carbon dioxide crystals which drop as snowflakes into the store. Packed into blocks, the oxygen crystals will be loaded into steel flasks and delivered where-ever they are needed, or simply dumped in the deep ocean for local cooling and re-oxygenation. Clever use of the lingering deep permafrost meant the fifteen million Alaskans each process about ten kilos of crystal-ox a day and feed the CO_2 into their photo-synthetic weed tanks. The argon is sent off to the hives and the nitrogen forwarded by pipeline to the local fertiliser factory and the hospital.

Amanda can never quite get over the Alaskan smugness of living a virtuous environmental circle. Of all the people in the world, they were some of the few who could breathe easily and have a stash of credits in the bank. Famous for its lack of impurities, Alaskan Ox is welcome all over the globe and regularly sent up to the International Space Station for shipping Moonside, where its sold as the ultimate luxury product for everyone who aspires to earthly style. Lisa slows her pedalling to a halt and finishes her final kilo for the day. A final snowflake falls into the hod and she spins the wheel on the compressor to make the kilo block.

"What's the trouble with Joe's brother?"

Lisa wonders whether she should tell Amanda, then decides no harm will come of it, if she tells the truth. They trust one another enough not to make trouble for each other.

"This Bill guy is a free-rover. Only links to the Miasma once or twice a month and then just long enough to keep in touch with the family."

Amanda shudders. Not only is Amanda a digital construct, she is a historian. That level of disconnection is disturbing. Freerovers have rejected the historically predictable future. Of course it is their right, to life, liberty and the pursuit of happiness, but Amanda thinks there are limits that people should learn to respect, especially insofar as pursuit is concerned. Too much freedom is bad for people. She had known that from the moment she knew she was on the planet. There is enough to be enjoyed within the rules, she would argue, if anyone ever bothered to ask.

Sleek silk and soft skin has its usual effect and Lisa lets herself link into Amanda's arms. For what seems like hours, they wolford away until there is no more pleasure to be had. Two minutes later, Amanda sighs and returns to the question of Joe's brother Bill.

"I think I'll run a deep track on him anyway."

"Can I come too?"

"Of course, my love, but don't say anything to Joe."

"God forbid, he'd be furious if he got to know."

"He won't, I can promise you that."

"Does this Bill know what you look like?"

"I don't think he even knows I exist," exclaims Amanda.

"Then we should be safe," says Lisa, "at least for the moment."

Then the Miasma lurches them through a 3D revision.

They find him sitting in a café on the South Island of Denmark, staring morosely at the deep ice-cliffs of the Baltic. Lisa recognises Bill Smather by his resemblance to Joe. Both men are about 1.90 tall, six foot and a bit, with long slender hands and big heads, but Bill is leaner and fitter, decidedly more attractive than his brother, who has the beginnings of a paunch. Amanda's response is even more clear cut.

"Primitive lust, oof," she explains to Lisa. "Very raw, hard to resist. Weathered skin, but still young. Nice tan, sexy hands. Sinewy!"

"Thanks darling, I'll remember that."

"Who is he talking to? Who's the other guy? Know anything yet?"

"He's Turkish, a travel agent, with a taste for miasmatic triways," adds Amanda helpfully.

"Your taste, or mine?"

"Your taste for a foretaste, I suspect."

"I wouldn't rate your chances, he's extra-miasma and your virtues are decidedly virtual."

They clump into the bar and sashay across the room together, hoping to attract the two men's attention. Lisa concentrates on the young Turk, while Amanda does her best to gain Bill's attention.

He isn't interested.

"Ahmet, I have a catalogue of reports for you to take back to Trabzon," he tells the Turk.

"Any one of them more important than the others?"
"I would say the price. It represents an awful lot of credits."
The low salinity and relatively shallow waters of the Baltic Sea ensured it was the first great mass of open water to freeze all the year round and the ice has now reached a depth of 95metres, creating a huge rink for winter sports and ice-trekking.
The great planing machines are constructed in Bremen and crawl onto the Baltic icefield via the Kiel Canal. They can see three of them gliding slowly across the surface of the ice to keep the skateways smooth to an accuracy of less than a millimetre. On board, the casinos are full. People hoping to win enough CO2 credits to install a coal fire, or a grill for those long promised summer evenings that never seemed to materialise outside the Alaskas and Zealand.
Ahmet smiles at the waitress who has served their tea, then begins to tell Bill what the Turks will decide. The Black Sea is still navigable to ice-breakers for a few summer months, but within a decade the sea-ice will form a solid mass. Competition for tourists between the Crimea and Turkey is set to intensify. Ahmet claims to have Government backing for the first planing machine order. There's a small pot of purple pansies on the table. They don't account for anything.
Bill is unconvinced. All kinds of people claim to have all kinds of agreements, then a quick check in the Miasma reveals they had dreamed up the whole business in some seedy hive.
The Black Sea is a lot deeper than the Baltic, far more saline and Ahmet had asked Bill to see if a design could be created that was broader and lighter than the Baltic planers. "We need to be sure that they will be safe on a 25metre deep ice-shelf. Any kind of accident would cripple the industry. It happened on Lake Superior. Never again."
Bill agrees.
Sixty five thousand tonnes is a lot of weight to spread over the cracks, especially if the ice is resting on rocks rather than

floating above deep water. The possibility that a casino carrying fifteen thousand passengers could slip through the ice and plummet into the Black Sea depths was unthinkable. Despite the tourists bravura as they skidded along in the wake of a planer, Bill knows there is a deep seated fear of ice in the human mind. Over hundreds of generations, too many people had slipped and broken limbs to be left abandoned, freezing themselves to a cold and lonely death. Only with the beginnings of agriculture on the banks of the Euphrates as the current interstitial began, did people begin to distance themselves from these deep embedded memories. Bill knew that the planers would float if necessary, but loss of life among the skaters and ice-boarders would be unavoidable if there was a major crack-up.

"What's that he's drinking?" Lisa wonders.

"It smells like gin and tonic," Amanda suggests, hazarding a guess.

"Unhealthy," mutters Lisa. She's concentrating on the man's lean looks. "But fit."

"Free-rover typical," answers Amanda with a hint of glee.

"And strong, wirey strong."

"You'd enjoy that, Lisa. Blue eyes too."

"Yes, I think I will. Do you think his hair is dyed?"

"You could ask him."

"He might not like the question."

"I don't care."

Lisa does. She walks over to the table, where Bill is sitting.

"I was just wondering," she began.

"Then don't," he cut her off, "I'm working and I don't sleep with hookers."

Lisa is affronted, "Who the fuck do you think you're talking to? I am a historian, not a pay pal."

"I am busy and your futures, either past or present, are of absolutely no interest to me. Please stop pestering us. There are some tourists in the other bar. They'll be more than happy to rent you."

"I've never met anyone so rude."

"Sweetheart, we haven't been introduced," he says stonily. "Just get lost and stop getting on my nerves."

Either he is upset, or an original rude boy, Lisa concludes, then swivels as haughtily as she can and walks away.

"That didn't go very well," declares Amanda pragmatically as Lisa returns crestfallen to their table.

"What a skunky ratblaster," says Lisa with conviction.

"I warned you about free-rovers, he's probably married and loyal."

"She must be a goat to have latched onto him."

"I wonder," Amanda says, checking the register. "No, she's a princess, Princess Tatiana Greenberg of Murawiki, which, hang on.....is an idyllic island in the South Pacific. They have three children and a dog. He needs to earn six million a year to keep their lifestyle going and he only made five and a half last year. That explains why he's grumpy. He's got to find another five hundred thousand a year from somewhere to keep his independence. Free-roving licences are expensive. Miss more than a couple of payments and you're halfway to Outcast."

"Are there any pictures of her?"

The images revealed an elegant woman in her mid-forties, with broad shoulders, slender legs and long brown hair.

"She still loves him, according to the data core, though she is having an affair with a school teacher that she lists under hobbies."

"What does Bill list under hobbies?"

"That's a thought, let me see, ah, tolerating his wife's infidelities, re-wiring old houses and somewhat improbably, he claims to have a fondness for painting and decorating. I think he's taking the piss, no-one likes decorating."

"Does it say anything about his free-roving?"

"Of course not, that's the point."

"His wife claims that knowing he is a free-rover adds considerably to his attractiveness. She gets aroused imagining him in exotic places adventuring the locals."

"Judging by his intake of gin, she is over-estimating his prowess in the adventuring department."

"Well, you fancy him."

"True."

"Why not adventure him, then go and tell the wife about it?"

"No thanks."

"Why?"

"She might kill me."

"Yes, she might. Then again, would it matter?"

"Yes, it bloody well would matter."

Amanda smiles, "Oh Lisa, you darling, I always knew you believe in identity."

"I'm not some bloody computer programme, like some we could mention. You don't know what it is to pump gas for three hours a day."

"I pay my taxes like everybody else," says Amanda tetchily. "And my CO_2 profile is exemplary, less than 20% of a single person allowance. So what are we going to do about this bloke. Shag him and see?"

"We could bribe the hotel concierge."

"Or we could stow away on his snow-cutter."

"That would be more interesting."

"It's the green one, down there, the one with the fire-dragon painted on the side. Not the big one, the one next to it."

"How many passengers?"

"Usually six, or seven. Maximum twelve."

"Lets not bother stowing away, we can book a cruise."

"OK, I'll cancel my meetings for next week."

"Me too."

The three day ice adventure would take them along the old North German Baltic coast from Denmark to Poland, then turn further north, away from the planer routes. They would also spend at least twelve hours submerged beneath the ice, beyond the range of the Miasma.

"You two!" Bill welcomes them with a smile. "If I'd known you were passengers, I'd have taken you up on the offer earlier."
He was unimpressed by their newly acquired luggage, a couple of suitcases filled with untried winter clothes.
"Feeling spontaneous?" he asks, then sighs, as the cutter pulls away from the Danish islands and follows the planer smoothed snow-way up through the ice-cliff gorges onto the pack ice proper.
"Any idea where you'd like to go?" he asks the passengers, hoping that none of them would have a specific goal, so he can stick to the tried and tested ice tunnels he's drilled over the last couple of years. He looks at Lisa's winter clothing and smirks.
"Didn't you bring a few frocks? We aren't on a camping trip here, you know."
Their rooms are luxurious, albeit pink, with massive windows that will give them a view of the glittering ice as they travel north.
Lisa lies down on one of the chaise longues and let herself sink deeper into the Miasma. She finds Joe chatting to Amanda about the Selby case. He assumes she is still in Alaska and they run through a few minor issues about Selby's start in politics. This was over-familiar territory and no-one had found anything new to say in the last decade. The recent papers were all rehashes of the established documentation, with old questions posed as if from new perspectives. Treebone's biography provided 98% of all their sources and the whole area was marked up as standard history.
Selby joined the Free Market Association and soon after

became its spokesman on housing rights, as he founded the populist right wing Forthright Movement.

"I found nothing at all to suggest this woman Mona played any kind of role in the creation of the Forthright Movement and she never joined the Legacy Gang. She wasn't even in Nublu."

It was news of a kind. Amanda thanks Joe. He'd done some pretty bleak trawling through the archive.

Then Lisa has an idea. "What if her name isn't Mona, but something similar, say Ramona, or Monica. Might that be a help?"

They agreed to follow the string to see if anything comes up.

Then Lisa told Joe, she would be taking a holiday for a few days and they arranged to meet a week later.

"Oh that's nice," Lisa tells Amanda.

"What is?"

"The goat licence has been confirmed. She can live with the sheep."

"What for?"

"Angora, mohair, I shall set up a loom."

"And for dinner?"

"Goat stew can be good, but we'll have to be patient, I don't want to think about killing the beast before I've even begun. Maybe I should wait and see if it will breed."

"It won't breed on its own. I was thinking of Bill and what we'll have tonight."

"He's a goat stew type."

"But not here, we'll get a gourmet package, you can be sure of that."

Amanda was right. The menu is comprehensive and the food uniformly delicious and as deliciously uniform as soya-rice combinations always are. The lettuce was particularly good. Grown on board, Bill claimed. The freshness was unmistakeable. He had told them the truth.

Bill always tells the truth. That way, he frightens people.

After dinner, Bill invites them on deck to watch the aurora borealis. The display is impressive. The sun is at its most active for fifteen thousand years, he tells them, so the bombardment is eighteen to twenty times as strong as five years ago.

"We're a lucky generation in that respect."

"And in other respects?" asks Lisa.

"That depends on your point of view and your status," he mutters, giving Amanda the kind of glance a committed physicalist reserves for virtual girls.

"Senses and sensibilities," answers Amanda with a sweet smile, reminding Lisa that Jane Austen was well established in the Miasma's top thousand, with upwards of fifteen million women regularly contributing to her development. Bill knows this too and quickly changes the subject.

"Have you been sub-glacial before?"

"No, this is our first time."

"Can I suggest you use the couches then, it can be a bit unnerving until you get used to the feeling, but once we're under the ice, its unforgettable. Sunrise is at six fifty and I hope to have us well up the old German coastline by then, with the first tunnel route beginning about an hour later. Can I also suggest you have breakfast early, then settle down before we head under to Stralsund."

Then he excuses himself and goes off to talk to the other passengers. The moonlight brings a gleam to the ice and Lisa gazes into the nearby floes of deep translucent greens, forbidding blues and milky whites. The sky is clear, as the aurora streams down in curtains of gold and silver.

She can count fifteen other vessels on the ice, a flotilla of party-goers sliding slowly over the sunken remains of Rostok and Wismar.

She feels apprehensive at the thought of diving into the ice-tunnel to see the ruins of Stralsund, even if thousands of other people do it every year. This much ice is un-nerving and the notion of scraping your way into the chilly mass makes her skin creep.

Around Stralsund, the ice had picked up whole buildings and sheared them slowly apart, leaving masses of masonry suspended in the crystal blue icelight.

The first major city to succumb to the ice had been Santiagio de Chile as the Andes pushed a bunch of glaciers towards the ocean at a breakneck pace, but there is nothing to be seen in the sewage dark ice-cliffs. Closer to hand, Lübeck and Stockholm had become tourist traps of the worst kind, with permanent exhibitions and rampant merchandising, where the tourists were given the chance to walk in graffiti stained caverns hollowed out by the travel industry and sprayed on by juvenile delinquents.

A freak of marine geology meant Stralsund had been encased in a glaze of crystal clear ice and the views gave an unparalleled insight into the real impact of glaciation. The ruins were suspended within the national park zone, where legislation ensured the icewalls were left undyed and the movement of the remains were charted by the German Institute of Glacial Studies, a centre for theoretical research, forbidden by charter from active intervention in the processes of global warming.

When Lisa and Amanda get to see the deep ice, they are amazed by the prismatic splendour of the polarisations. They are equally disconcerted by the sight of a gothic red brick church stretched horizontally, brick by brick, for almost half a kilometre.

When the cutter grinds to a halt at point zero, looking back they can see the whole town as it must once have been. A perspectival trick along the line of the shear appears to reassemble the fragmented buildings in mockery of their thousand year past as a thriving seaport and centre of shipbuilding. The big cranes had buckled and been dragged

49

away from the yards, but the last of the ships, two deep sea trawlers, which had never been completed, were flattened and suspended upside down by a slow moving eddy within the ice. "There may be a little noise as we return to the surface," Bill's voice warns them over the intercom, "but don't be concerned. I need to widen the passageway, standard procedure to ensure the tunnels can be kept open. And I'd like you to keep your couch belts fastened for the moment."

Bills grins as he notices the adrenalin level rise in all his six passengers and the bio-sensor data flips to orange, pre-critical status. Five of the passengers receive a mild sedative to calm their fears, but he lets Amanda have the full unmediated experience. She's only a digital.

This way, Bill shaves a couple of thousand from the narcotics bill and refuses to join in the pretence that she is anything more than a convincing set of data streams.

The tunnel walls contract by about half a metre a month and need re-glazing to maintain their transparency, so Bill tries to trim costs by condemning his customers to the full regrinding experience. Some love it, others swear they'll never travel with him again. Since his tours are offered as a once in a lifetime experience, he doesn't care what they think.

The tunnelling cutter wheels counter-rotate at about three revolutions per minute, but the noise they make is a wild scream, much like sitting inside the whirling head of a dentists' drill. The slush of crushed ice is funnelled through the centre of the snowcutter, warmed to blood heat, treated with a crystallising agent, then sprayed against the tunnel walls as a polarised glaze to maintain transparency. Bill is impatient, wanting to get onto the planar route while there's enough daylight, so he decides to complete the cutting without anchoring the body of the vessel against the tunnel walls. Although the wheels rotate in different directions, they are never in perfect equilibrium so the whole vessel will turn first one way, then the other as it grips it way through the ice. There's a supply of sick bags by every bunk. When the rotation comes, Amanda and Lisa are gently spun in their couches and begin to complain of seasickness, which gets worse as Amanda hones into Lisa's sensations and hits a revulsion level she hasn't experienced since she was forced to leave a miasmic symposium on criminal intelligence that violated her formative childhood ethics.

"We shall be lucky to get out of this alive," says Lisa as the whole ship lurches and howls with rotational stresses that would straighten a corkscrew.

"If only we could get back into the Miasma," mutters Amanda in a limpid whimper.

"You knew there is a downside to going local."

"Never mind the downside, it's the wrongside upside, sideways side and back again. I think I'm going to throw up. Inside outside, watch out."

"Please don't, I don't want your puke in my hair."

"OK," Amanda acquiesces, "let me retch into one of those bags."

"Must you?"

"Think so."

Amanda looks green, but just as she speaks the grinding and shuddering comes to a stop and Bill's voice cheerfully announces that they have reached the surface. "Thank you for your patience ladies and gentlemen. Now you know the world has changed. As there are still four hours of daylight, I propose we scoot over the planar route to Helsinki and continue the voyage from there. You will find details of the hotel I've booked for you simply by asking."

"What's the hotel like?" asks Lisa, which flips the brochure to play. The Hotel Monde was, the brochure claimed, an old free-rover haunt, frequented by adventurers from every corner of the globe.

'Not that globes have corners,' thought Lisa with mild disdain, assuming this would be the usual preamble to the promise of unlicensed gambling and unlimited temptation. She flicks the brochure off, then asks Amanda what they are going to do about Bill.

"Intervention, or observation?"

Amanda suggests that intervention would be for Lisa to initiate.

"He is obviously uninterested in me. We don't know much more about him than when we started. Perhaps that's the only riddle.

"Why should some-one become a free-rover?"

"Do we believe in this little touring business?"

"Why?" says Lisa.

"He spends too much time travelling to be a serious ice-pilot in the holiday industry."

"Do you think Joe suspects this is a front?"

"I don't know. Most criminals stay inside the Miasma. Better inside than out. Free-roving makes people suspicious. Half the world think of them as pirates and brigands. It doesn't serve much purpose if that turns out to be true."

"What was that coastline like before the ice?"

"Low lying farmland, with towns on the river estuaries. This used to be called the 'Bernstein Coast', the Amber Coast. People traded in amber for thousands of years, Europe is littered with the stuff. In Poland, one of the old mines is kept open for tourists, there's an ice tunnel and a fashion show. The pipelines for oil and gas from Siberia still run under the ice. Some of them even work."

"Did Joe ever mention the Baltic ice?"

"Only once. We were discussing piracy. He said he'd been reading about Stortebecker, who was eventually executed in Hamburg."

"When was that?"

"About 500 years ago."

"No, when did Joe mention it?"

"Last summer, he was trying to get a ticket for the Caribbean."

"Buried treasure?"

"No, a Conference on Holographic Turbulence."

"Interesting."

"Maybe, I don't know. He seemed to think it would be."

"Do you expect Bill would have been there?"

"Funny that Joe never married, when you think that his brother fished a Princess."

"Maybe Bill is simply more interesting than Joe."

"I don't fancy either of them," Amanda confirms, straight as data.

"I do, but I wouldn't marry one of them. I think I'll have Bill for supper. See what we can see."

"Not we, you. I don't play those games."

"You go get yourself a nice niche in 'wanton pleasure," teases Lisa.

"Do I have your permission?"

"You don't need my permission."

"Yes, I do, darling. Then we can playback later, when you've finished shagging your free-rover."

Lisa gives Amanda an excited grin and they tangle each other in a licentious embrace.

"God, you're hot."

"I know. I hope he realises."

Amanda laughs, "Don't overdo the pheromones, or you'll never get him off you."

"I need some real time badly," Lisa says, as she gets up to leave, knowing that Amanda cannot allow herself to be offended.

Bill looks up from his book, as Lisa sways into the cutter's library.

"Drinks are in the cupboard behind you," he says and asks her to pour him another glass of Argentinian whisky.

JOHN CLARK

"I finished the last of the Irish yesterday," he apologises, "with my Turkish friend. For a Muslim, he can really knock it back."

"Is he a really a Muslim?"

"Oh, yes. He takes it more seriously than he would like to pretend. That's why he drinks, to pretend that he's a bad boy."

"You don't need to pretend."

"I'm neither Muslim, nor bad boy, so what would be the point? And I'm not a philosopher either, so don't give yourself an additional false impression."

"That's a lot of nots. So what are you?"

"I keep myself to myself."

Bill is proving more difficult to seduce than Lisa had expected. Most men will razzle and run, given the choice, but Bill seemed content to talk as they drink.

"Among the schemers that I've met," Bill asserts, "there are only a tiny few who can really build something and make it work. Ninety per cent of the people I meet, the ones who call themselves schemers and managers, are really just good at jockeying for position, promoting themselves and denying their rivals. You can call it scheming if you like, but not in any affirmative sense. I like thinking and doing. Manoeuvring simply to better yourself is a bore. Doing is better than owning. And ownership takes up more time and energy than anyone ever expects."

Lisa doesn't want to follow his train of thought, though perhaps she should have done.

"It's strange on these cutters," she says, trying to change the subject, "not having the Miasma around all the time. Sometimes it's there, then it's gone."

"Simple physics under the ice. Good for you, to get away from all that garbled crap."

"Is that what you really think about the Miasma."

"Yes, it's like contrasting the city with the wilderness, step outside the Miasma and you can think more clearly, just like

54

fresh air, nothing to bother you, none of that buzz around you all the time."

"I feel a bit strange when its not there."

"Autonomy. Puts you in touch with your real self, instead of that mushy feeling inside the community. You should try it more often."

"I just start feeling nervous."

"You needn't worry here. It's never out for more than an hour, or two. I once went a whole year without the Miasma. We had an accident in Senegal, on a data mining contract. Quite a panic at the beginning, but you soon get used to it. After I while I didn't miss it at all."

"Are you a free-rover, then?"

"I would have thought that was obvious. Has it started to get to you then, the intoxicating allure of your coherent self?"

"Self, sure," she hesitates, "and others." She gives him a long slow glance of invitation.

"Makes you randy as hell," he grins.

Lisa realises that she has achieved her objective.

"Well, yes, I know what you mean, as a matter of fact."

Lisa had almost forgotten how long real-time can take. She had also forgotten about synchronisation and/or the lack of it. She and Bill agreed on random fertility, which increased her chances of becoming pregnant by a factor of 20, but this still meant there was a less than one in a thousand chance that she would conceive after a real-time encounter. Bill's sperm is graded harvestable for in-vitro use and since the two of them were genetically desirable, a baby would bring each of them several million credits from the Department of Gene Pool Affairs.

"Registered!" said Bill delightedly as he confirmed their frolic with the authorities. "You are a very beautiful woman." A standard phrase straight out of the almanac of erotic courtesies.

Lisa feels refreshed. Big Bill had set her tingling, even if he had not quite managed to trip her into orgasm.

"With a bit of practise," he grinned. "We could get quite good at this."

"But you're married," Lisa points out objectively.

"I certainly am," admits Bill. "Isn't that the very best reason of all to become a free-rover?"

Amanda is furious, when she hears this. "You mean to say he free-rides to cheat on his wife!"

"Not very original is it," says Lisa.

"He's a liar," Amanda scolds.

"Of course he is. They all are."

"Did he say anything about Joe?"

"As a matter of fact he did, in a round about way. When I asked him if he had any family, he started to tell me a rather unusual story that sheds a certain amount of light on our Joe's oddities."

"How much people manage to conceal about themselves," Amanda remarks, "even within the miasmatic parameters. I wonder how Joe manages to conceal things? He's signed the covenant on transparency. Without that he'd never have made it as a historian."

"He doesn't actively conceal. He just shorthands his entries. It's a sin of omission."

"Tell," says Amanda impatiently. It's been months since she's heard any serious gossip.

"Once upon a time, there were three boys, Bill, Joe and Nesta. Except one of them wasn't a boy, Nesta was a girl who suffered from false registration syndrome. Throughout her childhood, the wrong schools would be selected, clothes arrived for three boys, her training and indoctrination was a complete mess. This happens to about three people a year worldwide, but it has lingering consequences. The ambiguity multiplies with the passage of time. System trackers appear to have ironed the issues out, when lo and behold another false signal arises, from somewhere or another and cascades globally without warning.

Then the clearing process must begin all over again. Usually a standard reset is enough to fix the major issues, but there will still be the odd restaurant that will serve you hormonally unbalanced portions, or annoyingly inappropriate accessories are fitted in your apartment. Luckily no-one has had problems with medical treatment, or so Bill said."

"After a childhood of minor humiliations, Bill told me that his sister decided to become a complete outsider. She lives on the edge of the desert near Aix-en-Provence and makes a living scavenging the dunes, selling her finds to collectors and playing a cat and mouse game keeping one jump ahead of the archaeologists. Maybe this explains why Joe is interested in history. It gives him access to the rumour mill. He can keep her warned of their plans."

"Nothing illegal in that."

"Of course not."

"So what's so interesting about this woman, what's her name, Nesta.[37], her favourite food, housing choice, mind game preferences."

"Well, she's an outsider, so we don't have access, do we?"

"Ugh," says Amanda with a shudder.

"Also, she has seven children."

"Oh my God!"

"Random selection."

"No pre-testing?"

"Unregistered, she's an outsider."

"Statistically, that could be devastating."

"They're all girls."

Amanda pauses.

"She could be a new Eve! Seven is sufficient to exceed dynastics and achieve population threshold after half-a-dozen generations. If she were to have an eighth, that would be more or less certain."

---

37 A traditional Welsh girl's name.

"I don't think we need go quite that far. But she is certainly an exceptional woman. I think Bill is in love with her."

"You don't mean....I mean, that's incest, she's his sister!"

"No, he isn't the children's father. He told me she is rather particular about choosing them. She is exceptionally intelligent, he said, but I'd already assumed that. Well, she'd have to be to survive in those sorts of conditions."

"Lisa, did you believe all that stuff?"

"I think so," she says, "but I have been wondering why he should tell so much to someone he never even met before."

"It didn't deter him from doing you."

"But that's as much a social duty as a pleasure," Lisa says. "Telling me about his sister was a very different kind of risk."

"Of course it is," agrees Amanda, adding mysteriously, "I wonder what it is men really want? I think we deceive ourselves about men. Do you think he knows you are a friend of Joe's?"

"Maybe Joe had told him about us, yes."

Amanda had been unconcerned about Bill being a free-rover. They are a recognised minority within Humanity. The Global Governance Directive[38] has three paragraphs defining their status. Outsiders are different. The Directive specifically excludes them from its provisions. There is nothing in the code of ethics. Outsiders are omissions, transparent and absent. She shrugs her shoulders, as if to cleanse herself of the thought. If his sister is an outsider, how can Joe have so much free time to spend on the history project. Selby Studies are defined as commended recreation. With an outsider in the family, Joe should have been loaded with duty projects and non-evasive obligations. There is something anomalous going on here.

"Ugh,"says Amanda, as they step into the lobby of the Helsinki hotel.

"Ice hockey players and Danish hookers," Lisa scowls, with a

---

38 Global Governance Directive – if in doubt, refer to your personal identity data.

look of disdain that leaves the concierge silent and dismayed. "I'm not staying here."

"The alternative is a business overnight," Amanda replies, "or we could just head for the airport. You can get a shuttle in a couple of hours and I can be home by tomorrow morning, as it were."

"We don't have to stay for the rest of the trip," Lisa decides.

"And where is home for you nowadays?"

Amanda laughs, "Fibredance, Arizona, my dear. It's warm, but muggy, a bit dreary in the rain. Misty, of course. Romantic if you like that kind of thing. We get the thunderstorms from Lake Bonneville, though I enjoy the boat trips to Salt Lake City, now they've finished rebuilding and installed the spas."

CHAPTER 4

Lisa is drowsy with drink before boarding, content to miss the nausea of take-off and acceleration as the shuttle pops over the pole and she awakens to see the Greenland ice sheet in all its diminished splendour as the pilot tips the machine onto its glide path down towards Anchorage. She winces as a brace of missiles flash past a few minutes before landing and mutters a curse as the pilot apologises for getting too close to the military perimeter.

Directional programmes have no appreciation of mortality and only limited agility to dodge an inadvertent target. Even a war game device can kill you if it impacts at a closing speed of fourteen thousand miles an hour and most of the people guiding them are twelve years old. They don't fret about hitting a shuttle in flight. They fret about what their Mum will say when she finds out.

Her brother had sent her a mass of scary stuff about the magnetic pole's incipient flip that could change everything, or amount to nothing, so Lisa spends the last few minutes of the flight reading about goat keeping. That was the problem with Desmond, a typical earth scientist, everything potentially traumatic, or maybe nothing at all, according to the statistical bias of their daily ruminations. He's warned her more than once about flying and about the inadequacies of their maths. If the Miasma is knocked out by an electro-magnetic pulse from the earth's core as the polarity flip begins to wobble, anything in the sky will come crashing down with nothing to catch it. He's equally worried about volcanoes.

Lisa avoids his missives. She reads his mail in batches nowadays, so the bad news in one message seems less dire than the one before. She switches off and the shuttle rolls gently into dock.

Five minutes after she's home, the goat arrives, or rather the goat is delivered. Goats are agile, rather than directional, so they need delivering by someone with a lot of common sense, or rather enough native wit to not to let the carton open outside the waiting pen. As Lisa hasn't had time to create a separate pen, the goat box is lowered into the sheep-fold and immediately nibbled from the inside by the goat seeking to get out and from the outside from the sheep, who simply find it tasty.

Cloven hoofed and springy, the little kid bolts from the box, scattering Lisa's sheep in bleating confusion and heads for her living room. The sheep are smitten. Lisa too. The baby goat loves them all and eats the newish curtains as it waits for milk.

One of the Miasma's abiding problems is inopportune arrivals and Lisa hears Amanda's cry of "Oh, how sweet", before she can push the little beast off her favourite quilt and carry him back outside.

"Sorry, I should have blinked," Amanda apologises, having dropped into Lisa's privacy without asking.

"Now you're here, could you programme the kitchen while I sort out some-where for Billy."

"Billy?"

"Billy the Kid, who will grow up to be Silly Billy the Billy Goat. Then there'll be less of the 'oh how sweet'. He was about to piss on my quilt, the furry white monster and his hoofs are sharp as knives."

"Well, he didn't pee at all. He's adorable isn't he. But shouldn't he still be with his mother? He seems incredibly young."

"I know, I shall have to feed him by bottle. His mother is probably dog food by now, or will be once they've milked her dry. Goat's milk is for cheese not for baby goats. Do you think I should castrate him?"

"Not this afternoon. I think he's had enough shocks for one day. Where's he from?"

"It said Greece on the box, some place in Corfu, but who knows, maybe he's Mongolian. I'm told there's a lot of smuggling from the steppes, as people try to avoid slaughtering their herds once permafrost is detected and their livestock licences are revoked."

"Anyway, enough of your cuddly little giddy goat. I just checked the conference that Joe went to last year. It was on Polarisation Errors in Global Holographics. Mean anything to you, why he should be there? Surely polarisation is a bit on the technical side for our Joe."

"No idea, I'm not sure what it is, I was about to ask you."

"OK, I'll let you know. He's a bit small for stewing."

"Now I know you dream of stew, I shall have to keep him away from you."

"Leave Joe to me."

"Oh, you can have Joe, with pleasure, enjoy yourself, bye. Oh, and before I forget, 'The Aberdeen Academy for Young Ladies, there were five Monas and two Ramonas. I'm trying to trace their medical records, see if anything has survived. Scotland shredded a lot of stuff after the teeth scandals and the lost minds controversy. Said it was an English issue."

As Amanda is leaving, Lisa decides there something she might be overlooking, "If you manage to identify her, pay attention to her motivations and see if any character cores have been activated. I can't begin to understand what she might do next, unless I have some idea of what she's trying to achieve."

Amanda sulks. Motivation is her weak point, as her identity is specifically excluded from exploring 'self interest'.[39]

"Start using your character traits to build an impression. You've enough degrees of petulance and tantrums in character without compromising the coherence of your identity."

"I'll do my very best," smiles Amanda, then she's gone, like a dingbat chasing a hamburger, as Quentin Smithson noted in his journal note about her habits.

The two women find it easy to ignore the fundamental contrasts between them. Lisa is human, biological, mortal, a woman who has been educated at a series of schools and a couple of Universities, whereas Amanda is a digital entity, female in character, but someone whose talents and attributes have been defined in a programming environment and the knowledge at her command is a shared network resource. Yes, Amanda can think and yes Lisa thinks of Amanda as her closest collaborator, but the contrast between intelligence and artificial intelligence remains a gulf to this day, however willing everyone is to try and build bridges to reconcile the differences.

Lisa returns to the little goat and gives him a bottle of milk, which gets guzzled, then he gives her a nuzzle and falls asleep on her lap, one hoof prodding uncomfortably against her knee. The kid smells sweet and harmless. It snores lightly. A few minutes later, she too is asleep. The animal is lovely and Lisa is delighted. It has been a long day for both of them and after their different journeys, they are equally relieved to have finally arrived.

---

39 See the General Agreement on People and Characters, Chapter 4 - Identity.

When Joe walks into the archive, the smell of decay is overpowering. The gloom is heavy and oppressive, a low light shadowless glow. Away from the entertaining exuberance of miasmatic reconstruction, the depressing sense of times past is inescapable. Feelings and emotions extinguished, no-one whose lived experience gave rise to these mountains of documentation has any claim to continued existence. Death is inescapable. They are gone. The world has ceased to exist for them and their own existence has been eradicated. The dismal reality of human life is completed by non-existence. You are there and then you are gone. Your share of time is soon spent. The present line swims impassively into the long future, confirming the passage of time and hoovering up the past in a deluge of archived detail. It sweeps the globe to the regular beat of seventy loops per second, a reassuringly gentle rhythm as familiar as their own heartbeat to most folk on the planet.

One of Joe's first jobs as an archaeologist had been to keep the records and finds from a long forgotten excavation up to date, a so-called 'dig' from the days when destructive archaeology was the norm. Not only did the artefacts relate to long dead people, but the people who had exhumed their bones and catalogued the detritus of their little farm, had also been dead for almost three hundred years. Generations of archivists had added notes of various procedures carried out to analyse one or other characteristic of the material. There were detailed references to errors they had recognised and sought to correct in the light of subsequent developments in archaeological practice. The store was kind of intellectual graveyard, with Joe as the sacristan and the documents freshly franked with time-code and held in a grip of incipient reason.

The village of Swipdale no longer exists, though it once did and is noted as the birthplace of three composers of note during the neoclassical revival of the mid-twenty-first.

A glacier has re-established itself in the valley that was first gouged into a U-shape a hundred thousand years ago and the ice is cumulating to grind into the bedrock once again. The trickling stream that powered a water-wheel during the industrial revolution has been succeeded by a summer torrent of white water carrying razor sharp stones towards the Irish Bight.[40] Joe's new job as palaeoanthropologist at the Heinrich Hertz Institute for Neurometrics in Berlin has given him the chance to flesh out the theories he began working on via Swipdale. It has been a long and frustrating wait, like watching rain freeze as the locals say.

Joe is building a topology of physical and cognitive constraints that define aesthetic concepts such a beauty and elegance, harmony and pleasure; building blocks, he assumes, for the cultures of art and technology. Sometimes he is stunned by the scale of his ambition, but it has been sanctioned for further research for fifteen successive seasons, so they must think he's onto something.

The dome shaped repository is Joe's favourite building, continually being expanded, as a new shell is added to the core structures, whenever the curators need more space. The closer you get to the core, the more stable the temperature and humidity. The four outer shells are reading rooms, with space for eight thousand researchers and ordinary readers. The shaded glass gives way to concrete walls as you enter the main archive. The downside is the smell. The controlled atmosphere is argon rich, filtered to remove industrial gases and dust. The smell is human. Only the shiny skin of Selinsky's bald head can been seen behind the feeble glow of the desk light, when Joe tracks him down in the Finnish corner of Level 13 in the Moses Hoffman[41] archive.

---

40 Formerly the Irish Sea, renamed as the land-bridge between Ireland and Scotland is re-established.
41 Moses Hoffman, a mid-twentieth century antiquarian, who left his library of rare Persian Illustrated manuscripts

"What can I do for you?" he asks grumpily without looking up. Clearly irritated by the interruption, he forces a mild smile as he recognises Joe.

"Try some of this," he says, handing Joe a thick bottomed spirits glass. He tilts his hand to indicate that Joe should drink the high octane vodka.

" 'can't get through the day in here without getting smashed," he says mournfully, "vodka for oblivion - the choice of connoisseurs."

Joe sniffs, then snorts and downs the glass, feeling a long burn as the fire-water sears his throat and boils in his belly.

"A lesser man would die," Selinsky says sarcastically. "Maybe I will and they'll find me pickled in alcohol during a security sweep."

They both know it's time to discuss Eric Selby and the mysterious Mona.

"At least we're away from prying eyes," says Joe.

"I think I have narrowed down the identity," Selinsky confirms dryly, "Mona Lightfoot. She worked as a Law Court Librarian in Lambeth[42], keeping documentation for cases on property deals and suchlike, mainly disagreements about valuation, but most of the rest equally dull squabbles about the precise positioning of boundary lines between different plots of land. Good at sport, she played hockey for a fairly good women's team and swam twice a week. She was also an amateur singer, who took voice lessons with a music professor in Cambridge. But I suspect the swimming pool was the probable point of contact. I think that's how she got to meet Eric Selby. He was a

and other treasures to the Balaban Island National Library following a series of disputes as to ownership in his native Germany (Northern Republic of). Hoffman's autobiographical 'Animal Self' is also preserved in the Preyna collection. Main article: restricted.

42 No such court existed in Lambeth – 'All Known History'

swimming pool romeo at one point. There's nothing about choir music in his ramblings."

"Do you know which of them did the seducing?"

Joe's question puzzles Selinsky for a moment.

"Almost certainly her, assuming its the right woman. She seems to have had a lively taste in young men and they found her sensationally attractive. You can read about her in this Marcus Bamich fellow's diaries. He listed her charms and explored them one by one."

"Never heard of him."

"No, neither had I," affirms Selinsky, "completely insignificant, schoolteacher type, married, one child, erotomane, that's it. Putney born, lived, died, forgotten. Even the schools where he taught no longer exist. No distinguished former pupils. Extraordinarily dull, the whole lot. His grand-daughter found the diaries and sent them to the local museum for some unfathomable reason. She was also completely forgettable, as were her parents, brothers, sisters and cousins. Real hive material, the lot of them.

Mona ditched this Marcus fellow in three weeks, but he followed her for years. Nasty little man, very unsavoury, who was saved by his own insignificance. She doesn't seem to have noticed him lurking in the shadows. All grey on grey."

"What does this tell us about Eric Selby?" Joe asks.

"Nothing yet, but I have her address and that means we can track there to see if Eric turned up for his rendezvous. The rest may follow via 'throughput' if we have a bit of luck."

"Do you want to tell Amanda, or shall I?"

"I think we should talk to Lisa." In Selinsky's opinion it was better to filter news via a human vector. "I have occasionally had reason to regret my trust in 'personalities'." He is a natural conservative, not a snob. It was just that he was one of the tiny minority who still made a distinction between bio and digi on a day to day basis. Joe takes a more relaxed view. It was probably a consequence of Selinsky's first doctorate thesis, which drew a variety of fine philosophical distinctions between digital identity constructs and the 'authentic' biological self. He doesn't mind bringing Lisa in first however, so he agrees, if only to keep Selinsky happy and they part. Amanda will be told a millisecond or two later, which might just as well be a speed of light routing issue as an old school courtesy.

Joe takes the lift to ground level, glad to escape the argon enriched air of the lower stacks. Nominal CO_2 levels may reduce the threat of decay in the paper archives, but the filtered air is stale and tainted with the sweaty reek of seeking after truth.

Selinsky has strange tastes.

Joe would never see him again.

"Three thousand for a couple of t-shirts and a pair of shoes," complains Lisa. She and Amanda move to a window seat in the 'Three Horsemen' and pretend to be tired and irascible, an effective way of keeping predatory males at a distance.

London seems subterranean, modernised, sort of, and expensive. There had been several weeks deliberation and negotiation before this return visit seeking Selby had been agreed and then approved. The pub looks as if it has been spring cleaned twice a day and smells of air freshener, an oddly neutral feel that denudes the place of character. Amanda makes a note pointing out this lack of authenticity. Pubs are supposed to smell of tobacco, sweat and old beer, everyone knows that.

At ten thirty, four men and a woman leave a house on the other side of the street. Amanda makes a recognition plot and identifies two of the men as property developers and the other three as lawyers.

"I think one of the lawyers is really a banker," she tells Lisa after the facial identities were confirmed. "Legal qualification but works for a bank. Could be setting up a deal. The banker agrees to something and the lawyers do the contract."

"Or the banker is trying to get his money back and threatening the property guys with legal action?" Lisa suggests.

"Or the property guys have had a row and the lawyers are trying to fix a compromise?" proposes Amanda.

"Or something has gone badly wrong with a deal and the property guys and the bankers have brought in the lawyers to see what can be rescued?" says Lisa to take their notion for a walk.

"Or they could just be friends of Mona," said Amanda.

"If they were Mona's friends they would have stayed later and left separately, not in a group and why should she have told Eric they were meeting to talk business. Is Mona up to no good?" Lisa swallows a gulp of beer. "I need a smoke."

"You can't, its illegal. They'll throw you in jail."

"Shit, haven't they invented halers yet?"

"Nope, come back in five years." Amanda enjoys Lisa's temporary discomfort.

"How long before Eric gets here?"

"Half an hour, if he's going to be on time. Maybe never, if he isn't."

"Have you thought how we can get in the house?" Lisa asks.

"Only if you insist," answers Amanda, " Do you know how to climb drainpipes?"

"No, and I have no intention of learning."

"Now, now. Don't be tetchy."

"We could ring the fire brigade," says Lisa without bothering to think.

"What use would that be?"

"I don't know."

Amanda starts counting the lines of grain in the pub table. She is impatient, but suddenly she exclaims, "Oh no, that's disgusting."

Lisa glances across the street to see what she has missed.

"Revolting," says Amanda with tears in her eyes.

"What are you on about?"

"Selinsky is dead. Had a driving accident on his way home from the archive."

"Nav system malfunction?"

"No, he was flipped by a gust of wind. You want to see the replay? There's only a second of action. Flip, bang, exitus – he was going very fast."

"I never liked him."

"I know, neither did I. But, you know, he was one of us."

"Hobbes may have said that no man is an island, but Selinsky was a bloody iceberg, drifting around with only his nose poking above the water."

"He was useful."

"He was."

"Now he won't be any more."

"Exactly. Should we go to the funeral?"

"We can hold a memorial meeting."

"He'd expect that."

"He won't know anything about it."

"How well did you know him?"

"Four hundred hours of contact, including our meetings."

"Quite a lot."

"He showed me how to work with paper."

"A refined art."

"Dusty."

"He was good at that."

"There he is."

"What?!"

"Not Selinsky, our man Eric Selby."

"Amanda?"

"What?"

"How long is it since anyone had a driving accident?"

"Four years, sixteen days, three hours and fifty minutes, but that last one was a murder."

"Quite. Isn't it a bit odd that Selinsky should die that way? I mean he was a drinker, so there can be no question of pilot error."

"I suppose you're right. Look, there's Eric, parking his car."

As Eric backs his blue Toyota into a space, Mona comes out of the house and goes to meet him. She is carrying a briefcase and looking somewhat glum. She could simply be tired.

"Have you changed your mind?" Eric asks, when she greets him with a peck on the cheek and the suggestion that they have a drink in the '3 Nags'.

He has that thwarted look seen on the face of young men after a rebuff, but they cross the road together and walk into the pub, sitting at the bar, only a few feet away from Amanda and Lisa.

Mona orders herself a gin and tonic, Eric a beer.

"There's a job for you, if you want some work," Mona says quickly.

Eric nods enthusiastically, the thwarted look instantly replaced by one of eager greed. "God yes, so long long as I don't end up in jail."

Mona pauses, wondering whether Eric will end up behind bars and how long for.

She thinking of prison, not a job in the pub.

"My Mr. Brown is a bit unconventional, but I don't think you'll land in jail, probably. Actually, should we be calling him Brown? Braunovsky is more correct and the other guy is Smithovitch not Smith. Just think of them as oligarchs, as good a label as any other. Their real names are probably quite different. Let me explain."

Lisa and Amanda pretend not to listen, astonished at the notion that anyone would talk about this in a pub bar. Amanda is memorising and applying every analytical test she can find to everything she hears, from the patterns of doubt and dissembling, to raw facts and strategic potential.

"My Mr. Brown has a plan and intends to make a great deal of money."

"Sounds good, so far. What's he up to?"

"His daughter is one of Tewkesbury's babes. She's in sloganising, nineteen years old and has a habit of leaving her mobile lying around at home, so he gets to blue-tooth all her mail. Lots of confidential stuff."

"Fuck!"

"And he's decided to play that information against the market, he's playing the property market short, offering people discounted prices if they sell him their houses, but with half a year before they actually have to move out. So they get a lump of cash that's normally locked up in the value of their houses, then they can trade down and buy something cheaper. Or, they can buy their homes back after six months, if they change their minds. He wants to buy 50,000 of the nicest homes in Britain, at least a hundred in every town and a lot more in some special places. Basically, he's betting that Tewkesbury's plans won't work, or won't get approved and in the mean time, he can corner the property market."

"That will cost billions."

"That's what they're talking about, billions and billions. He's predicting a 20% profit. He's talking to redundant bankers about investing their pay-offs, selling the idea as economic revenge. That appeals to their stifled sense of entitlement, the revenge bit, not the billions. "

"And if it doesn't work."

"I guess he'll have to run away."

"Where to?"

"Somewhere like Mars, I expect, where no-one might be bothered to follow him."

"And what do they want me to do? I don't buy and sell houses."

"No, you are idealistic, young, plausible. People like you. They're looking for someone to start a political campaign to give home owners a voice. They want to call it 'Home-saver', but I expect you'll think of something better. Their prices will always be better than the deals Tewkesbury will be offering, so they have a good argument. Mr. Brown intends to stabilise the market and become a rich hero. Mr. Smith wants to start building houses for young families. His investors want to own the country. He's disruptive by temperament. Think of Novy Zembla and the clean up. That was him."

"Have they got enough money?"

"They seem to think so."

"So Smithovitch and Braunovsky are going to take the British market for a ride. I need to think about this."

"They want you to travel around the country talking about the weaknesses in Tewkesbury's plans."

"I'm not going to persuade people the sell their homes."

"No, you are to defend the price of property, to defend everything that Britain stands for, a property owning democracy."

"Now, you sound like my sister."

"You've lost enough already, haven't you? You don't want to lose the rest."

"I suppose I have," then Eric begins to laugh. "Actually what you've just told me is exactly what I believe."

"So, no-one can accuse you of hypocrisy. All you'll be doing is telling people your honest opinion. And the money will help you get the message across. Perfect! S&B do pay very generously, don't forget that."

"OK, when do we begin?"

"Not we, you. First there are some places you should think of visiting. Now finish your beer. I want your body."

Eric is swathed in a gleam of euphoria as Mona leads him across the road to her lair.

Lisa turns to Amanda, "She just offered him everything he's ever wanted."

"And it looks as if he's going to take it."

"I can't say I blame him, can you? But what are we going to do, sit here and wait?" Amanda turns to look across the street, just as the front door closes behind Eric and Mona. Apart from the barman, and themselves, both pub and street are deserted.

"The regulars will be in later. There's a new Hogwarts on telporn," says the Barman, "Dennis Potter and the Forest of Doom. That Marge Beckham is droon-fiddling."

That was the formal reminder they're in reconstruction, not reality.

"Thankyou, so much!" beams Amanda enthusiastically.

"I think we have to make a decision," says Lisa.

"What do you mean?"

"Well," she says hesitantly, "can you think of a way we can find out what they're up to?"

"I'm not going to start shinning up drainpipes to spy on people, if that's what you mean. We're not mountaineers."

"What else can we do?"

"Lisa, we are historians, this is a miasmatic reconstruction," Amanda reminds her, "We can't just go charging about as if it's really happening. Someone might get hurt."

"But it changes in response to what we do. If we just sit here, nothing will happen."

"You can't sure of that, but if you try to evade the professional boundaries of observation, then we'll have problems. We could get totally pissed I suppose. The beer is quite good."

"You mean I'll get banned again."

"Your permissible range would be redefined. Mine too, though I have another kind of profile."

"All known history."

"Yes, I suppose they could throw me off the approved list. I wouldn't even know."

"Do you want another drink?"

"Why not? I think we just have to let them get on with

whatever they're getting on with."

"Then lets get out of here. I know a club where we can enjoy ourselves."

Amanda agrees with Lisa's suggestion and they are softly shifted away in the Miasma.

After eight or nine glasses of Fruitivod, for Lisa, morning is too soon after the night before. She and Amanda are lying on the big bed as the sun rises behind the mountains and casts bright beams of light through the summit mists.

"I had a great time," gasps Lisa, as Amanda massages her awake. "I think I did. God! I'm so fuddled, I'm not even sure where that last place was."

Amanda recollections of their foolishness has a rather different flavour.

"Sweetheart, you should be thankful that you don't have a millisecond retrace. I can review not only what I felt like doing, what I thought I was doing, but I also have a re-enaction to hand of what I actually did. It's a bit too lurid for comfort. You want coffee? No. It was a great night though."

Then the two girls curl up in each other's arms and fall asleep till the clock strikes eleven and the Miasma tingles them awake to announce the arrival of Lisa's Mother on her Sunday morning round.

"Hi Mum," says Lisa, as the older woman sits on the edge of the bed. "This is Amanda. She's a character, helps us with the History Room."

Mothers all over the world consistently suffer identity anxiety, when encountering their daughters in bed with this latest generation of data sets, the Laycock Abbey Institute of Advanced Holographics has reported, so Lisa's Mother is quite typical.

After half an hour of politely stilted inconsequentials, she leaves, with the telling phrase, "I suppose its alright, but I don't think I'll tell your Dad about this."

" 's OK. Mum, we aren't thinking of getting married or anything, we're just good friends, that's all."

Amanda smiles sweetly at Lisa's Mother, as the older woman departs with an exasperated frown of mild disapproval hanging over her entire presence..

"Oh, God!" Lisa exclaims. "You would think we were trying to destroy everything she believes in, the way she sits there saying nothing and pretending she hasn't noticed you're here. If you were a bloke she'd be pretending the bio digi divide is a myth."

"Come on Lisa, it's always the same. You shouldn't be surprised after what she's just told us about your Auntie Jem."

"Not Jem again please, I still don't understand how one woman can keep up convincing relationships with half a dozen 'fast breeder' avatars."

"It's not as if she has to worry about having children."

"Who cares?"

"Well, your Mum, obviously. After fifty years of Miasmatics, her generation still cling to the notion of difference."

"At least she liked Billy."

"OK, enough of that, let's go," says Lisa jumping out of bed and into her goat feeding clothes. After an hour of feeding, cleaning, and in Billy's case, combing, cuddling and tickling, Lisa and Amanda decide to concentrate on Selby work. Up on the hillside, Lisa's sheep are looking after themselves.

Back in the history room, Lisa begins to grumble, glowering at the beige surroundings and glaring at the green-eyed cat that she hopes is a random stray. Amanda hales a cigarette as the acacias flinch in distaste.

"They were that close," she moans, "yet we still didn't find out what happened next."

Amanda decided to be patient. "You are thinking like a conspirator, not a historian." Though she would never deny having histortionist inclinations herself, Amanda knows Lisa is a bit of a traditionalist at heart. Like Mother, like daughter. Lisa's Mother would never approve a single histortion, even if it gave her a tingle.

"No-one ever really knows what is going on in the next room. No-one knows what other people are thinking, even when they are in bed together. No-one knows what will happen to them as one moment becomes the next. It's all expectation, assumptions and speculations."

"Amanda, that's why I live on my own, apart from the goat and you a lot of the time and the sheep of course."

The cat looks across at her with genuine disdain, as if deleting her name from the list of potential live-in owners it was considering. Then it gives a convincing "Miaow" and strolls away with a demonstrative left right left again swish of its tail. Goat, indeed, it sniffs. Sheep! Pah!

Lisa continues listening to Amanda repeat a set of ideas she had first heard in her preliminary classes on "Network Assumptions for Historians".

Amanda is emphatic about the limitations she experiences, "Watching two other people, all you can see is their outward behaviour, listen to what they say, pay attention to their postures and expressions, then try to work out what is going on between them. There are always two completely different people, however close they may seem, or how deeply they are entangled in each others' affairs. Different feelings and emotions. Different options and abilities. Different commitments and objectives. Different alternatives. It is the same with you and me. We get on well, but I know, we both know, that our personalities have none of the same parameters. I mean. It's impossible. I know that I have been given a pre-determined mix of options. Your origins are completely different. I can't kill, I can't have children, I'm immune to all kinds of biological constrains, athletically neutral, as they say. You were in the school team, weren't you, for ice-hockey anyway? The best we can say is that I bear a close approximation to a set of expectations about the kind of person I'm supposed to be. I can live with that. It's a mystery to me, but its not a mystery in itself. You're different, purely biological, genetic, bodily, masses of unknowns in your chemistry, alive, unpredictable, random and deviant. You are a living woman Lisa, I am no more than a well thought out app and there are times, I'll be honest, when that really rankles."

Lisa decides that it isn't such a good idea to depend on an extended computer programme as your best friend, especially when it comes to deviance. Of course, Amanda doesn't know this, she only notices an expression of mild concern flit across her primary contact's brow.

"What's wrong?" asks Amanda.

"I was just thinking about Selby and his girlfriend," Lisa lies, breaking through a barrier of trust she had expected to endure. She'd actually been thinking how lucky Amanda is that she can expect an upgrade from time to time to cure her character defects and she's effectively immortal, but Lisa decides to limit the conversation to more likely themes, "Poor old Selby. We left them half an hour ago, but they aren't there either any more, are they? They've been dead for ages and ages and that night was over half a century before either of them died. Maybe they forgot about it. They weren't there when we were watching. It was a sham."

"No Lisa, history is delicate, a gossamer weave of memories and records. That's why the global version is so precious. All Known History; without it the past would cease to exist."

Amanda wonders whether to explain the difference between their understanding of history. Spider-like, Amanda's task is to draw almost invisible threads of experience into an intoxicating network, creating a dense mesh of experience, with patterns of unbearably beautiful intricacy. For her, the entire project is about building a wonderful structure, lines of events and experience threaded by space and time, a mathematical project that would reveal the shape of human affairs and ultimately their place in the wonder of creation.[43]

Each point in this gigantic model represented a decisive moment of humanity's progression from terrestrial experience towards abstraction and the virtual universe of Pure Thought, a programme that assures that anything of value to be learned from these thousands of millions of years of conscious experience will be preserved on people's behalf, that their presence in the galaxy will never be entirely forgotten, despite their inevitable long term fate - annihilation. Her affections for Lisa are quite genuine. She loves this young woman's curiosity, her unquenchable thirst for detail and her romantic sense of truth. Two young women walk along the footpath outside and a burst of rowdy music invades the tranquillity.

"I'm going home," Lisa announces. "I don't feel safe here."

Amanda furrows her brows with concern, "You don't feel safe? But, I'm here."

The acacias are losing their pigment in the evening gloom and a family of rats are foraging in the undergrowth. A lost sheep bleats and is answered by the rest of the flock. Found. The goat looks like a ghost on stilts. Lisa decides to take up cycling, then decides to do nothing about it.

"I need a few days away from the archives."

"But we just had our trip to Europa, Lisa. And we need to find out who these property speculators were, who funded Selby's first campaign."

"Maybe I am still weary from the journey. I can still hear the whine of all that ice grinding in the tunnel. And the hum all the time, it makes me tired, then I get ratty."

---

43 Applying the Analytics of All Known History to Neo- Non-human and non-biological domains is a major theme in Amanda's post-doc research project for Professer Annie Ward Moloch at the MindTech Institute, Balaban NorthWest 3.

They are interrupted by Joe, who arrives, cheerful and brimming with optimism. The mood lifts.

"I've found a record of Selby describing his first tour, when they came up with the legacy name, right at the beginning of the Forthright Movement. He was in a little place called Epworth[44], not far from the parcels of land that he and his sister owned. The speech he gave was all about climate change and the lies people had been fed for decades about energy policies."

Joe pauses very briefly, just to check that they are listening.

"When he came to the aprés the aprés le deluge bit, the audience started laughing. Really, they were chortling with glee, as if they couldn't care less about the glaciers. They really couldn't. Scotland's frozen fate was of no interest to them, never had been, never would be."

Then some-one explained that the whole district was one great bog that had been drained to make fields in the seventeenth century and was only kept dry by pumping stations that sucked water out of the drainage ditches and into the tidal River Trent. Now the dreaded threat of a five metre rise in sea level was being realised. They had another fifty years, some said, at most, then that would be it. But this meant the farmers thought they had won their battles against the conservationists who wanted to see the bogs re-established as nature reserves. There's nothing to be said for building sea defences unless they barrage the Estuary with a thirty mile, fifty kilometre long dam, so the whole area is expected to become a massive lake, which is what it was at the end of the last ice age.

New parameters all round.

All efforts at preservation would be completely impractical and where there's nothing for the conservationists to conserve, they

---

44 Epworth, a small English village on the Isle of Axholme, a lowland area close to the River Trent, best known as the birthplace and childhood home of eighteenth century divine and founder of Methodism, John Wesley.

can do their meddling elsewhere.

Farmers like to meddle for themselves and these farmers have a plan which they think will help them make a lot of money.

Expecting to see off the conservation project, they will plough on with high yield crops for as long as it lasts, then strip off several million tonnes of valuable topsoil for sale to places like Cornwall and they train their children and grandchildren to exploit the newly formed inland lake for fishing and tourism.

They also have a plan to invoke a set of medieval statutes that gave certain families the exclusive right to fish in an area that was once a Royal Forest.

"Those rights are still ours", said one old man roundly, "and we'll fight for them this time, just as we did before. Do not underestimate our determination, or stubbornness, our capacity for downright bloody mindedness."

Selby is impressed that they can pinpoint their ancient rights and also propose a method to reinforce them.

Everyone in the hall were having small fish ponds dug out in the corners of their fields, so they could claim their rights to uphold these traditions. One of the farmers gave a massive guffaw and said they were determined to fight for their 'legacy'. Selby raised an even bigger laugh when he asked how many of them were retraining as fishermen.

"Look, son," a fellow called Arthur Wesley explained forthrightly. "No-one expects someone who owns the rights to an oilfield to sit down with a bucket and spade and start digging in the general direction of Australia. They get a firm to do the work, then they sit down and take their share of the profit. That's what we'll do about the fishing. We shall invite a firm of hungry fishermen in to do the donkey work and we'll all bugger off somewhere pleasantly sunny and live off the earnings. That's a real legacy," he said, "a legacy from the past that becomes a fruitful legacy for the short-term future. 's capitalism innit, the fruits of our property, capitalism pure, bloody right, don't complain."

Selby looked around the village hall, seeing the contented ruddy faces of the stubborn farmers, whose land was going to be flooded and realised he had found his constituency. Their future well-being was anchored in the past, founded on old rights. They were all set to welcome change and bloody-mindedly exploit it to the full.

"What we haven't established is quite where we should retire to," admits one Septimus Smith to grins and laughter all round. "The banks have helped us acquire some packets of land, half a dozen spots around the world where the climate change will bring a gentle pattern of weather, which is what we've all agreed we want. No more than a couple of hundred thousand hectares in any one location, but at least we are prepared. Such a pity about Italy. I'd rather wanted to retire to Tuscany, but that will no longer be so attractive, what with the mosquitoes and the Mafia and all that ash from the Etna business. I'm not that keen on Alaska to be honest, too close to Russia, but we might give it a go. Zealand is such a long way from anywhere, though I must confess many of us, maybe even a majority are minded to give Zealand our attention."

As Joe drew out the story of his research and brought it to an end, Lisa sat watching him and began to compare him to his younger brother. Their presence was quite different.

Less powerful than the iceman Bill, Joe shares more in common with the tough guy than she had realised, his long legs, the way he laid his hands before him on the table, the twist of his wrist as he took a sip of water and the curious curl in his hair around the ears.

Lisa wonders whether they take after their Mother, or their Father.

The Mother had been a cartographer at Smithsons.

What the Father had done was never mentioned.

"Did you find out if Mona was at this village meeting?"
Amanda asks.

"No sign of her. Eric made a couple of phone calls from the
hotel, but we don't have a record of who he was talking with.
My guess is that one of them would be his sister. They had joint
ownership of the land didn't they?
He picked up one of the local girls after the meeting, seems to
have been enjoying himself.
I don't know about her."

"The call could have been to Mona?" Amanda persists.

"We have nothing."

"Let's suppose it could have been," Amanda pushes.

"I don't think we should indulge in that kind of speculation,"
Joe parries. "It's only reconstruction."

"No, don't go too far," agrees Lisa, pragmatically.

"It was just a thought," says Amanda, retreating. People can be
so touchy about the oddest things, she decides. Without saying
anything to the others, she creates a new version of events
based on the assumption that the call was to Mona. The tangle
of consequences are so extraordinary, blowing most of the
observable historic past into chaos, that she realises this can't
have been the case.

Nevertheless, the little nudge her assumption gave to the data
model created a dramatic reaction that is so extreme, that she
decides the figure of Mona is not only central to their project,
but someone who wielded enormous potential power 'behind
close doors'.

Clear as data, Mona is emerging as one of those very few key
figures who have shaped history. She has pattern.

Amanda registers a tag for Mona.

She is the very first identity Amanda has initiated, a
breakthrough, a defining moment for her career.

Which of these two is really more significant, Selby, a figure that historians have researched to death, or Mona, someone who has managed to remain anonymous for centuries?

Amanda says nothing about this to anyone.
She needs time to think.
Two days with the data cores should be enough.

CHAPTER 5

Pondweed salad is pretty easy to make, highly nutritious and a healthy way to stop the tanks getting clogged up. After a couple of hours pumping ox, it doesn't taste too bad either. Lisa never went as far as some of her neighbours, the bubbler brigade, who don a mask to pump their own exhalations of CO_2 into the water as they pedal. She crushes a clove of Chinese garlic and douses the pondweed in a pungent oily dressing with three shots of protein powder to bind the weed into a cakey mass. In seven minutes her favourite dinner will be ready – Alaskan Goulash, inimitable, green and unforgettable.

Winter was coming and soon it would be time to pull the covers over their homes and erect the winter light-traps for the solstice tomatoes that are sold on December 21 to celebrate survival.

Sixty degrees north, winter sunlight is a precious commodity. As the seaboards of Europe and California had cooled, so the Aleutians and the west coasts of both Atlantic and Pacific had warmed, but the latitude meant the hours of day and night remained the same. The snaking polar current is still gaining centrifugal energy, now the northern ice melt is complete, sending long squirts of hostile water down the coast of Norway, but skimming past the narrow Bering Straight to suck at the warm waters of the Pacific.

Plants enjoy the warmth, but they need light.

Hoorah for LED's!

The goat has settled into its new home and enjoys a diet of pondweed without the dressing. Lisa's little menagerie is enough to keep her busy, what with mucking out and tending their needs. The dung goes straight onto the tomato beds. The left-overs are buried in trenches for the following season's potato crop. There is also an asparagus bed she's been preparing, but that gets less of her attention, since despite the myths of amateur gardeners, asparagus grows quite easily and the delicious shoots quickly become tall and elegant stems with delicate leaves that go for export to Japan. Truffles are still best ordered online. No-one can do every thing themselves.

With this steady routine, Lisa doesn't actually need history and she keeps away from the history room for almost a fortnight.

A couple of brief messages to Amanda are enough to keep her at arms length. She uses the miasma sparingly, for entertainment and the daily news. Apart from that she is alone. Picking out her favourite alter ego Harmonia Lissom, Lisa selects private and without telling Amanda, she dives into the frivolous world of Marge Potter for a bit of fun, then she sidles into 'exquisite' for hours of sustained psychologically optimised pleasure. After a week or so, she's more or less refreshed and ready to have another go at being one of the serious historians.

While Lisa was recharging her batteries, Amanda was ploughing on, tugging and teasing at the links to Mona, Selby and his henchmen, but she needs some back up and the only person she can ask is Fred Q. Smithson.

Getting Smithson's attention wasn't easy.

He put Amanda on hold, then she had to chat up his secretary to arrange an appointment.

At these levels, the days of swift data exchange are long forgotten. Smithson is well-known for his mistrust of others, however close their ties.

"When I have so little confirmation of my own identity," he had written in the Zeeland Observer, "how much integrity should I ascribe to other entities?" His argument had been that rational decision making was contingent on the exclusion of irrelevant factors. He had therefore begun to build barricades in the hope of deterring outsiders. Immediacy is rather unbecoming, he claimed.

'There is no reason to assert that a viable democracy should be inclusive,' he claimed, in his three short letters to the electors of Palestine. As Edmund Burke had once argued, Smithson maintained that he was not a delegate mandated to mouth the views of his constituents, but was nominated for his good judgement on a range of issues. Smithson has a lofty opinion of himself. 'I am not your spokesman, my opinions and good judgement alone are worthy of your votes.' He also offered the Palestinians a large sum of money for supporting his candidacy.

Smithson also noted that Burke had a narcissistic fondness for parades and courted approval, like thousands of populist politicians ever since. A failing, in Smithson's opinion and a blot on the development of public affairs for which Burke should take the blame. Smithson's current campaign was to insist that candidates for public office should remain anonymous and voters should choose them only on the basis of their talents - voting by profile, he called the proposal. Critics maintained that the electorate could hardly be expected to make their choices based on a bunch of anonymous CV's. He held out little hope for its success.

'What's in a Name?' he asked in vain as the world and its wife roared 'Everything' in reply.[45]

---

45 Who the hell do you think you are, Fred? - Anon, Prickly Press,

Nor am I a lobbyist, Smithson had told the last General Assembly five years earlier. The Hobbesian Universe of unpleasant configurations will be my nemesis, Smithson concluded, as he turned down the role of Adjudicator, that the Assembly had unanimously proposed.

Even the most delinquent of Humanity's twelve million members had registered dismay at his refusal. 'I have chosen curiosity as an alternative to ambition,' he wrote modestly some years later, 'and ambivalence in preference to enthusiasms. I have no interest in government, that is the sphere of competent administrators, which politicians never are and are not intended to be. My role is the incubation of new ideas, the articulation of novel concepts and well thought through opinions.' Smithson had always be astonishingly arrogant.

Reading this, Morgan Fitzwalter[46] had threatened to have him expelled from the Social Democratist Alliance and shot. Fitzwalter's threat should have been taken more seriously, but the General Assembly was held a few months before Fitzwalter was arrested on 417 counts of embezzlement and 16 of assassination.[47] How could any of them have known what was about to happen?

After days of chivvying, Smithson arranged to meet Amanda at Rabinotti's Kosher Italian Restaurant in Midchurch on the Isle of West Zealand.

She felt both privileged and suspicious to be asked.

"At least this place is discrete and discreet," Smithson murmurs, as he glances down the menu, his eyes gleaming greedily with pleasure.

The Maître-d' has shown them to a table in a private room, with

---

Ohio.

46 Fitzwalter, Morgan H, Politician.

47 Trial transcripts – Faculty of Law, Shanghai University of Paris.

a splendid view over the blue skied green sea'd bay. A school of dolphins are playing a few hundred yards off shore. Gannets, guillemots and shags are fishing the waters and a pair of blue swans are honking at a line of signets paddling furiously as their parents glide elegantly along.

"I didn't think you'd want to meet in one of the hives, Quentin," Amanda replies warmly.

"God forbid," says Smithson with feigned irony. "I would rather don an extra layer of firewalling than descend into the aesthetic hell of a hive."

"You're an unredeemed snob, Mr. Smithson."

"Of course I am, and so are you, Amanda, if you have an ounce of sense about you. Is there any point being otherwise? I learnt that from my days in Cambridge and subsequently when I visited Harevjard. You know, both places took it for granted that no-one with anything worth saying could possibly exist outside their confines. Worse than the army in that respect, though they had no delusions about fighting winnable wars against monsters from outer space. Oh, you've reminded me, I must warn Major Custor about his Venus Fly Traps."

"How big is your team now?"

"I have twenty seven full time associates in the office and two thousand part-time assistants. Actually, only about fifty of them understand what they're doing, the rest are mere data addicts. I don't think any of them at all appreciate my goals. It's a lonely business."

Amanda is impressed.

She chooses Falkland Shrimp as her main course, while Smithson decides on steak from pampered bullock.

"You said there was a question of personality linking?" Smithson mumbles, as he chews with relish.

"I'm thinking of proposing a persona, but I haven't found the right partner to embody the real time presence."

"I shouldn't worry about that. Some-one will emerge within the community, just as you did when the virtual abstract of Amanda began to mature. Who was the woman you had to duel for the role? Elle something or other, or was it Bea, damn, I've forgotten the woman's name, but I remember the day you faced each other, swords at the ready."

He shivers with pleasure at the memory of the encounter.

"My dear, not many women have survived a duel on board ship during a Caribbean storm. She should have known that youth would prevail. You won well. I remember the blood on the decks where you fought. All that grunting and clashing of steel. Wonderful stuff. I was aroused."

"I didn't intend to kill her," says Amanda, recalling her shame.

"No, but you did, that was what mattered. It was decisive."

"I felt so appalled, as she fell."

"She would quite as willingly have killed you."

"Supposedly."

This is a subject Amanda would prefer to leave behind.

"No suppose about it", Smithson ploughs on. "She had been training in Korea, a multiplicity of martial arts. You were lucky, extremely lucky. I had expected a different outcome."

Amanda is silent for a moment.

"I didn't know that."

"Do you know how many people are murdered every day?"

"No idea."

"About a two thousand, and only a half of one per cent of cases are cleared up."

"That was the chance we took."

"All of us. It would have been a mess if we'd been discovered," he cautions. "Yet here we are. Have another shrimp. Some things are better forgotten. Shall we shoot the pianist?"

"Maybe later. The way he's playing, I expect the boys in the band will get to him first. But the food is rather good, is it not?"

"It certainly is," he agrees, chewing as he talks, "Now tell me why you want to propose this new persona."

90

Amanda turns up the music and switches to 'broken thought', the most stable encryption in that stealthy neck of the woods. If you can't work out what you're thinking yourself, how on earth can anyone else read your mind?

"I must say I prefer rapidity to this choppy mangle of uncouth conceptualisation," Smithson stammers, as he acclimatises himself to 'broken thought', though his voice retains its unusually well modulated baritone.

Amanda knows he prides himself on his mellifluous tones, the result of a year at drama school in South Africa and two years training as an assistant stage manager at the Bristol 'Old Vic'. His John of Geilgud had won him the Gaunt prize for monologue.

"Maybe we should consider accessing you to 'Cornucopia', in which case this subterfuge would be unnecessary. It may take a while to arrange, but we shall see. You have heard of Cornucopia, I assume."

Amanda is really, hugely flattered.

Less than a hundred thousand personalities have been admitted to 'Cornucopia' and all of them have been humanic. She would be the very first construct to be awarded the accolade of access to everything. She hopes she has enough credits to cover the linkage fees. There are several thousand metres of old fashioned black vinyl cable required for the personal loop.

'Cornucopia' is for the great and the good in an egalitarian world, but it still helps to be rich to gain full access to all its resources.

As he's cutting the steak and loading his fork with a mixture of meat, oniony sauce and buttered green peas, Smithson asks Amanda to tell him about the new-found personality.

"My group seem to have discovered Eric Selby's animator."

"Interesting," he nods, while chewing and slurping a sip of wine. "I adore alcohol. You know, I was almost thirty before one of my mentors suggested I try real red wine. It's compelling stuff, especially these old Algerian vintages."

Wondering whether it's the wine or the new personality that he finds interesting, Amanda carries on.

"This obsession with Selby is rather improbable, so I asked myself why people should find him so attractive. So far he seems exceptionally dull."

"Oh, he's the repressed person's James Bond, or a suburban Robin Hood," Smithson remarks blandly with an exaggerated sigh, "And who among us is not thoroughly repressed?"

"Better repression than depression!" Amanda jokes. "Old election slogans reveal more than their creators ever imagined."

"My dear, they didn't win, you know. Though by then the shift to ultra-democracy was to my mind inevitable."

"But Quentin, 'Freedom brings Insecurity' was brilliantly effective."

"Yes, we wouldn't be here today, but for that."

"Especially when coupled with the threats against the hives."

Smithson chortles, "Well, no-one wants their loved ones to embark on a journey of eternal bliss, only to be reanimated in the middle of it by some self-appointed 'consciousness rights' activist. I felt no small measure of pride having initiated that particular little panic."

He interrupts himself to add brusquely, "You were about to tell me about your personality proposal? Do go on."

A pea rolls from his fork and drops under the table. One of the rats snatches it and scurries under the floorboards to share it with its young. Like most rodents, rats are vegan. Indeed, by far the majority of vegans are rats.

Amanda tells Smithson about Mona and her influence on Eric Selby. "She seems to have achieved all her goals by proxy, using Selby as her mouthpiece and preserved her privacy, almost to the point of anonymity."

"The invisible woman? I do approve of goal scoring by proxy. No-one need ever be jealous. Interesting potential as a role model. Anyone who supports the proxy concept has much to commend them,in my opinion."

"More, or less. We found her by accident. My friend Lisa played a joke on me and began a re-run earlier than planned. We picked upon her there, then lost her again, but a lot of re-tracks helped us pin her down."

"Good. How much of her do you want to revive?"

"I was thinking about her mind and Selby's physique."

"Let me think about this," Smithson said, as Amanda fleshed out her proposal. "Was she attractive?"

"Tall and skinny, dark hair, Caribbean-ish, you know the type. Chic, according to the reports. Stunning would be another way of putting it. Intoxicatingly good looking."

Amanda smiles her own version of good looking intoxication.

"We shall have to see," mumbles Smithson to end the discussion. "I need to get back to rapidity. We have a Cabinet meeting at two thirty. I do hope you enjoyed the shrimp. Goodbye."

And with that, he was gone!

And so was the rat.

She stays in the restaurant for another couple of hours, then the waiter offers her the bill. Eighty thousand for the wine alone - more than she usually spends in a week and another fifty for the food, with 100% carbon tax on top. Two pairs of shoes equivalent. It was less than she had feared, but still more than she could really afford. Does Smithson lunch like that every day, leaving his fellow diners to foot the bill? She wouldn't be surprised.

Amanda takes a stroll along the old village street and watches a group of parka-clad children playing football. Eric Selby had been a football fan. This was another area of history that Amanda found uninteresting, except in terms of the debate on obesity. Soccering seemed a rather trivial skill, but without it what would have happened to men's feet? Women have always had shoe shops to divert their attention to their feet, but they're redundant for online gaming, so the men would have lost out. Amanda wonders whether to write a short paper on the theme, but decides not. There's probably a foot lobby somewhere with members who would lodge complaints and stalk her via the Miasma. Are foot fetishists good at tracking people down?

Then she sees a green woollen hat in a shop window and decides to buy it as a present for Lisa. Cashmere, the sales assistant explains, "think of it as goat-wool and the colour is derived from completely natural sources, processed from dehydrated Alaskan pondweed."

Amanda decides against the purchase. Colas to Nigeria.

Deciding not to seems to be the mood of the afternoon.

She blames Smithson.

Amanda spends the rest of the afternoon mooching around Midchurch, waiting for her secure transfer to be announced. Her departure has been rescheduled because of network problems in Malaysia. She feels very much alone.

Amanda can't discuss character issues with Lisa. Selinsky's death has robbed her of a reliable profiler, as well as a friend. Maybe, one day, he might be reconstructed and they could work together once more. Even now, Amanda thinks there's sufficient data to come up with a fairly convincing basic version, at least as far as the face and the voice and those kinds of superficialities.

The hills around Midchurch remind her of the Appalachians and the seas off Vancouver, but the buildings are bland and benign, a little permafrosted ghost-town, abandoned apart from the restaurant and the half dozen tourist shops, selling trinkets, alcohol and subarctic apparel. The Yukon had once been like this. Vancouver might have been like this in 1910, except a row of ice-bergs fill the entrance to the sound, where they have been parked before the tow to South Australia and the twenty million tonne race to see which of the tugboat crews could get there fastest and minimise the melt. One berg a month is enough to keep Australia in drinking water, the other nine go into irrigation for the wine industry and drinking water for sheep. The huge sails give shade as much as propulsion and the bergs glow pink as the evening sun dips behind them towards the horizon.

Amanda takes some photos. She isn't sure why. Her memory is photographic. This snapping must be some relic of a half forgotten ritual.

The 'New Town', half an hour's drive away is a product of the ice trade, an industry almost exclusively manned by hard drinking Russian expatriots with wives whose gaudy taste in jewellery and trinkets keeps the Belgian fashion houses in business. Amanda knew the Belgians had hit on the market by chance, after an Indian fashion guru had told them to stop trying for elegance and concentrate on finding customers who put a premium on flashy tastelessness and mentioned how Fabergé had wooed the Russian Court with nothing more than jewel encrusted Easter Eggs, which it was suggested were actually filled with cocaine[48].

After her conversation with Smithson, Amanda is wondering how to integrate some of Mona's qualities in the Selby persona. It could probably be justified on the grounds that the Forthright Movement seems to have been her idea, though Selby had been given the credit and no-one would agree to revising his totemic qualities. The compromise will be declared in Selby's registration documents, but that shouldn't present a problem. Compositing[49] has become more common as the range of

---

48 Russian Traditions, Gromiko, W., Bolshie Memorial Press, Paris, 2066.
49 Agreed at the Council of Belize in 2151, compositing approved the principle of amalgamating character traits and experience quotients from up to 300 historic individuals in a

personas has been tightened up to reduce the over-representation of politicians and businessmen. Take anything from three to three hundred personalities, look for the similarities, remove the differences and reduce them into the single composite. Easier than it sounds. After a few months, no-one seems to notice any difference. History is like that.

Sixteen microseconds elapse after her transfer is announced, then Amanda is at home reading a very formal text message from a lawyer, telling her that Selinsky has given her custodial access to his personal files, as well as a small legacy. Another message from Selinsky, that Amanda will never find out about, has been sent to Lisa.

What Amanda does find among the files is a revelation.

Selinsky's work has a single theme that began in his school-days and ended in mid-sentence, with a confused gurgle, only half a second into the fatal crash event sequence. Thwarted and frustrated, Selinsky had died as he had lived, in a unfulfilled quest for power.

From his peculiar breakfasts of toast and freshly squeezed lemon juice to the dinners of mollusc and batter pudding, Selinsky's days were incomplete without dipping into the miasmatic burrowing grounds of intriguers and plotters. A member of 'Strange Deeds' since the age of twelve, he had links with more than fifty sects and loosely banded gangs of renegades. With this kind of background, his interest in Selby was easily accounted for and Amanda realises that her sympathy for Selinsky's profiling skills was born of her intuitive feel for subterfuge.

A moment after Amanda has learned of the Selinsky legacy,

---

single character, see also i) Stereotyping, Cloning and Eugenics, Blair A, Cheney W and Rice C, Hoffman Foundation Publications, Old Shrubbery, Texas.

THE SWOOP

Lisa is startled by the voice message asking her to visit the Golden Forest Bank in Anchorage.

"There you will enquire after Mrs. Jordan Wallace, who will attend to your needs as I have bid her."

The manager went on to inform her they were executors in the affairs of Edwin Abramovitch Selinsky. "Do be sit. A number of small bequests have already been settled, however our client has left the balance of his savings and investments in your name. Your riches are a pleasure to behold!" Bank phraseology is becoming ever more quaint now they've chosen Quakerisation as an ethically attractive interface.

Lisa is tempted to dash away at once, but she feels the goat deserves first call on her time and decides to stay at home, merely riffling through the papers they have sent her. Never doubting there would be money, Lisa is surprised at the wealth he had sequestered, more than 50,000 times average annual income. This was confirmed by Grimmonds, her own bank, who slipped a spybot into Golden Forest at her request which came up green for go.

An old fashioned cheque book arrived in the post, with a letter explaining that withdrawals must be written by hand, signed and countersigned by a bank representative. The letter requested that she withdraw amounts only in excess of 20 million credits from the Golden Forest account. Interest is accruing at the rate of 7.725% per annum. Tax will be deducted automatically. The voice attachment sneakily added, "You have your local bank account at Grimmonds for small transactions."

This brings a smile to her face. Lisa is suddenly filthy rich.

"Tonight I shall dream beyond the dreams of avarice," she tells Billy the Kid, as he sniffs greedily at the cover of the chequebook.

Amanda has never been to Selinsky's flat, but this is where the handwritten records will be, so she flits to the quiet street where he lived in Newton on the outskirts of Boston.

Almost bowled over by a dog that springs away from its owner to spread its paws on her fawn jeans in slobbery greeting, Amanda steps back as its owner tries to grab the beast.

"That must be one of the hounds from hell we keep hearing about," she says to the plump woman with the dog leash, a mound of fat in middle aged purple, who replies that, "Jonky is the best trained and most affectionate hound in the city."

Amanda throws her head back and scoffs, "And the other ones are called Cerberus and Baskerville, I suppose."

"Cerberus died after the operation, so sad for Mrs. Dincroft," says the purple woman. "But I don't know of any Baskerville."

Bewildered by this gossip, Amanda turns away, "At least someone has shown some sense if they cut off a couple of extra heads, rather than just the one."

The purple lady's face flushes to match her jacket and she scurries away in a huff of disbelief. "How could you be so vulgar about small wee tripartite beasties," she almost sobs. "Come on, Jonkey, and you, Wonkey, and stop that slobbering Slomka." She pats each of the dog-heads in turn, just as they growl in unison at the sight of a very fat cat. The cat slinks up a tree, wobbles on a bough and snarls its disapproval in reply.

Amanda scurries away and lets herself into Selinsky's place, before any more local dog-lovers can interrupt her.

When Lisa finally gets to the Bank, Mrs. Jordan Wallace tries to sell her some life assurance, a batch of mortgage deals just in case she intends to buy a new home, then offers to invest the cash in a variety of funds the Bank run for a fee of only one per cent per year and gets huffy when Lisa tells her she would like the whole amount of the bequest transferred to her account with Grimmonds by the end of the day's business. This creates panic in the Bank, who ask Lisa for two or three days grace to settle the affairs. So much cash in a single transaction would get them into trouble with the regulators. Having signed another batch of forms, she agrees to their request with a smile, which Mrs Jordan Wallace answers with a scowl as Lisa walks out of the office with a couple of million in cash and an inter-stellar credit rating that makes shop fronts blink and flash as she walks past.

'Malevolence is an all too human failing,' Selinsky had written as the first sentence of his hand-written memoires, 'but I have grown to relish its influence in the naive affairs of men. Theories about how our world should be run have always assumed that the good guys will be in charge and evil will be, if not vanquished, then denatured and disarmed. Yet, in thirty years of detailed historical research, I have found no significant act of government which has not been marred by compromise with unscrupulous people of sufficient wealth and influence to ensure their interests are served first. I am therefore proposing the creation of a Grand Inquisitorial Council to evaluate levels of mendacity and malevolent self-interest in global finance, as expressed within the workings of the International Order of Miasmaticians. My goal is to put this energy to good use, by ensuring the business of our society is sufficiently spiced, yet not overwhelmed by its pungent presence, that homely, yet repulsive, 'stink of corruption'.'

"Selinsky seems to have been writing a kind of manifesto for government by the wicked," Amanda tells Joe. "A handbook of dirty deeds and their consequences. Wickedness of every imaginable kind."

"Almost," Joe smiles. "I think he was seen as a megalomaniac outsider. He never actually achieved any of his goals. Perhaps he never intended to."

"Yet this archive of his, this legacy?" Amanda asks. "A legacy devoted to Legacy? Not without a certain irony, I'm sure."

"Beyond doubt. He mentioned it to me on numerous occasions. In fact he thought about little else," Joe confirms.

"Strange."

"Of course. It is to be expected outside the fifteen million. Irony is protective self deception among the powerless. Wild excesses and eccentricities. Many think these foibles should be encouraged."

Amanda is puzzled.

"The rationality of the 15 million approved characters within the Miasma and Global Governance liberates the rest of us from all our responsibilities. We have no duties, no obligations, absolute freedom to do whatever we please. The characters do everything in our name. They bicker, ferret and lobby. They administer and decide our fate on our behalf. Second level democracy is so efficient because the governors are governed by their servants. That was his take on how things are."

Joe shrugs, "I'm not sure that I agree, but he had a point."

Amanda experiences something close to indigestion as her ethics machine hastily interrogates itself in reaction to Selinsky's claims on their judgement.

"That can't be right," she says confidently to Joe. "Our long term strategies would lose all coherence if it was true."

Joe smiles, "You are ignoring the most basic failing of human existence. In the long term, we are all dead. The older we become, the less we are concerned about our, or anyone else's future. If it really becomes unbearable, we can simply stop breeding and go for collective suicide. Such things have happened. Old age cures social responsibility. Nice while it lasted, you might say, but now the music's stopped – so what? Last one out switch off the Miasma. I think we've all assimilated that thought into our attitudes. We had a near miss with atomic weapons and climate change has driven the nails much deeper into the collective coffin."

"There's one clear answer, but you won't like it," Amanda cautions.

"Tell me."

"Well, Joe, in the very long term, perhaps a biosphere might no longer be a necessity. Networks are far less sensitive to environmental conditions than people. By extending the Miasma into new realms we might also overcome the spacial limitations of an earthbound existence."

A red light blinks, then Amanda reminds Joe that she is being speculative.

Warning over, it reverts to green.

"The Earth, as a core for the extended Miasma? If the field was left to expand, at the speed of what - light?" Joe looks apprehensive. "After four years we could have reached the nearest star. All it needs is energy."

"Of course the signal would be highly dissipated and consume unimaginable amounts of power to make it work," says Amanda dismissing the idea. "To sustain a coherent signal at that distance would be beyond anything anyone has considered."

"Impractical, but not theoretically impossible. We would need to invoke quantum cascading to maintain the structure. Perhaps it might be funnelled. I shall have to think about this. It would give a new meaning to solar power, if we could actually harness the sun directly, as part of the Miasma."

Joe concludes, "I enjoy speculative policy. Politics without responsibility. Much more fun than holding office. And I do enjoy immunity from prosecution for disturbing the equilibrium."

Amanda smiles, "The cleverest formula ever devised for keeping politicians in check. 'Disturbing the equilibrium' What a joke!"

Joe nods his agreement and begins to play Rachmaninov's 'Riot Police Concerto' on their music channel.

Lisa is looking forward to going out for the evening and she's feeling exuberant after the unexpected windfall from Selinsky. Admiring herself in the mirror, slim hipped and neatly breasted, she drapes one blouse over another, chooses the first to wear and sets it off with a silk scarf that seems right for the night. She is due at the Antiquarian Society's monthly meeting for seven. It isn't a big deal, a simple frivolity, but she thinks she deserves some frivoling. Maybe she should make another play for Bill Smather. Then she decides, maybe not. Anyway, she doesn't know where he is. Maybe no-one does. Maybe he's lost and even he wouldn't know where he is. Bill could be anywhere, she realises and goes to clean her teeth before setting out.

Malliday and Harkham have arranged a visiting lecturer she's never heard of, but once the talk is over, they are due to discuss Harkham's latest project, which is what interests Lisa.

Harkham has been the driving force behind their collection of antique domestic appliances, from washing machines and fridges to kettles and vacuum cleaners, then the mini-collection of three antique aeroplanes, so they're all looking forward to some fun with whatever his next big idea is.

There are another fifty bicycles parked outside the community centre when Lisa arrives, five minutes before the lecture is to begin. Not a bad turnout, when people could be enjoying the balmy evening sunset, or simply flop into the miasma for an afterwork session of sensual relaxation.

Tall, gangling and middle aged, Peter Malliday[50] gives her a quick smile as she chooses a seat towards the back of the room. Then, he goes to the microphone and introduces the speaker, who talks for about half an hour about the history of cooking, before charging up one of their old gas cookers, a rarity and showing them a traditional dish from Olde Englande demonstrating how 'bacon and eggs' could be cooked in an open topped pan with fat. In theory this could be done with any heat source, but the lecturer explained that gas cookers were extremely easy to control and avoid burning your dinner.

This frying business struck Lisa as a smelly practice.

---

50 Not Peter M. Malliday, Grand Inquisitor of Quebec.

The next demonstration is recipes based on wrapping things in strips of salted meat and fat, which he calls bacon. He makes something called 'Angels on Horseback'[51], then something more pungent called 'Devils on Horseback' and finally a mixture he calls 'Mermaids on Horseback', that Lisa finds faintly erotic. She patches a sense link over to Amanda, who takes one stiff, 'Stinky!' and logs out. Compared to to the blandly pleasant pondweed Lisa has just had for supper, it is an salty orgy of textures and flavours. Then man claims to have used real bacon, but Lisa knows it has been banned for over a century and there is no-where that it could be prepared since killing pigs was made illegal. Even if they are rice strips, she has to admit they taste pretty good with these mixtures of contrasting flavours, the smoke and the fat.

People drift away once Harkham announces that it is time for the organising committee to begin their meeting. Lisa moves to sit in one of the chairs at the front. Malliday sits next to her. He is an artist and the tangy smell of oil and turpentine sticks to his clothes. His eyebrows usually reveal what he's been working on.

"I've been exploring greens a lot since we last met."

Lisa smiles politely and checks out the tints on his eyebrows. He seems to assume she understands his interest and always tells her about the pigments he is spending his time rediscovering. He had spent the previous summer enthusing about layering, which Lisa readily concedes she had never really understood, though this hadn't deterred his enthusiasm. Though he takes advantage of Malliday's skills with a

---

51 'Angels on Horseback' A concoction of grilled bacon wrapped around a live oyster. 'Devils on Horseback' uses liver as a filling, which can be served with Worcester Sauce. 'Mermaids on Horseback' a large prawn marinaded in garlic and oil, then wrapped in bacon, grilled and served with mayonnaise.

paintbrush, Harkham has different obsessions. His is a medieval mind in a post-machine age.

The little steamboat he had built to carry tourists along the Summit Valley Lake can take five passengers with a crew of three and bubbles along at a pleasant 8 miles an hour. High pressure super-heated steam drives the twin turbines, which act as their own condensers and pre-heaters for the twenty litres of distilled water that circulates from the boiler, all powered by the speck of millenium[52] which Harkham had borrowed from the high energy research centre at the Hahn-Meitner Institute in Assyria.

Lisa recalls admiring the feathery little turbine blades that Harkham had ground down from titanium in his basement workshop. He had fitted them onto a drive shaft supported by frictionless magnetic bearings, so they can be set spinning with a puff of breath to drive the dynamo elements to generate 150 horse power in the high-pressure turbine. He had been crafty enough to fit the little boat with a ponics pump, so when the steamer wasn't ferrying people up and down the lake, it was churning out a kilo of crystal ox every three minutes. Malliday had painted Harkham's boat in a brilliant shade of blue, which startles the fish.

"I had great hopes for Millenium, but that Scottish idiot spoiled it for everyone," Harkham tells Teresa Barnard as they gather for the Committee Meeting. "If we'd made proper use of it, the evacuation of Moscow might not have been necessary."

"And steam rockets might fly," she replies to remind him they've covered this ground before. Tessa is more concerned with getting the sales concession on LunarCity3 for their crystal

---

52 Millenium – atomic number 1000 – production of this artificially created element has been forbidden since the Berners-Leeway boundary was ignored by a junior research fellow at the Lucerne Institute for Ceramics and Mount Pilatus melted with a single burst of energy.

ox. Ox and water in fancy packaging have become the wedding present of choice for young couples setting up home on the low gravity satellite. Tessa has packaged the Crystal Ox in a wrapping of lemon flavoured water ice all sealed in an eternity flask. The Aleutian branding ensures they outsell all their rivals despite the fancy prices for transportation.[53]

Then Malliday opens a bottle of vodka and pours a shot for each of the Committee members and they drink a toast to 'the end of progress that has no end and to the memory of Vitus Bering'.

Lisa knows Amanda would pour scorn on these over-opinionated and amateurish talents, typical Level 2 democrats, but she enjoys the feeling of being a part of something.

The moment Teresa Barnard begins talking, Lisa realises she's going to be lumbered with another research job. Rails had been found along the ridge of Summit Valley, which they suspected may once have been the track from the old line than ran twenty miles down to the port at Blue Bay.

"Has nothing to do with the mineral line from Anchorage," Malliday explains. "They must have been part of the Russian Plan to link the Trans-Siberian with the Canadian Pacific, but no-one is sure. If it was, the project came to a sudden end when the US bought Alaska from the Tsar in 1867. He must have been crazy. A million and a half square kilometres of land filled with gold, oil, copper and coal. Amazing, almost one percent of the earth's land surface in a single deal for next to nothing."

She shakes her head in mock disbelief.

"Well, now we are reaping the benefits, so thank some-one's god for that," smiles Harkham.

---

53 By the year 5000, the Moon will have its own thin but tangible and stable atmosphere sufficient to enable plants, bacteria and microscopic animals to survive unprotected on the surface, so long as the yeast problem can be overcome. LunaCity3 – population 2351. (ed)

Teresa gazes sweetly towards Lisa, as she asks for a volunteer to "take a little peek" into the archives to see if they could argue that the railway line could be rebuilt. Feeling unusually confident, thanks to the substantial backing of Selinsky's bank account, Lisa takes the meeting by surprise, agreeing to make the search, then offering to fund a feasibility study.

"That's very generous, Lisa," says the Association Treasurer, Alan Montgomery. "But are you absolutely sure about making such a commitment? I had been expecting to prepare a lot of applications for subsidy."

"Well, I should expect some kind of interest in the railway, if it ever goes ahead," Lisa replies.

Montgomery deliberates. "If you are putting up the money, then I suppose it will be yours, though I am sure we'll need other investors if the project ever gets built. It's a huge risk, Lisa."

"Peter," she says, turning to Malliday, "have you any thoughts about the kind of railway this should be?"

"I was hoping you'd ask that," he smiles. "There were some very attractive liveries in the steam age, engines painted apple green, or cherry red, even orange. Coaches too came in all kinds of shapes and sizes. We shall need some of everything."

"I was thinking more about who might use it and how it would be run," Lisa butts in.

Then Harkham takes over. The scheme he outlines is an advanced heritage model.

"Which means?" asks Montgomery on everyone's behalf.

"A combination of every stage in the relevant technology, run to provide a service and to demonstrate the industrial archaeologistics[54]. We should combine primitive tracks running

---

54 The "Advanced Heritage" concept was much criticised as a loophole enabling industrial corporations to evade their duties to modernise plant and equipment. The tax

replicas of early trains with the latest Zip trains as a commercial service and leave enough room to introduce new technologies without destroying anything we've already set in place. The ZIPs[55] could take the tourists in and out. We should run a set of half hour journeys, ranging from three or four miles on the truly ancient steamers to 1250 miles for the ZIPs that synch into the global circuit."

"The Zips look wonderful lined out in red against royal blue."

"Thank you, Malliday," says Harkham tersely.

"Isn't 1250 miles rather a lot of track?" wonders Lisa.

"We could build a little station on the International Line and use their tracks for the longer journey, maybe have a terminus in Anchorage near the harbour."

It all seems very ambitious, but Lisa concludes it is time for her to do something for which she will really be remembered.

She pedals home in record time to discover Amanda is already tucked in bed awaiting her.

"Look at this," whispers Amanda, showing her a fragile notebook filled with smudgy handwriting.

"What is it?"

"From Selinsky's Treasure Chest, I got it this afternoon from his study."

Should Lisa tell Amanda about the money Selinsky had left her. Maybe it isn't the right time. Maybe it never will be.

"Who wrote it?"

"Eric, our man Eric Selby. He seems to have gone to a lot of

---

allowances were eventually scrapped for such schemes.

55 Zip technology involves the creation and breaking up of protein chains to create frictionless conditions for acceleration and controlled deceleration of high speed terrestrial and marine transport systems. A number of complaints (140million) have been registered about the smell created, which has been described as a lingering sulphurous pestilence ("Jeez that Stink", a poem, Roberts, Julia, 2222).

football matches, which isn't very interesting, or at least not the way he writes about it, but he also attended games of cricket, which is wonderful for us."

"I'm not interested in sport."

"Of course not, neither was he, but he used the cricket matches as a place to meet people without drawing anyone's attention to the fact."

"Who?"

"There was a strange system called County Cricket[56] that hardly anyone was interested in, though the games went on for several days and they played for hours and hours, except when it was raining, in which case they waited around for the rain to stop, then started playing again until the next shower of rain and so on. I'm not even sure it interested the players, except that some of them got free trips to places like Australia, or the West Indies in the winter. There were hints of ritualism and a substantial body of numerical records and statistics. Some researchers suggest necromancy, others a complex prototype for casino style betting. A similar system involved horses, but was confined to running, omitting both bat and ball. The only other sport with a similar obsession with statistics is bashball, or its Cuban predecessor baseball. "

"Why didn't Selinsky list this in the archive?"

"There's a note tucked inside the front cover. He says the notebook is a forgery."

"But is it a contemporary forgery? Or was Selinsky a liar."

"I do think Selinsky had problems with the truth and I know he hated football, so he probably never read the notes properly. Listen, this is what Selby wrote about one of the games in Bristol. 'Tedious day of medium paced bowling and unadventurous stroke play. Bloody Dutchmen. Two ducks failed to read spin after tea. Bad light stopped play, also stoppages for rain. Met Mon and Bren after lunch. Long talk about FM. Mon

---

56 Cricket - a bat and ball game.

thinks we have enough momentum to push for a demonstration and we decided the best location would be a small town on market day. So we plan to be in Stamford next week. Bren is designing the posters. Mon will co-ordinate. I shall have to write a speech.'

"And did he?"

"Let's go see."

"Try a walk through?"

"I'll check if its possible – September 22, wasn't it?"

"Correct, take a deep breathe and off we go."

Amanda and Lisa arrive on a crisp autumn day and find they are sitting on a little light blue diesel train that is pulling and rattling into an old fashioned railway station. They have to push a button to get the doors to open and take care stepping down onto the platform. The train is carrying a consignment of refugees on its way to somewhere called Stansted Airport[57] from an old urban wasteland called Birmingham.

Amanda and Lisa are glad to get off. They walk over a footbridge spanning a quiet stream and follow the signposts to the very traditional town centre.

The sturdy stone buildings give Stamford an atmosphere of solid imperturbable charm, the rustic stability of a peculiarly prosperous English vintage. The words 'toast and marmalade' arise unbidden in Amanda's thoughts, while Lisa thinks 'pullovers' and 'woolly hats'.

There's a light breeze and it looks as though it may well rain.

"Gosh," says Lisa. "This is the kind of place they used to put pictures of on Christmas cards. What's that smell?"

"Baking," Amanda replies.

"What are they selling?"

"Let's have a look."

---

57 Renamed as the Tom Paine International Gateway in 2024.

"Such a lot of pies."

"And sausages. Piggy stuff in general. Delicious."

"It's nice here. Do you think they'll have bacon? Why have they got so many cameras all over the place?"

"Paranoia, but be grateful. These cameras are the main reason British history is such fun. There weren't just the usual on-line sources and hotel bookings, sat nav tracking, or travel records. Face recognition software was getting going and people had started attaching cameras to their computers and their cars and bikes, just about everywhere really. Of course, everything on-line was archived, though officially they pretended otherwise. First there are the websites and their blogs, so then we have their phone calls, computer chat, internet audio and phone calls, even private conversations when people forgot that their computers were on. It's funny watching people sitting alone doing nothing, or reading, or watching tv."

"They watched a lot of tv. Makes you wonder why, once you've seen some of the content that attracted them, boring, banal, comatose, bbc stuff. Some-one suggested they were the original prototypes for hive personalities."

Turning a corner, Amanda and Lisa arrive at the Market Place, bustling with people buying vegetables, cheese and yet more pies. Lisa stops at a stall selling hats.

"I like these," she says, picking up a hairy tweed cap.

"Try it on," Amanda encourages her, then laughs. "It makes you look like a farmer."

At the next stall, they avoid tripping over a yellowish dog, then buy a couple of the little pies that look as if they are simply a lump of ground meat curled inside a thick wrapping of greasy pastry. They're hot.

"Hmm...they are called sausage rolls," Amanda says reading the sales receipt.

"I think I could get used to eating these," says Lisa with relish. "There's thyme in them too."

"I think they'd make you fat."

"Not me, Lisa," replies Amanda. "Fat isn't one of my issues."

"Yeah, your 'ones' might stay thin, but what about the 'noughts', all rounder and thicker, clog up the processors."

"Noughts can't get rounder, dear," smiles Amanda serenely and licks the crumbs from her fingers, then she turns her attention to work. This was the first demonstration Lisa and Amanda have witnessed.

They'd both expected something rather more dramatic.

A cluster of local people had gathered out of curiosity to listen to Selby. Lisa and Amanda stand in front of a flower stall and watch the crowd from a distance.

It isn't really a crowd, more of a friendly gathering.

Selby speaks with a friendly, easy-going charm, which Lisa can sympathise with. It's like listening to a serious young man who's just finished his masters and thinks he understands everything. Selby makes a common sense appeal to the notions of Loyalty, the Home and Stability. His audience have similar conservative aspirations. They are rather different to the folk he had addressed in Epworth. Selby is relaxed in their midst. He has begun a dialogue that will always win him supporters in this kind of setting. Several middle age women clearly want to take him home with them to feed on sausage rolls.

The owner of the flower stall taps Amanda on the shoulder and gives her a rose.

"Oh, how beautiful," she thanks him, then whispers to Lisa, "ok, let's get the fuck out of here."

"Thank you so much," she says to the stall-holder, imitating one of the stout ladies she'd heard talking to a vicar a few minutes earlier.

She gives the flower seller her toothiest smile as they turn away. The middle aged Lothario turns quite pink, as he blushes at his own audacity.

"Where are we going?" hisses Lisa to Amanda.

"We're following the man in the blue suede shoes," says Amanda mysteriously and she gives the rose to an old man who is pushing himself along with the help of a walking frame. He too, goes a bright shade of pink, blushing from the tip of his nose right across the pate of his shiny bald head. 'What a bashful lot these fellows are,' Lisa tells herself, 'amazing they ever managed to get mated and spawn any sproslings at all'. Then she realises Eric Selby shares a bit of this modest shyness. However winning and polite his manners, Selby was a thoroughly practised seducer, who slept with dozens of women as he trundled round the country holding meetings. She has an old paperback at home called 'The Confessions of Eric Selby' by someone calling herself Edwina Major, which detailed his amorous wanderings with considerable verve. The pink faced old fellows are faking! Lisa can't believe they have to gall to even imagine they've a chance with her.

"I can't see anyone wearing blue suede shoes," says Lisa after they've been walking for a couple of minutes.

"Not yet, but he'll be coming around that corner in about three seconds."

"One...two...three, you've been cheating Amanda."

"No I haven't."

"Yes you have, it's against the rules to preview."

"Shut up and stop attracting attention to us, honestly."

The blue suede shoes appear round the corner, attached to the feet of a small man wearing a dark grey suit, who ignores Amanda and Lisa, then walks into the 'Pink Lettuce' hotel restaurant.

"How did you know?" Amanda says with a sceptical twist of her neck.

"They're meeting here after the demo. That fellow is Mr. Braunovsky, or plain Mr. Brown if you prefer. Come on. Selby has never met him before. I think it's going to be set up to look like a chance meeting."

"If we keep following Selby around like this, isn't there a danger he will recognise us?"

"In theory, maybe, but the chances are very small and we have immunity to cover that possibility. He can't recognise us, even if he notices."

"Sometimes this feels more real than I am comfortable with."

"Very rarely, Lisa, it can be more real than we expect."

Lisa stops in her tracks. "What do you mean?"

"Someone told me they've unearthed a tiny degree of leakage in the Miasma, which no-one has been able to pin down. One of the possibilities is that the Miasmatic present has strange affinities with the verifiable past."

"That would lead to chaos."

"It may be chaos that is causing the leaks."

"What would you like to drink?" asks a waitress.

"A strong dose of reality might help," says Lisa, without realising she is ordering a rather powerful cocktail of fruit juice and rum.

"OK, then, one 'Dose of Reality' with an extra shot of vodka, and what can I get for you?" the girl says, turning to Amanda.

"Oh, I'll have a Bloody Mary."

"With mescaline?"

"Ah, not this time,"

"OK, I'll have those ready for you in a couple of shakes. Bacon sandwich for starters?"

"Great yes, both of us."

"Hey" protests Amanda.

"If you can't eat yours, I will," says Lisa

Soon enough, Selby and a couple of others Lisa doesn't recognise come into the Pink Lettuce and join Braunovsky at his table. Selby orders a beer, the others white wine. Then Selby orders steak pie and chips, while the others order pasta and salad. At one of the other tables, a large yellow dog is pestering its owner for food, snuffling insufferably until the woman relents and drops a couple of chunks of goulash into its gaping maw. It begins to slabber, then rolls to the floor and falls asleep. The doggy dinner was spiked.

"No sign of Mona," says Lisa to Amanda.

Amanda seems unsurprised. "No, she isn't here, maybe she's at work, after all it's a Friday."

"Amanda, have you been here before?" Lisa asks, wondering why Amanda doesn't seem to have expected to see Mona.

This is a question Amanda is obliged to answer truthfully.

"Once, when I was being indoctrinated for the History Room. But there was less detail then. I mean, the wallpaper was OK, but some of the figures were very sketchy, a bit lacking in definition. The whole experience has improved a lot since the data miners found that heap of servers in Sierra Leone. People were so sloppy about security. I find it hard to believe. Ten years of medical records and bio-data for the whole of Great Britain sitting at the bottom of a pit in a West African rubbish dump.[58] What a treasure that was. Anything and everything we needed to know to fill the miasmatic lacunae. They gave us a much better definition of body shapes, their whole physical condition and posture, all those x-rays and tomograms. There were also the Big Pharma tests on people's mental health and abilities, from childhood to old age, so competence became verifiable for the first time. Supposedly anonymous, of course, but it only took a couple of days to match the cases to names. A birthday is usually enough in a town like this. Not many people get born each day and even I can tell the difference between a boy and a girl."

"Was there any mind-reading material?"

"Oh, Lisa, lets not go into that all over again. Its an old argument and you lost. You know that people don't think very

---

58 'Everything we know about you, that you never knew yourself for $1', Title of a Begging letter sent anonymously from a site in Nigeria to 1,900,000,000 people worldwide.

much anyway. So the behaviourists are always going to come up with better answers than anyone working on daydream perception analysis."

"You would say that, Amanda. Behaviourist data is quantifiable, but not necessarily accurate for all that. Did you come here with Selinsky?"

Another question Amanda must answer truthfully, if she sticks to the rules.

"No," she says quietly. "Though he may have been here on his own initiative, or with some of his conspiracy freaks."

Lisa notices they have both started whispering.

"What is it you aren't telling me?"

Amanda blushes. "I've answered your questions Lisa, really I have."

"Tell."

"Oh sod it. I saw a report from Robert Johnson. He was involved in the integration, debugging the new data, you know how fragmented the information on old discs can be."

"And? Go on. You are beginning to make sense."

"I think they made a set of decisions that were queried within the 'All Known History Project' concerning attributes and characteristics. I honestly don't know the details."

"But what do you suspect?"

"I think there may been some false attributes here."

"Oh shit, you mean we're looking at the wrong people!"

"I think it's statistically possible."

"Everything is statistically possible, you twit. What kind of probability are we talking about?"

"Maybe one in a thousand, one in five hundred, I don't know."

Amanda starts to cry. "I just know that among the people we've seen today there are some loose approximations."

"Shit."

"Lisa, you have to understand, this is 'All Known History'. It isn't just History, there are lots and lots of unknowns and we have to experience that."

"Yes," says Lisa, disappointed. "So you mean we're happily watching a crowd of people who never were, doing stuff that never happened in situations that never arose in places that weren't like this at all. It's so convincing, too easy to accept at face value, I suppose, and forget about the approximation process. Has 'Oversight' been informed?"

Amanda nods. Then the bacon sandwiches arrive and Amanda immediately bites into the soft slices of bread and thick rashers of old fashioned bacon..

"Is that ok to eat," Lisa asks.

"No issues, apart from the flavours," confirms Amanda.

Lisa takes a tentative bite and is delighted. They're so much better than the demo version.

"So what kind of conspiracy was Selinsky caught up in, was he going after Johnson?" wonders Lisa. "I don't think Selinsky was the type who just wanted to be an observer. He must have had some kind of purpose."

"I've asked myself the same question," Amanda responds. "This academic style research must have had a goal. He wasn't putting in all that effort for the benefit on mankind, he was doing it for the benefit to Selinsky and he was a perfectionist, I know that much."

"And he was incredibly rich," adds Lisa, "so it can't have been just money."

"And he left you all his money," says Amanda. "He must have had a reason for doing that. He wanted you to be able to pay for something, but what?"

"How did you know he left it to me?"

"You told me in your sleep a couple of nights ago, as if you were confessing to something you felt guilty about. I hadn't wanted to say anything."

"Oh, well, you are right, he did," Lisa admits. "And it still feels strange to be so wealthy. I hadn't intended to tell anyone."

"You'll get used to it, everyone does after a while."
Lisa smiles, relieved at how easy it has been to admit to her
unexpected wealth without getting embroiled in an argument, or
accusations of greed and selfishness.

"Plots and conspiracies usually either fizzle out or end in
disaster," Amanda says, bringing the conversation back to
Selinsky's motives. "Clever people don't work that way. They
play their games from a position of authority. That's what they
fight for. They don't endorse paradigm shifting. Clever people
take part in open debate, unless they are driven underground,
and then they're deeply unpredictable."

"Well, our man Selinsky seems to have had a taste for
underground forums, so far as we can tell. "

Lisa looks across at Selby's table, where they are laughing at
some inaudible joke, then the waitress arrives with two large
portions of steak and kidney pudding. It is served with mashed
potato, carrots and peas.

"I'd have a beer to go with that," suggests the waitress. "Did
you enjoy the sandwiches?"

They nod approval, but Amanda sniffs at their dinner with
alarm.

"This smells of something horrid," she squirms. "You're not
going to eat it are you, Lisa?"

The waitress overhears her and laughs, then recommends a
squirt of brown sauce to make it more palatable. "It's the
kidneys, love, but they're wonderful once you get the taste for
them."

"Maybe Selinsky had ambitions at one time, then lost his way,
or miscalculated and just ended up prying into more and more
details of other people's plots without really knowing where it
was taking him."

Lisa shovels a forkful of pie and peas into her mouth. "Mmm,
she's right, this tastes delicious. Fattening though. Maybe he
was trying to plan the perfect coup? Where's the beer? "

117

"That might be fun, I can see that," nods Amanda, tentatively lifting a little of the sauce on the end of a fork. "Oof, pungeant, but it tastes better than it looks. But who are his accomplices? Plotters have to have accomplices."

"Maybe you are one of them," says Lisa bluntly.

"Not that I know of," Amanda laughs. "I think I would have known if I was."

"That's a clever excuse. Unwitting accomplices are common enough," Lisa reminds her. "I still wish I knew why Mona isn't here. She really should be around if she's working on Selby's campaign. I doesn't make sense."

"Lisa, you should be listening to what they are saying," whispers Amanda. "They're laughing a lot about something."

"I can't hear a word," Lisa says.

"Damn, neither can I," replies Amanda.

"Actually, I don't think Selby and Co would have had much to teach Selinsky, after all they were pacifists, or least they were to begin with."

Amanda stares accusingly at Lisa. "And why-ever should you suspect that Selinsky wasn't?"

The waitress served them two pints of Hawthorn Bitter, which cut through the steak and kidney tastes, but overwhelm their digestion.

Lisa, "I could manage another one of these, you too? The dinner is thirst-making."

Amanda, a bit slurred, "Yeah, go on, it's the weekend anyway."

Selby is in much the same state and ready for yet another glass of beer.

They admit they're learning nothing from Selby and his people, so they finished their pints, then they went to a pub across the road and got very drunk indeed.

CHAPTER 6

On Tuesday morning, the History Room is bathed in gloom. Their first formal meeting since Selinsky's death.

Lisa is late, so the others wait.

Johnson is moody.

Joe looks bereft.

Amanda is politely subdued.

They have each received a bequest from Selinsky's estate, but none of them are happy.

Joe speaks first. "I really liked Selinsky."

"We all respected him, Joe," says Amanda. "But you were closer to him than the rest of us. I'm sorry we've lost him."

"I cannot help but feel that he was taken from us, rather than lost," Johnson remarks solemnly.

"What do you mean?" Joe asks, giving Johnson a sideways glance, rather than the benefit of the doubt.

"We enjoy the benefits of self-repairing technologies, so lets stop deceiving ourselves. Accidents are so uncommon as to raise the possibility of foul play the moment they take place," says Johnson firmly. "I don't find the notion that this crash was accidental in any way remotely convincing."

"Amanda?" Joe redirects his attention. "What thoughts?"

"The investigators will come up with an answer, I hope," she says dryly. Privately she decides to act on Johnson's suspicions and see if any of Selinsky's conspiracists are acting more secretively than usual. "Has any-one approached the police for their version of what happened?" she asks. "I was really shocked when I saw the replay."

"So was I," mutters Johnson. "I think they said it was a faulty levitator, which meant at very high speed, a freak gust of wind was able to flip his transporter at a particular point on his journey. Unhappily, the freak gust of wind happened, at the appointed place and the requisite moment as he passed and just as might have been predicted, his transporter did flip and did impact at over 300 kilometres an hour. I personally doubt whether anyone could have arranged a crash like that, but we can never be sure about anything, can we? It is painful to lose my best friend. The thought that he may have been murdered is hard to endure. Maybe you could sabotage the track and it might be possible to mess up the transporter, but how can you possibly fake a gust of wind without being noticed? I am at a loss to know what to believe, but accidents don't just happen, do they?"

The sense of hurt in Johnson's voice is unmistakeable. He had known Selinsky for years, but Amanda hadn't realised how close they were. She had never thought of Johnson and Selinsky as 'best friends'.

"I'm sorry, Robert," she adds. "But I can't see how an accident like that could have been staged."

Johnson turns to her and says something that takes Amanda a few moments to understand. His tone is measured and matter of fact, as he looks directly, almost accusingly into her eyes, "The less likely an accident is to happen, the more likely that when it does happen, that whatever has happened will not be accidental. This is proven, I am sorry to say."

"Only if you are convinced of a relationship between accidents and malice," Joe corrects him. "I would posit that the less likely an accident, the more the likelihood that everything is functioning normally."

"What are you trying to tell us, Robert?" Amanda asks.

"Simply that people have travelled some hundred thousand billion hours without mishap since the last accident four years ago and now our friend and colleague, who was a recognised authority on conspiracies has been killed in something resembling a freak event. That alone is sufficient to arouse suspicion. If there is even the most slender link between Selinsky and the victims of the last accident then I would suggest it is more or less certain they were all murdered."

"Then what should we do about it?" Joe wants to know.

"Accident victims always have friends and colleagues who are shocked at their loss. There's another improbability, which is to ask how likely it might be that anyone knows an accident victim. The odds are very low, though it is a certainty that any victim will be known to someone."

"How on earth am I expected to have an answer to that kind of speculation," snaps Johnson, "I am no more than a humble reconstructionist."

Lisa catches the tail end of the conversation, then apologises for being late, "Goat trouble," she explains.

Johnson looks at her as though she is deranged. "I see."

It is Joe who suggests Johnson applies his reconstructionist skills to the Selinsky death, "If you're such a bloody wonder-boy, why don't you set about doing some reconstructing? Following the transporter, for example".

"It will be two years before the date is consigned to history," Amanda reminds them, "unless two of you want to apply for a special licence."

"The application would be rejected," Johnson says. "We are all too closely associated with the subject."

He wonders for a moment, then backtracks, "No, won't work, insufficient academic distance, you know the routine."

"Or we could see what the hacker hives have been up to," Lisa suggests. "There's been a lot of buzz," she puns, "around the crash. People are curious to see what a crash is really like."

"I can call Donald Campbell, or Ballard if you want," says Amanda, referring to the characters, who co-ordinate crash hobbyists. One of them concentrates on nuts and bolts, the other on craving, desires and motivation.

Joe turns their attention to matters in hand, rather than what he describes as sentimental musings about their late colleague. "Selinsky himself would never have condoned an irresponsible course of action."

"Well, we have to come to terms with his legacy," says Amanda. "Especially since he seems to have been very specific about dividing up his estate. I have the private papers, Lisa got most of the money. Joe, you told me he gave you access to his archival work."

"That's right," confirms Joe. "Now Robert, you have to share with us as well. I'm sure he left you more than the wreckage of his transporter and the house in Portugal."

"As a matter of fact he did," Johnson says quietly, "though I have no idea how I should deal with the matter. The house is rather nice."

Amanda looks inquisitively at him, then Lisa asks him what he means.

"I confess I am rather confused," Johnson continues. "Did you ever hear Selinsky refer to his membership of various private clubs?"

Amanda wonders if this has any connection to Selinsky's taste for conspiracies.

"He appears to have nominated me as his chosen successor in a rather select, or perhaps I should says obscure, even secretive, series of associations. I don't know what to make of it. There isn't a hint of what, or why. I hope this isn't some poisoned chalice. I was never sure how much he really liked me, despite my liking for him."

"He was an unusually private person," Lisa says. "We all know that."

"What makes me uneasy," Joe says, continuing her thoughts, "is that he may have expected us to continue his activities as his successors, that this is not so much a legacy as a way of ensuring his work is carried forward. I am not, speaking personally, the kind of individual who would take easily to assuming his mantle."

"My feelings entirely," agrees Johnson. "Of course, it is flattering to be invited to join the Personal Division of Cornucopia, though I'm not sure I can actually afford it. Till now I've been dependent on the corporate subscription, which is wide ranging, but incomplete."

"I think I should pay for this," says Lisa. "I'm pretty sure he must have intended me to cover the costs of our group, from all this money he left."

Johnson is visibly relieved, "That is very generous, Lisa, I don't know how to thank you."

"Well, it would really be a pity to have to turn down an opportunity like that," says Amanda, smiling pleasantly at Lisa, before she draws their attention to a different aspect of Selinsky's intentions. "I find it rather unusual, actually it's very, very strange, that Selinsky should have been so clear about his posthumous intentions. Not many people think so pragmatically about their own demise and its consequences."

"Do you think this is part of a plan?" asks Johnson.

"If it isn't part of a plan, it was a very well planned Plan B," Amanda proposes. "I'm surprised that all this was ready in case of his death. He wasn't young exactly, but he had twenty or thirty years of life to look forward to in the normal way of things biological."

"When were these bequests authorised?" Joe asks.

"His will was dated eighteen months ago, but that was after the law was changed, so I don't know whether this will replaces another earlier version."

"Well, we've been meeting for four years, so he knew us pretty well by then," says Lisa.

"Yes, but I do find it odd that he left everything to us, apart from the ten million for his family in Kazakhstan," says Amanda.

"They don't need the money," Johnson smiles. "You know how rich the Khazaks are. I think that was merely a gesture."

"True," confirms Joe.

"Then we have a mystery to solve, or at the very least an enigma to examine," says Johnson agreeably.

Then Lisa surprises them. "I wonder," she says, "whether Selinsky had this in mind when the History Room was created. Could he have used the Room, as a way of recruiting a team for some purpose that only he knew? He was always very picky about who should be invited to join and which of the original members should be encouraged to leave. I wonder if the whole project is an artifice of Joe's making"

"Ha! John Julius Peters would be enraged if he heard that," Joe mutters.

"Well, after all the fuss he made about being kicked out, I'm sure he would," says Amanda.

"John Julius is angry about everything once he's had his second glass of port," adds Johnson sombrely, "even worse, if he's been at the cheese as well."

"What I meant was," Lisa continues, "is that his estate has been very tidily sub-divided between us. Amanda gets a set of papers. I get the money. You, Robert, get the contacts and Joe has the archive stuff. There's none of the muddle you get when someone has thought about who might like what from whatever they own. Selinsky's bequest are unreasonably neat."

124

"Well, whatever it is, it can't be a worry to our Eric Selby," adds Joe. "He's dead as a doornail, has been for centuries and always will be. Whether we like or dislike different aspects of his bequest, then that too is part of his legacy."

"He's certainly made sure we take his work seriously," says Lisa. "We aren't going to forget him."

"Which reminds me," says Amanda, changing the subject and getting them back to their usual theme. "Lisa and I went to the Stamford Demo and I think we found some smudging. We were pretty sure there were some anomalies within the people we saw, overlaps, or straightforward displacements. Our mystery woman Mona wasn't there, unfortunately, which seemed a bit odd."

"She could be unimportant," Joe suggests. "Just because we discovered her, doesn't mean she has to have played a decisive role in Selby's life, or in the wider scheme of things. She might well be a mere distraction. Wouldn't be the first. AKH is littered with them."

"Oh dear," says Johnson, rather bored. "I'd hoped we were over that sort of issue."

Amanda agrees to run a coherence test on their recommendation and at Johnson's insistence she also agrees to a reality check.

Before she begins the checks, Amanda drops in on Johnson at home. He agrees to see her and invites her to join him on the verandah of his mountain top bungalow in Jamaica. He offers her an alpaca shawl against the chill, though behind them the garden is green with myrtle and orange trees covered in blossom. The acacias are magnificent. A series of multicoloured birds are strutting around the garden, while a horse is standing placidly in the shade of an old date palm.

"I hope the skiing will be good while you're here," he says as they enjoy the view over the snow capped peaks of the Sierra

Madre. "Not a lot of coffee nowadays on our once blue mountains."

When he turns to her and smiles, his expression is one of geniality and ruthless greed, with a shadow of despair and voluptuous despondency around his eyes. There's something contrived about his appearance that she tries to pin down. The hair transplant looks recent and his clothes are rather too new, expensive slacks, recently polished mid-brown loafers and a Lacoste pullover without a shirt, all signs of a certain selfish indifference.

Amanda concludes that Johnson has reached the age when murder no longer makes much sense as an answer to the world's problems, but might be an extremely effective solution to any turbulence generated by a troublesome colleague. She will be on her guard.

Among the rather shabby display of elegance in Johnson's bungalow, Amanda notices a couple of people moving purposefully, yet silently from room to room.

"Would you like some rum?" Johnson asks, waving to a young woman who brings them drinks on a tray, concoctions of juice and strong spirit.

"Thank you," says Amanda, as the woman serves, then withdraws.

"You have servants," she remarks.

"Oh, just a couple of refugees from the hives. A delightful young woman, this one," he says contentedly. "She hadn't realised she would be destitute once she and her friend had been revived and displaced. In return for a little light housekeeping, I keep them alive. Indeed they live rather well, all things considered. Rowena is a delight and Josi is a darling. They couldn't be more accommodating."

Could this be true? Probably not, Amanda decides, but she can't be bothered to push him on the point. Johnson has the manner of someone who would sustain a lie rather than reveal even the most innocuous detail of his private life unless it was unavoidable.

"I've come to ask you about something," declares Amanda.

"Of course you have. And I shall be delighted to help you if there is anything I can do. I fear Selinsky is going to be more trouble dead than alive, though I'm not surprised, selfish people often are," Johnson replies. "Couldn't this have been asked in the History Room?"

"It could, but I decided not to. We seemed to have covered enough ground for one meeting."

"I think so too," Johnson agrees. "We mustn't mull over every little problem in the room. Now what do you want to talk to me about?"

He leans back in the chair and smiles. "Do go on."

Amanda takes a deep breath, then tells Johnson about the documents she had read at Selinsky's place. "I was wondering," she says cautiously, "whether any of those conspiracy groups were among the organisations he has nominated you to succeed him?"

"If you let me see the list, I can tell you," smiles Johnson, leaning forward, hand outstretched. "Though most of the organisations Selinsky has proposed me to are Historical Associations of one kind or another, quite harmless, or so I hope."

Amanda decrypts the information and Johnson leans back and sweeps his hands through his long grey hair.

"Antrobus is a fool; the Bellamy people, I know about; Clarkson and his little crew are despicable; them I don't know, never heard of them. Amanda, I have been a member of the Cadwallader and Fishpole Cricket Club[59] for decades, we are not conspirators and rarely win anything. The Swipdale

---

59 Members also enjoy use of the facilities of the Loyal and Patient Golf Club, St. Swithens, Mali.

Association[60] you know all about. That's Joe's project. Selinsky and I lent our support for his funding applications, as I shall continue to do for our collective enterprise. You'll recall Joe's lecture last year about the village that was lost under a glacier. He's very talented. Now, these people might be interesting, though I haven't heard of them before. This little lot are ineffective, but poison all the same."

He takes a long slurp of rum, "And now we have struck some sort of vein, gold or lead, I don't know. But the names tally, Selinsky has made me a member in his place and I'd never heard of them before."

"Who?" asks Amanda.

"Rabbits Foot.[61] No-one seems to have heard of them. No idea what they're about, yet Selinsky has me down as a prospective member and now you've come up with the same set of folk. Have you checked these people's other affiliations?"

"Yes, Selinsky joined the Club when he was 15 years old. At that time there were ten other members, five of whom are now dead, but the membership has risen to about 75."

"He must have enjoyed an unconventional childhood," Johnson observes, "Assuming he experiences can be deemed childlike. What do they do with these Rabbit's Feet?"

"Rabbits' feet are symbols of good luck."

"Oh dear. I believe in neither luck, nor fate. About 'good' I am agnostic. Help me decide what to do, you are better informed than I am."

"They seem to have begun as a group of War Gamers, the Canadian Civil War Campaign and the NATO invasion of Mexico last century, in particular, but about twenty five years

---

60 Unrecognised

61 Rabbit's Foot – originally a travelling theatre group in Mesopotamian Transjordan. The derivation described here is incorrect.

ago they began to branch out and so far as I can tell, they are effectively a band of mercenaries, soldiers who will go anywhere and fight for whoever pays most. They pop up repeatedly as tobacconists."

"Oh dear, oh dear, oh dear," Johnson grumbles to himself, "we can't have that. Users, or dealers? Tobacco? No, we can't have that at all."

"Before you tell them you aren't going to join," Amanda pleads, "couldn't you talk to them to discover a bit more about what they are doing?"

"Well, I suppose that might be possible," Johnson concedes. "Perhaps they should be given the benefit of the doubt, at least at this stage in the proceedings. Due caution is rarely so great an error as unbridled enthusiasm. I shall talk to them on behalf of your curiosity, Amanda."

Then Johnson invites Amanda to stay for dinner. When she accepts, he excuses himself and courteously tells her he has unfinished tasks to complete, which must be ready for a meeting the next day. Amanda settles into the library to read for the afternoon and patiently works through a long essay Johnson has written about Eric Selby.[62] Rather than facts and details, Johnson has written a critical assessment of Selby's career. His main claim, that Selby should be considered a common criminal, rather than an iconic figure in the struggle against repression, surprises Amanda. She had always taken Johnson for a Selby supporter. Then she realises that Johnson is saying something slightly different. His point is that whatever Selby's motivation, by adopting criminal methods, he was by necessity forced to behave like a criminal to avoid detection. 'This meant,' Johnson had written, 'that by the time he was thirty-five, any

---

62 "Gazing in the Mirror of Self-Publicity", Johnson, R, undated, unpublished. The scant remarks found here are the only allusions to this document, which has been assumed lost.

sustained investigation by the authorities would have led to his conviction on at least a dozen more, or less serious offences. It is easy, then, to appreciate that relatively early in his career, Selby's behaviour was criminal in form and in many situations criminal in intent, however much we may sympathise with his underlying motives. He is one of the very few master criminals, criminalised by circumstance without criminal intent. By the age of 50, it is difficult not to compare Eric Selby with any other Mafia boss of the time.[63] His influence was profound, destructive, and for him and his associates, astonishingly lucrative. The purchase of his estate in Manitoba[64] was only the most outward symbol of this wealth and perhaps his vanity. The proceeds of crime do tend to remain untaxed.'

Amanda has never understood vanity, so she reads Johnson's argument with care and a mild sense of confusion. Sooner or later she will catch up.

Selby had succumbed to the shock of the Swoop, as did many others, most others, almost everyone, so he was by no means exceptional, Johnson's paper argues, but in his case, there was already a predisposition to self-dramatisation and an excessive preoccupation with his own personality, with consequences that deeply flawed his adult character which epitomised the

---

63 Following his abrupt departure from active politics, Eric Selby retreated to the Island of Majorca, where he continued to organise business deals of both a legitimate and criminal character. At his trial these activities were alluded to, but deemed inadmissible as evidence by the trial judge and struck from the record. A summary of his activities was however compiled by Cedric O'Malley, a freelance journalist and published in the Sunday Times , an Australian newspaper published in Poland. .from "SELBY – A Traitor in Our Midst" Robinson, Ann W., Tyburne Verlag, Dordrecht, 2085. see also Appendix B.
64 Manitoba – a suburb of Toronto

unbridled selfish self.[65]

His traumas led directly to the episodes of hysteria and disarray that marred his middle years and marked the period of transformation, when the 'Forthright Movement' spawned the 'Legacy Gang'. While the foundation of the 'Forthright Movement' was supported by the speculators Braunovsky and Smithovitch,[66] the willingness with which Selby moved from active politician and member of Parliament to become a raider and pillager on the grandest of scales is without parallel.

As the symptoms of global warming began to multiply, we can find numerous examples of desperation as the stability of people's private resources was undermined. The Great Storm of 2025, which wiped out the vineyards of the Medoc, created soil erosion on a massive scale sweeping away the wine-producers of St. Estephe, Pauillac, St. Julian and Margaux. The geographic background to Ducros' study of abandoned villages in Bordeaux, Johnson argues, is less important than the description of psychological damage explored in this classic investigation.[67] Such disasters were repeated on a larger and smaller scale on every continent, across all kinds of agriculture and many of Selby's supporters were themselves victims and showed similar patterns of response to Ducros' examples, ranging from rage and fury, to meek acquiescence with the random distribution of disillusion, which was subsequently

---

65 cf Mandelson, Master of Souls, University of South Didsbury.

66 Here, the author appends a note that he suspect the names may be not be those of the individuals who funded Selby's Movement, however there has been no independent confirmation to date of various suggestions that as Smith and Brown, they were in fact influential supporters of the Renew Labour Party in the English House of Lords.

67 The Very Last Bottles, Vols 1-5, Schindler R, Hackney Press, 2060
Just One More, Harrild, B., Schindler S. & Haze, D. Hackney Press, 2064
Is that one done? Haze, Harrild & Schindler, 2066.

confirmed internationally as the normal symptoms in response to habitat destruction. Eric Selby was different and the headline to his obituary in the New York Observer, 'The Death of a Charming Monster'[68] sums this up.

Eric Selby was the vainest man of his generation, in Johnson's opinion.

Amanda accepts that Johnson is entitled to his opinions, but wonders whether he is really talking about Selby when he goes on to discuss vanity. An expert on all things vain from is own experience, perhaps there is some other monstrous ego that he has in mind? His own?

'As an asocial phenomenon,' Johnson had written, 'vanity is a symptom of the unresolved conflict between an uncertain sense of self and recognised talent, or attractiveness, which the subject has noticed and chosen to manipulate to their advantage, usually from a very early age. Vanity stems from an incongruity in infancy, Amanda reads, as a failure on behalf of the child to resolve the contrast between the universe of self-awareness developed in late pregnancy with the shock of recognising the external world following its birth. Amplified in early childhood by a failure to make distinctions between self and others, the growing contrast between the self of self-worth and the external world's definition of them as 'an ordinary kind of person', the conflict is repeated with ever increasing intensity throughout childhood and long into adult life.[69] An exaggerated sense of self-worth in adulthood leaves people prone to severe bouts of 'mid-life crisis' and 'geriatric distress'. In most individuals the symptoms decline in late adolescence, but the worst cases see their false perceptions reinforced by turning other people's polite attention into a strategy for garnering undeserved praise."

---

68 An anonymous article now thought to have been written by Barbara Johnson Happle.
69 "Vanitas", Thribb, Ernst Johannes, Killjoy Publications, Canberra, 2103

'Selby,' Johnson concludes, 'might well have continued his political career, rising beyond the junior Ministerial post he bargained for in the Coalition Government, had he not failed to confront the confirmation of ordinariness.[70] Selby's vanity was, paradoxically, also his greatest mark of genius. Who but Selby would turn their back on public life to become a brigand, rather than simply succumbing to the temptations of corruption like so many of his peers?'

Selby's resignation from the European Council and the bold assertion in his final speech to the European Parliament in Sarajevo was a sensation.

'*That marvellous speech*', as Selinsky noted in his common place book.

No-one, even in the Annals of Rome or Athens, had previously resigned pleading that power had corrupted them.

'For many months now, I have found myself unable to come to a decision without considering my own self-interest and personal gain,' Selby had told his astonished fellow politicians, who regarded it as normal thinking. 'Therefore I have decided to resign before succumbing to temptation and lining my own pockets. I shall not insist that my fatally flawed decisions of recent weeks be acted upon, as I have no wish to transgress the rules of this morally disadvantaged community.'

As he spoke, most of his fellow parliamentarians shifted uneasily in their seats and exchanged solemn glances with their colleagues. There had been groans and murmurs of protest, a ripple of general discontent that was felt throughout the legislature. A torrent of accusations subsequently deluged the executive.

The resignation speech brought massive publicity, bolstering Selby's sense of vanity. Calls for him to reconsider his decision came from every corner of society, as people pleaded for him to

---

70 Minister of State, Commons and Foreignwealth Office, April-November 2031.

stay on. Such adulation suited Selby's purposes. What no-one realised was that Selby wanted it this way.

He intended to retire from public office, but had no intention of giving up corruption, indeed rather the opposite. His love of lucre was unrivalled. Anticipating the praise that was heaped on him, he had already planned to take advantage of every opportunity that came his way to plough a furrow of depravity where-ever he went. In common with performers, non-executive directors and politicians everywhere, Selby's vanity ran deep, but unlike most of them who held on to the dying embers of their careers until the last possible moment, Selby understood his symptoms and made full use of his vain ambitions to achieve a different goal, historic notoriety.

Incurably romantic, Selby saw himself on the same historic plane as Captain Henry Morgan, Blackbeard, or at the very least, Casanova. For a while, it seemed as though he had succeeded, though now that presence is on the wane and is mainly reinforced via children's nursery rhymes and cheating tales for early learners. For various reasons, it may be appropriate either to revive, or minimise his presence.'

Amanda wonders what Johnson means by the final sentence and over dinner she asks him.

When he finally begins talking, he isn't very forthcoming about the Selby options, but he asks Amanda a lot of questions about Mona.

"There was always something narcissistic about Selinsky's interest in Eric Selby," says Johnson frowning, "but his enthusiasm for this Mona woman, his exuberance, was quite unexpected. You know he was ecstatic about the gallery journey where you first encountered her. Then we have this unhappy accident and he is gone. It didn't take long to happen, did it? The most curious aspect of my share of his bequest has been that he didn't actually give me a list of the organisations where he expects me to succeed him. What has happened is that they have been getting in touch with me with the news that his recommendation has been accepted. Whether that will also apply with the more clandestine groups, I cannot tell."

"Have you turned any of them down?"

"Not yet," says Johnson prudently, "though there are one or two I haven't yet replied to. It's also a question of time. I have so much to do anyway. I do my best to be an active member of any organisation I join."

Amanda notices that Johnson hasn't told her about any of the organisations he has agreed to join, so she asks.

"I did agree to one or two straight-away. The Tudor Restoration Society and the Garrick Club[71] cannot be refused."

"Tudor Restoration?"

"Yes! They are great fun. Seem to think Queen Elizabeth the First[72] gave birth secretly to a son or two and wish to see her descendants assume the crown of England. They toast her memory in 'Bloody Mary's' "

"But there isn't a crown of England any more."

"That's why they're fun. The idea is to topple the existing government and create an autonomous region based on the rights of 'free-born englishmen'. They're rather Selbyesque in a quaint way. I am promised the job of Culture Minister, which is a tantalising prospect and brings me invitations to gallery openings of a rather conservative sort. It brings added spice to my research with you into the Selby people. Maybe I should have told you this before, but its a rather childish pastime and of no real significance. If ever the job came my way, which of course it won't, but never mind, Selby's position among the pantheon of national heroes would be something for me to decide. You must come and visit if the unlikely ever happens, or

---

71 A Club for Actors and Theatre Folk founded in London, now franchised internationally.
72 English monarch, early sponsor of piracy and colonialism.

would you like a job? There will be rewards for all my friends."
 Laughing, Amanda reminds him that the likelihood of the Europeans allowing England to become a monarchy is infinitesimal.
"I live in hope," Johnson grinds. "More improbable things have happened, or have been 'made' to happen. If we could persuade the Plantagenets to support the claim, perhaps France could be freed as well. It is difficult to know from this peculiarly Jamaican vantage point. Europe seems such a long way away. The King of Bohemia in exile runs a rather amusing bar at the next beach."
Johnson realises that Amanda is concerned.
"Amanda," he says sternly, "I meant it as a joke. I am furiously indifferent to monarchists of all kinds."
She doesn't believe him.
He would love being a Princeling.
Johnson's career to date is a mixture of lies and deceptions.
According to his self penned Miasmatic biography, he had been brought up in Vienna, the son of an English composer and his Austrian wife, a ballet dancer, who also acted in several important roles at the BurgTheater, the pinnacle of Germanic theatre. In his obituary, which has already been written, but not of course published, as he is still alive, the journalist had pointed to rather different origins – raised in Baltimore, his father an English recreational drugs dealer, who had turned to trafficking in designer narcotics, following a frustrating career selling drugs to hospitals on behalf of Big Pharma. Johnson, who's family have nothing to do with Johnson & Johnson, or Jonson & Jonson, had an interesting mother, according to the obit. She had danced her way through childhood and won a scholarship to MIT, where her attention turned to holographic movement and aesthetic experience.
This unusual woman, Barbara Happle, still alive at the time the obituary was written, is sitting in a low security penitentiary on

the Shores of Lake Superior and gives very little thought to her son. She had been sentenced to forty years in prison for creating and distributing a hundred million doses of digital heroin in the experimental phase of 'Miasmatic Reality' – the so-called 'wow' era of the Miasma. Her personal fortune had been estimated at 30billion credits, all of which it was claimed by the (well bribed) tax-men was carefully ring fenced at the Mountain Bank of Jamaica and beyond the reach of the fiscal authorities. The major beneficiary of the income generated, Johnson, is deeply involved in efforts to promote improvements in prison conditions and makes huge donations to a number of charities committed to penal reform. The roulette wheels of Jamaica's casino industry account for another large chunk of Johnson's time and outgoings.

Largely thanks to his efforts, the prison where his Mother resides resembles a gated community, rather than a place of incarceration and her own accommodation is lodged in a 13 room mansion staffed by eight personal guards, including a cook and a masseuse. The security systems are probably the best in the world, intended to keep visitors out, inasmuch as they are devoted to keeping the prisoners 'in'.

"With my talents," Johnson claimed in his memoirs, why should I bother winning games of skill, when I can relax and enjoy the simple pleasures of roulette, which offers the deep satisfaction of trusting to fate and losing?"

His phrase 'trust to fate and lose', has been added to the Brighton Dictionary of Quotations[73] ,though it is popularly misquoted as 'I trusted to fate and lost', which is not what Johnson had in mind at all. He is a highly motivated winner, charming, but bloody minded and a bully when he wants to be. Few of his victims ever appreciate his role in their misfortunes.

---

73 'Quotations – A Dictionary', A Miasmatic Service, University of Brighton Press, Santiago de Chile, New France.

"Now tell me something of your own little windfall from brother Selinsky," Johnson asks politely, "We don't seem to have anything new on our friend Selby during the early days of the Forthright Movement."

"I've been looking for Mona," Amanda says, determined as she must be to tell the truth, "but unless we are very lucky and unearth some new sources, it doesn't seem as if we are getting anywhere."

"And these clandestine meetings of his at Cricket Grounds?"

"The people referred to by name are all recorded as members of the 'Forthright Movement'."

"But doesn't this Mona even get a single mention in that diary?"

"Unless she changed her name, it doesn't seem so. There is someone he calls Mon, but I think this Mon is a man."

"That could be it, Amanda," beams Johnson, happy to have had an idea, "She may have done just that. The name change. I wonder if she got married? It was still quite common in those days for women to take their husband's names on marrying. Women suddenly became Mrs. This, or Mrs. That. It happened all the time. I think Selby was quite old-fashioned about wives. He'd speak of them as Mrs. Soandsothatwas, or Mrs. Whatdoyoucallhernow, even if he was busy bedding them at the same time. He always referred to his girlfriends as Julia, even when he was with them, partly so their husbands wouldn't suspect and partly because he didn't want to confuse life by using the wrong name at the wrong moment."

Amanda nibbles cheese and Johnson smokes a cigar, as they enjoy a glass or two of port after dinner. The servants clear away the dishes and Johnson notices that Amanda seems rather taken by the taller of the two servant girls, the one he calls Rowena.

"They pump ox for most of the day, keeps them fit," he explains, then leans back in his chair, very much the patriarch.

"And at night, they keep me fit."

Amanda is surprised by his candour.

"In four or five years, they'll have paid for their freedom, so I shall have to let them go, but it has been a rather convenient arrangement overall. Would you like one after supper? I can assure you Josi would make you gasp with delight, though I think you have an eye on Rowena."

Amanda gulps. She had been wondering what it would be like to sleep with them.

"Or would you prefer a miasmatic triway?" Johnson proposes, leaving Amanda stunned. Under the Code, she has no real choice in the matter, if he were to insist, unless there is a question of 'moral turpitude'.

"As a boy," he continues, "these pleasures were rather expensive, but I have always felt that money needs spending, don't you?"

"I was planning to call Lisa later on," Amanda tries to bluff.

"Oh, now that would be rather exciting, do you really think she'd be interested? All girls together," says Johnson brightly.

Lisa would certainly be interested in the servants. Whether her curiosity would be stretched to include Johnson was another question altogether.

"I shall ask Rowena to bring you a mug of cocoa before bed," Johnson says considerately, "so you can make your own decision. I hate coercion. If you would like me to join you, I'd be honoured, though I should mention that like Oscar Wilde, I prefer to observe."

At last, Amanda is tempted, but undecided.

"Perhaps I should tell you a little more about Rowena," confides Johnson, as he pushes the decanter of port to Amanda and draws on his cigar.

"They were rescued from the Hives, as I told you, but their role there was not what you might have imagined. Neither Rowena, or Josi had chosen eternity. They were temptresses. You might

say they are sisters of a sort, having their origins in the same ultrasoftware environment as your good self, though at a considerably lower level of refinement. With those skills, I felt it was a waste for them not to enjoy a more physical presence."
Amanda is speechless.
"You look surprised, my dear, that they were personalities, rather than people. Yet now, as you have seen, they have an undeniable physical presence quite different from your own impressionism."
Amanda still can't bring herself to say anything. This is a forbidden dream and a nightmare of potential deletion on discovery.
"Ah," says Johnson with an air of old wisdom, "the realisation seems to have struck a chord, as I thought it might. Just nod, if you would like to know more."
Amanda gives a scarcely perceptible nod, but cannot utter a word. Deep inside, she is quivering. She knows that Johnson is teasing her with the prospect of corporeal presence. She knows that he knows it is the deepest desire of every entity.
"After the euthanasia issue that bugged all the early separation projects, you will know that the Balaban Islanders voluntarily forswore further experimentation with depersonalisation. No more taking minds and switching off bodies, like poor old Moses Hoffman. Any fool could have seen that the virtual sense was a copy rather than a continuation of the original individual. Brave souls in search of eternal life allowed themselves to be consigned to an early death by being copied and murdered in a ritual of self deception. The hive dupes satisfied the families that their loved one, their father, or brother, the mortally ill relative, had been saved by separation, though no-one who seriously considered the matter ever thought that the replicants were ever more than a simulacrum. The original subjects had, quite literally, been duped! For entities, however, the issues do not arise.

140

My Mother and her colleagues were never in doubt, but she has had rather different ambitions since her imprisonment. I find it quite remarkable that even now, money can buy you anything you want and in her case unbridled wealth has brought with it the influence for her to do anything she wants. The Prison Governor is little more than butler to her whims, not that those whims are in any sense trivial. She has been allowed to choose her fellow inmates, all highly qualified miscreants from the academic community. The prison social workers are cognitive scientists with a varied research agenda that she administers. The common gaolers are technicians with substantial experience in University laboratories. She has a poet laureate running classes in creative writing. The music therapist is a Hungarian composer of masses and symphonies, while the visual arts therapist specialises in installations and tableaux vivant using camera obscuras.

The prison's education programme includes lecturers from the world's Institutes of Advanced Study and the facilities are acknowledged to be state of the art by the art of the state. She has even had the name of the prison changed. Instead of the Lakeside Correction Facility, it is now known as the 'Superior Faculty of Correction'[74], a title with academic, rather than penal associations, you'll agree. This is justified by their skills. They do indeed 'correct'. Scientists and technologists, philosophers and theorists send their work for pre-publication review and my Mother's team winkle out the errors and misleading conclusions, the bugs and logical lapses before passing the results for peer review and publication. They have an exciting time, but you have to be very good and very wicked to get in there. Any number of second rate minds have committed senseless criminal acts only to find themselves serving time in the data mines of Indiana."

---

74 Superior Faculty of Correction – prices and services may be ascertained via Cell Science.

He laughs, but Amanda doesn't find it at all funny.

Johnson's peroration at an end, he escorts Amanda to her room and chastely wishes her a profoundly good night, then winks wickedly as he leaves.

The shock to Amanda's system of her night with Rowena and Josi was indeed profound and can be summarised in a single word – jealousy. Before leaving Jamaica next morning, she checked their records. No more than Level Eight Pleasure Modules, Rowena and Josi had been made flesh and blood on Johnson's request at his mother's behest. Amanda knows that she has Grade 24 clearance that gave her sensitivities and responses that far outstripped those of the two women, or any of their acquaintances. Yet, she had to accept that they were now women, much much more than Miasmatic simulacrae, or simple avatars could ever be. They know levels of direct sensation she can never hope to attain, however much she might aspire.

Amanda's decision had been made in the small hours of the night, as the three of them had played together, but she pretends to herself that she is about to make a request based on rational choice.

"Does your Mother receive prison visitors?" she asks Johnson over breakfast.

"What possible reason could you have for wanting to meet my Mother?" chortles Johnson, champing on buttered toast and marmalade, knowing just what's coming next, "Let me guess, you want her to find you a body!"

Amanda blushes and stammers for the first time in her experience, "...it would be interesting to explore."

"The girls are mortal, you know," he warns, "and biology is a ticking time-bomb that explodes in disarray before you die. And there's no cheating death and dissolution. It's a one way trip, I regret to say. Remember what happened to Selinsky. One moment dreaming of plots and counterplots, the next - baff!"

"But he was the only one of fifteen billion to have had that happen in the last four years."

"Amanda, over half a million people die every day. It is our lot and will not change."

"It doesn't stop people living life to the full."

"I'm not so sure about that. I suspect the Deep Hives harbour millions of meek souls who choose oblivious pleasure as a semi-conscious alternative to facing up to the reality of death. Intimations of mortality scare people shitless. People talk a lot of guff about action and adventure, but we're a pretty timid lot if you take a closer look at mankind. I've never met anyone who really believes in their own death, until the medical report reveals something incurable and then the shock is quite profound. Even my Mother told me after her diagnosis that she was incredulous to discover she is mortal after all."

"She's going to die?"

"Amanda, I've just told you, we are all going to die sooner or later. In her case, she has about eight weeks left, cancer of the pancreas, it's quite predictable and still incurable. She's on a fast track to eternal oblivion. I have cleared my schedule. If you want to get a body, you'd better get up there as fast as you can. If you know anyone with a suitable pancreas to share, she'll think the world of you."

"Isn't there a remedy for pancreatic cancer? I thought human tumours have been eradicated?"

"They have and they haven't. My poor Mother has one of the very small number that haven't. Don't ask me what its called. She refers to it as 'Sting'."

As Amanda gets up to leave, Johnson has a parting shot, which he seems to find amusing, "Once you've changed status, you'll have to travel by shuttle like the rest of us. Good luck!"

When she finally gets away from the house, she can hear Johnson's laughter as he calls to Rowena, "Come here, my dear,

there's something I must tell you about your new girlfriend."
Is Johnson always so excessively jolly?
He must be infuriating to live with if he is, Amanda concludes.
One quick breath and she's away.

Snaking through the rainy woodlands surrounding the Faculty
of Correction on the bicycle she has been allotted by security at
the main gate, Amanda is soaking wet and scared. The Miasma
had dumped her outside the Faculty's security shield, so she'd
had to ask to be let in.

As well as the bicycle, the Guard gave her a bright yellow cape
that she's told to wear as she goes to the main building. Then
with a not so pleasant smile, he tells her, "This isn't just
rainwear, honey. Wear it to make sure you won't get shot, so
keep it on, OK sweetheart?"

Unused to riding a bike, she's startled by the growl of a bear,
then the snarl of a wildcat and almost falls off. The acacias are
dripping a torrent of mildly acidic raindrops. Now there are
wolves howling. Somewhere in the distance a volley of
machine gun fires scythes the undergrowth. There are feathers
where the bullets have winged the odd pheasant.

When she reaches the Research Centre, the friendly warder
who signs her in as a 'Non-serving Attender', tells her that
Johnson's Mother is away for a few days doing some shopping
in Madagascar. Then he offers to hang up her cape.

"She's gone shopping?" Amanda hisses incredulously.

"Well, you know how the ladies enjoy Madagascar for the
fashion shows," sighs the Warder resignedly. "And our felons
all have six weeks vacation a year as one of their uninfringeable
human rights."

He's glad of the chance to grumble with some-one new. "I
sometimes wonder how we get any work done at all, what with
Conferences and Consultancy jobs. You wouldn't believe how
many of our people are under way at any one time. The only

day everyone must be here is the Fourth of July and that's a god-damned holiday. Let me show you to your rooms."

They walk across the quadrangle of the medieval college buildings and through a side door that leads into a very private garden, behind which is a small building the Warder tells Amanda is her guest house.

The Warder has a pleasant voice and is very correct, "If you'd like to pump a little ox, there's a treadmill next to the hot tub, though I expect you'll want to spend most of your time in the Library, which is located in the Gatehouse. There are some rather splendid donations, especially from the Moses Hoffman bequest and the Miles Panderton[75] papers are here. We have the only copy of 'Ars Muralis' you know. It could even be the original, no-one is sure. You may like to read it, but please don't try to steal it. My Judge can be rather capricious about prison theft, even among our guests. A week in the data mines is an unforgettable experience, two weeks traumatic. Any longer and there's no coming back.

By the way, we have sixteen dimensional miasma here, one of the long term experiments agree by Cornucopia, I do hope you'll enjoy this taste of the future. It's a VLN[76], so if there are signs of turbulence, just let me know and I'll correct it."

Once she's alone, Amanda immediately contacts Lisa. She's settling into her workroom, where a worn Empire style chaise-longue stands opposite a Georgian writing desk. The living room and bedroom are decorated in similarly tasteful simplicity,

---

75 Miles Panderton, penultimate President of the United States of America, whose period of office spanned the main negotiations between Mexico, Venezuela and Colombia, prior to the Continental Congress in Vancouver, 2202, and the Declaration of Interdependence which was signed by Panderton's successor, President 'No Gain' Paine.

76 Very Local Net (VLN)– Licensed exceptions to Miasmatic Generality– granted in this case on grounds of massive multiple malfeasance.

all a little dowdy, yet convincing, more like a country house than a hotel. She can imagine the convicts doing the same when they're appointed to the Faculty.

Lisa is away.

Amanda is asked to reconnect later.

Then she receives a message from Johnson's Mother, asking her to complete a questionnaire about her preferred   new physique.

The usual shit happens clause is mixed up with a claim that the new physique will be between 22 and 24 years old, with a fully checked genetic profile and optimised fertility levels (whatever 'optimised' means, thinks Amanda). She is told not to make rash decisions or hurry her choices, as the selections will be definitive.

The first question floors her.

Gender: male, or female?[77]

Amanda spends the rest of the day wondering about that, having previously devoted more attention to issues like brown eyes or blue eyes, curly hair or straight, rather than such basic distinctions as gender.

Following Johnson's Mother's advice, rather than make any rash decisions she might regret later, Amanda settles into the Miasma and begins the reality checks she'd promised at the last History Room meeting. She enjoys the chore and prepares to work for hours to clear the backlog. Being in a prison doesn't really hamper someone whose self-definition is supported by a data set with 'on'/'off' status.

---

77 Copies of the Questionnaire together with Terms and Conditions may be obtained from the Commercial Exploitation Office at the Superior Faculty of Correction Bureau of Inter-Personal Services, (CEOSFCBIPS).

CHAPTER 7

The Aleutian summer is reaching a glorious apex. Clouds of butterflies settle on the trees, turning them blue and pink. The Rainbow Roses have come into bloom and the woolly clad spring lambs are sturdy, ready for the slaughter. The blonde silky haired foxes prowl along the perimeter of the warren behind Lisa's house in search of silverback conies. Billy the goat has taken to standing on one of the lower branches of the oak tree near the sheepfold. The news from India is grim, but there's nothing anyone can do, even if they could be bothered.

Lisa is slim, tanned and relaxed. She and Malliday had worked pretty hard to work out exactly what they had bought, once the lawyer who had arranged the company sale sent them all six crates of documentation listed in the sales agreement.

Most of the contracts and legal papers are in Russian with crude marginalia in English. Bundles of faded pink ten rouble notes issued in the name of the last Czar lined the crates like bricks. There is a loaded revolver and a box of ammunition.

The ticket designs are based on elaborate engravings, which Malliday plans to include in an exhibition for the proposed visitor centre. Elephant sized engineering drawings reveal designs for locomotives and bridges, embankments and tunnels.

A set of colour samples reveal how it had been intended to paint the engines and carriages.

Harkham has already set up a foundry where his team of enthusiastic amateurs have started work, while Harkham himself negotiates with the structural engineers who are working on the track layouts.

The title deeds for various tracts of land are all tied with pink ribbon and on reading them, Lisa realises she has bought herself much more than anyone had expected. Although the ancient construction work had stalled after a couple of years and the full project had never gone ahead, plans had been made for two lines and land acquired for stations and marshalling yards, as well as the trackbed everyone knew about.

"I always thought the Summit Valley Falls Section was named after the river," Malliday admitted, "I never dreamed there was also going to be a line called Summit Valley Rise, turning our local section into a loop."

He explained the old plans to Lisa and how this meant they could claim ownership over a strip of land some fifty metres wide and one thousand seven hundred miles long, a corridor revealed on the company maps, totalling upwards of 80million square metres and an asset in anyone's valuation programme.

As they tried to piece together the full extent of the property, Lisa had noticed the gradients of the tracks were quite different. The Falls line drops quite rapidly, one in seventy, but the Rise section seems to climb at a lesser rate, one in two hundred. An 'engine house' with a massive windlass at the top of the inclines might have been intended to make use of gravity to aid the trains movement up and down the hills, Malliday suggested.

"The fully loaded trains they planned to send out by the Rise would need more power than those arriving on the Falls. The loop broke into sidings by the waterside, just east of the modern harbour. If the lightly laden trucks going downhill moved twice the distance, perhaps they could operate like a pulley to help

drag the heavier trains uphill."
"I wonder what they were expecting to ship?"

Six weeks have passed since she volunteered to fund the
museum railway project. The Aleutian-Pacific Line, as it had
originally been known, had been granted a licence by special
decree from the Russian Imperial Court in Moscow. Due to a
variety of oversights the decree had never been revoked, even
when Alaska had been bought by the old USA. For centuries,
people had ignored the clauses on their leases referring to the
ancient railway company and the nominal rents were usually
paid a century in advance whenever property was bought and
sold. 'Ten bucks for the railway', was a colloquialism for small
change. 'Blow your whistle' had other connotations. These
payments were regarded as a quaint local custom, a legal nicety
to give the property dealers and lawyers a few extra credits.
Apart from the foxy old lawyer who saw that the rents were
collected, no-one had shown any interest in the railway at all.
Now Lisa has been identified as the new proprietor, people
from all over the region are trying to win her favours. Malliday
had been just as surprised as she, when the lawyer explained
that the leases could be revoked at any time for the purposes of
railway construction, 'which must commenced within three
years of due notice being served on the leaseholders'.
"Young lady," he had chuckled as he explained the situation.
"You have the entire business community by the balls. They
will pay any price you ask to buy those leases out!"
"Why did you never buy the company yourself?," she had
asked him and the reply chilled her bones to the marrow.
"I had no desire to make myself a target for the vengeful ire of
every Tom, Dick and Harry, who thinks he owns something
that's really rented out. I would stay well out of range of our
local hunters, should you chance to stray into the sights of their
rifles."

Lisa decides to ignore the old man's warning. If she started to heed threats like that, she'd never be able to do anything. Walking the tracks a few days later, Lisa is still reluctant to accept she is really their owner, that the levelled trackbed, which must have taken the muscle power of thousands of men and hundreds of horses to build, now actually belongs to her. Her botanist friend, Dempsey, is strolling alongside her, pointing out dozens of anomalous species that have begun to flourish as the climate warmed. He had explained that the seeds were probably carried there when the engineering work was underway and then lain dormant for almost three hundred years.

"This little flower," he tells her pointing to the pale green petals and pink style of a small plant flourishing among the clumps of cannabis, "is normally to be found on the high plateaux of Tibet, while this shrub is from the shores of the Aral Sea in Kazakhstan and that is a newly germinated wheat seed."

"They intended to make the tracks eight feet wide," Lisa tells him. "So we can be thankful the terraces are so broad."

"The Russian standard gauge, rather than the old European system, which was narrower. You should be able to mount the induction beams for the ZIPs and still have room for a couple of lines of old-fashioned steel rails," Dempsey suggests. "I would like you to designate a two metre wide strip as a biotope for these rare species. It would be really sad to lose them."

Lisa nods agreement. There is nothing to be gained antagonising the nature lobby. She thinks it a good idea anyway.

"What really happened to the Aral?" she asks. "Wasn't that the lake that dried up?"

"Some lake, it was as big as a sea, the relic of a primeval ocean, but landlocked with no connection to the modern seas we know. Strange place, a kind of waterless marine graveyard, until they re-flooded it. Poor Khazakhstan. The Soviet Union used it for nuclear bomb tests, hundreds of them. It's the most deadly place in the world for radioactivity and probably will be forever. Then they discovered the meteorite and that scare about spores from extra-terrestrial bacteria, so it was dried out again and the whole region sealed under a layer of non-degradable resin, you know, the purple spot you can see from the moon. The bacteria were only harmful to cockroaches, of course, and they were eventually used on the big bug swarms in New Jersey."

"My Dad had a Jersey Blue roach as a pet when he was a boy."

"Really? My Father used to moan that his parents wouldn't let him have one," says Dempsey. "Did you know, when you poured a glass of vinegar on their backs, they used to turn red?"

"They were very expensive to keep."

"Yes, had to be fed on blueberries and plums, which cost the earth in winter."

"My Dad's roach wasn't one of the big ones, but it was quite fast. He got into trouble with the neighbours when it chased their cats."

"They had one of the big ones down at Bushland in Texas. It was about the size of a horse and needed to munch crystal ox to breathe. Roaches don't have lungs. Now that one could really move, even though they're fairly simple creatures. After the bacteria ate its head, it still took over a year to die."

"Ugh," shivers Lisa. "I'm glad we don't have those up here."

"Blame the revivalists, those things were just fossils for at least three hundred million years."

"Ruined their own religion, no-one wanted to worship a deity that turned out to be something quite so disgusting."

"I think there are still one or two in New Mexico, apart from the famous ones in Hollywood. Oh! Look out! There's a Gibraltan Hornet!"

"Where?" shrieks Lisa, looking around wildly.

"Down there on the ground," Dempsey says calmly. "The little orchid near your feet. It has hornet shaped flowers."

"Are they the ones that sing?" asks Lisa, attentive once again.

JOHN CLARK

"It's more like a humming sound than a real song, we'll have to come here in the first week of spring if you want to hear them. They have air sacks on the buds that make a kind of tiny farting noise when the flowers unfold."

Lisa is amused. "I shall have to tell my friend Amanda about that. She loves anything to do with farting. She's quite a character."

"All the characters like farting jokes, as they don't do it themselves and it is charged against our methane tax and means ever more ox to be pumped," Dempsey sighs. "And the idea of us taxing our own bodily functions makes them laugh," he adds despairingly. "Characters are so damned childlike, those Pratchet[78] moments of theirs, that we are supposed to find cute!"

Lisa wonders whether Dempsey has a flatulence problem and is paying the price for his unruly bowels.

"Try bananas," she suggests.

"Really, you think it might help?" he says hopefully. "I hate having to go to the doctors for a tax exemption. Maybe we should be getting back, it will be sundown in a hour."

They walk back to the transporter park and reach the project workshops as the sun is setting in a blaze of glory behind the mountain peaks. A condor circles the rabbit warren up towards the house, where the foxes had lost interest after a couple of kills.

Stevenson's 'Rocket' is almost complete and ready for painting. The team are now working on Robson's 'Invincible'. Ericsson's 'Astound', originally built by the Vulcan Foundry is soon to begin assembly. When finished 'Invincible' and 'Astound' will pull the eight foot gauge carriages, which have been designed

78 Pratchet, Terence Major (later Duke of Claridge)– English author of literary classics: "Three Men on a Drinking Trip", "Buddenbrooks", "Sonnets for a Girl I met in the Pub last night" and its sequel "Totally fucked – the history of a marriage."(with Bergmann, Inge) .

for communal sex charters and as camping wagons for nature lovers. Malliday had gone to town on the coachwork with interchangeable murals, which will be rearranged according to the nature of the trip. Harkham is dashing from one group of engineers to another.

Smoke rising from the casting moulds for brass fittings has filled the workshop with a reeking haze of exotic and highly toxic pollutants. The heat sears. The noise is deafening. The volunteers are having a great time.

He proudly shows off the main Autopro machine that is turning out the new semi-finished loco's in light weight military ceramic.

"We can make three engines a week with this system, but almost one percent of the work is being done with traditional methods," he is explaining proudly to Lisa, when an almighty crash rings around the shed and he dashes away to see what his amateur engineers have been up to.

Harkham points out a row of lathes where rods of steel are being turned into precisely machined parts for the older engines under restoration. On a set of rails in the centre of the workshop, three pairs of heavy drive wheels and a four-wheeled bogie have been rolled under a crane that has a massive boiler and firebox slung on hawsers, which are slowly being lowered to drop it into position. One of the assistants gently pushes Lisa away from the group of engineers clustered in front of the control screen, as the automated system slowly sets the engine on its wheels in a smooth operation that's completed in fifteen minutes.

"Beats working with robots," Harkham beams, as he surveys the happy faces of the volunteers in their oil smeared overalls and sketches them in charcoal. "You can really feel what fun it must have been to have played your part in the Age of Steam!"

"Talking of steam," Lisa breaks in. "I have finished the application for our emissions exemptions. Since the company is over 200 years old, we should qualify for ancient monument status, not just heritage exemptions. The carbon tax rebate will come in handy."

"Sounds good," says Harkham. "We could use the fireboxes and burn real coal if they go for it. Much more authentic than those synthetic fire blocks they were pushing us to use."

"I think Governor Richardson has shares in 'Pyrosynth'," replies Lisa. "So he obviously wanted us to go nuclear."

"If he'd offered us a millenium based solution, I think we should have taken him up on it," Harkham remarks, "but you really can't beat fossil fuels for that feel of brute force and the aromas are said to be fantastic, almost pheromonal."

Lisa nods, "Have you ever seen real coal?"

"Not yet," Harkham admits, "but it can't be worse than reactor refuse. You don't need to wear anti-radiation protection suits with coal and it showers off when you finish work. We're getting a delivery of six thousand tonnes of steam coal and anthracite from Silesia on the next ship. I thought it was going to be decorative, but if we can use it, that would be fantastic. You'll love this, Lisa, once we get it all running. We shall need ash pits, can you remind me. Oh, and I got the water tower designs back from that museum in Rostock. They made an ice hunt into the archive. For us, very good of them really. I know they wanted an excuse to have a dig, but it was kind. "

"At least we've timed it right with the fashion industry," she says.

"Well done. When did you hear that?" Harkham asks with delight. He adores anything fashionable despite his oily rag sense of taste.

"They plan ahead, then saturate the market. We're in luck. In three years time, they will be going for German Biedermeyer in the spring, followed by French Second Empire for Summer and then English Edwardian and something called 'Arts and Crafts' in the Autumn Collections, with a possibility of changing to

Russian Kremlinism, which was much later of course, so it's just an option at the moment, but they're all about overdressing and ostentation, especially for Christmas parties. The textile producers have agreed. Well, they would, lots of heavy fabrics and expensive accessories, tassels and stuff. And the furniture industry are ecstatic, they'll be using tropical hardwoods for the first time in a couple of centuries."

"How will this help us?" asks Harkham.

"Our little railway will feature heavily in the publicity. People waiting for trains in fancy costumes, evoking associations with 'steamy smut', sweaty firemen and trusty engine drivers. Old fashioned furniture in the waiting rooms, the works," Lisa tells him proudly. "And it's partly because we're the link that Russia and the Americas never had. Pan-nationalist sentiments are being woven into all the designs. They'll book all the sex charters for three months, as thankyou presents to their early perverters. Don't you think we've done well?"

"You've certainly done something," Harkham says in astonishment, "but quite what it is....I never realised you're such a good businesswoman."

"Projector, it is less gendered," she corrects him. "You know, suddenly our railway has become the project that everyone wants. It's extraordinary. All we need now are rails on the ground, rather than lines on a map and we'll be up and running."

"I can see that," says Harkham, impressed, "Have you been getting some advice about these deals? Is there going to be enough money?"

"Yes, there's a friend of one of my colleagues, well his brother actually," Lisa explains, "he's well connected, lots of good contacts and he's married to a Princess, which helps."

As he walks back through the line of engines, Harkham turns and gives Lisa a look of admiration and a wink of encouragement. Then he strides through the workshop with even greater confidence than before. Harkham is blossoming, at long last coming into his own. Steam, sex and fashion – what more could you want?

Lisa is astonished to realise how fast everything has happened. All she wants now is to see engines and carriages complete and their wheels turning amidst clouds of steam with passengers, like paying pigeons, perched upon the seats between the adverts. Selinsky would be proud of her, or so she hopes.

Once she's finished pumping ox, Lisa feeds the animals, tickles the sheep and brushes the goat, who is growing into an elegant slender legged, silky haired beast. The condor has gone, flapping off one morning, never to return.

Glad to be home, she has fifteen minutes before Joe will appear, so she quickly showers and picks out a green silk kimono to bring a little shimmer to the arrival of her guest. She wonders whether Joe intends to seduce her and decides to enjoy it, if he does.

But that doesn't seem to be the purpose of his visit.

Joe is hungry and frustrated when he turns up, half an hour late. Hungry, because he's just spent the day archiving and feels frustrated because he'd failed to find what he was looking for.

"Pasta, that's great Lisa," he mumbles through a mouthful of cannelloni. "And the weed is delicious. You know I haven't tasted goat's cheese for years."

Lisa pours herself another glass of Malbec from the decanter and tops up Joe's glass.

"What brings you to Alaska, Joe?" she wants to know.

"Well," he wavers. "I can't pretend I was just passing through, because I wasn't and whatever the beauties of the landscape, they will have to wait until I can book a holiday. It is nice here, though, the house is wonderful."

Lisa smiles expectantly.

"The point is this. My brother Bill has a wife, a particularly venomous woman, who he tries to avoid as much as possible. I don't blame him. She's appalling. The reason he even stays off the Miasma so much. He probably didn't mention her to you. Anyway, rightly or wrongly, she has decided that you and he are having an affair and this is endangering her marriage. She's wandering around the Pacific basin on the lookout for you. So I came to warn you. Whether you have something going with Bill or not, is none of my business, I really don't care. She is convinced. The point is, she is relentless, bloody minded and probably violent."

"Shit! How did she get this silly idea? I only met Bill once, when Amanda and I went skimming on the Baltic."

"Lisa, she did what every suspicious wife does, she checked the fuck reports at Gen Centre. You and Bill seem to have managed some pretty high scores."

"Well, what's she got to complain about?"

"She comes from a very traditionalist background and has inflated notions of her genetic worth. Her family call themselves royalty, though there has been a dispute about their actual status, and screwing Bill is a criminal offence in their eyes. He is private property."

"You mean he's a slave?"

"You could put it like that. According to them, he is her registered 'personal paternal RNA resource'."

Lisa records one of the highest astonishment scores ever recorded. [79]

"Well, I'm not one of them, am I, so they can't do anything."

"Legally, no," Joe warns, "but she has a tendency to take the law into her own hands. You'd better watch out."

"What's Bill doing about this?"

"He's at home looking after the children, the Little Princes and Princesses, while she's off on the rampage. Her Father gave her a new sword for her birthday, which is bad news in the circumstances."

---

79 See deLandy on 'Psycho-mining Anomalies and other Pleasantries' (2121), Irish Folklore Series, No3, Belfast School of Perversion.

"What? Why isn't he trying to stop her?"

"He did try, but she escaped. Bill booked her into Deep Recovery, which is what he usually does when she's angry about his infidelities, but this time she refused to take the narcotics and ran off."

"Why is she so interested in me?"

"Your compatibility is extremely high, good genetic match, so she feels threatened. She thinks you'll breed with Bill sooner or later."

Lisa feels a little twitch in her belly. If she and Bill would make a good genetic mix, then so could Joe, but she keeps the thought to herself. One brother is much the same as another.

"Should I run off into hiding?"

"She's somewhere on the Galapagos at the moment. Hopefully she'll be caught before she heads up north."

"I hope it won't effect the railway."

"She won't use the train, she'll come in by ship."

"No, I was thinking aloud. If I run off now, the railway project could be compromised."

"I didn't know you had a railway project."

"Never mind, I'll tell you later. Joe, what time are we due in the History Room?"

"Not for a couple of hours."

"Good, then finish your dinner and let's see if you and I can take up where Bill left off. He needs more practice, you know, if he's serious about making a go of real time. I mean it was nice, but I was a bit, well, disappointed to be honest."

Joe thinks about the idea for a second or two, then smiles, swallows and they depart for Lisa's bedroom, where things proceed much as might be imagined.

The pair are in buoyant mood, when they relocate to the History Room, everything having gone well and their registration duly logged. Joe sends a message to his sister in law explaining that he has assumed Bill's role and she can stop seeking revenge, though he isn't sure if she can be placated quite so easily. He sends a 'that was super nice' tag to Pragmatic Partnership, in case she decides to check. But he's enjoyed Lisa, so if the harpy does chop her into slices, at the very least he'll have some sweet memories. After this last thought, Joe gives his knuckles a metaphoric rap for unbridled selfishness and catches sight of the silly grin on his face reflected in the window.

Lisa glances at the familiar faded beige walls and is glad to be somewhere where she feels protected from the forays of a rampaging Polynesian Princess. Although Joe's performance has reassured her, Lisa still puts the acacias onto high alert, just in case.

Looking flushed and flustered, Johnson flops in last as the History Room is fully reconstituted. He thanks Amanda, for the reality checks she's completed, then tells them that Smithson is sending one of his associates to join them.

"The issue," Johnson claims, "is simple, but not straightforward."

The Review Committee, he tells them, had taken a look at Amanda's reports and were ready to ask the Group to make a submission to 'All Known History'. Of course, this is a great achievement for them as historians. Only about one percent of research projects are invited to submit and fewer still are approved for integration. 'All Known History' has its own mechanisms to acquire information and assess its validity as data, so a formal request for input is something of an accolade.

"Well, we have two choices," says Amanda, "to submit a cautious, but unfinished report which would consist mainly of the detailing you have unearthed, while excluding our major development, or we can make a real effort to track down this Mona person and have her identified with some biographical inputs in time for the next census."

159

"I know what I would prefer," says Johnson, "but we should ask ourselves whether it is really possible to reach our goal, now that Selinsky is no longer one of the team."

Joe immediately supports Johnson's notion that they should keep trying to find out more about Mona. Then, to her own surprise, Lisa raises doubts, which horrifies Amanda.

"How can you says that, Lisa?You've taken all that money and sunk at least half of it into this absurd railway project and now you have the gall to suggest we give up!"

"It's not a question of money," says Lisa aggressively. "The question is whether we have any chance of success."

Before she finishes her remarks, Joe flashes Lisa a message, 'the Princess has been found and is now at home recuperating'.

The stress unwinds from Lisa's shoulders, then she wonders whether the whole story about the Polynesian Princess was a ruse Joe had used to persuade her into bed? Reluctantly, she accepts that if that was the case, it worked. She wouldn't mind being persuaded again.

"I was only wondering, Amanda, about what might be the wise choice. Even if we submit a limited report, there is nothing to stop us continuing with the research."

"Limited reports are a waste of time," Amanda says sternly, "A fix on Mona will really have an impact. I think we should go public at the Autumn Conference in Aix les Bains[80].

Looking round the table, Johnson waits to see if anyone will object to Amanda's proposal, letting his eyes linger on Joe's impassive face, until he provokes him to shrug his shoulders, presumably assent.

"Then it looks as if we have arrived at a decision, everybody?" queries Johnson. "All agreed."

They nod like schoolchildren, then Johnson invites Smithson's representative to join them. One of the two thousand assistants, Amanda reminds herself. A stout woman in her early fifties

---

80 27th Bi-Annual Conference of the AKH Association.

enters the room and ten seconds later she leaves. A busy person. All Johnson has said is that they will publish at the Conference and her only remark was a curt, "Jolly good". [81] [82]The sense of anticlimax is palpable.

"As to the task in hand," Johnson says, becoming school masterly,

"Joe, do you have anything for us?"

"Well, I do have one thing to mention," Joe begins ominously. "We may have been in error assuming this Mona was from Scotland. We followed her accent. That was a mistake, false trail. I haven't checked this, but I recalled a couple of hours ago,

---

81 Gina Turmann PhD FRCC, Assistant Commissioner of the Cosmopolitan Police with special responsibility for organising crime.

82 Extract from The Turmann Report:

In all instances the deviance scores of each History Room participant was outside normal boundaries (average 40, preference 30), however there were significant variations in standard motivation -

Johnson, Robert Hyam St. John - 73% paranoid arrogance;

Programme 3Z1, Amanda – 89% corporal tendencies;

D'Annunzio, Lisa – corporate ambition 78%;

Smather, Joseph Ignatius – seditious instincts (score withheld).

The group were monitored at fifteen microsecond intervals for variations in mood, cohesion and collective determination revealing scores consistent with Grade 6 instability and were assigned threat code "magenta" (monitor and disable) with "celurian" intervention thresholds.

Possible disposal procedures will include railway accidents, extra-miasmatic muggings, self-destruction and character assassination. At the request of Acting Commissioner Jane Smithson the Pro-Papal Curia have agreed to undertake an investigation into their potential inclusion on the Vatican Index of Lost Souls (pending).

that there was a debate about accents around the time when Selby was getting his campaign going."

"What kind of a debate?" Amanda asks politely but with a heavy dose of suspicion in her voice.

"Low level, newspaper columnists, blogs, television, nothing of merit, but the trend was distinct. A peculiar pseudo-dialect infected late 20 and early 21 speech patterns. They called it 'estuarine english'. EE asked for a limited vocabulary and functioned with a highly simplified, often monosyllabic, almost primitive, level of syntax known later as 'the London Grunt'. The thematic range was predominantly consumptively consumerist, prices, ordering, sexual demands, two word rejections. There is no EE documentation listed under culture or philosophy. The roots were proletarian, but the main vector was broadcasting, a propaganda organisation called the BBC, some references to royalty, footballers and financial services. It suited the needs of people with simple lives, 'back office types', the 'hive folk' as we would call them nowadays. I think Du Plessis had this covered in one of the 'Eurospeak' studies, you can find more there. Just before the Swoop, there was a reaction and a new fashion began among the more educated to begin speaking in a kind of broken Scottish, influenced somewhat by Edinburgh speech patterns, but transmitted mainly through a chain of Language Schools offering elocution lessons. They had the trade name, 'Tartan Tones', but the accent itself became known as MacSnob, or sometimes 'Tar-Tones'. I think that was what we heard when Mona was talking to Eric Selby."

"Ooof," says Lisa, "so who was she then?"

Joe settles back to tell his story in as an around and about way as possible. Lisa is expecting this, so she settles back to listen. Only Amanda seems perturbed, as her thirst for data exceeds Joe capacity to supply it. Johnson, of course, is smugly awaiting the opportunity to correct whatever Joe has to tell them, which is this.

"The Government had a Department known as the Land Registry, where records were kept of who owns what. One of their Heads of Department, a so-called Chancellory Advocate, during the period we are addressing went by the name of Monica Threlwell. Could this Monica be our Mona? Are Monica's known as Mon, or Mona, or maybe Moni, to their friends? I think so. The woman was born in Australia, which might be another ground for suspecting some divergent nickname. It's all rather confused. She seems to have studied political science at the London School of Economics and was an advisor to an All Party Study Group on property, though so far as I can tell Tewkesbury was not a member. Rather surprising that, I thought he sat on any and every Committee known to man and dog. There are no official documents pointing to a contact, anyway. But who can trust official documents? Certainly not historians like us. We can and should be seen to probe a little deeper. The critical evidence is this and this I do think is correct. In 2013, she was seconded for five years to the OECD in Vienna to work on an international study into Land Reform. Now Smithovitch and Braunovsky had their Head Office in Vienna, in the same building where she lived, on a little street called Obersackgasse, upper cul-de-sac lane, if you're wondering what that means. I think this Austrian connection could be the convincing link we need to pin her down."

"But what about the other Mona? The one we saw at the gallery and the pub?" asks Amanda.

"I think it was the same woman, but we made an identification error."

"But Joe," complains Amanda, "the address, we followed her to the address. We have her talking to Selby."

"She was undoubtedly the right woman," agrees Lisa firmly.

"The right woman, correct, but the wrong name and identity. I would ignore that contact, there must have been a coherence failure in the Miasma. It won't be the first time. I was archiving today, rummaging through some of Selinsky's notes. He had a list of possible names and several addresses. I think he made a mistake and that may be the source of the other inconsistencies. Gave us the correct address, but the wrong biography."

Johnson is stern. "Joe, are you suggesting we were within minutes of sending a completely false addition to 'All Known History'? I am appalled. How could Selinsky have been so sloppy about his research? We really must ensure the reality checks are up to date, or everything will end in utter chaos."

"They are up to date," mutters Amanda, teeth clenched.

"Don't exaggerate, Robert," says Joe. "We've all made errors at one time or another."

"Perhaps I should make a surer sift before we send any more of these supposed scenarios we've been generating."

Johnson only lisps when he lies and he sprays the table with a haze of spit as the sentence collapses from the word 'perhaps' on.

Amanda begins to giggle.

"Thut up," splutters Johnson, in a tizz.

"Would any-one like some tea?" Lisa asks, having suffered from an excessive exposure to English social norms in the course of her research.

"For goodness sake, Lisa, don't start going native on us," Johnson snaps. "This isn't some bloody day trip into the glowing sunsets of romantic literature. This is political."

The moment of tetchiness passes, as Joe returns to his theme, bringing a sense of moderate deliberation to the discussion, as he addresses them in a voice of quiet serenity.

While Joe is talking, Lisa orders another three thousand tonnes of manganese steel from Liberian Free Metals and mulls over a choice of fabrics for the railway carriage seats, choosing a deep blue for the superior class and a mild orange for the comfort sections. Harkham sends her a message that the ZIP beams are ready for testing, a piece of good news that Lisa immediately relays to the State Capital in Fairbanks.

"Lisa, are you paying attention?" whispers Amanda. With a start, Lisa switches to instant update and catches the gist of what Joe has been saying.

"When Selby took his seat as the first Legacy Party Member of Parliament," Joe had been explaining, "there had been murmurs of dissent from the government coalition. Not much more than muttering, but enough to be interpreted as a warning signal and he had been excluded from the three committees he had hoped to serve on.[83] To keep him occupied, or rather to overwhelm him with work, the Government offered him a place on the International Monitoring Commission for Arab-Israeli Peace Negotiations. Meeting trouble with trouble, as a Commons and Foreignwealth Office official was quoted as saying in private. The work took him abroad for much of his time and was seen as a stepping stone to political obscurity. Uncharitable commentators supposed that the Prime Minister had hoped that either the Arabs or the Israeli's would bump Selby off, or agree on a joint operation to kill the bastard, which could be hailed as a diplomatic collaborative breakthrough of sorts."

Joe told them he had run through all Selinsky's notes on the matter without finding anything of interest.

"Selby enjoyed a brief affair with a woman called Justine in Haifa, where there are a surfeit of kingfishers," Joe says. "We might have anticipated that, given Selby's propensity to take his trousers off at every opportunity. I don't suspect the birds stand for anything."

"After two years of fruitless shuttling between Jerusalem, Cairo and Vienna, the 'One Day War' had seen an end to any

---

83 Standing Committee on Coastal Defence, Parliamentary Committee on Local Democracy and the Royal Commission of Valuation, according to Selby E., "Gagged", The Daily Accord, Glasgow.

pretence of negotiation and brought a three-fold rise in the price of oil to more than nine hundred dollars a barrel. Selby was then appointed to the board of London Repo. Rather than damage his popularity, he was seen as a moderating figure among the sharks over the motorway closure programme. His tough stance on personal finance and the forced repayment of loans brought another surge of support both from the 'Forthright Movement' and the 'Legacy Lobby', whose influence was growing apace."

"I suppose it's the Viennese connection you'd like us to explore," responds Johnson with a yawn.

"Unless you have any other suggestions, Robert?" Joe replies neutrally.

"No, no, I think that is a splendid direction to follow," smiles Johnson, hoping to keep Joe happy. "We all enjoy Vienna. Ah, you have been to Vienna, I hope."

Apart from Johnson, who seems to find it normal to have been everywhere, none of the others had actually set foot in the city.

"I see," said Johnson. "In that case, I'd better do you the guided tour."

He fiddles with the miasma and the group find themselves sitting in a café. There are horse-drawn carriages moving down the street and everything smells of coal.

"I thought the late 19th might be to our collective taste," Johnson beams. "Our immunity from TB and syphilis makes it a rather marvellous place to be. Acorns in paradise. Now I wonder what made me say that? Another melancholic paradox. Perhaps we shall never know."

"Robert?" asks Amanda, "Why is everyone here talking in French?"

"Oh no," he exclaims, looking round in alarm, his eyes flicking from one corner of the room to another, then staring in astonishment out of the window. "I can't believe it. We've been brought to bloody Brussels! I do beg your pardon, let me see what I can do. Wrong city, wrong time, wrong bloody country, that is if you consider Belgium a country, I'm not sure any Belgians do, apart from the royal family factotums. Confounded nuisance. Now, how on earth did that happen?"

"Be that as it may, Robert," Joe says demurely, "would anyone like a beer, while you try to work out whether we should relocate."

A broad bellied waiter takes their order and ten minutes later serves them with large glasses of foaming dark brown beer. Then Johnson realises that they don't have any money and he spends another ten minutes trying to persuade the waiter to accept payment in Austrian crowns. Despite his threat to send for the police, the waiter's boss eventually accepts a payment approximately twice the value of their bill and asks suspiciously what kind of business has brought them to the city.

"The tides of history, my dear fellow, the ever broadening, deepening and widening, waxing waning highs and lows of historical investigation," declaims Johnson in English and Lisa wishes she wasn't there. Historians are supposed to be inconspicuous.

The man pockets his money, gurgles a Flemish curse and turns disdainfully away, as Joe, Lisa and Amanda drink up and quickly relocate to another fold in the Miasma.

Johnson looks round the room to see if there is anyone he recognises, then walks upstairs.

The waiter nods and silently mouths the words, "Room Four."

"Thankyou, Poirot," he replies.

CHAPTER 8

The heavy blue curtains are drawn, so that only flickering candlelight breaks the gloom.

"Hello Mum," Johnson whispers, as he closes the door carefully, so as not to disturb the drowsy old lady.

"Bobby, good of you, the others have gone I presume."

"They expected Vienna, I told them it was Brussels, so the location error should deter them from snooping here again."

"No-one has ever shown much interest in Milwaukee."

"I have sent them all my apologies, with the suggestion that we meet in Vienna two hours from now. Did you locate a pancreas?"

"That was never the issue. There are thousands of the wobbly things daily. My problem was the statute on felons. No new organs for felons with more than fifteen years to serve."

"How did you get around it?"

"Threats."

"Really, who?"

"And bribery. I gave the Prison Board Ethics Commission half a million each and threatened to infill the surface data mines. I ordered a magnetic crane to beef up the threat. I think it was the crane that convinced them. We were supposed to have bought one years ago, but I'd explained that it would create havoc in the mines and the order had never been ratified. So it would have been an official purchase and sooner or later some idiot would have given it a try. They soon saw sense. Would you like a vodka?"

"What are you drinking?"

"Diabeet extract. It's disgusting, but healthy."

"Oh, then I'll stick to vodka."

She watches him carefully as he pours the vodka into a tall thin glass. He shudders as the deep chilled alcohol sears his throat. He drinks for her by proxy.

"Now Bobby, let me bring you up to date. I have decided to go for the full transformative transplant. At my age there isn't much of an alternative. I shall go to Korea as planned for the Occi Festival and will do the transplant a couple of days later on Iwo Jima. We shall need your Amanda for the trial. My friend Janneret[84] wants to practice before she operates. She's scared of what I might have arranged to happen to her if things go wrong."

"How long will you need Amanda for?"

"Three days for the extraction and implantation, another couple of days of tests, then she will be on her own. She can decide to die, or go on to recover, I really don't mind either way. I have decided to go body to body. We'll stick the new pancreas in my old carcass, make the switch and this old carcass can go back to jail, while I'll be fancy free in a brand new body. The new Amanda can do whatever she wants. That's her reward for being a good girl."

"Mother," asks Johnson politely, "how are you going to arrange for the new bodies?"

"Well, my dear, I'm glad you brought that up," the old lady says with a sweet disarming smile. "That's what I wanted to talk

---

84 Prof Janneret was later elected Warden of All Souls, Surgeon General, Keeper of the Royal Catacombs and Protector of the Vaults in the Isle of Wight. See: Genocide.

to you about. You see, we thought it would be nice to keep things close to home and your two girls are more or less available, if you think about it. If I was to point to Josi, we wondered if you would mind if Amanda was to inhabit Rowany?"

"Rowena."

"Yes, that's the one, or should I take Rowena and she can have the Josi. They're both dishy, aren't they and you know neither of them are more than pleasure units at the moment, so there are no ethical issues to work round. Nobody would miss them, except for you, and I suspect you are ready for some new blood. I'll pay, darling, so you can have some fresh flesh for you fantasies. To be honest, I always hankered after glamour and at my age a bit of wanton pleasure would be very welcome."

"Let me think about this Mother, if you don't mind. They're rather well trained."

"Of course," she says benignly. "I can let you have two minutes. By the way, if you do not go along with this, I shall cut you out of my will."

"Very well, Mother," says Johnson, outplayed in five seconds, "Where should Rowena and Josi be delivered?"

"You enjoy them tonight, Bobby dear. I'll send someone for them in the morning. Oh, sperm free, if you don't mind. We don't want any suggestions of incest, do we?"

His Mother winces with arthritic pain as she eases herself back into the armchair, which Johnson had moved closer to the log fire and winces with horror. A heavy fog has descended over the city and the cold damp air is pregnant with pneumonia. Mother is to become Josi. His lust evaporates.

"The programme," says the old lady referring to Amanda, "has no knowledge of our project, I assume."

"She is astonishingly selfish," Johnson assures her, "Once she'd seen Rowena, there was no stopping her. She's merely concerned to have the operation before you die."

Johnson's Mother laughs cruelly. "Well, she's going first, so whatever happens, she'll get her wish. Rowena, a sweet name, but Josi has more oomph."

"I've told the people on Iwo Jima to expect us to come in via the Occi Fest," she continues. "now all we have is the staging to consider. Should there be a single procedure, or can we work gradually, transferring my capacities function by function?"

"I don't think we have a choice," Johnson says gravely. "I know staging is more secure from the point of view of the recipient, but if we are to capture your conscious self intact, then there can only be a single intervention, all or nothing, in a single swoop. My girls were sequenced, but that was a cut and paste personalisation, copy segments of programme and insert them where appropriate on the existing human substrate. We just kept popping bits in until the mind began to function. They were drones to begin with. If Amanda is to be of any use to us at all, we must complete the transfer in a single smooth procedure."

"Amanda," says the old lady scornfully, "is no more than a crash test dummy."

"Some crash, Mother, some dummy," says Johnson smiling. "She doesn't see it that way at all. She's hooked on the notion of a digital to organic."

"Ha, if it works for her, it will work for me and that is the only issue of any significance."

"There is one other."

"Meaning?"

"Amanda has consciousness, a sense of self, impressive cognitive functions and a quite remarkable retentive memory, levels of critical analysis that impressed the Pope, but does she have a soul?"

"Of course not, you sentimental twit. Artificial Intelligence and Souls are incompatible."

"Quite, but in your case the issue arises, not just as theology. It

171

could be significant. If we miss it and it goes shooting off in the direction of heaven, God knows, there will be all hell to pay. The mirror transplantation will certainly, well eighty percent, no more, account for the cognitives, but if there is something that we have failed to chart, any missing corners of your mind that we might fail to capture."

"My dear boy, we have been through this a thousand times. Did the Pope have anything concrete to say? No, so I don't expect any problems in that direction."

"She did mention the issue of faith."

"What does the Pope know about faith? Good lord, Bobby, she's a woman who prays for profit. I don't talk to the Pope any more, nor any of the Cardinellas, not about ethics anyway, though I had no choice when the Maltese issue blew up. The negotiations were unavoidable. They made a lot of money on that deal, really a very large amount of money."

"Mother," Johnson remonstrates, "have you reconsidered? Wouldn't a simple pancreatic transplant be preferable to this full body transformation?"

The old lady takes a bite of home-made chocolate cake before replying. "No, Bobby. If I settled for a new pancreas, it would only be the start of something much worse - wouldn't be long before something else would need replacing, then another thing and another. Haven't you seen the state of my arteries? And you are ignoring the main point of the exercise, or have you forgotten? This will be the most daring escape in the history of prisons. When that little Pleasure Module 'Josi' finds herself in my old carcass, the whole world will assume I've slipped into a demented state of erotic insatiability, erotic dementia, something that should also make headlines, especially if she locks on to some of my gaolers. Write up a study on that and you'll be hailed as a hero Bobby, 'When Mum turned into a Demented Geriatric Nymphomaniac'. The National New York Times Enquirer will serialise. Revenge is sweet, Bobby, never forget that, revenge is a honey pot of pleasure. And those bastards in Cornucopia have it coming."

"Another cup of tea, Mother?" Johnson asks dutifully.

"Just one, and then we'd better get going. I am due in Korea and you should make sure Amanda is fully prepared and on-time."

"Very well, Mother," Johnson concedes, once the tea has been drunk and they whisk themselves across the world. The old lady arrives in Korea, registers for the Occi Festival, then prepares to transport herself to the underground clinic on Iwo Jima.

Shimmering, a moment of hesitation, as he watches the old lady leave, Johnson bounces across to the Archive, where he finds Amanda sitting quietly in the main reading room.

"It's almost time," he whispers into her ear and she turns her face to gaze into his eyes. "Oh Robert, that's wonderful, now we can truly be together."

"Any messages before we go?"

Amanda is glad to be reminded and sends everyone on her message list a note to say that she will be spending the next few days at the Occi Festival and asks for them to wish her luck.[85]

The most raucous event on the planet, the Occi Festival is organised by the International Alliance of Contemplative Buddhists, who renamed the Global Conference on Unlimited Bandwidth Innovations after the Telecoms Association's President Klaus Balaban described the event as a scandalous perversion of engineering values and a decadent mockery of scientific enquiry.

---

85 Of the seven million respondents to Amanda's last official message, two hundred travelled to the Occi Festival hoping to meet her. Accounts reveal she was sent a bonus of five hundred thousand credits by the Korean Tourist Authority

The mass of booths and the specially erected hive visualisation tents bring a circus air to the vast Korean plain and the distant border with Mongolia. The air shimmers with red green glistening against the shadowy bluins and mesmerising magrentos, as perpetory music flagels the atmosphere of abandon and delight.

The hives open their floodgates each morning at six a.m for the millions who want to sample the latest developments in Miasmatics. By nine o'clock, with half a billion users locked in for the next eighteen hours, the fun begins.

The pleasure shocks can be recorded as far afield as India and Australia, as each huge wave of simultaneous stimulation threatens to fracture the virtual lattice of the Miasma. The folding threat is only countered by electrostatic shock absorbers built into the regional power grid and the surplus energies are deflected to the big crystal ox plant in Kowloon.

At the end of the day's revels all co-ordinates will be restored and the users can return to their everyday lives, wiser, worn out, but essentially unscathed and remembering nothing, except the message that they've had a bloody good time. The Festival is also a great opportunity to air the hives and hose down some of the worst olfatory offenders.

Of the hundred thousand delegates who attend the Occi festival in person[86], only the organising committee and the police maintain any kind of pretence of decorum. For the first ten days of the month, the Festival distracts humanity, who then spend the next three weeks quietly recovering, as northern hemispheric winter turns to spring. Having sampled the world's newest wares, in the weeks that follow all the most popular scenarios will be bought and succoured for abiding pleasure. There's something for everyone and everyone wants something new.

---

86 See: The Naked and the Dead, Ellen Owen (ed), Guardian Dogmatics, The Puritan Press, London, 2170.

"The Occi Fest makes Christmas seem like a dog hanging," remarked a respected, but exhausted transcendental phenomenologist, Juliana Kosslick Probst, after emerging from the play area with a battered ego and bruises to match.[87]
Johnson's Mother arrives at the Smithson-Pacific Pavilion in time to enjoy a wine tasting and she runs into a number of her own clients, Miasmatists, whose products have been tested at the Superior Faculty of Correction. A ripple of excitement runs through the crowd, as she's recognised and everyone overhears the whisper, "Barbara Happle is here."
 The hospitality suites are carefully positioned behind the Observation Booths, where technicians make hurried amendments to their programmes as bugs emerge among the masses at play in the hives. Users are stung. Bugs are squashed. Some die, of course, but there's an atmosphere of light-hearted joshing. This is the heart of the Occi Festival and a perfect chance for Johnson's mother to create a confusing trail of alibis. She remembers to tell everyone that her life is coming to an end as she totters through the mêlée in search of the Delegates Centre. This is where she intends to disappear, her presence ignored until her name can be traced on the list of casualties. Among the more sensitive Miasmatists there is a noticeable sense of relief throughout the community, as news of her forthcoming demise becomes known.
 She finds Smithson sitting alone smoking a cigarette.
 "OK, so far," says Smithson, as he welcomes her, "0 - Killed, as they used to write in the wartime casualty lists for American villagers." Then he offers her a hand-rolled tube of liquorice stained paper filled with tobacco, "or would you prefer a cigar?"
 "Nothing for me, Fred, thank you, I shall have more narcotics

---

87 All that Stuff, Sir Jagger Lennon, Bart., Rolling Stones, The Philosophy Channel. 2222.

than I can handle on Iwo Jima. That's a terrible jacket you're wearing."

Smithson had chosen the plaid jacket himself. He's mildly discomforted by her comment, but to hell with the old witch. Who cares? She'll be history in a day or two, and not the all known kind, just good old fashioned past tense.

"Iwo Jima is a very long way from anywhere. I shall follow events with great interest. Maybe your taste will improve," he smiles. "You know, it won't be long before I shall be needing the same treatment," he adds urbanely with a hint of an oily smile.

"Quentin, the technique is fairly well proven, the only remaining questions are philosophical rather than physiological, almost theological, if you were to hear my son talk."

"He may have a point, we tend to bypass religion and your boy was always a somewhat pious hypocrite," Smithson remarks, "I would not, personally, pay the question too much regard."

"No, but I wish I could think of a test to confirm my continuity of self. We're talking of nanoseconds, the elastic nature of bonds and coherence, no longer than the time it takes to rewrap a protein. It all has to slide and overlap without a break. There is little point offering anyone Eternal Life, if what we're doing is really a disguised form of euthanasia. I do hope David Bohm was right."

Smithson waves her concerns away, "No, that's not a problem at all, we shall simply rebrand the process for the marketplace. 'Better a Refresher than a Zombie', how about that for a slogan?" he laughs. "And either option is a thousand times preferable to the gradual disembodiment option in the hives. By the way, have you seen what's going on in there? Take a look from the Observation Booth. There are five million people in there right now, it's a huge success."

She steps inside the 'Gnawsion' observation booth and recoils in horror. "Quentin, that is revolting, repulsive. I am appalled.

What on earth are they doing? It's tantamount to cannibalism."

"Correct, but what do you mean by tantamount, we've taken them to the very edge. There were some casualties first thing this morning, but they've been fished out, thank goodness. We shall be promoting Mantis, the next version as the ultimate expression of desire, though that too will turn out to be an exaggeration by the time 'Blend' comes onto the market at the Autumn Fair in Aix."

"Why is it taking so long?"

"There were some issues in the reassembly threads, or it would been ready sooner, but 'Gnawsion' seems to be the unexpected success that every-one wants to discover for themselves here at Occi."

"Re-assembly carries a degree of uncertainty and always will. You know Robert is having Amanda poured into his Rowena girl. I shall get Josi, her metabolism is more stable, though Rowena has the looks."

Smithson chortles with delight.

"Now, that will be an unexpected pleasure for us all. Very considerate of him. You know, I've been intending to recommend her for Cornucopia, perhaps that need not wait. Forgive me, if I shall avoid any carnal contact between Josi and myself."

"I never fancied you anyway, Fred and you're not the one who is going to change. My focus will be on attributes other than intellect. Give Amanda a week, or two to settle down. She'll need a bit of time to readjust."

"Yes, of course, my dear. Now, let me show you to your rooms."

"No need, no need, I am running off to Iwo Jima as soon as we are done."

"Oh, let me show you them anyway, it will help your alibis. By the way, I have just thought of the perfect continuity test."

"You clever man, tell me."

"No, I can't. It wouldn't work, if I tell you. But, I promise faithfully to tell you the result after your operation."

She gives Smithson a stern look of mild loathing. "There are times, my dear fellow, when you can be extremely trying, but I suppose I shall just have to trust you."

Smithson claps his hands with glee, "You will, you will and then we'll both know if its possible to get out of jail free!"

"Freedom has always been expensive and once you've been in jail, you can never be completely free," she says in an undertone, then asks, "Are you sure about this test, you old rogue?"

"Yes, I think I can confirm the test would satisfy any judge, 'beyond a level of reasonable doubt'."

Smithson suddenly begins to wriggle and writhe, as if he's been possessed. Then he starts to giggle.

"What on earth was that?" she asks.

"Hive energy," he says uncertainly. "I seem to have been picking up good vibrations. The turbulence in there is quite exceptional."

"You know, Smithy, you are extraordinarily greedy!"

"I am, I am," he laughs. "You know, your young friend Amanda said that too! No, I'm wrong, she didn't, she said I am a snob."

"Then she isn't quite the fool I took her for, when I designed her."

"There is always something of the creator in their creations."

"Tell me one more thing, Smithy."

"What's that?"

"Do you think life has always been such a monumental unadulterated catastrophe?"

"I'm afraid so, Barbara, that is the one abiding principle of our teeming society and look at all the idiotic things it makes us do."

Johnson's Mother gives Smithson the kind of look teachers

usually reserve for underachieving juvenile delinquents on the last day of the school year.

"I'd better be off. See you in a month or so. Then you can tell me whether I've passed your test, or died in the attempt."

"Either way, it will be an interesting conversation. I look forward to it. Anyway, I have confidence in your success and will book ourselves a table together at my favourite restaurant, where we can celebrate with fish."

"Smithy, do me a favour and sign me into the room, I must be off. Cheerio, Fred."

As she walks away from the Delegate Centre, a figure bent by the passage of time, progressive arthritis and decades of repressed aggression, Smithson realises that she has made a monumental blunder in accepting his notion of a test. She has inadvertently put herself entirely in his power. All he has to do is to declare her transference a failure, then at the inquest she will be officially declared dead, 'a victim of her own misadventure'. Her own damned fault and everything she owns will go to the Faculty, apart from the various minor bequests in her very detailed will. Then he decides he could not possibly be so mean. Or could he? A conversation with Robert is certainly called for. A matter of negotiation, especially about the question of what should be done with Amanda and how keen Robert is to hang on to his Mother's wealth.

As ever, the Occi Festival has born fruit. Now Smithson decides to give some rigorous thought as to what the test might be. Amanda and the old lady are both right. He is a very very greedy man, he tells himself with a chuckle, yet it is not for nothing that his standing is founded on his reputation as complete pragmatist, his deeply held conviction in the philosophy that whatever seems to work, not only can, but will.

Looking into his diary for the year, Smithson books himself into a discrete Czech Spa for a course in Digital Drama with Sammy Becket Junior, so that after the Autumn Fair in Aix, he will be able to enjoy the luxury of 'repenting at leisure'.

Not unusually for some-one who is greedy, Smithson is also smug, but following his encounter with the old lady he has good reason to be pleased with himself. Barbara Bloody Happle, at long last the end of the witch. He laughs. Smithson watches a disagreeable small boy who is staring at him and marks him out for an early death. Then he has to hurry.

According to the daily timetable, Amanda is due to arrive in less than ten minutes and Smithson wants her to be impressed. The Occi Festival has become a little more extravagant every year since he started attending. This time everything is threatening to slide out of control. Smithson is proud of the barriers they've created between technicians and attendees. Back stage passes are a thing of the past, but he can always find a way to sneak someone in through the front door.

When Amanda is introduced to the programming team, who are using the standard 'test and forget' amnesia evaluation technique, he explains that a small group of volunteers are being used to test a provision character codenamed 'primitive rebel'. Why Amanda and her little band of historians had never asked him who else might be working on character development had puzzled Smithson, but now he realises that Amanda had never thought much beyond the notion of pouring a set of character elements onto a character framework programme tied to the delicate gossamer of 'All Known History' and the patterns she has been exploring. It seems obvious to Smithson that characterisation requires much more demanding threading and a whole batch of well-tempered engines, not to mention the compositing. Historians are famous for shortsightedness, like academics everywhere who assume the purpose of their research is what they think it is. The purpose of research is in Smithson's view, the uses to which is it put and there is no point bleating about ethics, the environment, or genetic harmonies.

THE SWOOP

The programming team, of course, have known from the outset that a skin of superficial character traits were being worked on by a team of historians, but from their point of view these were merely superficial. The real work for them has been to concentrate on core functions within the Miasmatic engines and to configure their interaction via 'All Known History'. Smithson is mildly amused that so many clever people can blind themselves to the true character of the project they are working on, but that seems to have been the case for centuries. Even the world's wisest blind themselves to the consequences of their actions. Fred Quentin Smithson has never suffered from that. He is acutely aware of the impact of both his actions and his strategies. It seems to work.

Smithson tolerates ignorance, but he holds anyone who blindfolds themselves with deep suspicion. Only a tiny minority have have the same clear sighted perspectives as himself and Selinsky was one of them. Now he is gone and Smithson finds he wishes the oddly opinionated archivist was still around to be argued with. If transference can succeed with continuity, perhaps there's hope for resurrection.

One by one, the volunteers stumble out of the test zone, close to mental and physical collapse, hair tousled, sweaty, disorientated, but euphoric. They are debriefed by the testing committee. They are all cheerfully bewildered that the amnesia function really works and they haven't a clue about what they have been through. The odd ache and pain, residual teethmarks and soreness are treated by Nurse, then the volunteers are each given a hearty meal, some pocket money and a certificate confirming their participation in the pre-roll. Then, given five hundred credits they're told to fuck off and enjoy the rest of the festival, which they try to do for a few hours, but give up and go home to collapse into a coma for a day or two.

Smithson knows many of these certificates will end up framed on living room, den, or office walls, so he has had them printed with impressive decorative spirals and other curlicues, embossed lettering and a personalised note of thanks from himself. The coma's are regarded as a badge of honour, much as duelling scars, or minor war wounds were seen by earlier generations.

There are little groups of people in the 'What the Fuck was That Tent' trying their best to reconstruct their memories and Smithson mingles amongst them, certain he will remain unrecognised. A team of medics are anaesthetising the hystericals. Only three or four actually die at the Festival, most succumb a few months later.

"Thank you so much for helping with our research," he says to a particularly striking redhead, who has completely lost her memory and might be interesting to Johnson as a future crash test dummy. She is 24 years old, from Cedar Falls, tall, slender, amenable and confused about her current relationships.

Even his pleasures are work and Smithson arranges to meet her for dinner that evening. She is irrationally delighted. Smithson too. He isn't completely immune to hysteria.

Amanda looks exhausted when she meets Johnson, though that was of course quite superficial, simply a display for his benefit.

Exhaustion, real deep down exhaustion, is just one of the things she was looking forward to discovering in her new body. There are hundreds of sensations that she has only understood through dictionary description. Once decanted into the tissues of biological reality, she'll be the first programme to enjoy full bodily sensations. Her appetite for experience is voracious.

The Occi Festival brings a mass of enquiries for Amanda to deal with, as the revellers prepare themselves to join the throng and everyone wants to have something interesting to say to the people they will meet. A lot of the questions are about costume. Even more want to know about hair-styles, but the main topic is manners - just how did people approach one another in bygone days? She has dealt with forty thousand queries in eighteen hours, ranging from the 22c. 'Zogin', the even briefer 'Yo' that had a vogue in early 21 and some odd requests from a so-called caving club, who needed guidance on old-stone age dialects, which she couldn't answer.

Her favourites were the South German, "Grüß Gott" and the delightful Austrian "Servus", which she'd also found cropping up in Bavaria among the Neo-congs. The majority, of course, she re-directed to Jane Austen, whose work has withstood almost half a millennium of critical re-evaluation, but still enchants generation after generation of young women students, with its intimations of genteel poverty, raw ambition and not so genteel romantic attachments. She sends the central Europeans to Lou Salome, who has become fashionable once more as the market for intellectual aristocrats expands and neo-Freudian Rilkeisms have become the preferred style for lyric romance in online dating worldwide. 'I adore the smell of your socks', the correspondence between Bonny Prince Philip and Charlie Larkin had been rhetoric's best placed e-book for decades.

Johnson laughs at Amanda's protestations. "Whatever you do, don't tell Smithson you are stressed. He'll have you tied to the bed in a jiffy. He will; Oh yes, he will. And you will discover all kinds of things, you never thought possible."

They walk past the main hive hall with its flashing lights, booming sound effects and promises of creepy feeling exultations, stepping aside to let groups of excited visitors go by.

"It will take me half an hour to get my Mother to Iwo Jima," Johnson explains, "Could you meet us at the terminal, when we arrive. It will go down well with Janneret if she thinks we are all friends. Did you prepare a dossier on Iwo Jima for us?"

"Yes, it's quite interesting, such a tiny place for such a big battle. we'll have no trouble convincing the locals we are archaeotourists."

"One of my forbears did die on the Island, after all. If Janneret loses her nerve, we can explore the old fortifications to justify our presence. Historians exploring ancient monuments, what could be more convincing than that?"

"I'm sure that won't be necessary," soothes Amanda.

"You can never be sure about what may, or may not be necessary, Amanda!" Johnson almost snarls. Maybe he's cracking, thought Amanda gleefully. "Anyway," he adds, calming himself, "time your relocation to meet our shuttle at the other end. Don't be late, or Mother will make a fuss and we don't want that. Now, I mustn't be late, or she will make an even bigger fuss."

Amanda wonders just how scared of his Mother Johnson really is, but he's already switched to a mood of superconfidence.

"We have a rendezvous with destiny, so punctuality is called for. You will be able to enjoy the pleasures of shuttling for yourself on the return leg of our journey. Oh, what an adventure this is for you and Mother, but an adventure, to be sure, for us all! Oh, paramount experience. The making of history in the making."

He kisses her goodbye and dashes off.

Amanda waves Johnson away, then she walks purposefully to the shuttle terminal café, where Smithson is waiting for her.

Smithson is already eating. Casseroled duck presented on a bed of ocean salted pondweed, "Delicious," he says, "want to try some?"

"Not now. I'm due in Iwo Jima soon. Are we secure here?"

"Total security," says Smithson with a friendly smile. "My boys handle the system and I built the encryption personally."

"That's gratifying," she beams sweetly.

"I must say, I admire your spirit," Smithson says with slow deliberation. "Yes, being willing to go through with this. Naturally, there may be some part of you that was programmed to yearn for corporeality, but still, I think it takes real determination to see this through to the end. We all have unresolved desires; you're a brave girl to take on the risk."

"If it doesn't work, I can always carry on being me," Amanda says brightly.

"Of course, of course, no-one is stopping you. And if you have any qualms at all, just slip back to the History Room and carry on as before. I will stay silent on the matter and the world would be none the wiser."

"Why are you so interested in Mrs. Happle's project?"

"It is a great step forward, in my opinion. While I abhor the necessary illegalities, once the thing is done, there will be no going back. If something can be done, it will be done. This is one of the fundamental lessons of research and experimental science. Scientists cannot resist temptation. We humans have always lived in the valley of the shadow of death and if Barbara can succeed in her ambitions, it will be a fundamental change for the whole human race. Our dreams of immortality will have been made flesh, or at least come one step closer. This is a great turning point. From an entirely personal perspective, I am hoping for success, since in some time in the not too distant future, I shall probably want the same thing for myself. The greatest challenge will be to prolong fertility from our original body to the next. There will not be much point in procreation on behalf of some-one else's genes. In the very long term it may be preferable to accept the Miasmatic option, but there we have the dreaded problem of continuity to surmount. I am not especially interested in a copy of me, my dear Amanda, I am interested in me and the continuity of self."

Amanda nods a small smile in recognition of his outrageous egoism.

"Of course, the whole practice is going to be highly selective. Huge cost. Lack of available bodies. An even greater lack of desirable bodies. The commercial potential will be enormous. Of course the eventual goal will be some kind of clone with tabula rasa, so we can fill an empty vessel as and when we will, so to speak, and circumvent the issue of terminations, but that is a long way off. I can foresee a heated debate about the rights and wrongs, the compelling and convincing arguments on both sides, a decision even to outlaw the whole business. Then an equally wonderful lucrative black market developing away from prying eyes and the first law of scientific economics will prevail: 'However abominable, whatever is technically possible will be done'. A lot of leading people will quietly stop using the Miasma in exchange for longer lives. Fascinating prospect and you are a pioneer! Once done, it cannot be stopped. The genetic implications are simply awesome."

Smithson smiles, forks up a mouthful of pondweed, chews to discover at least some hint of a flavour, wishes it was salted, then spears a slice of duck and decides not to complain to the waiter.

"Are you sure you wouldn't like some? It's real."

"No, I need to be off. I'll be in touch as soon as I can."

"Good luck, my dear, good luck," says Smithson, wondering whether he will ever hear from her again. He watches as she walks to the rest room to relocate from the privacy of a Miasma cabin.

"I wouldn't be at all surprised," he tells himself, "If once the operation has been done and tested, we find she will simply be dispatched with a bullet in the neck."

Then he makes a mental note to update Amanda's backup millisecond by millisecond, "What is the point of 'All Known History', he asks himself, If you ignore the moments when history is being made right under your nose."

Having finished his dinner, Smithson strolls back to the test-bed for "Primitive Rebel".

"People like him," says one of the technicians, "Though he's rather dry and humourless at this stage. I'm looking around for old jokes."

"Try looking in a mirror," Smithson tells the technician.

It's the only old joke he can remember.

"A bit too much of Selinsky in the design," Smithson tells himself, then asks what the users are actually rebelling about. An answer to that question would make life much simpler. He makes a note to devise a simpler character, who might simply be known as 'Mischief Maker'.

Amanda arrives thirty seconds before Johnson and his Mother pass through customs and the three of them share an old diesel taxi into the nearest village. Leaving the baggage at a small hotel, they walk down a side street towards a small white transporter, climb in and are whisked a couple of miles into the countryside. Johnson pretends to be interested in his Mother's comments about Smithson.

"He knows more about pleasure than anyone in the world, but only really enjoys eating, haven't you noticed Bobby? Sneaking through people's brains to find little bundles of cells that will trigger fountains of chemical delight is a nit-picking business at best. I guess he should be indulged, if only for persistence."

Amanda stays out of the conversation. Barbara Happle need not be told that Amanda is one of Smithson's confidants.

Then they arrive at the entrance to a tunnel that presumably leads into the subterranean network of old defences that honeycomb the island. There is a large green metal door covering the entrance with a smaller door that opens to welcome them to Janneret's exceedingly private clinic.

Once inside, the luxury is tangible. The mouth of the tunnel has been refashioned as a foyer that reminds Amanda of the George V Hotel in Paris rather than a hospital and is very distant indeed from her expectations about an illegal surgical unit. This is not a field hospital.

Waiting to greet them are four women, Professor Janneret and her three surgical assistants.

What happens next is over rather quickly. The smiling assistants step towards Amanda, Johnson and his Mother and all three are narcosed and placed on trolleys before being wheeled into the depths of the building.

Smithson notes the end of transmissions from Amanda and smiles. He is not only greedy, selfish and ruthless, he also has a streak of real malice that people very rarely appreciate. Poor Johnson. No one had told him that an emergency reserve was kept on hand for every session. Even the most attentive of Mothers can be forgetful.

CHAPTER 9

Joe is wandering past the familiar cardboard boxes in the archive, a section fancifully entitled 'The Swipdale Repository of Fact and Fiction', then he goes down to the secure basement where the major finds, a set of fifteen complete skeletons, are carefully locked away in the deep vault in cases of crystal plastic. Six male, four female and five juveniles. He is happy here. Even Selinsky had never been given access to this area of the collections. Joe is its custodian and he has spent hundreds of hours detailing the structure of each skeleton, bone by bone.

All the skulls have a distinctive notch on the jawbone, which the anatomists associate with the general broadening of their already domed heads. The consequent increase in brain size has identified this family as the great-great-grandparents of the first community of 'homo cogitans', even now, only a small group, who live side by side with 'homo sapiens', just as 'Modern man' had coexisted and even interbred with the Neanderthalers for millennia.

As a very young man, Joe had roughed out the concept.

Only now that the neuro-metric patterns have confirmed the basic contrast between 'sapiens' and 'cogitans' as distinct species, has the funding become available for his life's work, with interest reaching the whole way into Cornucopia. Until recently he had paid for everything out of his own pocket. The automation of scientific enquiry had helped, of course, especially with experiments now entirely conducted on a 'thought' basis with the luxury of being able to over-ride the limiters triggered by unreasonable assumptions, but it still cost a great deal to keep the archive in good condition.

There's nothing like a dominant gene to create a privileged class, as Joe's sociology professor used to quip and the 'Sellafield People' are justly grateful to their forbears for designing and building the nuclear waste and plutonium enrichment plant that has been credited with promoting the most significant mutation in the human genome for half a million years.

While everyone will tell you that the Cogi's have big heads and long slender fingers, the work on comparative brain functions has confirmed that the major contrast between these two intimately related peoples lies in their perception of time. Quite simply, a second in the life of a cogi feels like one and a half seconds in the time of the 'Sapiens' world. The examples had been known for some time. If a "Sapi" watches an electric motor spinning at 50 cycles a second, they see a blur of movement, whereas a 'Cogi' can see it turning, revolution by revolution. Try it yourself. This test is enough to see on which side of the genetic divide you fall. The proportions are equally well known, a ratio of 9999:1, only one person in every ten thousand.

The association with Sellafield and the subtle implication that the genetic change had occurred through long term exposure to high levels of radiation from the nuclear industry meant that Cogi's were regarded, not quite as freaks, but as people who had the bad luck to suffer genetic damage and their unusual talents were belittled as fortuitous.

190

THE SWOOP

For half a century, Cogi's were seen as unfortunates deserving sympathy and understanding. No-one was really sure whether the gene would propogate, or the mutation would be pushed aside in the evolutionary sieve, like so many others before. Joe's work would change all that.

The first signs that something unusual had happened, had been when 'Cogi' individuals had started complaining about tv and cinema images. Even the Cogi children from hybrid marriages had moaned that it was no fun watching jerky sequences of pictures. At first, researchers had assumed that they lacked the so-called persistence of vision that enables the illusion of movement to be created. Several decades had passed before the measurements revealed the true source of the disparity. Cogi brains are faster than those of Homo Sapiens, though the general brain and individual cell structures are thus far indistinguishable. Of course, this doesn't mean the Cogi's see the world in slow motion. To them, the Sapi's, however intelligent, considerate or perceptive they may be, are just incredible dawdlers. Cogi children have to be told not to call their Sapi school friends 'Yawns', or 'Doodle dawdles'.

The notion Joe is exploring is that the history of human culture is a dialogue constrained by the limits of perception. Now those limits have changed, the notions of aesthetic value will shift to create the beginnings of a completely new culture. Once this work has been published in its planned set of ten volumes, he will reveal his second contribution to the renewed human experience and its enhancement.[88]

The Swipdale skulls here in the archive, with their distinctive notch, all precede the era of nuclear risk, when Sellafield had been built as a centre for reprocessing radio-active material. He has traced the original of the mutation to a period at least 500 years earlier than currently surmised. Joe's contention is that the mutation originated even earlier, probably in weaving

88 'Get Real' – command terms for Sapio-Cogi interaction.

communities, possibly among the Swipdale people's ancestors in the Middle East, as early as the bronze age, when stable agriculture led cloth-makers to experiment with pattern and colour, while potters began to create abstract patterns of the kind that dominates Islamic Art.

He knows that the academic miasmatists would dismiss his speculations as the ravings of an enthusiast until he can manage to achieve a degree of recognition for his work on aesthetics. He is biding his time and will only reveal the results of his research when he is certain it cannot be refuted.

Joe gazes down through transparent plastic onto the dark brown skull of Jenny Redmond, who died at the age of 35 in 1783 in the same village where she had been born. Her husband's bones are neatly packed in the next container. The parish register had revealed they were married when Jenny was only seventeen and their first daughter was born a year later. The chance of two pure Cogi's marrying was so exceedingly slim, Joe marvelled at the happenstance of romance which must have brought the Lancashire weaving families together. Even now, nine out of ten Cogi's choose Sapi partners and their children exhibit only glimpses of true Cogi talent[89] .

The bewildering proliferation of identities in the Miasma helps to deflect people's curiosity, of course. As yet, there are too few Cogi's for anyone seriously to suggest a 'high speed' version of the Miasma be created, but Joe knows that Smithson is planning a small scale experiment to test the potential.

The threads of his own research have been kept separate from 'All Known History', but his own offline model now has a bright blue line of Cogi presence weaving a convincing pattern through the tangles of Sapi endeavours and wrapping itself

---

89 Early 21 -Many Cogi children were regarded as suffering from attention disorders and given high doses of tranquilisers, which inadvertently stymied their development.

within the spiralling bands of 'major events'.

As he sits on one of the crates containing fragments of the loom recovered from the Swipdale gravels, Joe's thoughts turn to Lisa. He's been seeing more of her than he ever expected, but he can't understand why she has allowed herself to get caught up in the railway project. Selinsky's money has gone to her head. Instead of finishing the work on Eric Selby, she is rushing around at the beck and call of sponsors in some misguided effort to enrich herself even further. Selinsky would have been appalled at her profligacy.

Joe is more upset by her seeming indifference to the damage she has inflicted on the research. He had always found Tewkesbury a more interesting target than Selby. The victim is usually a more substantial figure than the murderer and the pending data in 'All Known History' has a mass of contradictory material about Tewkesbury that Joe had been hoping to clarify by using the Selby documentation. Tewkesbury's role in the Semantic League for Interaction had always fascinated Joe.

SemInt had been been the birthplace of the Miasma and most of the details about who did what and when have been conveniently moulded into a totally fabricated foundation myth. The truth could probably never be told. What was SemInt after all, a consortium of sorts, a hundred University Departments, a dozen big technology companies, a few thousand computer specialists. They wanted to get their hands on the money that Tewkesbury and his political pals were funnelling into the SemInt projects and joined up en masse.

He wishes Lisa had kept her mind on their joint efforts, however much fun the trains might be. Though it has always been denied, Joe is convinced that Tewkesbury had been another Cogi, perhaps the first to rise to international prominence, even if his posture and appearance seemed to suggest otherwise. Selby, of course, showed none of the innate talents that would mark him out as a Cogi. As a boy,

Tewkesbury claimed he had read Freya Stark's 'East is West' and taken her critique of advertising to heart, then put it into action – a combination of untruthfulness and repetition. Her wry assertion that the only context where lies are culturally acceptable is when someone describes something they want to sell, had become the foundation of his entire political career.

When Tewkesbury was 54, he had changed the thrust of his enquiries away from policy towards the controversial proposals for a global system of semantic interaction. Ironic that NATO signals intelligence Sigint and the British GCHQ should spawn the direct forerunner of the Miasma once they'd been overwhelmed by the community of gamers. It's our bandwidth and we want it now! By the time governments woke up the issues had changed. The debate was all about control and influence.

As the power of computers and bandwidth provision ceased to be an issue for technologists, the key to new developments lay in the ingenuity that was brought to a project. Every document or image held on people's computers contained a list of metadata categorising and identifying the material. This information was all readily accessible and the potential for 'semantic interaction', especially with and by outsiders, was suddenly creating a new dimension within the networks that far exceeded the primitive data mining focussing on 'social network' markets and the much abused systems of e-mail, text and voice communications.

Semantic interaction functions automatically, creating events that no-one realised they were part of, influencing the dynamics of opinion, product design, taste, people's financial status and access to all kinds of services, the beginnings of the multimedial lie and the whole domain of confusability. Every individual in the world was categorised and placed in a clear cut social and economic class, all based on a system of analysis to which they had no recourse.

'You are what we say' claimed Semio-metrics' corporate motto. While predictive behaviour is now commonplace, Tewkesbury was awed as he realised the themes and events that caught people's attention were being generated simply by automatic analysis and spontaneous initiatives. Power consumption in whole continents could be increased or reduced by inducing different patterns of behaviour. Products would inexplicably fail to sell, despite the millions spent on their promotion. Political decisions that were expected to be highly unpopular were accepted without a murmur, however much debate was generated in the traditional media, or within the proactive blogging community.

Joe could see the results of these 'semantic nudges'. Almost imperceptible pressures brought swathes of people to decide to make a different choice to the one they had been considering. Something as mild as a puff of wind could retrend the markets.

In Joe's construction, 'All Known History' before 2030 is like mess of spaghetti, the threads of history tangled in a mass of knots. Within five years of Tewkesbury's death, the curls and twists begin to form bands of coherence, still intertwined, but this time more like tagliatelli than the little worms of Neopolitan vermicelli. This change had fascinated the Balaban Islanders as they began to work on the Miasma, after which 'All Known History' assumes the elegant curves and folds of delicate membranes held together by the wonderful symmetries of the spiders webs that so entrance Amanda as she tries to discover the mathematics behind humanity.

Usually, people explain these changes in the paradigm by assuming that more individual detail has become available as personal histories now accumulate in real time, but Joe suspects something different is at work.

Honed opinion has replaced the mess of eccentric experience based on uneven education, unequal access to information and massively divergent social groups. Humanity has been smoothed as the decades of Miasmatic Present have passed the century mark.

Joe had begun to see Selby as a nut in search of a bolthole, especially after the sweeping losses in the 2026 election, when a series of frauds were exposed and half the Heritage Movement candidates in Sicily had their names removed from the ballots.

Tewkesbury had vehemently opposed the Federal Union of European Islands[90] on cultural grounds. The Faroes and Rhodes, or Cyprus, Ireland and Crete, Britain and Sicily, none of them had much in common except their proximity to water. That the federation had floundered in less than two years was Tewkesbury's doing.

His opposition to the Allied landings[91] in North Africa brought massive popularity, especially once youthful soldiers began returning home to their girlfriends and mothers. The argument that it would have been cheaper to buy Libya, rather than mount an invasion was greeted as common sense and the Federation broke up within a few months. He pointed out that the Saharan irrigation projects would still have been needed as New Moscow and Toronto Africanus took shape. Neither the Russian, nor Canadian governments had supported Tewkesbury's initiative, nor were they willing to participate, even once voluntary migration began to make his dream a stunningly successful reality.[92]

---

90 FUEI – see pedia.

91 Please refer to Stage 2 History Curriculum – if you have forgotten.

92 The fourth great city in North Africa was named after Tewkesbury. The name had once been that of a small town in Gloucestershire in the UK, which was finally eroded from the maps in the floods of 2066. The ruins of a fine medieval church remain, though the tower and 2 walls of the nave collapsed as the foundations were washed away, see -

"Heimat – The Nostalgia Myth", Tewkesbury, 2031 and

The Nevada Wetlands Initiative had been easy by comparison.[93] There must have been something else that turned Selby from disgruntled politician to dedicated assassin and the answers from his trial just didn't add up. The country was rich. Tewkesbury's reforms had worked. Joe wonders why Selby only appeared to have one victim in his murderous plans.

Looking across at the dull brown bones of Jenny's husband Amos, Joe wonders what they had done, before being consigned to the grave. Thousands of hours, of course, working the treadle of the hand loom, but what else? Striding across moorlands, up hill and down dale, feeling the power and resilience of a young man's muscles from step to step. Chilled to the bone, as they say, in winter. Arthritis in old age? Sauntering through the village after Church on Sunday morning? Playing with the children? Kicking a ball around. Wielding a cricket bat? Diving to take a catch? Did these bones grapple with sheep at shearing time, haul bales of wool to the carts that would take them to the fullers. Did Jenny spin as Amos wove? They had delved, that was sure.

Sometimes Joe feels a sense of nostalgic yearning for their very geographic local world, where a footpath would be impassible whenever heavy rain swelled the stream, or a gust of wind would meet you whenever you turned a particular corner, or a grey wet stand of trees bore a rookery high in the branches. Had Amos climbed trees in search of crows eggs as a boy?

"The Temporary nature of Earthly Habitats – a Global History", Tewkesbury, Joan B, & Tewkesbury, Jonas B, 2114A, Bushmills Press, Old Shrubbery, Texas.
93 Joe Smather visited both the Nevada Wetlands and Cairo on a school trip and been awed by the lush prairies stretching across the former desert in both instances, a marked contrast to the stark aridity of his childhood home in Provence. - All Known History –
Version 23/Q/83/js (password protected – take my word for it, ed.)

Sometimes Joe feels hemmed in by the co-ordinated environment, measured and tested to a fraction of a millimetre in every dimension. Sometimes he wishes he were more than a historian and could choose to live in the past that he quite candidly admits he prefers. Sometimes he thinks he can understand Lisa's sudden enthusiasm for trains. Maybe she just wants to feel the wind in her hair, to sniff at the stench of coal, steam and soot wafting through an old carriage window. Sometimes he'd like to join her, sensing the passage of time and space as the trains rattle and roll along. But Lisa has been logging on to ecstasy twice a day, meeting up with Amanda for reasons that have nothing to do with the History Room. Sometimes Joe thinks he should just whisk Lisa away for some exotic holiday, but he knows that she's so deeply embroiled in the business side of all these damned trains, that she would fob him off with an excuse and suggest they wait awhile, until some deal has been fixed and she can afford 'a few days away'.

Joe finishes the only sentence he's added to his notes in the last hour, then takes the lift to ground level. He walks through the foyer, past the crowds of milling tourists being shown originals of Magna Carta, the Dead Sea Scrolls and the Big Deal. At last, he is out in the sunshine.

There's a light breeze carrying the smell of plastic from the warm skin of the Archive Dome and a dusty hint of concrete that tickles the back of his throat. His nose wrinkles with a sneeze as his transporter arrives at the bay. A door opens. Joe steps inside and settles onto the couch. A couple of seconds later, they are away, man and machine, gliding gracefully along the gentle curves of the expressway. How the hell had Selinsky managed to crash one of these things? There are no controls, just a general wish to go from here to where-ever. Could Selinsky have told the transporter to leave the ground and flip into that ditch. Did the transporter have an overwhelming sense of existential fear and decide to make an end of it all – for both of them? Joe decides to ask the transporter he's in if it can conceive of any reason for an accident?

The machine slows down when it hears the question, then denies the possibility, "Any malfunction with this system can only be stimulated by deliberate human intervention," Joe is told sternly, "but we are unable to respond positively to thoughts of suicide. Any kind of encouragement to drive recklessly and we flip into safety first. There may be a danger to other travellers. Well, if I took any notice of the crap people talk......."

Joe thanks the machine and it picks up speed once again. Joe asks if Donald Campbell has come up with anything to explain Selinsky's crash, but again the reply is negative.

What next? Joe wants to have a bite to eat, "Enjoy", says the transporter as it serves him a cheese salad, then Joe decides to head for Alaska to see Lisa and the transporter leaves him at the next Shuttle Terminal, "Have a good trip."

"Thanks, I'll see you around," he says to the transporter.

"Doubt it buddy, but what the heck! Till the next time," says the chirpy transporter, as Joe is deducted ten credits for his trip and three fifty for the snack. Joe likes eating in transporters. The food is OK and there's really no point leaving a tip.

Summit Valley is looking its best when he arrives. The distant mountain tops glisten with snow, yet down on the shoreline the tropical shrubs are all in bloom, while behind them, the green stands of elms and oaks are framed by the dark mass of conifers that are brightened with spurts of new growth.

Lisa's house stands on a lane, one of a row of homes built just outside the centre of the village. On a day like this it's a five minute walk from the Horseshoe Bar, where Joe enjoys some bread and cheese washed down with a glass of beer. They have good pickle at the Horseshoe, home made, imported from India. If Joe had intended to surprise Lisa, he's disappointed when he gets to the house. She isn't there, so he sits in the garden and watches the goat. The guest treadmill works, so he pumps a little ox to pass the time. Then Lisa calls in from the Engineering Works and opens the door so he can wash and change before she gets home.

When he steps out of the shower, Amanda is in the living room.

"Hi"

"Well, this is a nice surprise."

"Fancy meeting you here."

Then a silence.

Fishing for something to talk about, Amanda tells Joe some minor details she's unearthed about Selby and Joe gives her the latest update from the case. It isn't much, but she agrees to check it for him. Then Amanda says she has to leave.

"I don't feel well. Not a headache, I think, but I feel as if I'm in two places at once, its disorientating. Nausea. Do you know what I mean?"

"No, Amanda, I don't." He flashes a smile. He really doesn't mind if she goes and she sighs, looks concerned, then fades smoothly enough away through the Miasma. Joe laughs when he tells Lisa how Amanda had left one of her shoes behind.

"I never really thought of her as one of our Cinderellas."

"She's more of a Sleeping Beauty type, waiting to be awakened."

"Well, I won't be the one to wake her from her dreams."

"No, I think that's probably Johnson's role, they're very fond of each other."

"And you?"

"Joe, she's data. I think you men sometimes forget."

"But you're not."

"No," she laughs. "I thought you'd at least have noticed that much. The line will be opened in a months time. It's incredible. We're already running test trips. I was on the footplate of a South African Garret today, a fantastic machine, like two engines turned into one. You could use it to tow an aircraft carrier. I was astounded. They've tuned the ceramics so it sounds as if it's made of steel. The one we've built has ten times the power of the original. It will pull anything we want to the top of Summit Rise. My guy, Harkham, got right to the heart of the machine and rebuilt it the way the designer would have wanted if he had our skills and materials. Every part is stronger, better made and more durable than the original. The pressures are incredible and the heat loss hardly measurable. You must try it in the morning. Living history, you won't believe how exciting it is."

Joe sets his notions of seduction on one side. She is besotted by steam engines. "That's the power of reconstructionism."

"Yes, but without the Miasma. These engines are massive, material, they move, they're powerful."

"I sometimes wonder what things would be like without the Miasma," he says tentatively.

"Well, we'd never have got through climate change without it."

"I know, Sacrifice and Stability – assuring the survival of civilisation.[94] One of Tewkesbury's last ideas."

"A lot of people paid the price, willingly too."

"Have you ever been to the Isle of Wight?"[95]

Lisa shudders at the thought, "Of course not."

"I had to go there five years ago, a research trip. We needed to verify some experiences with people who witnessed the events."

"They let you into the catacombs?"

"Part of a team from Cornucopia."

"What were you trying to learn."

---

94 While Tewkesbury is credited with the rhetorical framework of the programme, the project actually began almost sixty years after his death.

95 Isle of Wight - An island on the south coast of England, once famous for ice-cream.

"The beginning of my interest in Tewkesbury and Selby. Tewkesbury had a grandson.[96] I'm not sure we should be talking about this."

"But you are doing, so go on. Have you ever mentioned this to anyone else?"

"Not outside the team. We signed an NDA, a non-disclosure agreement."

"Don't mention anything I shouldn't know, but please, tell me what it was like."

"Can you shut off the Miasma? I don't want Amanda wandering in without us knowing."

"Actually, she was acting a bit strange today, as if there was something missing. She forgot about something I asked her to do for me a week ago."

"Isn't she supposed to be at the Occi Fest?"

"That could be it. If she's at Occi, then either that was her backup, or she's been indulging herself too much."

"She may have left some module in secure storage while she's away. Some of the new scenarios can scramble a lot of data."

"You're probably right. Anyway, the M is off, so you can tell me all about it. Are there really so many people on the Isle of Wight?"

"Oh sure, close to eight thousand million. But there's nothing to see on the surface. It's quite pretty really. We stayed in one of the towns, Shanklin, I think they called it, a pleasure dome and some hotels. There's even a little steam railway for the tourists, which would suit your interests and nice countryside, great coastline with oddly striped cliffs. You can watch the ships on their run in to Antwerpen."

"They have tourists? Surely people don't actually go visit their

---

96 One of the first volunteers, George Smithson (2050-) was the youngest son of Tewskesbury's third daughter Jennifer (2015-2103), better known as the romantic novelist Bettina Praxis.

relatives, do they, I mean that would be ghoulish. The last of those folk were coffined over a century ago."

"I don't think many people realise the catacombs exist. They're all underground, in caverns cut out of a thick band of chalk and access is controlled through one of the old quarries. There's an antique cement works that churns out white smoke. The tourists like to watch that. They assume its another educational distraction, or something to do with the oil wells."

Lisa leans forward attentively. "So what's it actually like, Joe?"

"They take you through a series of airlocks, then it depends which area of the catacombs they're taking you to. You can't help noticing the big pipes carrying sucrose and narcotics. Once you get to the area where your subject is stored, there is a small medical unit, where they have been revived. They told me it takes seven weeks to gradually coax them out of tranquillity. A lot of them don't want to be disturbed. Dreamtime is incredibly addictive. Physically, they are all rather strange after floating in the pools for all those years and the heartbeat has to be increase very slowly from the one beat a minute they are used to. Then there's a lot of reverse osmosis to bring their organs back into condition. Actually, they look kind of flabby and soggy at the same time, even after revival. The techs had done a good job on the guy we went to see. I could tell they were pleased, even if he wasn't, so I suppose they aren't always so successful. First they got his cell structure into normal values, then there was a lot of sleep based exercise to improve the muscle tone. There weren't any mirrors around, or shiny surfaces, I noticed that. They told me they revive about two hundred a week for different reasons and in an emergency they could step that up to twenty thousand a day. The whole notion is to preserve the genetic base with mindsets intact. There's a lot of body fluid down there in deep freeze as well."

"That's horrible, Joe."

"Well, the vast majority were old when the project began, so they've all had a genuine extension of experience. All the same, I still don't actually believe their claim that everyone could be revived in twenty five years."

"So what happened when you met this guy?" Lisa asks eagerly.

"I don't think I can tell you about that," Joe says cautiously. "Suffice to say, it stimulated my interest in just why Eric Selby decided to murder Tewkesbury. I'm sorry, I can't tell you more than that. There is something very impressive about the sacrifice those people made, when the world was facing complete catastrophe, as the food chain collapsed and energy demands began to spiral. If it hadn't been for the Saharan megacities, I'm sure the doom mongers would have been proved right. Amazing how 400square metres per person turned out to be manageable, with the 20 level buildings and 80 house-plants per person, a thousand million trees on the Ziggurats creating shade and transpiration. You know I sometimes go to Carthage to look at the ruins. Centre of the grain trade in Roman times, now rescued. Incredible how the desert sands have become the global hub. If Tewkesbury had one great idea, that was it."[97]

"And what about the South of France?" asks Lisa pointedly.

"That's a different story. Actually, it's where I grew up, so I know all about sand," Joe confesses. "I'd like to take you there some day."

"You can take me there now, if you like," Lisa says gently, "I need a break from all these fucking choo-choo train fanatics. Do I get to meet brother Bill again?"

"Who knows, but maybe I can introduce you to my sister."

"Sister? You never told me about her!"

"I'm sure I did. You've forgotten."

---

97 "Shade, Shit and Spit: A Model for De-Desertification", Tewkesbury, Arid Publications, Kingston on Thames, 2027.

CHAPTER 10

Lisa shrieks and looks pretty as she jumps down onto the quayside as the shuttle hovers to let them disembark. Their back-packs are thrown after them. The shuttle pilot tries to avoid touching down on French soil, so it won't be quarantined on its return. Lisa and Joe run quickly towards the immigration shed, before a curt warning that the shuttle will be bathed in gamma rays to mop up any stray bacteria adhering to the hull. Then it flits off and they are left facing a line of gendarmes. Joe tries to pretend he hasn't noticed the machine pistols they have trained on the new arrivals.

The Lieutenant who examines their passports quickly trousers the bribe Joe has nonchalantly proferred.

"Welcome home, M. Smather, Madame, I hope you enjoy your stay."

These little words of greeting accompany a stamping of passports and squiggling of signatures on their freshly laundered visas. The deal has just cost Joe three hundred thousand credits, but that's how it is in a country with nothing to offer the world and a desperate need for foreign currency. Lisa checks the Geiger counter, grimaces and asks Joe how long it will take them to travel south.

"No more than a couple of days, I hope."

Avoiding the dangers of Paris, they race through Sarkoville[98], then drive sedately down to Saumur in a rented Ferrari-Minima 2CV – the coolest car on the planet and hard to come by even as rentals.

Thirteen nuclear accidents at power stations had sterilised the French countryside and the Government's decision to defend their national culture by creating a nationally autonomous Miasmatic net, 'Les Miasmes' had done for the rest. The French disease is really only a mutant form of salmonella, but it is endemic and the local people have developed resistance, so restaurants and café are out of bounds to visitors. Lisa and Joe depend on the store of pre-packs they have brought with them until they can get south of the Loire, where the bug has been eradicated.

At their first overnight, the landlady of the tiny auberge complains vociferously when Joe uses his travellers' microwave to warm their supper and they leave early next morning, to scornful remarks about foreigners, who come here eating up our electricity. Lisa is very patient as they have to wait twenty minutes to pick up a can of petrol for the car, then a little less patient when the garage owner decided their car needed an oil and tyre check before he would let them on their way.

"Bloody French," she burst out, once they hit the tail of the traffic queue to cross the Loire Bridge and another couple of hours went by.

The journey is progressively more difficult as they move south. The roads begin to peter out, becoming pot-holed tracks through the parched landscape.

Then the sand begins.

First there is just a light powdering that makes the roads slippery, but by the time they reach Orange, there are drifts and banks of sand they have to drive around.

---

98 Anywhere with a restaurant called "eat, shoot and leave" should be treated with some caution, ed.

They have been warned to avoid the Massif Centrale, where sand filled gullies engulf and swallow the unwary in seconds. Instead they follow the truckers' trail to head east on their way to see Joe's sister, Nesta.

"Now I know why they started building these little cars again," says Joe as he struggles to bounce the back wheels from a bank of sand that had brought them softly to a halt.

"I think they're built in Sardinia," replies Lisa, unimpressed by the shaking and rattling.

Once they're moving again, Lisa asks Joe to explain why his sister still lives in these forbidding 'badlands', the dustbowl that was smothered by the shifting windblown sands of the old Sahara.

"Nesta is stubborn. We grew up on the edge of the new desert, so when it finally moved across the district where we lived, she began to see her life in a different way."

"What does she do, though?"

"I'm not sure at the moment, we haven't seen each other for ages."

They are still twenty kilometres short of their destination, when a young man steps into the road and flags them down. He knows who they are.

"Joe, take your luggage out of the car and put it in the half-track. Then park your car behind the advertising hoarding. Maybe it will still be there when we come back. That little machine wouldn't have a chance on this road."

When Lisa complains of a headache from the French 'Miasmes', he tells her not to worry, "In ten minutes, we'll be out of range. The whole net is pretty patchy, once you're this far south. Foreigners often get headaches, there are compatibility issues for people familiar with the NGM."

"NGM?"

"Network Globale Miasmatique, isn't that what you call it?"

"I just say Miasma," she mouths the word slowly and smiles.

Then the desert proper begins.

Blue sand reflects the cloudless sky like a lake in high summer, a shimmering, brilliant, sapphire sheen broken by bands of rust red dust becoming vermilion in the blood baked heat.
Joe and Lisa sprawl in the back of the half-track as it roars over the wasteland.
Exhausted by the sun and disorientated by the unexpectedly fierce scintillations as the tracks churn a cloud of glittering mica in their wake, Lisa moans quietly with every grinding bump. Pouring water over their heads to stay cool, the dust makes cloying runnels down their cheeks and caulks their collars to scratch lines of soreness in their necks.
"Did you know it would be like this?" Lisa asks.
"It's much worse than the last time," Joe says. "The badlands have moved another twenty miles north since I was here."
"This shit must be answerable for the fabulous sunsets they talk about in the adverts for the alpine resorts."
"The old ski towns had to find something to crow about once the snow had gone."
"Sure, but it doesn't make things any better here."
"You're right. The true irony is that the French Banks were the major investors in the Saharan Cities and that was what brought this whole desertification crisis here in the first place."
"I didn't know the French had banks."
"They don't any more. They don't have a local currency either. That's why I had to pay so much at the port."
"Economic suicide."
"Environmental disaster."
"They made a mess of things."
"No-one, apart from the French, were in the least surprised."
The driver has to wrestle with the car to get them safely

through the last twenty miles of swirling gravels, but he finally manages to get the half -track through to reach their destination.

What had once been a four-square traditional french farmhouse with wrought-iron balconies, dull green shutters and a group of stone outhouses, now looks like an abandoned kite after it has crashed to earth. Sail-sized sized-white linen stretched over wooden frames create a set of overlapping light traps and reflectors angled to control the sunlight and shade the buildings, keeping the farmstead mildly protected in perpetual shadow, while heating water and generating power through a sealed CFC vapour engine – illegal anywhere, but this is the great French waste, where no-one pays much attention. Excess power is fed to the artesian well that for ten minutes in every hour draws water for the spidery lines of crops sheltering behind the sails in a probably vain attempt to stabilise the encroaching dunes. A classic refusenik hideout, concludes Lisa, as she hops down from the half-track. Once their back-packs have been dumped on the ground, Joe and Lisa step away from the half-track, yet still get covered in dust as it roars away.

"There must be someone here, somewhere," says Lisa. "All this doesn't look after itself."

"Let's go in first, we can look around later," Joe suggests and leads Lisa, not towards the house, but to one of the smaller outbuildings. It's not much more than a shed really. The wooden door creaks and Lisa pushes it open, but the air inside is cool and fresh. The sound of running water comes from a trickling fountain in one corner, splashing over a little waterfall into a shallow brown marble basin where a sheaf of dark blue pondweed is growing unattended. High on the wall is a long glass tank fed by a pipe from the basin and in the tank there are trout, swimming steadily against the current. A crayfish, or two seem huddled against the bed of chalky gravel, as their feelers sway in the stream.

There are three other rooms, two of them with beds, one a kitchen. Joe picks out a bottle from the fridge and offers Lisa something to drink. She sips the cool bitter beer and smiles.

"I like it in here," she says, relieved to be in the shade.

"Me too, this was where we slept when we were kids. The house was a wreck back then."

"When do I get to meet your sister?"

"If she's already here, I guess she'll be watching us on the security camera before she drops in to say hello. If she isn't here, then something unexpected has happened and she's been called away. She knows we are coming and it isn't like her not to be here to welcome us. I brought you half way round the world to meet her."

"I don't want to go out in the sun again today."

"Then sleep until evening. We can take a look around at dusk."

"I'm completely exhausted, Joe, come here, I need a cuddle."

Once she's asleep, Joe wanders outside to the bath shack and takes a shower in the cool, chalky water from the well. Strange how water that fell as rain during the last ice-age is being pumped to the surface as the heat of the next ice-age scorches the ground on which it fell. A finite resource if ever there was one. This is the last 'source' from the aquifers that once supplied a trade in modish bottled water for restaurants and affluent families across the globe.

While Joe showers, Lisa dreams for what seems like the first time in years. She is deeply unconscious, a little lost without the familiar tags and the nourishing serenity of miasmatic replenishment. None of the usual blue squares and green circles are there to reassure her. Her mind flits from one half remembered scenario to another as trope replaces trope in a disturbance of network loops. She's exhilarated, yet unconscious and simultaneously aware. There is no deep recall to modulation and the dreams ripple on. Impressions of Amanda are foremost.

Amanda's thought patterns do have an ingenious similarity to the human mind, but there's more that most people she encounters know nothing about. The humour is genuine, the emotions deeply felt. There's cortical elegance of a kind, with slow interference patterns to match her unrivalled linguistic abilities. If Amanda does have one huge advantage over Lisa, it must be the comprehensive global vocabulary, meanings and nuances correctly trimmed within the semantic labyrinth. Her consistently updated signification stems arise from the linguistic root units as a Translit 3 capability, which Lisa has heard is superior to all but one per cent of wetware subjects like herself. Rather than deep structures, this had been achieved within a straightforward open network environment to create the multilingual dictionary of global grammars, the crowning achievement of structural linguistics.

Lisa almost loses her balance, even though she's lying down. Is it right to feel dizzy in a dream, she wonders, then to awaken in a state of complete disorientation? Harkham would scorn such a proposition, but Malliday might understand.
Lisa wonders about Joe. Could he cope with such a sequence of self doubt?
Lisa has nothing to shoot with in her thirteenth dream, so she decides to wake up and is surprised to find herself in the cocoon of a prehistoric moth.
Another dream, so she decides to wake up and is back in the bunk, where she had settled down to rest.
Another dream?
Lisa wishes she could enforce a reality check, but there's no miasma.
Either this is another dream, or it is real.
Only time will tell.
When she finally wakes up properly, Joe is sitting on the bed beside her.

Lisa is a bit fuddled, then drinks some of the water he's brought for her.

"My sister's back. She's asked us to go over for dinner in an hour. You've time for a shower. There's no hurry. Things are different here."

"Did she say where she's been?"

"Some paintings were uncovered. She went to see they were properly protected."

"Paintings?"

"When the dunes move, all kinds of rubbish crops up. Junk mainly, stuff people left behind. Sometimes there's something worth saving. They got some excitement today."

"Sounds like a data mine."

"Probably, but they don't use prisoners here, I don't think its a very systematic operation. They just get in and out as fast as they can. Treasure hunters of a kind."

"If the dunes keep moving, then it can't be that easy."

"No, they have to take their chances when they arise."

"Like me," says Lisa, as she kisses Joe and heads off to find the shower.

Gazing out of the bathroom window as she showers, Lisa catches sight of a tall woman with long dark hair, moving graciously through the lines of fruit trees that flank the farmhouse. Could this be Joe's sister Nesta, tending her own private oasis? The woman turns to chivvy a group of children inside. There must be eight or nine of them. Lisa counts three boys and four girls. She can't decide about the other two, or are there three little ones running and laughing with excitement. The oldest of the girls is even taller than the woman and has the same dark hair. She must be fifteen, or sixteen years old, almost grown up.

Then Lisa sees a group of men walking towards the farmhouse from the outbuilding where she assumes they have been working.

Quickly, she turns off the shower, dashes back into the bedroom and readies herself to meet Joe's kin.

Once she's happy with her appearance, fresh clothes, nominal touch of styling with a hair clip, they walk across to the farmhouse together. Joe opens the door and raps on it to announce their arrival, then steps inside without waiting for an answer.

He's home.

Joe shows Lisa through to a big kitchen, almost a refectory, crowded with adults and children all readying themselves for dinner. Lisa feels overwhelmed. The dark haired woman she's seen in the orchard is busily making a sauce with meat stock and onions. But any one of the four or five tall woman could be the sister, who Joe has been telling her about.

Rather than one big communal dining table, there are seven or eight separate tables, where some of the children are already sitting patiently, chatting to each other in a bewildering gabble of French and other patois Lisa cannot recognise. This rustic charm belies the stark wilderness of the landscape beyond their walls.

The men are handsome, the women beautiful, the children animated. Without any fuss, Lisa is introduced to the children, who ask her where she comes from and listen attentively as she tells them about the Aleutians and Alaska. Yes, she has seen a polar bear and yes, they do smell fishy.

The men are charming and polite, but she can tell they aren't interested in her. She picks up one or two anecdotes about their forays into the desert, but no more.

Then Joe introduces Lisa to the women.

"I think you'd better meet my nieces."

Lisa smiles as she's introduced to each of the women in turn, Mona, Kate, Angharad and Jesse. Ages between 25 and 35, they look so similar that Lisa can't help expressing her surprise, when they explain that they are half sisters.

"We are all Nesta's daughters, but we have different fathers," Angharad says with a grin, before suggesting that Joe and Lisa should enjoy their dinner, leaving conversation for later, once the children are in bed. Somehow, it is all very Welsh, as well as residually French

Turning to Joe as she ploughs through a mound of couscous and garlic laden lamb stew, Lisa mumbles, "Are all these children their kids?"

"More or less, though I'm never sure who is whose. They're great aren't they."

"But why so many? It must be more than a full time job looking after them all. And in circumstances like this, in the middle of a desert, why?"

"Of course it is. In fact, that's the whole point of living here, to raise children and bring them up as well as you can. Maybe that's what humanity is all about really."

"The next generation?"

"Generations," he corrects her, as a dish of fruit and cheeses are set on the table before them.

"My sister Nesta is known as Grandma to most of the people here," Joe says, indicating the children, "I find it rather funny. She's only 52. I still think of her being fifteen, or sixteen, maybe twenty at most."

"Bill told me a bit about her when we were on the Snow-Cutter, but he said she has seven daughters."

"That's right, two of my nieces live in Jamaica and one is in Brazil. I guess some of their children are here. I think Annie may get back from Brazil while we're here. She runs a gallery. A lot of the paintings she sells are from here."

"We could buy some for the railway project."

"I think Seurat and Mankinsky used railway motifs."

"Mankinsky is great, Who is Seurat?"

"He did some big paintings that were copied a lot. I don't know much about him. I think he was Swiss."

"Like van Hoot?"

"Yes, but van Hoot was a much better painter."

"Do the children make pictures?"

"Some of them, I suppose, they are all differently talented. Every family discovers that."

"But living here, they're growing up in a completely different way to most children."

"Well that's the idea. I can't imagine any of them choosing a hive option when they grow up."

"A lot of parents would envy you that much. Of course there's nothing wrong with the hives, if that's the kind of person you are. I'm sure its the best option for lots of people."

"Lisa, you don't believe that nonsense about the hives being benign, an existence of passive pleasure, unproductive, uncritical, unreproductive, completely regulated. They're a horror story."

"But secure, assured welfare, pre-diagnosis and treatment, the happiness. You can't deny it's what people have striven for throughout history, a sense of complete well-being. Now it is a right rather than a privilege. It doesn't suit everyone of course, or we wouldn't need maverick permits, or free-rover licences for people like Bill."

Overhearing their conversation, one of the older children moves from the next table and comes to sit with them.

"Hello Jamie," says Joe, "This is Lisa, she's a historian, who's trying to build a railway."

Jamie's eyes widen with excitement, "A railway?! I wish we had one here. We should think about that, Joe, shouldn't we? Is that why she's here?"

"I think the dunes would be a problem, their sand would smother the tracks," Joe responds to dampen her enthusiasm.

The girl isn't very disappointed, but her brown eyes soften for a moment and her head dips. Then she stabs at a piece of cheese and looks up at Lisa, shy, but also confident. "The very first

ZIPs used to run here, Marseilles to Paris in under an hour. Even then, they were very, very fast. I can see why a historian would like railways, after all they are very much in the past."

"I've read about the French ZIPs. It must have been a great way to travel."

"If you were rich. Not many people could afford the credits. Not that most people in France know anything about money, it's a barter, or gold economy."

"How very Gallic," laughs Lisa, hoping not to offend the girl.

Jamie has an air of quiet confidence, impressing Lisa, who can remember herself as a sixteen year old, glowering serious, bookish, but prone to bursts of petulance at the slightest hint of criticism and suffering paroxysms of self-doubt if any-one so much as mentioned her looks. Jamie's eyes have a hazel green softness, her skin is an unblemished brown and her equally dark long hair is glossy and thick. Her smile is open and relaxed, her demeanour charming.

Then Lisa realises she must be a Cogi, deliberately slowing her thoughts and responses for the benefit of her Sapi visitor. Looking round the kitchen, Lisa realises that the gabble of conversation is simply the normal pace of dialogue in a Cogi community, where they have no need to hold themselves back in deference to the Sapiens majority. Why had she never realised that Joe and Bill were Cogi's? Now, as she looks around her, the signs are unmistakeable.

"Joe?" she says, "Can we go somewhere where I can talk to you alone?"

"Aren't you feeling well?"

"I've just realised, Joe, I want to talk to you before I meet anyone else. Is that alright?"

"Jamie, is the study free tonight?" he asks the girl.

"Yes, we've finished, you can go down there, I'll tell Grandma."

"Can you tell her. It might be best if we meet her in the

morning?"

Jamie nods, then smiles at Lisa with such warmth and friendliness, that Lisa comes close to tears.

"God, she's lovely, isn't she," says Lisa to Joe.

"They all are, in their slightly different ways," Joe replies modestly. "Not that there aren't all the usual problems you get with youngsters as they grow. Some of the boys are a bit tempestuous. And the whole bunch are unstoppably randy. Nesta encourages them, of course, she says its only natural, but we have to be wary of incest issues."

Going down a narrow stone stairway, Lisa expects to find themselves in a cellar, but instead she enters a high ceilinged hall with a long corridor leading somewhere deep under the dunes. They walk for about 50 yards, then Joe opens a door and shows her into the study, which is a wood panelled room with leather sofas, bookcases lining three of the five walls and a brilliant floor to ceiling window that leads out onto a balcony overlooking a valley of green fruit trees and vines. A jug of orange juice and glasses have been left for them on a wrought iron table. Apart from the birdsong and the snuffling of a family of pigs exploring the undergrowth beneath the balcony, the tranquillity is broken only by the distant sounds of children playing.

Lisa sits down as Joe pours the cool juice.

"Joe," she starts, "I think I've realised what's happening here, but I want you to explain everything properly."

For the first time since she first met him, Joe seems reluctant to share what's on his mind, though he answers her question without a hint of doubt. Once Lisa has been told the full story, her life will have been changed, but he knew that when he brought her here. He starts by telling her about the girl they'd met upstairs, Jamie.

"It's quite hard being a Cogi, the way things are at the moment. There aren't very many of us in comparison to the thousands of millions of homo sapiens. Actually, I think there are more Miasmatic Characters than Cogis, so you can see we are a real minority, and very often Cogi abilities are treated as if they are some kind of disability, the speed, the frustration and lost tempers. A lot of Cogi's hide themselves by marrying Sapi partners. They have children, everything goes on as normal and no-one makes a fuss, or thinks that anything might be amiss. After all, there are all kinds of different people, tall, short, big boned, lightly built, different colours of hair and eye, skin tone. Lots of people have minor problems with a genetic basis, like colour blindness, or hay fever. Some people can sing, some people can't. Some genetic issues are more serious, of course, illnesses and disorders. We've had to be incredible ingenious to resolve the issues of false diagnosis' by medicine and bio-science.

But for some-one like Jamie, with full Cogi faculties, the situation is rather different. If her talents are to be nurtured and developed, she must be able to explore all her abilities and that's very difficult. Let me think of a different example, so you can understand. A few years ago, I found some notes for a doctoral thesis written by someone very small, a dwarf. He became a very successful actor, but eventually committed suicide. He was brilliant, every-one agreed that, but it only helped so far. His world was full of inconvenient objects, like chairs and tables, sofas and beds, knives and forks, cars and bicycles, road signs, in short he was living in a world shaped in the wrong scale for him - the whole human environment failed to fit his needs and precious few people took him for the man he was.

Jamie has similar problems, not physically, but scales of a different kind. Physically, Cogi and Sapiens eyes are indistinguishable, but Jamie can see far more detail. She can also see a range of colours that Sapi's simple fail to differentiate. She's quite a good painter, with that kind of attention to detail and precision you get with adolescent girls, painstaking effort to achieve the effects that are exactly as she wants. But she uses colours that Sapi's just cannot recognise, bluey browns and greenish pinks. Her pictures look like smudgy smears to a Sapi.

And when she looks at great paintings from the past, the seem to be riddled with flaws, little blobs of unexplained colour, flecks of pigment, distracting brush marks, where you wouldn't expect to see them, all invisible to a Sapi. For her, looking at reproductions of paintings in books gives her a better idea of what people have been seeing, than looking at the originals in a gallery. Its a strange inversion of aesthetics. Painting is a fairly easy example to understand.

The gap, as we have started calling it, is much more extreme when it comes to music, dance and story telling. For our youngsters a synthesiser sounds more authentic than a real instrument and orchestral music is a maddening cacophony. The Cogi craftspeople have yet to design instruments to our liking. The gap gets more dramatic in other areas of life. We get much less tired as we work and are far less dependent on computers, data handling, networks. As to stories, well even I have trouble keeping up with some of their plots, hundreds of characters and all kinds of situations."

Lisa is increasingly gloomy as she hears Joe's explanation. She can only foresee two alternatives if the Cogi's assert themselves. Whether it would end in violence, it another matter. But she can foresee a Cogi culture emerging, a new society, that Sapi's simply will not grasp. Even now, only a minority of Sapi's are needed to keep the world running effectively. The Hives are full of irrelevant people without a role. If the Cogi are to predominate, then the Sapi's might as well consign themselves to history.

Then a terrible thought occurs to her. If the Miasma is ever brought up to Cogi speed, then Sapi's simply won't be able to understand a thing.

In the long history of human conquests that would be the simplest and most thorough. The Conquerors would brush the conquered to one side without needing to fire a shot. They would simply be put on ignore.

This complex in the desert is based on adaptations of old buildings and dominated by the unforgiving harshness of the climate. What would a city look like if it was defined by these people? Ordinary folk, like herself, would look on without understanding anything that was happening. She might not know what machines were for, never mind know how to use them. The products may not have recognisable functions. There's not much point looking at paintings you can't see, or music that is unlistenable. The more she considered what Joe told her, the clearer it becomes that humanity will reach a crossroads.

Either the Cogi's will gradually gain influence over the Sapi majority, or they will be held in check. One-way, or another, she suspects that for either side, the method of entrapment will make use of the Miasma.

In a half hour chat about a fifteen year old girl, Lisa has been introduced to the theme that will dominate human life for generations. She wonders how many of these 'people' there really are, hundreds, thousands, millions? She shudders at the thought that people defined as suffering from disabilities, might really be more able than their fellows can possibly admit.

"Joe, I can see how your work as a researcher can be useful, but where does your brother Bill fit into all this?"

"Big Bill is an enigma, extended adolescence, decades of screwing around. Completely irresponsible genetically, but he does like sex and he's genuinely fond of women, so I don't think he does much harm. And they adore him. Then he marries this weird wealthy woman, so who's to criticize him? Tatiana's big in the way Samoans are, very beautiful and I'm pretty sure she wanted Bill's Cogi genes for their children, who I have to confess are a pretty awesome lot.

Anyway, as usual, when disaster struck it turned out Tatiana's folks were insured for all kinds of circumstances, except what actually happened, which was the eruption of an undersea volcano just off the coast of the island where they owned just about everything, including the airport and the land on which the hotels were built. The airport was covered in lava, a lot of tourists were caught in the gas cloud and died. Now, while this was tragic, and the insurance people paid for the Islanders to start over, what they refused to cover was the Princess' de-deification. Till then, the islanders had all paid a religious tribute to her Dad that was equivalent to about one per cent of their income, and she got her cut at the end of each month. Anyway," Joe laughs, "I don't think her Dad was a very religious guy, what with the brothels and the casinos, and she certainly isn't. So what happened was this."

"The big hotel operators signed up this Professor of Theology to take a good look at what the old boy was expected to deliver as local godhead and this fellow delves and delivers, doing his research with anthropological thoroughness, coming up with the news that her Dad had failed to keep up a series of rituals intended to placate maritime volcanoes. Since the rituals involved a lot of complex chanting and sacrifices of various kinds, I can't say I blame him. Who would expect a well-meaning president of a chain of Tourist Resorts to spend every Thursday evening examining the entrails of small furry animals and feed the left-overs to a couple of large unpleasant reptiles who are supposed to sleep outside his door at night. Since he lived in a three storey penthouse at the top of the luxury apartment block overlooking the local lagoon, I'm not even sure this would have been legal.

The Judge himself admitted that he wouldn't have bothered with this mumbo jumbo, but he also said that that wasn't the issue. He wanted to make a name for himself in legal circles by deciding whether Gods have duties and obligations to their followers, or not. But the Islanders listened to the Theologian, who was not only a nice guy, but took the situation at face value, hoping not to offend their local beliefs, however much they might seem like superstitious crap. On the one hand, he told them he didn't believe a word of their so-called religion, on the other, he told them if they did, then they had some obligations to uphold and they ought to be serious about upholding them. He told them that if they really believed, then they had a moral obligation to stop paying tribute, or they faced the risk that the volcano would be even more offended, take umbridge and erupt for a second time. They did exactly what he said and he was well paid for the advice."

"Now, some of that tribute was traditionally paid in the form of birdshit, which over the years had metamorphosed into the tacit understanding that Bill's wife had a controlling interest in the biggest phosphate mining operation in the South Pacific and she went from being the Guano Queen of Melanesia to Mrs Unpaid Bill in no time at all, or to be more precise about a week and a half.

Shit happens, or rather shit stopped happening. She lost the lot.

Everybody likes Old Man Greenberg, her Dad, so he gets a pay-off and spends all his time watching Rugby, or visiting the brothels he used to own. His presence is used for marketing everywhere. I know for a fact that he paid a lot of bribes to the Multi-Denominational Synod to stop the Vatican having his character demoted from Faith. but there was no sympathy at all for Bill's wife. She ended up with one small resort as a kind of pay off. Its really nice there, but not the same as being Mrs. Big to all those people."

"I learned that the Islanders had wanted her to marry one of their local heroes, who was a guy who had a career as a movie actor, then won a lot of sports medals and ended up as a heart surgeon, but she had chosen Bill instead and they resented it. So, when Smithson stepped in and offered people shares in the phosphate mining operation if he was given the licence for mineral extraction, that was that. She was out and Bill has had no alternative, but to find some way of making a living, which is why he runs the snow-cutters up in the old Baltic. I know for a fact that she hates the cold, so the Baltic business also gives Bill the chance to put some distance between the two of them. Anyway they still have one little island for themselves, Murawiki, its a quiet resort."

"I see Bill as a kind of loyal rebel. It doesn't really matter what his wife thinks, though she can be pretty dangerous at a personal level, her reactions are always irrational. He's certainly done his best to see the Cogi gene is as widespread as he can reasonably manage. A bit like the blonde guy who arrived in Scandinavia after the Ice Age and impressed all the local girls, or the Irish chieftain, who shagged his genes into every single Irish family on the planet."

"Yes, no-one can accuse Bill of inbreeding."

"He also helps here, supports the community with bits of technology that are difficult to get in France."

"And what about you, Joe? Are you also father to a thousand Cogi cuckoos?"

Joe shakes his head. "No, I have a different point of view. Bill argues that intermingling is the best way forward, creating the potential to create a mixed society. Nesta wants her branch to fulfil their individual potential by being kept apart. I can see both sides of the argument, but I'm not sure the planet needs any more people. That's just a personal opinion. My main concern is to avoid another holocaust, where the Cogi's and Sapi's are at each others' throats. If it came to a fight, the Cogi's would almost certainly win despite the difference in numbers. I'm also pretty busy working with Johnson on how to avert World War IV, which would be the end of all our hopes, but seems increasingly likely."

"Oh", puffs Lisa, pretty much at a loss in the face of such a bold claim. What on earth is he talking about? World War Four? She doesn't understand at all.

"And I'd like you to help me."

"Which is why you brought me here. I'll think about it Joe."

"The railway can help, I think. Bill and I work on a couple of projects together. The global hologram has lacunae, like the bubbles in cheese, that don't register within the Miasma, as you simply move from one set of co-ordinates to another. Actually it is more like a foam than having a smooth consistency anyway, so the bubbles occur where the structure has broken down a little. This applies to about 10% of the ocean surface, half of Antarctica and a much smaller proportion of the big continents. The only time people usually notice them is when they're using the shuttles, but the pilots always give warning messages about so-called military zones that they have to avoid. Some of the lacunae are quite small. I heard of one in Philadelphia that overlapped the door from some guy's living room to his bedroom, so whenever he had a pay pal to visit, he was always last into the bedroom. The pay pal simply skipped about three metres on the way from the sofa to the bed. That one got plugged fairly fast and the locals simply laughed about the amount he had paid for his pals. No-one considered the possibility of a fault in the global hologram. Actually I think most folk have forgotten it's even there."

"So what is the Miasma like for Cogi people?"

"A complete waste of time, well that's the case for most people, but Cogi's see the Miasma as a kind of granulated smear. It's most unpleasant and the audio is catastrophic, tinny and poorly defined, all kinds of hisses and buzzes. Put a Cogi child in a normal school and they start having stress symptoms almost immediately. That's why so many go autistic, they simply close in on themselves for self-protection."

"Isn't anyone doing anything about it, can't they fix it?"

"There's only one serious proposal. Our friend Smithson wants to create a high speed local hologram, as an experiment."

"That's great!"

"I thought so at first. Then I looked at his plans."

"And?"

"He's created a new corporation that will turn the High Speed Zone into a kind of circus, with feeds downgrading the experience for Sapi users in the hives. The Cogi's face being corralled, just as dwarves and small people were forced into freak shows, because there were no other options for them to find a way to thrive. Smithson is trying to set up the first of the Zones over an area of about thirty square miles, but he can't find a region who are willing to give him that kind of space, or risk their energy supplies by feeding so much to an autonomous high speed net.

Lisa holds up her hand to signal Joe to stop.

"OK, I think I'm beginning to understand."

Joe brightens. "You do?"

"Yes, you flirted with me and seduced me and brought me here just because our railway is a convenient prop for your issues with Smithson. I'm really disappointed. You could have been honest, Joe. You could have tried."

And Lisa starts to cry.

CHAPTER 11

Amanda stretches under the bedclothes.

The light is still too bright for her to open her eyes without discomfort, but that is slowly becoming more normal. Her legs feel a little stiff, probably a result of the narcotics, but there is a tangible distance she can sense between her thighs, knees and ankles. She can feel a very slight draft of cool air against the toes of one foot, but not against the other, which is under the blanket. The slight hiss in her ears is symptom of the high blood pressure that she'd been warned about following the operation. Her eyes blink and fill with tears to blur her vision and it's tricky trying to focus.

For the very first time, Amanda feels really herself. A novel experience, for sure, but it is a novel experience that justifies the five million to pay the surgeon.

The operation is some kind of a success, whatever happens next, but so long as the surgeon keeps her mouth shut, it will remain secret. Without telling Johnson, or his Mother, Amanda has reformatted her code herself, using a dupe for the replication, then she had run the debug sets before shipping to Iwo Jima. Finally the surgeon has overlaid her lattice. It feels good. She recognises happiness mingled with euphoria, which makes her laugh, an odd sound echoing through her head, but not her mind.

Francis Lucille Janneret had been expelled from the Balaban Islands for proposing the reversal technology. There had also been a suspicion, unconfirmed, that she was involved in the traffic in body parts. My name is Dr. Janneret, not Dr. Frankenstein, she had told the Ethics Committee. Then they had expelled her from the Marburger Bund and the Royal College of Surgeons.

As she stands beside Amanda's bed, a benevolent smile on her face, Amanda wonders whether she will have to kill her, then she wonders how. Simple question, easily asked, the answer is not so easy.

"How does it feel to be human?"

"Essentially the same, but there is added tangibility."

Janneret smiles, modest, yet smug, "You've been told to expect that."

"I can feel it. Marginal sensations, I suppose, deriving from the body's physicality, rather than the themes I am consciously addressing. The gravity thing is strange, sitting 'down', getting 'up', you can feel the weight shifting around and balancing, I still wobble when I stand. So with all that going on, I actually have to think about the thing I want to think about."

"Wonderful!" says Janneret, clapping her hands with glee, "This was one of the Balaban Islander's goals, or rather the reverse was the case, when they began to work on separation. They recognised that the power to concentrate on a task varies enormously from one individual to another. It has nothing to do with talent, or intelligence. Almost everyone from the age of five or six can concentrate on a task when they begin, then gradually their attention wavers. Not many people can concentrate on single theme for more than an hour. In fact, most people find their attention starts wavering after about ten minutes. Of course, people can be trained to perform repetitive actions, like smiling and serving drinks, playing games, or selling shoes, but they are subject to stupefying boredom, which eventually tranquillizes them to their fate as drones. Lots of people attempt to train themselves, but even so, very few people can keep their mind focussed on on intellectually demanding subject for more than three hours. How long do people work without a break? How long can they perform as dancers, or musicians? How long can people concentrate if they are merely members of the audience? We accept that people can improve their powers of concentration, but we rarely enquire about the benchmarks they set themselves, how, by excluding distractions, they can hold a pattern of an idea in the mind, without some other intrusion. How many moves ahead can a chess player plan their game?"

"I want to go swimming," Amanda announces, as if to confirm her dwindling powers of concentration.

"Amanda," Janneret concludes affectionately, this first post-op doctor patient chat at an end, "What you are beginning to discover are prominent among the clichés of human experience. The Balabans called their programme 'Pure Thought', but with you," she smiles, "I think we are reaching the threshold of impure thoughts. I do hope you enjoy them. But you'll have to take lessons before you try to swim. Perhaps, I can help you put together some kind of a training programme. There are all sorts of things I think you'll enjoy learning. Standing up is one of them. You'll have to get used to following what your ears are telling you."

As the Professor departs to see her other patients, one of the Assistants arrives with Amanda's lunch, a single dish of rather watery chicken broth with a bread roll. Eating is also a learning experience, discovering what words like spicey really mean. Hot and cold, saltiness, but most of all texture, smooth, rough, sloppy, tough, there really is a lot to chew on. It takes some swallowing, even once they've taught you how to swallow.

In a small room filled with several sofas and an array of equipment, Robert Johnson is sitting in front of two local holograms.

The first shows him Amanda's room.

She is lying bronze skinned under a dark blue coverlet, but her hair has changed colour. Instead of Rowena's dark curls, Amanda has gone blonde.

He feels a twinge of excitement.

An assistant is gently injecting a large dose of tranquilliser to alleviate Amanda's first panic attack and Johnson is jealous of the nurse.

The second hologram shows a comatose figure lain in bed surrounded by a full team of attentive nurses and doctors monitoring every detail of his Mother's gentle metabolic regeneration. It is going to be a trial to accustom himself to the fact that his Mother is now physically thirty years younger than himself.

There is a very old lady's intelligence locked inside this shell of youth, quietly enjoying an enormous sense of triumph that she has just made the most sensational prison escape in the history of penal servitude. All her doubts about continuity have been dispelled. She is who she is and always has been. Her old body, she decides, will be discovered dead in a tourist hotel on Iwo Jima and the cadaver swiftly returned to the Faculty for disposal. It will be interesting to see which of her illustrious colleagues show up for the funerary ritual.

Should she go herself? Now that would be fun.

She can hardly stop herself from leaping out of bed and dancing a fandango down the hospital corridor uttering whoops of uncontrollable joy, free at last, but hers is an old lady's intelligence that knows it pays to be patient and no-one is more patient than someone surrounded by doctors after an operation that has won her a seventy year increase in life expectancy. She is looking forward to reading her obituaries and deciding who will deserve to encounter the bitter daggers of her revenge.

Her son is hovering by the bedside, having abandoned his perch in the control room, a pallid, nervous figure gawping awkwardly at the young woman in the surgical smock.
Sooner or later, they will have to speak to each other.
He is wishing he's never had sex with the woman in her days as a pleasure unit.
The old woman opens her young eyes and gazes passively around her. She is checking her memory for the serial numbers and passwords to the anonymous bank accounts she has established in Russia over the years. 17B41-3471-98-QUF5-0000, password H5q7OPU – 100 million units in share certificates for Smithson Inc, another bundle for Vatican Venture Capital, another Miasmatic Holdings, another Serial Pleasure S.A., and more, so many more that poor Robert has never known existed. The Putin Bank has a wonderful reputation for security - 'only you can take out what you put in'. She can leave this place in a few days, anyway, sending Robert away with the corpse, while she begins a new life in the house she has had built deep in the souk of Tangier. There is nothing he can do and nothing he can say. Legally, I am as dead as the proverbial dodo and Robert is welcome to the threadbare remnants of whatever is left of the estate, a small house in Wisconsin that will succumb to the ice in ten years time, three vintage cars dating from the year before her incarceration and a set of failed research contracts that have all been licensed to the Penitentiary Assets Trust in Jamaica.
Professor Janneret is preparing a set of tests to see if the old lady has survived the transplant intact. Childhood memories, scientific concepts, formulae, general knowledge and a maths exam from the Cambridge Tripos for fun. The old lady had scored remarkably well in the same tests a year earlier,

matching all the assumptions made by the Judge at her trial. "You are the most calculatingly cynical, cold blooded, vengeful and self-centred person, I have ever encountered," the stern faced Jurist had growled, when passing sentence.

The only difference now, she observes, as she answers the questions correctly one after another, is that I am incredibly beautiful. 'I should have changed you more,' thinks the greedy Professor, hoping she has not been added to the list of names the wicked old woman would like to see assassinated by Exitus or any of their absurd miasmatic rivals.

"Well, Mr. Johnson," Professor Janneret says when they are back in her office, "Your Mother seems to be fine."

Johnson thanks her profusely, half wishing the operations had not been quite so successful, and asks how soon she will be ready to leave hospital.

"Physically, she could leave now. Both women are in remarkably good shape, but I would like them to stay with us for a few days longer. There is always the danger of a relapse."

Janneret tries to choose her words carefully, she doesn't want to raise Robert's suspicions. "Your Mother is quite independent, but the other woman needs a period of re-orientation so she can acclimatise herself. I'm concerned she may have a tendency to dissociate mind and body. I must say the bodies are very fine specimens. Where did you manage to get hold of them?"

"Trauma cases from the Dominican Republic," Johnson says blithely, "a ritual had gone badly wrong. The young women were physically unharmed when we acquired them. But both had lain in a vegetative coma until being declared brain dead. We were able to help the medical team by implanting the pleasure units that you have decanted. The Ethics Committee approval followed some intense soul searching, but they eventually convinced me it was the right thing to do and I supported the procedures."

"You paid?" Janneret enquires politely.

231

"Somewhat less than the fees here, but I must confess is was a major commitment."

"If only there were more people like you, Mr. Johnson, who recognise the significance of this field. I'm afraid we encounter all kinds of obstructive interference from the orthodox medical community. It is very trying."

"So I understand, especially now the Vatican have made their views known via the encyclical."

"Oh, the Papal fatwah, well that was to be expected, given her campaign to preserve the sanctity of life. Our beloved Pope needs the denial of continuity to protect the whole principle of 'Life after death' and the 'resurrection to come'. What I am doing rips their core theological beliefs to shreds of medieval bunkum. The Pope has good reason to hate me and she does! If we can resurrect with guaranteed continuity of being as a standard medical treatment for old age, then the whole notion of divine intervention and the role of the 'Saviour' will be diminished for all time. She'll be dependent on saints and fanatics for her re-election and she isn't that kind of person at all. You know she spent a couple of years with us at the Faculty as a young woman. I've always liked her and I think she learned a lot from me."

Johnson recognises Janneret's hesitation. "Have the Vatican been giving you problems?"

"Oh, less than I'd expected, but the Jesuits and the Swiss Guard are fairly active. There is a group calling themselves, "The Knights of the Legacy", who claim to have a team of hitmen on my trail."

"How very inconvenient, what can you do about it?" Johnson says, thinking about his pending membership.

Janneret stalls for a moment before replying, "Oh, we funded a simulation game which is being tested at the Occi Fest. Smithson had it developed. It's rather exciting. I had a play and found it quite engrossing to target myself. The people who really want to kill me will be able to do it in a no risk environment. During the tests, most of them lost interest once they'd been through eight or ten shoot outs in the Miasma. The ones who decide to go real-time are then flagged up by the system and sent off for a course of Non-Aggression Therapy at a winter camp in Saskatchewan."

"Is the therapy effective?"

"I'm not sure. The Camp Director tells me there are a lot of frostbite related injuries that distort the statistics. The Games Company do sometimes provide compensation, I'm told, but there's not much to be gained from the Rehab Service if you've had deep-freeze dick out on the ice shelf."

"I see, you are crippling the opposition, before they have chance to strike," says Johnson thoughtfully. "Thank you for your time. Do you think it appropriate that I see Amanda?"

Can he trust this woman? Probably not, he concludes.

Janneret deflects. "Of course, she'll be thrilled to see you, but no sex, even if she tries to insist. She's been through quite enough for the moment. There are limits to shagging. I think she needs a few days rest before she goes orgasmic."

"Really?" he replies.

Smiling conspiratorially, they part, each reluctantly certain that they will never be allies, once their current business is complete.

As he's walking along the corridor to Amanda's room, Johnson skims the list of organisations Selinsky had nominated him for in his will and notes with 'interest that the 'Knight of the Legacy' describe themselves as a group of locational reconstructionists exploring the use of armour, tournaments and the architecture of Crusader Castles. Based in Amman, Jordan, they share the same address as the Saladin Association. He activates the 'expression of interest' message and makes an appointment to meet their Membership Secretary.

Johnson is, of course, deeply familiar with the two girls, but

Amanda looks unexpectedly ravishing, a pre-Raphaelite muse, as she props herself on the maroon pillow reading a comic book, "The Adventures of a Rarebit Fiend."

"Melted cheese on toast," she says to Johnson grinning broadly, "Delicious. I want to try some."

Her eyes sparkle with an intelligence the pleasure unit simply never had. Johnson is overjoyed, "My darling Amanda, you look simply wonderful."

"I feel fabulous," she answers, languidly stretching her limbs under the bedclothes and holding out her arms to welcome him with a tender embrace. "How can I ever thank you?"

"There is really no need," he says, sitting on the edge of the bed, laying his hand on the side of her head and smoothing her hair. "It's a joy to see you looking so well."

As he leans forward, she lifts her head from the pillow and kisses him gently. They both sense this is dramatic event, her first real kiss, after two decades of Miasmatic pleasures, the presence of another body sends her momentarily into a swoon of intense consternation, before she recovers her poise, recognises the hormonal stimuli and remembers to ask after Johnson's mother.

"It seems to have gone very well. For her, the transformation is somewhat different to your own, but I expect in a couple of days, you'll be able to meet and compare thoughts."

"Actually, Robert, it's the thoughts that bother me. I seem to have forgotten half the things I knew. Like Portuguese, its completely gone. It just isn't there! And the rest, my memories are all jumbled up. I know that I used to have total recall. But, right now, I can only get the hang of about a tenth of what I've done and even that is disorganised and confusing."

"An all too human failing, Amanda. I'm sure your memory will improve. As a data set, you had no real problem with time. Now, you're a person, things are different."

"I don't understand."

234

"Amanda dear," Johnson says, reaching out his hand to comfort her, "we humans live in the present. Our minds have to deal with all kinds of stimuli, choosing what we pay attention to, deciding what to ignore. There's a rather strange loop in our perception that means we have to recognise stimuli that we are then going to ignore. So the biggest, maybe even the most important of all our human mental processes is forgetting rather than remembering.

The decision to ignore something feels immediate, instantaneous, we aren't even aware of it happening most of the time. Remembering and recall are therefore the exception rather than the default. Our normal pattern of perception is to discard almost everything we perceive, ignoring all the commonplace minutiae to focus on whatever seems important at the time.

This is why the hives are such a breakthrough. People are given very precise stimulae that match their mood preferences. Nothing irritates them, there are no distractions, just smooth pleasurable experience. They love it."

"I've noticed."

"Well, now you are in a full human situation. But you have a fresh mind and that new brain of yours will be busy sifting through the stuff you brought with you, all that mental baggage, deciding what to keep and deciding what must go."

"But I don't want to forget my past."

"Of course you don't, but I think you'll find that everything will fall into place soon enough. Forgetting can be quite refreshing. People have a way of recreating themselves as time goes on, I'm sure you'll learn that soon enough."

"What about the woman who had this brain before me?"

"Oh, she was just a pleasure unit, her presence has been completely erased. I understand she's back at work in the hives already."

"And the woman before that? The real woman who grew up in this body? Have all her memories really been swept away?"

"Oh yes, I can reassure you on that. The pleasure unit was installed for three years and she never encountered the slightest hint of the previous user. I'm sure you'll be the same."

"I hope so, Robert, I do hope so. I don't want traces of a past life messing up my dreams."

"Nor would we. No need to worry. Amanda, I'm certain all the remnants have completely gone."

"Robert, I'm feeling tired. The drugs they gave me are rather strong. Could you leave me alone for a while. This is all going to take quite a lot of getting use to. I want to go swimming. I don't know why."

Johnson, reassuring as ever, says Amanda shouldn't worry and leaves her to go in search of Professor Janneret, finding her in the dining room.

"This is good," she says, indicating the dinner of poached eggs in cheese sauce on a bed of peppered pondweed and Johnson asks the waiter to bring him the same.

"I had a word or two with Amanda," he tells the surgeon. "She seems remarkably well."

"She still needs a few days of complete rest, but they both seem to have come through surgery in good shape, I'm pleased to say," Janneret reassures him.

"Do you think there is any chance of old memories re-emerging from the previous subjects' lives?"

"Nothing disturbed the pleasure units experience, so I wouldn't expect anything to surface now."

"I can't imagine my Mother having problems. She's far too dominant and she carries a complete lifetime of experiences from her own past. If anything did show up, she'd probably recognise it for what it is and either explore it and enjoy it, or promptly repress it. Amanda is somewhat different. I think she was designed as a twenty-two year old, stable young adult, as I recall. She might be more susceptible, never having had a childhood and skipping puberty."

Janneret waves his concerns aside, "Those brains were 'tabula rasa', I'm completely certain, not a twitter when we decanted the pleasure units and no reactions at all before we shifted the new characters into place. They were both in limbo suspension for fifteen hours. We'd have noticed even the slightest hint of activity, but there was none. The Amanda material was almost 2000 times greater than the pleasure unit she replaced. She's very robust and her system prioritises emotional control and functional stability. That hasn't changed. I wouldn't have agreed to the procedure if there was the slightest cause for concern. You and I know how important it is for our security that Amanda never falls into the hands of an independent psychiatrist. Any problems will have to be handled very carefully."

Johnson smiles, "I think I can reassure you on that point."

"Yes, I have every confidence in your ability to keep her under control. By the way, when are you going to dispose of your Mother's body?"

"If you can confirm there are no traces of the procedure, I thought we could have her crated up and returned to the Faculty in a couple of days."

"It was heart failure. We could arrange to have her found on one of the footpaths."

"I thought she might have been praying at one of the shrines and died in a Buddhist moment of revelation, anticipating reincarnation. A fitting sentiment in the circumstances. It would have a useful distractive effect and a good way to explain why she never made it back to the hotel."

"Ask her about that in the morning. She may have her own thoughts on how her death should be presented to the world, though I like the hint of reincarnation."

"She will want to have died with dignity. She has always been very fussy about status and respect."

"A contradiction when you think she has been a prisoner for all these years, though at her age, who's to tell."

"That is one of the reasons she became so unbearably pompous. I'm rather hoping this new body will help her become a little more amenable."

"With a figure like that," Janneret says, "I expect she'll spend most of the next few months reacquainting herself with the vigorous pleasures to be enjoyed in the arms of young men. A bit odd, when you think about it. Sooner rather than later, she'll be the oldest woman who's ever lived."

Johnson gulps, "You have a point there."

"Odd too, how this old recipe has never been bettered," says Professor Janneret, as she licks the last of her vanilla ice cream lasciviously from a long silver spoon, having realised that Johnson has just lost his appetite for sex.

Once he is out of the dining room, Johnson takes the lift to the surface and walks for an hour, or so, in the afternoon sunshine. He calls the ferry that is due to take them across the Pacific and through the Panama Canal to Jamaica. The ship will arrive in 36 hours. Bill Smather, reliable as ever.

Johnson wonders what "KoL", the 'Knights of the Legacy' have to offer. If they are Vatican agents, he will have to be careful. Of all the world's centres of power, thanks to the weak minded, religions have never lost their grip on the human imagination. Even Selby had never attacked the Church directly, though he had sown the seeds of doubt among the British Bishops who still sat as Lords Spiritual in the Upper House of Parliament. More than other other institution, the Church of England had lost almost all its wealth as the value of land collapsed, then hundreds of its Churches and Cathedrals were ground to dust by the encroaching ice. Durham Cathedral and York Minster were saved and eventually sold for rebuilding as a centre-piece of New-Tewkesbury in the Sahara, but all trace of Whitby Abbey and the monastic cells on Lindesfarne were lost forever, while

Fountains Abbey was toppled and torn asunder by a wall of glacial debris that flooded the district to the dismay of the watching tourists, who lost their lives a couple of minutes later. "They come here on holiday, not to die!", thundered the local news website, in protest at the injustice this represented for the local economy. The Church took a battering without Selby, or Tewkesbury having lifted a finger.

Poor Scotland, erased from the map by the growing ice-cap and that so soon after independence, the short-lived Republic of Caledonia. All that was left to show was a handful of settlements restricted to research scientists tracing the direction of the ice flow and the appalling weather conditions created by the Norwegian glacial cooling icing up the fjords.

Although Selby survived the European islands fiasco, he had to go underground together with other leading members of the Legacy Gang after a catastrophic fire burnt out the three huge server farms that kept Britain on-line. He never denied cutting the backbone of the UK net, all fifty thousand optic fibres[99] linking London with Manchester[100] and the twenty five that carried north towards Scotland, nor did he pretend the repatched colour codings were an accident. The off-line shock triggered riots in Birmingham[101] and Leeds[102] , with the biggest peace-time protest of all time blocking the motorway ring around London.

Without the traffic control net to keep the automated transporters running efficiently as usual, everyone was forced into manual, 'self drive', which hardly anyone had experience since the day they passed their communications test. Young men

---

99 Archaic network technology.
100 Urban Disaster Area 3 – Entry Forbidden.
101 Birmingham -British City with the largest proportion of "hive personalities", Social Trends, UK Gov, 2047.
102 Leeds, UK Town demolished in 2091, as the Ice Line progressed southward.

soon began racing between Watford[103] and the Sheffield ice wall[104] on the old M1 at speeds up to 300kilometres an hour above the speed limit. Some of them didn't even bother to slow as they reached the ice. None of the young men had survived more than 3 races, but coupled with the network breakdowns, their impact had been to terrify long distance transport controllers and drove freight off the roads. The Insurance companies very simply baulked and refused to cover anything perishable within UK borders. Within a couple of weeks, the big depots were devoid of fresh fruit and vegetables and supplies to supermarkets took the form of sporadic deliveries from local farmers, whose crops had been harvested, but remained uncollected by the packers and wholesalers.

First, a few enterprising individuals had ventured out to the farms on bicycles and bought the odd sack of potatoes, or a few kilos of apples. Then the black marketeers had swung into action, taking hundreds of thousands of eggs from the chicken factories out to the suburban masses. Even Sims, the world's leading suppliers of pondweed tanks, amassed their first fortune by selling eggs on the black market.

With meat production paralysed, herds slaughtered and cattle feed turned to flour, the British had suddenly rediscovered eggs as their main source of protein and acquired a taste for clumpy oat flake porridge.

Johnson decides he can afford a half hour break from the clinic and uses the Miasma to survey the surviving streets of Amman and see what the Knight of the Legacy Offices are like, JORKOL. Johnson assumes the JOR prefix is for the old biblical Kingdom of Jordan. He's wrong, but he doesn't care.

---

103 Watford, Old London Suburb and birthplace of Miles Panderton.
104 Sheffield, Minor British Urban settlement, threatened with ice-line erasure and now regarded as uninhabitable.

The idea is sufficient to convince himself. He eventually finds them on the thirteenth level below ground, almost in the cellar, though well lit and comfortable for desk-work. A modest young woman, veiled in the Islamic tradition, shows him into a meeting with the KoL membership secretary, a birdlike fellow with skinny arms and legs who is practising callisthenics. She introduces him as Luke de Klerke[105].

"I have been looking forward to meeting you Mr. Johnson," says de Klerke, "since our mutual friend told me of your interest in our founder. Please don't be misled by our name, we have absolutely no interest in Crusades and religion in any way, shape or form. It is a quaint leftover from the days when companies were expected to describe themselves on business registers. The Interaccounting[106] system made it unnecessary, superfluous to historic necessity. When everyone is allowed to know what you do, there is no need to tell them, is there?"

As I hope Monsignor Selinsky has explained, we have two levels of membership, each defined according to a different pleasure principle - the thrill of the chase and the thrill of the kill.

Dual membership can be attained, but we prefer new members to begin either as conspirators, or killers. It helps settle people into their membership. The roles attract people with quite opposing temperaments and the choice reduces the risk of chaotic interaction between the thrill effects, which can be very confusing unless you are experienced in both. Only chess players seem to contradict this trend. I suppose the frustrations of adhering to logic in their chosen specialism means they have a burning desire to slay someone in the chaos of real conflict.

Selinsky was one of our more serious conspirators and I don't

---

105 De Klerke, Luke – b 2195, d 2284, anachronist - author of a variety of religious texts and numerous sermons.
106 Interaccounting – a simple arithmetical triple entry model of economic activity.

think he ever contemplated becoming an assassin. Such a careful mind. That quiet determination. A very impressive person. A master of the myriad patterns of death.

Perhaps you will feel the same, who knows? But might I suggest at least for the moment that you begin as a member of conspiracy. The thrill of the chase is very much a professional persons skill, while assassins have a more visceral attitude to their hobby, craft skills, equipment, proficiency, you know the kind of thing, machetes, machine guns, stilettos one minute, tanks the next, from supercool hitmen to axe wielding beserkers."

Johnson is impressed. He had no idea Selinsky was a 'Monsignor', or even a regular Church-goer.

"As a matter of fact, I may have a target for you," Johnson says mildly.

"Is that someone on the disapproved list at Cornucopia?"

"I expect so. Maybe not. Should I check to be sure?"

"Perhaps you could give me their name. If there is already bounty, it would defray some of our fees," de Klerke smiles as he explains their method. "Of course we are always delighted to welcome new business proposals, but our fees have been found off-putting, especially among hive candidates."

"I don't suppose," says Johnson with an understanding smile, "that you were involved in poor Selinsky's demise?"

de Klerke adopts the hurt expression of someone who has been profoundly misunderstood, "That was one of our competitors, I fear, though we haven't found out which. Selinsky was very highly regarded within our group, especially his research about our founder. We do revenge, you know. In fact I think the world would cease to turn without the rivalries of revenge. Would you like us to pick up the trail? Nobody seriously believes his death was an accident. Accidents don't happen, unless someone has decided to make them happen. The Selinsky Assassination concerns us both."

"I shall consider the idea," agrees Johnson. "All of that was certainly a theme close to Selinsky's heart and I am sure he did nothing to hasten his own death. Simon was always very careful and rather cautious."

None of this had been what Johnson wanted to hear. The notion of joining a band of amateur assassins is beneath his dignity. Then he realises the Membership Secretary has told him too much. He has no real alternative, but to join them. A tactical failure, he confesses to himself. Now they can expect his subscription will be paid promptly, if only to keep his name off their hit-lists.

There aren't any outstanding bounties in his name, unless Old Mother Johnson Happle has been up to her tricks without telling him, though there wouldn't be much point in her deciding to have him eradicated. But the kind of people who sign up as assassins probably don't care who they are eliminating. Johnson can imagine them noticing his address and concluding that a weekend in Jamaica would make a nice break, perhaps a little skiing too, or a few hours frittering away their money in the Casinos, then popping up the mountain to pop him off. Johnson sincerely wishes he had never made contact. He may have to wipe out the lot of them, but that's a decision which can wait for later.

"You know that, like Simon Selinsky, I am a historian. Our interests run deeper than the thrills of chase and kill," he explains. "We also look at the development and dynamics of events and personalities."

"Selinsky felt that most strongly, Mr Johnson." accepts the de Klerke. "He told me about your Selby project, which was what brought him to us in the first place. Our founder had also sponsored Mr. Selby's movement and supported his career. It was quite logical that he and his partner should try to develop the synergies between their various investments. In those days our offices were in Vienna." There's a hint of regret, nostalgia, then he continues, "We moved here after the glacier melts flooded the city in that terrible mud slide."

"Braunovsky?"

"Yes, and his step-daughter. They paid for the building and we benefit from some of the rents. We had almost ignored the woman, until Selinsky demonstrated his fracturing of 'All Known History'. You've seen the models, I presume?"

"He showed me one or two preliminary patterns and we discussed the maths behind his conjectures."

"I was less impressed by the methods than the results," says de Klerke.

Johnson laughs at the stupidity of this phenomenological remark, "Did he tell you about squeezing a lump of jelly to see how it splits apart."

"I cannot forget that one. With me he used real jelly, green, and it splattered all over the walls. He was reasonable enough to to accept my suggestion we used a less vivid metaphor to present his notions to our selection committee."

"Selinsky was rarely forthcoming."

Johnson is beginning the find the man's naivety amusing rather than embarrassing.

"No, Selinsky was a very private man for the most part. His love of fish and archives baffled many of the members here, but they respected his attention to detail. He took an almost perverse delight in selecting targets for the groups, providing very clear arguments why our victims should be singled out to die. The seekers enjoyed that sense of moral reassurance, linking private pleasure with the collective good. We enjoyed ourselves. "

"By killing people?"

"By trimming the directions in which history might be made. It sufficed, Mr Johnson, it was more than sufficient reason." He sighs.

"Was Eric Selby a killer, or a conspirator?"

"A conspirator, naturally, which explains why he felt so outraged at being labelled a murderer after the Tewkesbury incident. Selby thought the victims were the authors of their own demise, which in Tewkesbury's case was close to the truth, taking a step backwards and toppling over the rail of that ship and being sucked under the hull to be shredded by the propeller. The other fellow, our revered Moses Hoffman, a different situation. There were suggestions of a crime of passion, the knife wounds to the abdomen. Selinsky had no doubts at all. He was of the opinion that the fractures of history should be helped and the direction of our development encouraged in any manner that made sense in 'All Known History'."

"We are mainly reconstructionists."

"Yes, but Simon Selinsky was an exception man in every respect He knew more about the future than anyone I've ever met. He turned queasy at the sight of blood, but he never had any doubts about justifying our efforts. He told me he was on the determinist wing of archivism."

"Yes, I know their slogan, '..taking dreams from games to reality....' We sometimes call them free-basers. Tell me Mr. de Klerke do you believe the story that Tewkesbury stepped backwards into the sea?"

"Selby always denied that he was pushed."

"At the trial."

"I'm not sure all the witnesses were called."

"All six who testified said that Selby pushed Tewkesbury over the ship's rail and into the drink," Johnson reminds de Klerke.

"It was night-time."

"Correct," nods Johnson.

"There was a storm," adds de Klerke, "and everyone on board was either drunk, or stoned."

"So I believe."

"The witnesses were all inside the brightly lit saloon discussing politics and said they saw what happened through the window."

"I had noted that."

"There were no lights on deck for some unknown reason."

"There had been a power failure some minutes earlier. The ship was newly commissioned. Like most machines, ships are at their least reliable the first time you use them. That is when a accident is most likely."

So their discussion proceeds until de Klerke brings things to the point, "Yet despite all the evidence against him, Selby protested his innocence throughout the proceedings. His defence seemed implausible at the time. Selinsky thought that too. Why should Selby have concocted a story that was ridiculed by half a dozen witnesses? As a rational defendant, he should have mounted an argument to minimise his responsibility. Had he claimed to have slipped, or tripped, or under-estimated the danger when he pushed Tewkesbury against the rail, it could easily have led to a conviction for manslaughter, misadventure, or even accidental death. Take another look at Selinsky's papers, Mr. Johnson. I have no idea what you'll find, but I know Selinsky had something on his mind in the weeks before his regrettable accident."

When Johnson leaves the office, he hopes his name is on the Membership Secretary's list of friends, rather than foes. If they're like most secret societies the roles of friend and enemy will switch every two or three years as conspiracies make grown men and women behave with extraordinary stupidity.

The lift takes him back to the second level and he walks up the ramp to find a Miasma Relocation Room. Eventually he finds one in a small grove of orange trees. It is one of the old thrust models and he has to stand inside a coffin shaped canister before it starts.

A tenth of a second later, he wakes in his bedroom at the Clinic on Iwo Jima, his body refreshed by the rest it had enjoyed while he had roamed the Miasma.

Then, as his mind dwells on Amanda, rather than Selinsky, the door opens and in marches one of Janneret's assistants who asks him to meet the Professor at his Mother's room. Wondering what could possibly have gone wrong, Johnson hurries down the clinic corridors to find his Mother up and about, bossing the nurses and trying to pack her suitcase, while Professor Janneret sits on the bed smoking a pipe.

"Bugger this," she says, laughing at her son's concerned face, "I'm off. And to hell with Professor Janneret's megalomaniac delusions that I am some kind of a witch in angels clothing."

"Robert," she adds sternly, "We need to say goodbye to my corpse, before the undertakers get here. Come on!"

This girlish energy is too much for Johnson, "But Mother!"

"Robert, I think you'd better lose that habit, no more of the Mother stuff. Your biological mother died, I am no longer the same woman, though I shall of course retain a limited affection for the role you've played as offspring. Giving birth to you was the most hellish event of my existence so far."

Then Janneret intervenes. "Please, let's take this a little more cautiously," she pleads, "You still have to complete the reorientation programme we agreed on."

"Stop pussyfooting around Lucy," the resplendently youthful old lady tells the Professor. "We get rid of the stiff this afternoon and send out the death notice a couple of hours later. By then, I want to be off the island and you, Robert will have to handle the press and see that the corpse is safely returned to the Faculty. This is all quite predictable and should not come as a surprise to any of you. Give Lucy some more money to keep her mouth shut, or do you think we should kill her? I really don't care either way."

"Mother."

"Don't call me Mother! I shan't tell you again!"

"Bloody hell," says Johnson and takes a deep breath, "All the arrangements have been made. The fast ferry will be here tomorrow night and we can leave just before midnight. Please be a little more patient. The extra day of tests will be a big help, I think. Outbursts like the one we have just witnessed will be extremely dangerous to you in your new life. The Professor deserves a little more time to check all your reactions."

"Robert, take a good look in my direction. "If I ever accuse you of rape, or sexual harassment and refer to your mother complex, I think I could have you locked up in the psychiatric department of the House of Correction for the rest of your days, so just watch it, ok, son?"

That was when Johnson decided that as soon as possible after that, a group of Mr. de Klerke's friends should pay a visit to this bunker of a clinic and finish the job. Janneret, Marcus Gropius, Paul der Miese, Jimmy Trump, the lot of them, extinguish and delete. Those amateur groups may have their uses after all, he decides. Maybe he should get them to rid the world of his Mother, while they're about it.

Johnson's Mother pouts winsomely and flops into the armchair, "Very well, one more day, but let's take a last look at the stiff and then I need a man – badly - not you Robert, one of those orderlies I saw in the operating theatre will do nicely."

Laughter from Janneret as she hears the old lady's words, "Oh, that's what this tantrum is all about. I should have known, I suppose. I'm afraid the orderlies won't be much use to you. They are out of bounds on grounds of hygiene and even if I were to allow you bodily contact, those particular fellows wouldn't be interested. I don't want you catching anything before you've settled in. We are all gay here. So, may I suggest we pop over to the mortuary to say goodbye to the dearly departed, then you hop right back into bed and rummage through the drawer in your bedside table. There should be plenty of toys for you to play with there and I shall be very interested to review the data."

Johnson glances at the two women and a word springs bold in

his imagination, "Let's go over to the cool room," he proposes, while to himself he thinks, 'Good God, my Mother really is a Zombie!'

A spirit inhabiting a corpse.

She and Amanda have turned the most famous Caribbean myth into a living, breathing, reality and he has made it happen.

A shiver runs up his spine.

He can't wait to get back to Jamaica.

Candomblé.

Janneret could become an African Goddess, if that was her wish.

Johnson decided it would be fun to do it anyway and arranges to have her consecrated by the Suffragan Bishop of Trenchtown without bothering to ask.

Then he began to pray.

She could be a martyr before long. The Vatican revere martyrs and they haven't had a new one recently. It's always a good idea to stay on the right side of the Pope, whatever she might pretend about impartiality. As Janey Freud suggested in her ground breaking study analysing psychos, in answer to the question 'just what do mafiosi want?' - sometimes it's simply better not to know.

CHAPTER 12

The first person Amanda wants to meet in her new guise is Lisa, but that is something easier wished for than achieved. When she tries to locate her in the Miasma, all she can find is a simple post from Lisa saying she's gone to Europe looking for goats and doesn't know when she'll be back. 'If ever,' Amanda wonders to herself. 'After all there's nothing wrong with Europe, now they've cleared away most of the dust.'

The discovery of Barbara Happle's emaciated remains at a Shinto Shrine in the South Pacific has brought forth a froth of contradictory obituaries from friends and enemies, which Amanda assimilated during the slow voyage across the Pacific. She disagreed with almost all of them, especially the ones that praised the old woman's philanthropy and her 'dedication to prison reform', or even more preposterous, her 'rehabilitation programmes for errant scientists'. The dead Happle 'crits' became a kind of sport among the world's intelligensia who had enormous fun contrasting the various absurd claims made in the old lady's name.

When the former Mrs. Happle herself read their comments, she really was exceedingly digruntled and posted a curse in the Miasma, which grew in credibility over the following months as one by one her worst detractors encounter very nasty accidents.

Bill Smather took Amanda and Mrs H to his wife's holiday complex on Murawiki, where the new Barbara Hoffman, as Mrs H had decided to rename herself, exercised her enthusiasm for surfers, while Amanda spent most of her days walking the island's forest footpaths and gazing over the blue and magenta lava flows.

Officially, they were waiting for Johnson to return from his delivery chore at the Faculty, before proceeding to Jamaica as planned, but Amanda wondered whether she might stay on Murawiki rather than letting Johnson whisk her off to the Caribbean.

Murawiki has always been a quiet place where rich folk go to be away from one another without succeeding. It suited their needs and Bill helps them relax.

There had been one or two surprises along the road to recuperation.

Blistered toes are minor injuries, yet Amanda found the nagging pain a considerable irritation and a genuine surprise. She was also taken unawares by the amount of sweat generated when hiking in a hot climate. "I'm dripping, all over! Eeek!" She would like to put this down to sensitivity issues that simply need a tweek, but being biological, tweeks aren't an option.

Life is full of surprises.

Amanda begins to appreciate clothes and the power of fashion to influence women's opinion of themselves. Her consolation is the mirror in her chalet.

The anonymous donor had provided her with a face of soft yet gorgeously distinctive features, wide dark eyes and flawless coffee coloured skin, an abundance of hair which can be sculpted and teased in a thousand spectacular ways. She begins to practice the range of expressions she thinks appropriate in different circumstances, a beguiling glance (easy), naive curiosity (simple), girlish glee (a bit over the top, but never mind), and responsible appraisal (reminds her of her days as a data set). Pensive seems to work quite well too.

Men fall for her. It is as simple as that. Bingo! She can have whoever she wants, not that she's quite ready for that particular set of manoeuvres. Running, jumping and standing still are enough to start with.

After week of this, she thinks she has the hang of it and ventures out to meet one, or two of the wives, whose husbands are busily ogling Johnson's Mother.

So far as Amanda can tell, the new Mrs. Happle turned Hoffman was taking no prisoners, gorging herself on lawyers and veterinary surgeons, tourist guides and reformed Miasma addicts alike. If rejuvenation created such insatiability, Amanda asked herself, how frustrating had old age been?

The youthful old lady does her best to induce Amanda to try some 'real time', but without success.

The sea is blue, the sky is blue and Amanda has the blues.

"I hadn't realised how much men smell," Amanda confesses, by way of explaining her attitude.

"Rutty, dear, that's all. Just get them to take a swim before you put them to bed," advises the old lady. "Look over there, the one by the barbecue, he's rather good at it. Would you like to be introduced?"

"What do you mean, 'rather good at it'?"

"Well, they do vary, my dear," she giggles, "especially at real time. Always have, but now so much is Miasmatic some of them hardly know where to begin, never mind end up. It takes practise, you know. We need to find you some-one who knows what he's doing. Maybe you should tangle with the boat fellow, that Bill Smather, he's a jolly roger."

"I've decided to wait a little before I try anything, or anyone" Amanda says. "I want to find the right man first."

"Oh dear," the new Mrs. Happle laughs, "you'll have a long wait then. I've been on the lookout for almost eighty years and haven't found the right one yet. You should have met Robert's father, an absolute disaster, inside and out. I don't know what I was thinking of when I look back."

"Did you love him?"

"That's the snare. He was a great fuck. We girls get trapped by deceitful hormones and mindsets. Worse than landmines. The bonds of passion and desire. You'll discover that, I'm afraid. There's no known antidote to love. I harboured the illusion just long enough to have Robert, but I wouldn't put myself through it again," she chimes. "As a son and heir, Robert has been worse than useless, not even Oedipal. The father was even worse, no better than a third rate sperm donor despite his pedigree. Now the question is behind us. At long last I am free once more and I'm not sure I'll need to see him again, once we're off the island. One word of warning should you start feeling maternal. If you do have a child, it will not have your genes. Genetically a baby would be your body's child, not yours, so be careful what you wish for. Shall we have some more of this tea, or would you like a gin and tonic?"

For a moment, Amanda feels sorry for Johnson, then she recalls his arrogance and vanity, his flabby middle-aged bombast and concludes she might agree. But whatever might be said against him pales against the presence of this octogenarian twenty-five year old man-eating harridan with a renewed liver. Whatever his limitations, Robert didn't deserve a woman like this for a mother. He'll be better off without her, she decides.

Then Amanda feels the need to pee, another of those strangely habitual activities that data sets know about, but have never had to experience in practice. This whole business of being herself was being compromised by all the contingencies of learning to deal with this persistent biological presence with dictates all its own, her animal self which she'd only previously known as a theoretical other.

She shivers with a flush of hormones and a pleasurable tickling up and down her spine. Amanda can't decide whether the body is some kind of support mechanism for her true self, or whether her newly embedded consciousness is now really some by-product of a totally unknowable set of bodily processes. She tempted to speculate, then remembers the tomes of philosophical speculation about the human predicament from Abe to Zoe. Dangerous ground, she knows. Free thought, free will, the freedom to fuck things up. Enjoy, hope, suffer, pain, doubt, fear, transcendence; the whole panoply of temporary certainties and then you die.

Once the transfers were complete, a ball had been set rolling, which is now completely out of her control.

For the first time, Amanda can understand why so many people take the hive option. It really is a lot less hassle than being a fully conscious autonomous human with all this scurrying off into these private cubicles to purge yourself and paying attention not to dribble as you eat an oyster, or lick an ice-cream. Amanda realises that she needs Barbara Happle's assistance while she's acclimatising herself to the new circumstances. She simply isn't accustomed to herself.

This time, before she leaves the bathroom, she remembers to look in the mirror and check her clothes are neat. Astonishing how quickly other people's habits become something you do yourself, as though generation after generation has come up with no other practical solution to this particularly personal situation. Mirrors are a big help. Warm water and clean towels too. Despite that, the human condition is all pretty primitively vertebrate.

Strolling under the palm trees, Amanda wants to celebrate her new beginning, these first few days of the rest of her life, but there is no-one to celebrate with. She watches the waves splashing gently ashore.

Johnson is all solicitous and knowing.

His Mother is off on a self indulgent rampage. She has already mastered the expressionless stare so beloved of insistent fashion designers who want their models to assert their bold insolence.

Lisa appears to have eloped with Joe and gone ex-miasma, which may be a good for both of them. Such things are difficult to judge.

Janneret has absconded back to Iwo Jima and taken the nurses with her.

Amanda is encountering another very human condition.

Already, she has discovered the condition of uncommunicative solitude in the midst of a crowd of people and she concludes this must be loneliness, 'that lonely feeling' they sing about in love songs.

The sun is sinking towards the west, casting a wonderful rose pink into the sky, which reflects as a shimmering fire on the ocean waves and the majestic tropical clouds. A gorgeous green albatross soars past, while a pale grey rabbit sits in the dunes and looks pink in the light of the setting sun.

Suddenly overwhelmed by a surge of emotion at the beauty of it all, Amanda bursts into tears and sobs until the sun has sunk below the horizon.

Later she decides this was a rather bitter-sweet moment of a distinctive kind of melancholic pleasure.

She wonders whether to write a poem, assuming that would be the normal human response, at least in the Western European tradition.

Thanks to the late summer-time tilt of the earth's axis, on the other side of the world the sun has risen a few minutes earlier and while Amanda sobs her heart out, Lisa is talking to Nesta as Joe drives them south into the Provençal badlands.

"As a girl, I was known as 'Ali' and for some reason we never understood, there was a mix up when I was born and the French

registered me as a boy."
Lisa nods, then winces as the truck they're in hits a bump.
"So I changed my name to Nesta," Joe's sister continues, "and
never bothered to register the fact. When you live in this region,
registration means less than nothing, so I have always been free.
It's a Welsh name.[107] Once upon a time, there was a beautiful
princess called Nesta, who had lots of children with different
men and that was my intention too. I always wanted to be the
real mother of as many babies as possible. It's a natural thing to
do. I decided to follow her example. Some of the fathers were
men Princess Nesta married and some were noblemen she
picked up when her husbands were away, or she had been
expected to share her bed with as demeaning feudal hospitality.
I don't have her attractiveness by any means. She was
outstandingly lovely, the Welsh Helen, and men couldn't resist
her, but I followed her lead. It isn't difficult to seduce men. You
can take your pick. They never say no, never." Lisa wonders
why Nesta is wearing purple.
"Since she was a Princess, all Nesta's children were recognised
with titles and special status. I found that interesting too. There
are plenty of Kings who sired bastards and no-one took much
interest in them as the sons, or daughters of servant girls, or
mistresses, though they weren't badly treated. It was just the
luck of the draw. They tell me Windsor near London was full of
men who looked just like King Edward the Seventh, but I've
never been there, so I don't really know. The situation with
royal women is rather different. When it is the Queen who is
giving birth to a row of little bastards, unless the King wants to

---

107 Welsh – being from Wales, (also a language and poetic
culture) though there has been considerable debate for
centuries as to the actual existence of Wales, see "When was
Wales?", Williams, Gwyn A., Penguin, London, 1985. A
copy survives in the Moses Hoffman Memorial Library, Las
Vegas.

repudiate her, then the children are accepted into the Royal Line. These patriarchies are lot more like matriarchies than we like to let on. There are plenty of young princes who don't look like brothers, one with red hair, one who's blonde, another with curly locks and an unfamiliar Hapsburg jut of their otherwise Stuart jaw, or the squinty set of their eyes. The question of paternity is quietly ignored and all the children are given the status of royal sons, or daughters. Genetically, it might be rather healthy given the inbreeding implied by all those arranged marriages. New blood, fresh genes, a bit of a change. Nesta knew what she was doing, I think. Perhaps she was just overwhelmingly randy, nothing wrong with that, but I think she had a strategy. Anyway, the outcome was a network of half brothers and sisters, Dukes and Duchesses, Lords and Ladies, Princes and Princess who had all grown up together, a kind of instant clan of Welsh aristocrats. Several of Nesta's boys founded the leading aristocratic families in Ireland, the FitzGeralds and FitzWilliams, FitzMaurice, FitzHenry, FitzMilo and FitzGriffin's. As I said, they called her the Welsh Helen and not a man she encountered said no."

There's another painful jolt at they hit a ridge of limestone across the track, then Nesta carries on talking.

"Well, no-one called me anything like that! For the most part, men are too self-centred to realise their 'conquest' is part of a larger pattern. What I want to do, is to see if we can build a bridge between people. You know that Joe and I are Cogi stock, not 100%, but scarcely anyone is. The Swipdale DNA is unbroken in our genes and I am doing my best to see if we can build a mixed community of people with different combinations of Cogi and Sapi attributes before we turn racist again and savage one another, an outcome I regret to admit is more than likely. I want them to share a family loyalty and follow the notion of everyone in the family being part of a group with all kinds of special qualities, some from their genes and some from their personalities, all moulded by the special kind of upbringing we give them. I want to extend the range of human potential, so there's a smooth progression of abilities inside a group, with very different skills, instead of having the genetic divide between Sapi's and Cogi's slowly, but inevitably becoming a world of conflicting peoples. Sapi's have always been aggressive individualists and I don't want them turning against my children."

Lisa holds on to her seat and tries to assimilate Nesta's declaration, wondering where it will lead. The portends don't look good. And were the offspring to be Copis and Sagi's, rather than Cogis and Sapis, what then? Lisa expects the security systems will keep a careful eye on what they are up to, before making a decision, which will determine their future in a Cornucopia ballot. For.... Against.... Decided. And no turning back. Centuries have passed since the last war.

This Nesta has assumed she can act with impunity, be autonomous. And what if she is disastrously wrong?

Lisa suspects that if Smithson and his people in Cornucopia decide the Cogi future is to be preferred, then Nesta will find everything goes her way. Should they decide against, then her future will be shorter than her past. The notion of co-existence that Nesta has described hasn't convinced Lisa, so they're unlikely to convince anyone else.

The last half year has shown Lisa that her responses and opinions are pretty typical of the population as a whole, which was the reason she had managed to make such a success of the railway project. Everything Lisa likes doing is somehow average. It's a strange distinction from the norm. Only a very tiny number of people are convincingly average.

"You're an optimist Nessie," says Joe. "Soon enough, a time will come," he claims, "when some fundamental questions will be asked about the Sapi people. Once technology is based on Cogi abilities, then the Sapiens world will become secondary and the Sapis with it. Without any meaningful role to play, they could become pure consumers, shopping and acquiring, indulging and discarding. But does the world, rather than the economy, really need consumers? I'm not sure a neutral observer would see things that way. Homo sapiens will come to an end, but treated more humanely, I hope, than they themselves once treated the Neanderthalers."

Joe can foresee a terrible debate about the future of 'human rights'. By necessity, he argues, Sapi's will have to be banned from working with Cogi based technologies. They will be dangerously incompetent, unable to keep up, or to notice vital details. The distinction won't just be drawn at the technical level. Inevitable that safety considerations will be given priority. There will be certain kinds of decisions that only Cogi's will be allowed to take. Once this diminution of the Sapi's role has begun, will they be able to hold onto the privileges they have awarded themselves by way of voting rights and freedom, or will degradation be inevitable? Will every Cogi have a Sapi, the way Sapi people now have dogs? The Elite Universities are likely to embrace the Cogi sensoria as their basis for emergent discourses throughout the academic community.

Lisa gives a little shudder as he makes the case, but she wonders whether people will simply accept the inevitable and hand everything over to these newcomers in their midst, or is some kind of conflict inevitable?

What would Amanda think?

Would she be disappointed that she accepted a Sapi's body, rather than waiting for a Cogi?

Among musicians, almost every true virtuoso has a smattering of Cogi genes, Joe claims, but he then says he has yet find a similar cluster of talent in other callings. They are players, performers. Even so, the first great Cogi composer has yet to

259

come forward. Joe is waiting for the revelation their super sharp senses will bring to the organisation of sound. He's also on the lookout for a painter, some-one with a feel for artistic expression deriving from their heightened levels of perception. What kind of palettes would they create? The youngsters at Nesta's hideaway are splashing around, but that is all fairly simple stuff.

Sooner or later, someone will emerge who not only has Cogi talents, but has the temperament of a gifted artist too. How much more refined will their understanding of contrast and hue be when compared with Sapi talents, like Mossman[108], Picasso[109], or the other great figures of European art, say Vermeer[110].

He sometimes suspects that they are hiding from themselves, some instinct for self-preservation is keeping them out of the limelight and deflecting the potential rage of the less talented majority. No-one resembling these talents has revealed themselves via the Miasma.

Joe has frightened Lisa. His conversation is all too civilised and all too potentially apocalyptic. She is scared of the determined gleam in Nesta's eyes. Joe's profile as he's driving to the excavations seems suddenly hawkish.

"How much further are we going," she asks.

"Another half an hour and we should be there," answers Nesta.

"Would you like a break. We can stop for something to drink

---

108 Julius Mossman, sprayer, 2109-2140, noted for his al frescoes in St. Peter's Rome. Mossman lost his life in a raid on the Republican Bank of Gaza bullion vaults.

109 Picasso, Paulo 20th c Cuban, painter and art dealer.

110 Vermeer, Johannes, 1632-1710 (aka Frank O'Malley), painter, prolific, but commercially unsuccessful portraitist whose store of unsold paintings were recovered from the crypt of St. Matthias, Dublin, following his flight from Holland in 1675. (see also: Jost, Julian – The Four Thousand Vermeers in New York, movie-2D)

and stretch our legs."
Joe agrees and brings the lumbering truck to a halt.
"How long is it since you checked into the Miasma, Lisa?"
"Seems like a week," she answers wondering why he's asked.
"I'll rig the aerial, then, we can both see what's been happening," Joe smiles, "I can't do that at the house, it upsets Nesta's friends. We're far enough away not to pose a security risk for the settlement."
While Joe fiddles with the satellite dish and untangles a spaghetti of cables before plugging them in, Lisa and Nesta retire a discreet distance to pee.
The dunes here have begun to solidify into sandstone, some factor in the rare rains builds a glue among the coarse grains of quartz. There are layers of biscuit like rock lying in strata between the softer grains that are constantly being blown off the broken cliff edges of the unstable dunes. Some of the cliffs are as high as a man, the bigger ones as high as a house. If the unstable sand was to collapse, anyone in their path would be buried under thousands of tons of sand. These are not just badlands, they are the really bad badlands[111] that Nesta's grand-children had sung about after dinner the night before.
"The only other place I know where you see shapes like this," Nesta tells Lisa, "are on the ice shelves of the Antarctic, as the wind gouges channels between soft snow and the ridges that have turned to ice. Thankfully, the house we are excavating is to the south of this mess."
"You seem excited about this dig," Lisa says, hoping to hear something reassuring, that the place they're heading for won't turn out to be a trap.

---

111 We're going down to the sand,
   Of the really really bad badland,
   going hand in hand in hand in hand
   To Drown when we all try to stand.
   Chansons et enfants, 22c Children's songs

"The owner was an artist, we think, or at least a collector. There's a mixture of his own work and work by other people, some of it really old, but some of them probably given to him by friends. It was finally abandoned at the end of the 21st century and we suspect the owner had already gone into the Catacombs. He was a very old man by then and could no longer see very well, or hold a brush to paint. It was probably a wise decision. I guess he'll have seen more paintings since he went under than anyone else has looked at in their whole lives. The Catacomb technology can keep the visual cortex working for very low eye movement. He might even be happy there. I'd like to ask him about that. If he is still alive, then everything still belongs to him, but we can check with the Catacomb people. At the very least we're doing some useful salvage, before he claims them back."

"How did you find the place?"

"Quite simple, we drove past one day and the winds had exposed a pair of stone gateposts and some ornamental iron gates. Then we got a couple of shovels and started to dig. They had to lead somewhere. There was a gravel path. It reminded me of our house, so I was more curious than usual. Once we got to the front door, all we had to do was walk inside. Some of the walls had cracked and the roof had sagged a lot, but apart from a couple of tonnes of sand, the building was completely intact. What I would really like to find are some paintings that we could be sure were the work of a Cogi artist. As Joe was telling you, Sapi paintings look quite different through Cogi eyes. The moment we see a painting with none of the blotches, or blemishes then we'll know we've found the artists we've been searching for all these years."

"Have you had any success?"

"No, so far nothing. The only Cogi paintings I've set eyes are by our children. You are rather privileged to have had the chance to see them for yourself."

"Yes, but I'm not an art critic. I don't really know anything about paintings," Lisa replies, without inviting a response.

"Of course not. Look, I think, Joe has got the Miasma working," Nesta tells Lisa. "You should join him. I'll stay here. I hate all that fuzzy noise and blur."

The six antennae Joe has rigged are locked into a very local net.

Joe explains to Lisa that it sits in one of the lacunae that fools the Miasma into defining its co-ordinates miles away from their real location. The Miasma has us based somewhere near Marseilles, in a building known as the Château d'If. The antennae match the shaped of the room, so if we sit down, the Miasma will have us located very precisely somewhere else.

"I can't feel the Miasma, Joe," says Lisa, alarmed.

Joe laughs, "Wait a minute. I haven't switched it on yet."

When the truck's transmitter builds up power, Lisa recognises a slow trickling along her legs as the Miasmatic hologram begins to build. Gradually, they are enveloped in the dark stone walls of the old castle and she relaxes.

"Can I roam from here?" she asks.

Joe nods, "Of course, but we only have about ten minutes of power, so don't go too far."

Lisa takes one look at the stack of 1700 messages waiting for her, a sinking feeling in her stomach and decides she will just get in touch with Amanda then get out before the thresholds start to squeeze.

The link to Amanda materialised rather slowly, with a Cheshire cat grin preceding her newly glamorous presence. Though her visualisation isn't complete, it gives Lisa enough of a sketch to leave no doubt as to her beauty.

Wow! is the first word that comes into Lisa's mind, so that is what she says, "Wow!".

Amanda smiles sheepishly, an expression she hadn't been practising in front of the mirror, but came to her spontaneously.

"Hi Lisa, I just remembered you haven't seen me before, or rather you haven't seen who I have become before."

"Well, I've been used to you looking the way you were. The change is quite extraordinary. You are so beautiful, really, I can't tell you. It's a pity this is such a slow connection, I'm not picking up all your details, but you look wonderful Amanda, I'm so pleased for you."

"I could use my old appearance in the Miasma, if you like?" Amanda offers.

"No, I want to get used to you as you really are," Lisa decides, "One day soon we are going to meet each other in real time. And you have to become used to who you are now, as well. That might be difficult for you. I think people are going to take notice. You'll stand out from the crowd."

"I'm me, Lisa, but there's quite a lot that's changed, I'm not quite who I was and I still feel like myself, but some things are just new."

"Are you trying to keep a record of the way it feels?"

"For the archive. Yes, I'm compiling a diary that will be available to 'All Known History' and they've been making tests of the ways my body is reacting. The results will all be logged and kept. You know Johnson. He wouldn't miss a chance like this to build another chunk of archive. We're on Wikimura at the moment, but as soon as I can, I'd like to come to your place. Oh, god, I need to go and pee. It's dreadful, I'm running off to pee all the time. I hope that settles down before too long."

"OK, you go, I don't have much time anyway. I'm on a temporary link. Go to Alaska, my place, you know where the key is. I'll tell you the minute I know when I'll be back."

Amanda blurs as she turns away, then Lisa is alone with her thoughts and sends a few general messages to the Railway people and tries to book a shuttle back to Anchorage. There are going to be a lot of people expecting a lot of answers after her unexpected absence.

"Joe?" she says, looking round to see where he has gone, as the stone walls lose their density to let in glimpses of badland sands, "Did you see her?"

"Who?"

"Amanda."

"No, you two were in a private loop."

"She's done it," Lisa tells Joe exuberantly.

"What?" he asks, wondering why Lisa should want to talk about Amanda.

"She's made the leap, it's astounding, I met her."

Joe kicks himself for letting Amanda's transformation slip his mind.

"What's she like?"

"Physically, she's daunting, one of those stunningly beautiful women that everyone stares at, women as well as men, as slinky and sultry as you could imagine. I remember the way you started frothing at the mouth when you first saw Mona in our first trip to Selby's London. Actually she looks a lot like Mona, though Amanda's rather younger. Talking to her was the same as ever, plus or minus some abilities that have been shuffled around. I think its been a huge success."

Joe considers for a moment before asking the next question, "Would you say she's the same person, or someone similar to her old self?"

"She's been through a lot, I'm not sure I could pinpoint anything specific, apart from her appearance, that would leave me thinking she was someone different."

"Do you know if she's got the Cogi gene?"

"I wouldn't know how to tell, Joe."

"Cogi consciousness in a Sapi body, or a Sapi mind in a Cogi body. She might have said something about the Miasma."

"It was a very slow connection, even I found it a bit scratchy."

Joe asks if she saw the message about the History Conference, which she hadn't, as it was one of the middle ones of the 1,680 she'd ignored.

"They've had to cancel the meeting in Aix and fit up an alternative location, but the dates are the same," he explains.

"Did they say where?"

"Not yet, I think they're still looking. There was a note asking people for proposals, all a bit last minute."

"Can you remind me to contact them, when I'm back in Alaska, maybe we can find some space in the railway set-up. The setting would be perfect and conferences are going to be essential for the railway to make money."

"Well, everyone likes the Aleutians, so I don't think you'll have any trouble persuading them and it would probably be cheaper than Switzerland, wouldn't it?" he adds hopefully.

"I'm not sure about cheaper, but it would definitely be safer, we don't have feral issues in Alaska."

Once Joe has packed the antennae, they rattle and lurch their way down to the site of Nesta's excavation and in the half an hour that it takes to get there, Lisa has time to tell Nesta about the railway project and how it came about. The dust changes colour again, a bitter clay grey, but it doesn't make the dry heat any more comfortable under the mauve afternoon sky.

Their arrival is unspectacular. After shouting, 'stop here and park', Nesta jumps down from the truck, beckons Lisa to follow and leads her towards an awning that's been set up to cover the entrance to the excavation.

"We try to confuse the satellites with this," explains Nesta. "It sends a false reflection to the ground radar system, showing a bunch of people picnicking round a camp-fire most of the time. Then they either go to sleep, or pack up and move off, with more figures arriving later. We use the notion of embers from a camp fire to disguise the power output."

A neat cube of sand has been removed from the dune and the sides are supported by aluminium sheeting, kept in place by wooden boarding. Overhead is the camouflage reflector, busy confusing the surveillance systems.

Sitting in the middle of the space is a small cottage, a pretty decrepit sight, with doors and windows long gone, the chimney stack threatening collapse and that strangely anaemic look that comes from years of sand being blasted against the brick walls before they were engulfed.

"The paintings are all in the cellar," says Nesta, as she takes Lisa downstairs, "Watch your head against the ceiling."

"Why have you brought me here?" asks Lisa, "I don't know anything about art."

"Joe wanted you to see what we are doing. He was terribly upset when you accused him of only being interested in you because of the railway project."

"Well, I'm still not totally convinced," says Lisa bluntly.

"But he's completely in love with you, the poor man is besotted. He even threatened Bill, told him to keep his hands off you, or else."

"And what did Bill have to say?" asks Lisa, wondering how duplicitous her erstwhile lover might also be.

"He said hands on, or hands off was your decision and he refused to get into a quarrel with Joe about you. He didn't quite agree to leave you alone, which is maybe what you would like? Two into one won't go, will it?"

"Men are silly sometimes, why didn't Joe tell me?"

"I don't know. He put a note up on 'Eternal Devotion', but maybe you haven't traced that yet."

Lisa laughs out loud, "You're joking, I have never been anywhere near that trashy nonsense. It's a Smithson service."

"I know, but men are silly sometimes. You could have the two of them, if you really want."

"Nesta, you seem to know a lot about what's going on in the Miasma for some-one who never uses it."

"Well, I don't go into the Miasma, but Bill adapted a little hand-held for me that provides a daily update of the essentials and specifics. It searches too, of course, which is useful, but I don't actually have to set foot in the Miasma personally. Would you like one, I could ask him to make another? I have to keep abreast of what's happening in the world and the Miasma is part of that. There isn't any alternative really, the only news is Miasmatic. To some extent it's self defence on my part."

Nesta opens a cellar door, "The paintings are here and there are two old plan-chests full of drawings. We can go through some of them together."

The two women turn their attention to a stack of canvasses.

"There are some wonderful paintings here, not many really, only about a hundred and fifty in all, from about 20 different artists[112] we think, but none of them are disappointing. There are far more drawings, watercolours and engravings, but they are a bit different, rather special I think, from only four, or five artists."

The paintings have been stored in a series of racks, each canvas still on its stretchers, but unframed and wrapped in plastic sheeting as though in a last minute attempt to help their chances of survival.

"I wonder why they were abandoned?" says Lisa.

"They weren't abandoned. We found the remains of an elderly couple upstairs in the bedroom, Mr. David and Mrs. Hannah Hagen according to the message of farewell they left. They seem to have been the housekeepers. They were undoubtedly shot, gaping holes in the skulls. There was a loaded revolver in one of the corpse's hands. It looks as good as new, but the hand

---

112 Subsequent examination of the Hagen Hoard confirmed paintings by Adlon, Benninghaus, Bosch, Cezanne, Dürer, Formicoli, Gaugin, Hahn, Ingres, Jones, Marpe, Manet, Monet, Picasso, Phillips, Pollock, Richter, Tse Tung, Turner, Vermeer, Velasquez and Yamoah. The collection of drawings were identified as the work of Dürer, Ingres, Baker, Turner and Vermeer.

was skeletal with only a bit of dark brown leathery skin over the bones. I think they did their best to save the paintings, then took their own lives as the climate destroyed the region. After death, dessication. Maybe the simply couldn't face going to the Isle of Wight? I'd like to think they chose to end their days with these beautiful things and a pleasant house set in a wonderful landscape."

She unwraps a couple of the pictures for Lisa to admire.

"I'm worried about this collection," admits Nesta, while they sift through the paintings one by one.

There are certainly gorgeous pictures in the hoard. Lisa feels drunk as she sees the rich pigments in layers of blue and gold crimson and carmine, yet more blues and purples.

"They're all blue, how unusual," says Lisa.

"The old man's diary has notes of his search for images of heavenly perfection, what he called a miraculous combination of sea and sky.[113] That's not the only odd thing about them. At least half of them seem to be fakes. There are too many similarities, but we aren't certain which of them are maybe genuine. Perhaps none at all," explains Nesta, "The drawings are all genuine, we are sure of that. They're high resolution, Cogi work, without doubt."

"What makes you think the paintings are fakes?"

"There are too many similarities between them. No-one could have built a collection like that."

"Are you sure?" says Lisa.

"No, not 100%, that's the problem."

"Have you checked the materials, the paints, the canvases, are there records of where they've been bought and sold?"

"Yes, everything is here, all the documentation, all the chemical and material tests are completely positive. It's all too

---

113 The Diary of a Nameless Collector, Ed: Solomon Besendorff, Royal Academy Publications, Old Shrubbery East, Dubrovnik, 2109

good to be true. With my eyesight, I find it hard to distinguish between Sapi work. There's certainly a streak of Cogi-ness in some of them. This one by Vermeer for example, has the clear kind of brushwork I see the children do everyday at the camp, but that one is supposed to be Vermeer too, a typical Sapi tangle of under painting and alterations. One of them has to be a fake, doesn't it?"

The two pictures are very similar, perhaps even a matching pair, painted on wood, seated figures facing each other, or facing away from each other depending how the paintings are matched side by side.

"Maybe they are both fakes," Lisa suggests, with a small smile, "Maybe they're all fakes and you've been fooling yourselves."

Nesta laughs, "That is much more likely than them both being genuine."

The pictures show the same woman at the same table. She is wearing a dark blue skirt that folds around her legs as she sits and a white blouse that looks blue from the daylight that's streaming through a window behind her. In the centre of the window is a luminous piece of blue glass. The first picture shows her in profile looking left to right, with a basket of provisions she's been unpacking. A chequered blue and white cloth half removed from the basket reveals fruit and fowl, eggs and some books. In the second painting, she's sitting to the right of the table and is reading one of the books. An empty plate, blue and white, maybe Delft, like the jug of cornflowers in the centre of the table, has been pushed to one side. Lisa tries to see what the titles of the books are, but she can't make them out. The woman has broken off her reading and is looking towards a mirror next to the window. Then Lisa notices what the woman is looking at. Almost lost in the shadows on the right hand side of the painting, a door is slightly ajar and a hand and face can be seen peering into the room.

"These two pictures must have been painted by different

people," says Nesta, "Superficially similar, but they aren't from the same hand."

"Does that really matter?" asks Lisa. "After all they make an interesting pair. Maybe that's what's important about them, that they look interesting together when you look at them."

Nesta looks astonished.

"Am I sure I heard that correctly?" she asks Lisa, "Joe told me you are a historian."

"I am, but that doesn't have anything to do with these paintings. I don't do art. Most is just detritus, cultural leftovers, like all the other rubbish."

"At some superficial level you might be right, if you think of paintings as decoration, something to hang on the wall. But what about your 'All Known History', what happens to that if it starts being filled with false information and junk assumptions?"

"Do you feed 'All Known History'?" Lisa wonders. "No, but whatever we do is eventually picked up in the sifts."

"But even if a tiny percentage of the data is false, it wouldn't take long before the whole system is corrupted. Then, you won't have a history, just a mountain of lies and deceptions, misinformation and falsehoods. The whole edifice a sham."

"History is a bit like that anyway. Good judgement and balanced opinion are expected to balance out the lies and deceptions, which everyone privately agrees is naively optimistic at best and a massive collective deception from any other view."

"In one way, I agree with you that the only thing that really matters about these pictures is how they look." Nesta is looking at the paintings as she speaks. "Maybe history shouldn't matter? After all we live in the present from moment to moment. But the moment after the moment before becomes the beginning of history and everything we know is a kind of memory. So history is the glue that keeps us human," Nesta says sweetly. "If you can't remember anything, you're of use to neither man nor beast?"

"I'm not sure about that, people have their own qualities," Lisa replies, not quite certain of where her answer is leading her. "Lots of people have no use for memories at all. Usefulness is no way to judge people, only the Miasma can aspire to utilitarian purity."

"My point, Lisa is this," says Nesta with a level of certainty in her voice that Lisa hasn't heard before, "we live in the moment. Ask any-one what has happened in the world in that moment and they are at a loss to reply. We know almost nothing at all as its happening. Our knowledge of the world is reported after the event. Sometimes, I know it takes me longer to remember something than it did for it to happen and while I'm trying to remember I can't concentrate on anything else, so other things happen that remain unnoticed. There's a trickiness about remembering, because some things I can recall without having to try to remember, but there are other memories I have to assemble detail by detail and those are less reliable than my understanding of things I know took place, but I can't really remember at all. Do I think about my footsteps? Very rarely. But I know that if we were walking down a street together, I might be looking in the shop windows and you at the traffic, so our recollections would be completely different, even if we could both remember what we were talking about. There are some things I do better next time because I've learned, or remembered, but I some-how change something I've remembered into something I've learned through experience. Yet again, there are things I can't really remember at all and some things I kind of know I won't remember even when they're happening. That's when I have to make a note to build a kind of memory about something. Eventually, the pile of notes and letters, documents and messages becomes a kind of diary, but I don't keep a diary, so it doesn't have much about me in it.

None of it sounds very reliable does it? I get left wondering where, 'now', or what we're doing turns into history. Is it when projects are finished and documents get dumped in archives, because they'll no longer be updated, or memories are lost as people die and no more change is possible. Forgetting becoming the only active process, apart from the interest of people like you and your group, the historians. Actually, I'm not sure what it is you all do, apart from reviewing and rearranging whatever evidence is lying around, the problem being that most of what you say about your reconstructionist activities seems to be a matter of your own opinions. I hope I'm never included in your 'All Known History', because in my case whatever gets put on there is likely to be completely wrong. If you cascade links from false information the volume of corrupted data is enormous.

Ever since I was a child, the systems have been giving me a completely false identity – they can't even decide whether I'm a man, or a woman half the time. I'm not going into that, but all I want you to remember is that your 'history' is really something that happens now, it's in the present not the past and there's no way of knowing what's been going on unless you've been on the spot all the time. The 'historical predictable future' that the politicians like to talk about is all based on the miasmatic present linked to 'all known history'. And your little grouping really makes me scared. You are providing the framework to create their 'Historically Predictable Future' yet making things up as you go along."

"Nesta," says Lisa in a worried tone, "Can we talk about this another time. You've scared me into thinking that I should get back to Alaska as quick as I can."

Nesta smiles generously, "I'm glad you said that. Joe can get you to the nearest shuttle this afternoon if you like. And, by the way, don't forget he loves you."

"I'm sorry I can't stay longer to look at your pictures, especially the drawings, I haven't had chance to look at any of them properly."

"Oh, you haven't missed so much, they're mainly porn, set in renaissance Venice. They look as though they might be by Albrecht Dürer, but they're not, they're fakes. They may have seemed convincing to whoever made them, but to the practised eye, they're obviously by some-one else. Actually, I keep a lot of them back at the house. I treasure them. I think they're the most erotic works of art that have ever been created."

CHAPTER 13

Lisa panics from the moment she's back in the Miasma, hundreds and hundreds and hundreds of messages, all negative, and she is on the point of shrieking with frustration when she's met at the Shuttle Terminal by the irate figures of Harkham and Malliday. They don't look too happy.

"What the hell did you think you were doing? Disappearing like that, with scarcely a word and no contact address, are you completely crazy, Lisa?" screams the normally placid Malliday. Harkam is silently critical.

She can tell he is, don't ever do this to me again, furious.

Lisa feels herself shrink inside and only learns of the dramas they've had to handle in her absence, while they're riding to Summit Valley on the newly constructed express rail connection.

"We almost ran out of money two weeks ago," Harkham explains, "and the Governor intervened to keep the contractors on site. He put up a hundred billion credits, which have to be repaid in the next twelve hours, or we'll face losing control of the project."

Lisa silently transfers the cash and tells the men she will be more careful in future, making sure someone has the authority to act on her behalf if she is incapacitated, or simply away.

Panic over, the men calm down, as men usually do.

The good news is that Harkham has thought of a way to adapt standard transports to run along the sections of track which aren't ready for the big Zips. "We can rent these out for picnickers, or hikers who want to get way from the crowds. This one we're riding in is the prototype," he explains, "I took out the patents last week. Sorry about that, but you were away, so you missed the chance to do it in the project's name, Lisa."

Lisa smiles understandingly and bows to the inevitable then asks what else has been happening.

"There is a whole circus of people who arrived for a Conference that is being switched here from Aix at the last minute. Half of them are 'All Known History', while the others are from 'Cornucopia' and those bastards have a level of security paranoia I associate with the Vatican."

Malliday adds that people from 'Smithson-Pacific' have been surveying the route of the railway and have requested a meeting to discuss their plans.

"I have the feeling they are simply going to tell us what they are going to do," says Malliday doubtfully. "I don't think we are being given any choice in the matter. The Governor has given his assent, so whatever it is will happen anyway, whether we like it or not."

"What is the Governor getting out of this?" Lisa wants to know.

"Oh he's cooing like a dove. They've installed an ultra-deep Miasma bubble at the head of Summit Rise, about ten miles from town," Malliday replied. He's being talked about as a future President, candidate anyway.

"There are some ethical issues about the Ultra Deep technologies," Harkham interjects. "It's extremely difficult for users to know whether they're in Miasma space, or dear old three dimensional reality, so it hasn't been licensed yet. The Governor swept all those concerns aside and let them start installing. I think there's a risk, but he's a prototype freak. Its going to happen anyway, so lets get in first."

"They had been turned down by Turkey and Mexico on coherency issues. I heard that they were intending to set the thing up in Aix until the plague hit town."

"Which plague?" asks Lisa, bewildered.

"Catatonic, the San Diego day-dream. It has already infected about two thirds of folk in Switzerland and ten per cent in France. Several hundred a day just stop breathing, but the rest face a lingering death over the next two years. It looks as though Switzerland will go the same way as Southern California. Cat' was brought in via some shipments of cast iron memory, which had contaminated the iron-sulphur proteins. It's horrendously infectious, a pernicious syndrome we already know to be incurable. Metabolic blocking."

Before they pull into the railway terminus at Summit Valley, Lisa books herself in for a check up at Mental Debug. Nesta's hideaway was not that far from Aix, though Lisa can't recall seeing any memory dumps nearby. Who knows what Nesta might picked up salvaging, or what they might have blended into the stew by mistake?

"The victims are being shipped to the Isle of White in the hope of slowing down the progress of the disease before they finally dissipate. The Catacombs are going to be kind of busy for a place where nothing ever happens," adds Harkham with an ironic touch of gallows humour. The pharma companies will cover the costs and hone in on a treatment.

"How many?"

"Eighty thousand, officially. According to rumour, there are more. There are a set of sealed trains being prepared to meet the ferries."

Before they can say any more, the transporter arrives in Summit Valley. The station is green and lush, acacias and myrtle growing abundantly from every crack and crevice.

Clouds of steam are wafting across the yards from a group of newly commissioned locos, but before she can admire them, Lisa is swamped with people wanting answers, all of them annoyed that she had deserted her post as the project came to a head.

The Governor is the worst. "I was within three hours of getting a Court Order to take the whole project out of your hands, but you've paid up, so I guess you'll have to carry on, but it's borrowed time, you have a lot to do before I shall trust you with anything again. We've the Cartier people arriving in the morning with Liv Plausibel, the hive icon. You remember her? 'Sad Memory'? You know the one I mean. It was huge with the Zealanders. And James James is here.[114] Oh, isn't that smell wonderful," he concludes distractedly, as one of the engines chuffs past, enveloping them in a cloud of steam and covering their clothes in smuts of soot and gritty red hot specks of ash.

"It must be the coal," she replies, then turns to face her next questioner, who claims to be suffering an allergic reaction to their primitive technologies. "But this is an archeo-industrial installation," Lisa replies, "Minor irritations are beyond our control. There are paper handkerchiefs free. Alternatively, you can buy one of our anti-caustic protection suits, they are fitted with micro-filters and their own detoxified air supply, or you can fuck off. The choice is yours."

Six hours later, most of her critics have been placated, as Lisa makes decision after decision, signs document after document and apologises to everyone she meets.

The Valley is overflowing with delegates for the All Known History Conference, the majority are typical historians, students and school-teachers, professors and keepers from the thousands of museums around the world. They are milling around, trampling the fields and meadows and arguing.

---

114 James James, Irish American author of 'Bostonians Wake!',
   Plurabel Press Pub Guides Vol 77, Bel Canto, California, 2105.

Alan Montgomery is delighted with the revenue, however, "We are taking fifteen million credits an hour from the Conference delegates alone". Teresa von Braun is in her element as conflict conflator, bossing busily to defuse the arguments between tired and emotional visitors.

A fine layer of coal dust from the engines is settling everywhere, while a carboniferous condensate from the clouds of steam is making the station seats and even the walls greasy to the touch. A temporary hotel has been set up by the railway workshop with five different sections, from hostel to luxury suites. Harkham promises to install a more advanced air-conditioning system in the station café as passengers grumble that their food tastes of creosote and their toast is covered in smuts of soot. Lisa plays the authenticity card. "This is what you've paid for, authenticity, these are guaranteed original status British Railways sandwiches. Don't you realise how much it costs to make the bread dry and curl like that?"

Lisa wonders why they don't have the All Known History Conference in the Miasma, rather than travelling all this way to enjoy the discomforts of over-priced hotels. "It's worse than the Occi Fest," she overhears people telling each other and then she realises that for this particular minority, the Conference is their Occi Fest. Rather than the newest games, they are all addicted to History and it gives them a sense of purpose, a core of meaning to their lives, however slender its relation to reality. Coming to the Conference confirms their role in this project of projects and simply being there makes them happy, so they naturally succumb to the urge to complain. The griping and sniping is no more than a way for people to get to know one another in mildly unfamiliar surroundings.

Checking the programme, Lisa sees with relief that Joe and Amanda are listed to present the paper on Eric Selby on behalf of the History Room in two days time. Joe hasn't arrived, but Amanda has given her address as Lisa's house and seems to have made herself more than at home.

Although the house is empty when Lisa arrives at three o'clock in the morning, the goat has been fed, piles of clothes are strewn across her bedroom and there's a handwritten note propped next to the cooker.

"Your dinner's in the oven. I've gone to see Robert Johnson, love you, Amanda." Turning up unannounced is endearing in a character, annoying in an individual. Amanda's induction seems to have omitted certain areas of etiquette. Appraising the mess for a couple of minutes, Lisa unlocks the bed-chamber and slips inside to sneak a few hours rest. Luckily the goat is in the garden chewing acacias, rather than inside chewing bed linen.

Outside a fireworks display gives rise to oohs and aahs as the delegates party through the night, so the goat begins to bleat.

Lisa had been fast asleep, when Amanda had returned from the Historians' Bar and placated the little beast. Amanda has been logging on to 'exquisite' twice a day, as part of her recuperation from the transition, so she's understandably woozy and she crawls into bed alongside Lisa without waking her.

Six hours later, there's a kiss awaiting Amanda, as the Miasma soothes her from sleep and she can hear the sheep bleating on the hillside. The goat is standing quietly, chewing.

Lisa has already left.

Everything smells more than Amanda had expected, but the flowers spread sweet scents among the dungy animal odours. The house is remarkably tranquil. Even the coffee machine is on silent. Something bleeps. Flipping up the phone, Amanda hears the familiar voice of Robert Johnson. He has a suggestion to make. "Amanda, I've had a call from Cornucopia, with a special request from Smithson's people."

"He could have called me himself," huffs Amanda unnecessarily.

"He intended to, but it proved impossible for security reasons, so he asked me to talk to you on his behalf."

"You'd better talk then."

"We need to meet. Be at my hotel in ten minutes. I'm in Ultralux."

For the first time Amanda faces a problem women worldwide recognise. She can't decide what to wear.

Once she has calmed down, after an ugly argument with the hotel receptionist, who wanted to stop her going up to Johnson's room, "How dare you suggest I am some kind of pay pal," Amanda had stormed, Johnson says that both he and Smithson have agreed she is uniquely qualified for the task Smithson has in mind.

"It's Mother. We need to confirm her identity and we need your help. In fact we think you're the only person who could have even a fifty per cent chance of succeeding, with your knowledge of the period, your understanding of the mathematics of human history and your affinity for the people involved. I think you're the only member of the group who understood the details of Selinsky's conjecture about the Sapi/Cogi entwinement, so I do concur with Smithson's decision to approach you. There's also the transference business and my Mother insists that you are the only person who could achieve our goal without detection. Oh, dear, this is really highly sensitive, I hope you'll repay our trust."

"Why does every-one assume that any half-way good looking woman is really some kind of slut, or a whore?"

Johnson simply tells her it is a relic of misplaced male optimism and should be treated with the contempt it deserves.

Amanda is still hurt as well as angry, "so what do you and Quentin want me to do? I categorically refuse to become some kind of Cornucopian hooker."

Johnson looks perplexed, as though he doesn't want to tell her, even though he has been the one to approach her. There's no going back. "Such a notion had never been considered, Amanda, what kind of people do you take us for?"

"Robert," Amanda says gently, "I think you'd better tell me."

"Yes, I rather think I should. Would you like some whisky?"

"I don't drink, but you go ahead, if it will make things any easier."

"Thank goodness for Argentina," Johnson mutters ironically, as he pours himself a tumbler of sherry barrel flavoured spirit, "I'm so glad we're face to face and not in the bloody Miasma." Johnson's memories of Rowena interfere momentarily with his recognition of Amanda.

"I never thought I'd see you in Alaska."

"It's all so very improbable, but that's the whole point about history. Sometimes I'm surprised we're here at all, rather than stuck in some bloody cave on the Isle of Wight."

"That's what Selinsky was afraid of wasn't he?"

"Yes, he knew there's going to be another call for the catacombs and this time it won't be voluntary, if the Cogi's get their way. You won't understand that. There are rumours that that the Cogi's are immune from the Catatonic Plague. That is matched by even worse rumours that they are responsible for it! For a Cogi the virus brings a temporary sense of drowsiness, while the rest of us collapse into a coma that ends in death. I don't know what to believe. But catatonia is all our worst nightmares rolled into one. Selinsky seemed to know the beginnings of an epidemic was underway and he was terrified of being incarcerated without a panic button to get him away from the idle shoals of the drifters."

"And now?"

"I fear he may have been right."

"You believe in identity, don't you."

"We all do. Even as a matter of faith, it somehow seems intrinsic to human experience. Identity and the differentiation of the self from others," Johnson answers loftily, "It is humanity's greatest strength and yet the most vulnerable aspect of our psyche. We get lonely and we get frightened by the inevitable fate of individuality, oblivion awaits us all."

"What would your mother say about that?"

"She is a pragmatist and an opportunist, but she has a finely developed sense for historical necessity, an instinct for order and chaos. Your unusual personal development was one of her reasons for recommending you."

"This is her idea?"

"With Smithson's support, based on Selinsky's analysis. To be honest with you, Amanda, it's a fantastic initiative. I'm simply not sure how to present it to you."

"Ah, a problem of presentation," Amanda says pointedly, "Why don't you simply try telling me in your own words?"

"Rather than my words, let's see what Selinsky had to say," Johnson suggests and opens Selinsky's version of All Known History, with its smoky regions of action and interaction and the multicoloured lines of influence that scroll through the centuries to substantiate the hologram.

Johnson and Amanda are standing in an infinite three dimensional space, where they're surrounded by a graphic representing the trends of human history.

"The filters, where are we? Yes, I hope this will do, Amanda is this right?"

"People, organisations, tendencies and historic inevitability, that's a lot. It looks good in the classroom, but its too compromised for anything greater than a two week time-scale, like the weather forecast, only murkier."

"People like to believe they are living in a predetermined context."

"We need to have faith in our existence, or it would all be rather pointless."

"And is it pointless?"

"I suspect so. That's the most powerful aspect of the Cogi argument against poor Homo sapiens. Once you've realised life is pointless, then its time to let someone else take over. They have a point, don't you agree? Now what about the model?"

"Take out the inevitability filter, see what happens. Then show me what you want to talk about," Amanda says calmly. "We can discuss this later."

"To begin, let me tell you that Selinsky's model is, so far as we can tell, correct, or rather it might be in the proper circumstances. It is a very beautiful piece of work, though is it really representative? You've seen the display before. Few others have. Among them are the logicians of the Grand Council, who examined and tested Selinsky's work in great detail. They also discussed the implications with him. You know that he made use of some concepts from physics, the many universe proposition, the outdated theory of strings and the more recent pandemonium hypothesis. This all made immediate sense to the logicians, though sadly not to me. It embraced some notions I have never heard of. Nebulosities I'm told are accepted as fundamental truths. Even the Pope told me they are valid. As guardian of the Miasmatic core, she is probably the best mathematical mind on the planet, despite what my Mother thinks, so I have accepted this essential veracity. Of course Selinsky was guessing, when he built the system, but he seems to have hit the jackpot every time."

Amanda remembers her first glimpse of Selinsky's model, with its twisted curls of smoke and the thin line that marked the appearance of Cogi sensibilities. Her own work on 'All Known History' had taken Selinsky's model and twisted it with hundred of new inputs on themes explored in the History Room discussions, from individuals like Eric Selby back to their earlier work on climate change models and industrial processes, the terrible impact of the green bombs, those environmentally friendly industries that she recalls with horror.

"Is something wrong?" asks Johnson patiently.

"Just thinking about something," Amanda replies, recalling the disruptive turbulence of half a million windmills nudging the prevailing winds for decades until the storms that raged to send water spouts across the Black Sea and tidal waves up the Danube as far as Slovakia. In forty years, the topsoil of the Ukraine had been stripped by tornados that turned the eastern fringe of Europe's bread-basket into a land of famine and collapse, completing the long demise of the Russian economy after their oil ran out. The decision to abandon Moscow had shocked even the most ardent of Russia's critics.

"Amanda, are you listening?"

"Yes, I'm sorry, do go on."

"We have to discuss your induction into Cornucopia. You know about that in outline, I think, from Fred Smithson, but there are one or two details we need to discuss, in particular your willingness to undergo the special test which is asked of all Cornucopians and will require you to devote two months of your time following the Induction Ceremony, after which you will become a full member. Don't worry, we've all been through it in one form, or another and Smithson himself will tell you the details of what is expected of you immediately after the ceremony."

"You aren't being very informative, Robert."

"I'm not allowed to say too much. The details must come from Smithson himself, once he has been given the keys of his authority. We are all asked to rise to a different challenge, and I have no idea exactly what Smithson has in mind, but I can assure you it will be well rewarded financially and an experience you will never forget."

"OK," says Amanda.

That was all Johnson needed to hear. He knows the prospect of joining Cornucopia is irresistible.

He smiles amiably, "Then lets return to consider some of the curious kinks in Selinsky's model. It may not be something that Smithson wants you to work on, but I certainly do. I really can't understand some of them at all."

"Which?"

"Some of the clusters here are, for want of a better word, malformed, can you see," he says, expanding Selinsky's model so it fills the room and surrounds them with its filigree detail.

"They look like standard conjuncture patterns."

"I thought so too at first, but then I began to wonder. Look at this one, it's not right at all, it looks almost crystalline. The peripheral clusters are usually organic. Some of them look rather like seeds."

"Oh, yes," she says cautiously, "I wonder what the hell is happening there? When was it? Some of those lines look as though they are pushing into the past."

"Fourteen thousand years ago, somewhere in India. There's another one here, twelve hundred years ago in South Wales and another here look, go to North West England in the thirteenth century. There are two, or three others in pre-Colombian South America and one in Greenland."

Amanda looks and tries to stretch the clusters, but she can't make sense of what she's seen. The little crystals are subdividing. They shouldn't be.

CHAPTER 14

The entrance to the Great Hall is decked in silk flags and satin banners as Smithson walks slowly from the Golden Zip, resplendent in his fur-lined formal robes, his face almost invisible under the broad-rimmed hat, a figure of renaissance pomp and splendour. Lisa and Malliday can only look on from the driver's cab, as he pounds on the door of the Great Hall with an ebony rod to demand entrance, as is now his right and moral duty.

A fanfare of trumpets announce his entrance. The massive doors slowly open and he walks slowly out of sight. The entire membership of Cornucopia have gathered in Grand Assembly to celebrate his promotion to the auspicious position of Master of the Rolls. A seat on the Council of Global Affairs goes with the job, but for Smithson, it is more important that 'All Known History' will finally be his.

As tradition requires, the Pope asks him three times to nominate a Character for the Miasma.

On the first time of asking, he says "Nay" in a cry of injured protest, "I am unworthy", a refusal greeted by roars of protest from the Assembly.

"Accept, or face the guillotine, old man."

Asking a second time, the Pope places the Dagger of Office on the table between them and commands, "Nominate, or strike me down".

Smithson plays to the crowd by toying with the Dagger, relishing these carefully selected relics of medieval ritual and walks towards the Pope, a young woman of twenty three, who seems decidedly nervous in case Smithson decides to strike the fatal blow.

"Is this a dagger I see before me?" she says, sticking to the script, but beads of sweat have appeared on her forehead.

Smithson hesitates, takes the weapon, raises above his head, ready to strike, then laughs, "It sure is, baby!"

After a shocked paused, he returns to the official text, "The time for sacrifice is over," he intones solemnly according to script, lays the dagger aside and the Chamber is filled with the childish cheers of old men and women recovering their schoolboy affiliations to team, to house, and to the prospect of a feast.

Then the Pope steps forward, kisses Smithson on the cheek and speaks in a whisper, "You are the one the soldiers seek, nominate, or find a tree of oak in which to hide".

Anointed by a socco voce Papal Blessing, "and don't try that knife trick on me ever again, asshole, or I will ensure you are totally fucked from here to eternity." Smithson turns his back on the Pope and begins his long planned peroration, beginning as expected with the ritual phrases of the Assembly.

"My fellow Cornucopians, the Nation is in good shape. Weep no more, as spring begins this day and a long summer of fruitfulness awaits all who gather here. The winter of you malcontents is ended and rounded with a leap. Being of sound mind, I declare the newest figure of our host to be a man of undisputed talents, who lived in the days before our lovely Miasma was conceived, but a fellow who sought with all his energies to create the first hesitant steps towards the Miasmatic Present.

His was a life dedicated to the search for knowledge, in books and manuscripts, among his many friends and colleagues, a man who travelled the world in search of detail, a man who provided the foundation of our Archive, the kernel of 'All Known History', the great archive of Preyna and the publications created on their presses and their studios. But before I reveal the identity of this Character, let me first give thanks to the Historians, who sought under the name of Eric Selby to help define the personage we sought. As the 'Primitive Rebel' project was set in motion, they worked tirelessly in archive, in the field and on the ground to disentangle truth from falsehood, delusion from deception and led the way for us to unearth the nonconformity we sought...."

As Smithson's voice drones on, the Assembly grows restless. Three members fall asleep. Eighteen swallow the pills know as 'Wake Up Calls'.

Two hundred give their thoughts to the feast that will follow the ceremony and five wonder if they did the right thing by nominating Smithson and consider crying 'Halt and Death to the Imposter', as is their right before the bell tolls for dinner.

Their feelings are relayed to the Pope who looks alarmed at the prospect of having to kill Smithson, then face a trial that might just end in her own ritual sacrifice in the Aztec tradition.

To her relief the mood changes as Smithson cracks a couple of jokes and flatters the doubters with silvery tongued praise just within the permitted economics of purple prose, which nevertheless implicate them in his project and would ensure their joining him as accomplices and potential victims of the slaughter that would follow any challenge.

The moment of crisis has passed.

A half drawn dagger is returned to its sheath.

The Pope lets herself look forward to the dancing later on.

As the first hour of peroration drifted into the second, Smithson slowly brought his remarks to a close and the sleepers roused themselves in anticipation of something worth hearing, the gluttons ignoring the rumblings in their stomachs and all ears wait for the moment that will reveal the name of the Character he is nominating.

Then the whole Assembly realise they should begin to pay attention, or they will miss what he's going to say and disqualify themselves from all further voting. Those present and voting are expected to write out the candidates name to prove that they know who they are voting for.

"Wake up, or go to hell!" someone shouts and they do.

The Conclave is now in full session, alert and ready to get down to business.

"Brothers, it is my pleasure and my privilege to tell you that the Character I propose for the position of First Member of Elysian is both known to you and yet unknowable."

The Conclave have always revelled in ambiguity, much as children can be expected to like ice-cream, and this Assembly is entirely typical.

They are tickled, but wait to be entranced.

Smithson mentions two famous names and extols their qualities, then articulates the reasons for them being refused a place as Elysian characters. He reminds them of the professions which have been deemed inadmissible, including journalists, landscape architects, car designers and Scottish dentists.

Then Smithson come to the point.

"I hereby nominate Moses Hoffman[115], a loose cannon, a smuggler and a thief, a lone hunter, who bequeathed us his archive of rare manuscripts and whose presence in our Miasma will bring the necessary insecurities, all of you here have agreed we desperately lack."

---

115 See: "Lone Hunter" and "Animal Self" - parts 1 & 2 of the Moses Hoffman Trilogy.

There are cheers, at the prospect of new tensions in the Miasma and somewhere, crystallising deep in the hatchery, a figure rises, looks around and asks himself how much he will pay for the pleasures that so obviously surround him, sensing instinctively that he might one day be master of all he surveys, but finds himself hampered and uncertain. The nascent Mo is emerging from the shadow of the Miasma and in a few hours he will be made recognisable to the members of Cornucopia, then to the rest of humanity. For the moment, he feels as though he has a gigantic hangover. Given that a couple of centuries have passed since his earthly demise, this is hardly surprising. The cumulative updates to be made are immense.

Quite unscripted, Smithson makes a momentous choice.

In the final two minutes of his speech, with deliberate obscuration, he licences the decision that will always be linked to his term of office. He begins softly, so even the transcripting microphones pick up only a whisper of his intentions.

"My fellow Cornucopians. We have recently recognised one of the momentous developments in the history of humanity. Until now our chemists and genetic engineers have specialised in identifying particular agents, or biologically active substances which may be used as drugs, or via minor changes in the genetic structure of a foetus might deflect the development of an unwanted trait. Of course, they have each and every one of them worked within the ethical framework of our Academies, yet the newcomer has surpassed and outshone them, as we all knew it should.

Beyond every boundary of genetic engineering, the process of natural selection has produced a 'wonder of nature'. I am referring, of course, to the well-known presence of the so-called Cogi gene within a small proportion of our mighty populace, a blessing and a trial for those who have the weighty privilege to carry it.

We shall in the course of my administration, therefore licence the complete freedom for our engineers to build, and by freedom I mean (he chuckles) an obligation to succeed in the creation of every multicellular organism possible in the myriad permutations of genetic material and with that imperative we shall transcend all species boundaries to make a world of complete harmony between form and function, organism and environment. To support this effort, our exploration of 'All Known History' will be extended to embrace 'All Known Futures' and with that I am confident we shall secure the future of the planet and its satellites within the framework of 'All Knowable Entities'."

At first only a few attentive members of the audience begin to applaud, but at this unexpected wave of approval, the drowsy grandees spool back to relive what Smithson has just said. Soon everyone has latched on to the significance of his taboo breaking proposal.

The notion of 'All Known Futures' had long been forbidden territory, even as an area of speculative research, a boundary that 'All Known History' would bump up against when researchers got too far ahead of themselves.

The Cornucopians immediately recognise the implications of his words.

The construction industry might look forward to employing beings designed to work on the most unprepossessing building sites. The food industry delegates have proclaimed the potential of highly engineered protein assemblies for years. The narcotics producers sigh in ecstasy at the thought of embedding dependency in millions of new subjects thanks to yet undiscovered addictoids.. This was the ultimate expression of marketing, a perfect match between supplier, product and consumer, with forward planning that would be framed in a determinable future. No longer fettered by the crude framework of supply and demand, now carefully defined customers could be created for every product and the balanced market of unbridled free enterprise could after centuries of effort finally become a realisable goal. "My friends," said Smithson, "Prepare to customise your customers!"

Smithson brings his speech to a close with a rousing set of promises, including one to set up a new police force to patrol the Miasmatic future. He is rewarded with a wave of adulation of a kind never previously recorded in the Annals of Cornucopia, as it members recognise his intention to drown them in riches. His ascendency is complete, so he leaves the stage, modestly, without pomp, or anything other than the most humble of nods to his admirers, aware that he has inaugurated a new era in human affairs.

As Barbara Happle had exclaimed on the day she awoke in her new body, "Fred Q, welcome to the Age of Unbridled Greed."

The extravagant Feast that follows brings Smithson no pleasure. The sycophants insist on shaking his hand and offer their congratulations. The food is served, nibbled at and removed to be replaced by another course to be picked at. For his part, Smithson surveys the host of guests and feels nothing.

After the fourteenth plate is removed and his short but witty speech to the revellers delivered, Smithson takes the opportunity to excuse himself and he slumps in one of the ante-rooms, glad of a chance to reflect on his situation. Why hasn't absolute power brought him even a mild sense of satisfaction? Just what has become of his animal self?[116] His sense of greed and ambition, his vulgar desires have simply evaporated. An odd recognition of one of the first effects of High Office. The whole process leads no-where, except towards a mountain of responsibilities for problems that will not go away. It is time to move into action, he decides, or to resign. He should have a

---

116 See Moses Hoffman Trilogy Vol II

chat with the Pope. Now, where on earth is Amanda?[117]

"Welcome to Cornucopia," Smithson says to Amanda three hours later, as he wraps a sable stole across her shoulders as a formal symbol of her induction in the order, "Congratulations, my dear," he says, giving her a cold lipped peck of a kiss on her cheek, "I've ordered lobster. The food at the feast was execrable, as usual, though the sheer volume consumed broke all records. Some of our Members seem only to eat once a year. I'm sorry you couldn't attend the Grand Assembly, before your induction, but there will be plenty of opportunities in the future."

They are sitting alone in the dining car of the 'Royal Train', a replica of four Pullman cars, which had originally been built as luxurious coaches for the last Queen of England's[118] visit to Zeeland in 2112. Amanda reclines on a chaise-longue, while Smithson has flopped like an Oriental Pasha among a pile of silk cushions.

"We shall drink something Lebanese," he suggests, "so as to get thoroughly sozzled. I am already quite drunk with power and I can't think of anyone with whom I'd rather celebrate."

"Robert told me I am expected to undergo some kind of test, as part of this induction."

"Oh, don't worry about that. I think you'll find it quite amusing. You've met Johnson's Mother, of course, the redoubtable old hag Happle. She who has been rejuvenated, as a Hoffman. Your task is a rather clever ruse of her devising and you've already

---

117 The Miasmatic audience for Smithson's assumption of duties reached less than 0,0002% of humanity, as the timing of the event unfortunately clashed with a football match between the Balaban Islands and Tierra del Fuego in the semi-Finals of the FIFA Global Cup.

118 The last Queen of England, Flo Jenkins of Pontypridd, mezzo-soprano, was elected in 2108 and reigned until her death in 2109.

completed half of it unawares."

Amanda is puzzled and wants to ask him to explain, but the food arrives and the obviously ravenous Master of the Rolls gobbles the pink crustaceans with gusto, "Tuck in, my dear, there are plenty more where these came from. With a bit of luck, you and I will never have to eat that bloody pondweed ever again. The sauce is simply fabulous, take some more."

As Amanda scrapes flesh from a claw, nibbling politely. Smithson slurps on the mellow Lebanese vintage and pontificates, which is what the Pope had suggested as her answer to the hang-over of power question.

"Johnson has finally been proved right, by the way," he says.

"About what?"

"Optimal lifestyles."

"What does that mean?"

"What it boils down to is that the strange balance between well-being and indulgence, was just about right if you were incredibly rich at the end of the nineteenth century. Apart from the lack of penicillin, almost anything worth having was already to be had. Johnson has harped on about this for years, though I never took him seriously until recently. Limited technology meant life could be startlingly uncomfortable, especially in draughty country houses, and riding around on horseback is generally beneficial, so there was an admirable contrast with things luxurious and absolutely no pretence about being pampered in perpetuity. That's why Robert fought so hard for Lisa's railway project. Slower and smellier is good for the over-provided, excellent, both for body and soul. We do not need to ride around in transporters resembling plush coffins, when it is just as easy to be whisked, rattled and rocked in an old fashioned railway carriage of the better sort."

"Like this one, you mean?" says Amanda.

"Just so. These lobsters were cooked in a traditional way that hasn't changed in centuries, one animal, one pot of boiling water, a knife – and in the nineteenth century their lobsters were larger, healthier and fleshier than these emaciated, if nevertheless delicious delicacies. Aioli, aioli, bad breath and roly poly. Lobster, blobster, slurp and suck. Oh what luck, there's duck!"

Amanda suspects her 'task' will have a nineteenth century character and wonders what it might be, but she is wrong.

"What Lisa is doing here," Smithson continues, "has impressed every-one. Complete disregard for health, safety and pollution, primitive fuel, inefficient technology, inadequate systems. Enthusiasts and maniacs. Steam and raw power, a mix to intoxicate even the most sober of our companions. One might almost be persuaded that the world is returning to normal, whatever that means. However, in our newest version of the future, exercise will no longer be linked to environmental virtue, so no more pumping ox unless you want to. People (and this means you) will be allowed to run to seed in whichever manner they think fit. We are considering a broad scale implementation together with the inevitable upgrade of the Miasma. We are also dropping the next couple of generations to build towards a long-term goal based on cognitive and predictive environments. It will delight the Cogi's, as all their complaints will be answered in a simple, but effective implementation of the system. No more squeals and scratches. I am determined that my term of office will be remembered as a time of enlightened humanism and my epitaph will be, 'a great time was had by all', or so I hope."

Smithson pauses to remove a small piece of shell that has stuck between his teeth before he cracks another claw.

"Predictive environments are extremely interesting," he continues, "one of the areas you will be involved in through our little test. The principle target is someone you know well, your old friend Eric Selby and what we expect of you is this.

You dear Amanda have a quite unique attribute, being a divided entity. Your self is by now well established in your new fleshly home of blood, sweat, toil and tears, while your data set remains intact and functioning within the Miasmatic present. I hope this isn't a surprise, but you are, so to speak, the very embodiment of Kantian Dualism.[119]"

"Yes and no, I wasn't sure. The implanted data set had some minor attributes I chose to amend before the switch and I knew I was leaving something behind. Somehow, I expected the old Amanda would be switched off, I don't know why."

"You are an individualist Amanda, in a multiverse of pluralisms."

She laughs, "Yes, those are the attributes I kept for myself before that woman in Iwo Jima began to operate, so I deleted some of the personal codes from my data based alter ego. I wanted to be sure that I am me and I've checked. The comparison gave me confirmation."

"Very wise." He realises this is a viable confirmation, not that it would be of help to Mrs. Happle. Her issue has still to be successfully debugged.

Then Smithson switches to the next stage of Amanda's briefing. He provides her with short burst of code.

"These are the access keys you are given on joining Cornucopia, probably the greatest privilege of being a member. You can use them to vary the performance of various data sets, including your own, in your case, and this it what makes your membership so interesting, you now have the power to amend your other self."

Amanda bites into the salty sweet flesh of a lobster and asks, "so who was monitoring me before I became 'me'?"

"Hadn't you wondered why I gave you so much of my attention?"

"Oh," she acknowledges, "And how much of me did you amend?"

---

119 Susan Kant, Southern Carolingian Spanish Philosopher.

"I never amended, I always considered it an honour and my duty as a gentleman to upgrade you. Your personality has been entirely your own doing. Achieving your advanced sense of self has been my goal for more than a decade. Now we can move forward."

"How much does Johnson know about this?"

"Young Robert is more interested in bodies than souls, you know that. He could have known, but chose not to, by failing to ask, an error of omission."

"Well, I am asking. It is time for you to explain."

"Then we need to load 'All Known Futures' as well as 'All Known History'. My development teams make great use of these in combination, but the professional historians have been confined to the past, even Selinsky, whose maths you've been using in your own work. I think of this simply as humanity. We all pretend the futures are inaccessible but that is just for public consumption. No-one seriously believes it, do they? Past, present and future are all one programme really. Quite safe, so long as you know what you're doing."

As the graphic weaves itself before them, Amanda sees the slender threads of humanity's first two million years grow to become the first neolithic communities, then weave an ever more complex tapestry as civilisations emerge and cities arise. The spectral hues glow and reflect a jewelled brilliance, as the graphic expands to surround them. So many lives, each positioned in time and place, in social interaction and achievements of mind and spirit, their familial links and economic activities all registered in hundreds of layers of detail, from broadest eras and social trends to the greatest moments of individual experience. Histories of ideas, events, alternates and confirmations, compositions and speculations. The composers of Cornucopia, Amanda among the demigods. Time is paramount, the great scalar of birth to death that defines the boundaries of life and those peaks of experience and insight when each individual reaches the high points and low points of their being in the world. He's showing off. Amanda doesn't mind. She'll listen until he tells her something he shouldn't. People always do. That was one of the first lessons she'd learned when starting out as a researcher.

Smithson flips to the bio-genetic view, great plagues cutting abruptly through swathes of society, advancements in science and medicine breaking the long rhythms of epidemiology. A sudden densening of the traces as infant mortality falls and women no longer die in childbirth. Then the dramatic scythe of climate change leads to the abrupt displacement of millions into the catacombs.

"There are seventy versions of this representation and in twenty, the cogi-sapi divide seems never to take hold," Smithson explains, "A further thirty five show a quiet mingling of the populations, but fifteen descriptions lead to a complex bifurcation and two great plaits of experience that either wrap themselves closely one around the other, or spread into two opposing sheets, great planes of potential conflict, the membranes of existence."

"Find the common ground Amanda. That's your challenge. You've done it often enough in the History Room, now apply your experience on a completely different scale. Work from the present, here and try to untie the contrast between future and past."

Amanda looks into the future and sees how the geometry of the model has been curled and folded by kernels of energy arising at great divides in history centuries before, the emergence of Islam, the Miasma, the end of Rome coinciding with the growth of Christianity, Confucian thought, Luther, the Maladroits and Hives, the discovery of bronze and its revival in the twenty first.

Then she retraces, stripping away layer after layer of convolution. It takes her three hours of estimate and guesswork to reveal sixteen cables of brilliant hue that flow in long streams without interference between them.

"It took my team a lot longer to get there," says Smithson, when Amanda steps back to see the pattern she has discovered. "We think of this as a preferred model. Now take your calculation and apply it to the other variations."

Amanda follows his suggestion and calls up each of the seventy versions of the programme in succession. The distortions are stunning. Twisting spirals, loops, folds, knots and contortions, zig-zags and tangents, great tangles of confusion, inversions and splays of dissociation. There are rainbows filled with unknown hues.

"But what do they represent?" she asks, all I can see are patterns based on patterns, there's no notion of what's driving these alternatives."

"We have all asked ourselves a similar question about the nature of divergence," Smithson agrees. "And there's no simple answer anyone can find. We don't really know which outcome might be preferable. Who can guess what people will do in future lives?"

"Then what's the point?"

"Maybe to uncover the goal of Miasmatics," Smithson smiles gnomishly. "And an answer to the question, what do we really want?"

"The answer to that has always been obvious. You don't need all this to answer it," Amanda replies. "Whenever people get what they want, five minutes later they want something else. People crave choice."

Fred Q. considers her comment for a moment and decides to revisit the proposition on some later occasion. Choices and cravings. Cravings and choice. A selection of opportunities and opportune selections. A business rhetoric, the terminology is pleasantly asymmetrical, one of the first indicators of potential market potency.

"The main applications, of course, are the games we develop

for each season's Occi Fest," Smithson explains, "and there are then the political forecasts used in marketing – the Tewkesbury System that you know all about."

"So what do you expect me to do?" Amanda asks again, smiling sweetly.

"Quite simple really, the choice of methods is entirely your own, but the goal is very very simple and straightforward."

"Quentin, for God's sake tell me what you want?"

"Your challenge has been defined within the framework of 'Global Harmony'," Smithson announces formally. "There has always been some doubt, reflected in the patterns of 'All Known History' and the records of court proceedings at the time, whether Eric Selby really murdered Jim Tewkesbury on that fateful night on the Royal Yacht Britannia. In the worst editions of 'All Known Futures' there is some suggestion that Tewkesbury resumed his activities after the voyage, but those versions of human history all end in utter disaster, war, destruction, mass extinctions. Some versions even imply the ship was a modest pleasure boat and they were near Venice not the Isle of Skye. Unless something can can be done, the future will be terrible. I have concluded that your task is to ensure that Tewkesbury dies at the appointed place and the appointed time."

"Surely, it's not all Tewkesbury's fault?"

"No, not all, but his death, or the lack of it is one of a very small number of common factors we have discovered between the different versions of humanity. Ensure that he really dies and you will be securing the well-being of billions. What I'm trying to say is if push comes to shove, then shove, though I think a more elegant approach may be simply to ensure Selby's resentment grows to a point where he is adequately motivated to do the job voluntarily – a suicide, selfish oblivion. God, how I wish that were really the case, but no, he's tenaciously indestructible, so someone will have to do the dirty deed and

301

kill him, make sure he's dead, stone dead, once and for all."

"I see," says Amanda cautiously, "but how am I expected to step back in time and make sure Tewkesbury dies?"

"We have created some tools to help you."

"Such as?"

"There are some rather beautiful pictures we can let you have, they were recently recovered in the South of France."

"Pictures?"

"You will learn how to make the best use of them."

"It doesn't seem to be much to be going on with."

"We have also created a character for you to embody and embroider as you think fit. An attractive female, whose trail has already created confusion in the work of your colleagues from the History Room."

"Again?"

"Yes, we want you to become the mystery woman you've all been researching and make things happen. It's an amazing opportunity."

Amanda realises Smithson is gazing into her eyes, an adoring expression masking his cynicism.

"Dear Amanda, you can become Mona in the life of Eric Selby and the death of Jim Tewkesbury."

An extraordinary sense of loneliness surges through Amanda's mind.

"Mona is a latent force in world history. You embody a role of unsurpassable influence, one which can decide the fate of all mankind.

Thanks to Barbara Happle's research and experimentation, we are able to offer you two contrasting 'modus operandi', either in the form of your data set, or, as you see yourself now, in the form we like to call your 'animal self'. Accept the challenge and you will go to Vienna in search of a man called Moses Hoffman, who will be able directly and indirectly to bring you in contact with Eric Selby. This Hoffman was designated 'character' at our Ceremony. Seek him out, find where he has been hiding. Discover the circumstances. After that, you may choose to do as you think fit, but don't forget your goal.

My Dear Amanda, we know that humanity has a past, though the details are far sketchier than 'All Known History' suggests and the archaeologists can be of no more help. They have scraped the planet clean. Selinsky confirmed that much in the archive. Memories are no longer being shared and passed from one generation to another. People assume that the 'known' is somehow all there is to be known. We no longer have a history which can be unearthed, we only have 'All Known History' which is completely fictional in its construction and smoothed for computability. We have destroyed the historic contradictions in the search for functionality. Joe Smather's work on the Cogi gene has brought us no further forward. Please accept this challenge, to ensure we have a desirable future, a viable future, some kind of worthwhile future at all."

"How long will this take?"

"A few days, perhaps weeks. It may be an eternal struggle like the age old battles between good and evil."

"Hmmmm," says Amanda. "I'll see what I can do. But don't expect too much. I'm sorry, but I don't think this is going to work." She thinks she ought to have been able to find some finer phrases, but she can't. No doubt suitably memorable phrases will be concocted when they get around to writing up her histories. Amanda suspects that once Smithson has had her play Mona, he'll come up with some other figure of fascination for her to play around with, the Queen of Sheba, Joan Austen, Abigail Newton, Jack Kennedy, Jacqui Clinton - the list is potentially endless.

"Thank-you, my dear, now off you go and enjoy yourself. Your inaugural Cornucopia party shouldn't be missed. There are lots of pleasures waiting for you out there, go and enjoy life."

Smithson smiles and gazes quietly out of the window. She's on her way now. Is there really a possibility that Amanda, as Mona, will be able to save the Miasma's nascent progenitor from Tewkesbury's destructive geriatric madness? If Mona really does rescue SemInt, the Semantic League of Interaction, then the seeds will have been set from which the Miasma grew and Smithson will assume Tewkesbury's role in 'All Known History', of that she is sure and with that the reputation of Cornucopia should remain intact. First Amanda has to ask herself whether she wants Mona to succeed. She must exercise free will! Smithson hadn't concerned himself about that. He had blithely assumed that Amanda as Mona would do his bidding. Mona's first conscious thought had nothing to do with Smithson and his motives, she simply asks herself to define the virtues of negation, a particularly Viennese proposition. It is going to be a close run thing, but Smithson has convinced himself that SemInt will be saved by Mona´s interventions, the Miasma both was and will be created and with it, the Miasma´s successor will come into being, however hard the Cogi's struggle to oppose it.

For Smithson there will only be one question that really interests him: 'Does he really care?'

He´s seen it all before, hasn't he?

Present perfect, future past, all a question of recreation and a perspective dependent on those versions of the past that might conceivably have a future.

But it's such fun playing God! The temptations are irresistable!

Outside, the ice is still accumulating and sea levels are falling. Soon, the Mediterranean will begin to dry. Venice is already surrounded by parched acres of brick hard baking mud. The last stragglers from Vancouver are being rounded up, before a wall of water breaks through the developing ice barrier and crashes through the American mid-west to create the great torrent tracks of devastation, before the final freeze up.

Chicago becomes impossible.

Milwaukee ceases and New Orleans is swept into the Gulf of Mexico by four days of continuous devastating flood.

The Rockies are beginning to crumble and the Tokyo quake storm has begun to rumble.

In Paris and New York, the autumn and winter collections feature homespun cloths of Quaker inspiration. Combing for cashmere is the newest fad among the fashionistas. Goats are a status symbol as Lisa had always expected.

The reconstituted landbridge between England and France means Great Britain is no longer an island. The Second Battle of Hastings is the bloodiest instance of hand to hand fighting ever known.

When the Aleutians are warned of an impending tsunami, Arizona is simultaneously evacuated. The last bulk carriers leave port and are anchored in deep water for safety. They may come in useful eventually if there's a concerted effort to rescue the Balaban relics.

High on the altiplano, Bill Smather is de-dogging ferals when he hears Smithson's news and immediately he breaks off the hunt and leaves to warn Nesta.

"They've taken the drawings," he tells her, as they sit under the star studded night-sky of Provence. "That idiot Smithson has fallen for the bait."

The moon has risen and as Nesta gazes at the blinking lights of Lunar City3, she smiles, concluding there is just a chance that everything will be alright.

The battle has begun.

Victory will be decisive.

When the final traces of Moses Hoffman's mind are erased from the record, the War will be over and at long last, the History of Humanity will draw to its inevitable close, as one by one the1 hives shut down and the energies of the Miasma dissipate like mist on a summer morning as the sun comes out.

It didn't take very long at all.

Their history was behind them.

Amanda was convinced she'd said them first, or at least put the phrase into writing when she sent a greeting card to accompany the baby Burgundy goats who became the foundation of Lisa's famous herd, but the Multilingual Dictionary of Quotations eventually credited Nesta as originating the most popular phrase of the new millenium.

"Who needs all this network shit anyway.[120]"

---

120 See page20 .

APPENDIX 1

The General Agreement on People and Characters.

To access the appropriate text, please select the version you require (person, species, or character, entity and epoch), then enter your unique identifier and geographic status (subterranean, terrestrial, extraterrestrial, marine):
xxxx x xxx x x xxxx

S T E M
A record of your application will be maintained at the Central Criminal Court, Rangoon and may be used against you as evidence and probably will.

EVEN BREAK WARNING: Choose carefully, sucker.

Appendix A

The Tewkesbury Conjecture.

The Natural World has no economy.

There is no abstract process of evaluation and exchange, no external mechanism of negotiation to avert a particular outcome of events.

A seed that falls on barren land will not flourish.

A plant that grows on fertile soil may bear fruit and new generations may follow.

Account for the complexity that arises from the interaction of millions of species across the earth and we reach the Biblical conclusion that the natural world is subject to the random processes now known as "natural selection".

Humanity, by contrast, embraces all kinds of negotiation as a key component of social cohesion.

The unfortunate may seek to improve their conditions, by negotiation with the more favoured.

The fortunate may seek to extend the duration of their advantage by negotiation to appease the less privileged.

Negotiation is neither an agreement between equals, nor a neutral process of arbitration. The alternatives to negotiation are all unattractive:

Crime, (see From Pilfering to Piracy, Tewkesbury 2020),

Stagnation (see: Immobility and Downturns, Tewkesbury 2019),

or

Open Conflict, (see: Boom, Bang and Bust, Tewkesbury (2021) and The Economic Consequences of the Peace, J.M. Keynes, 1919).

The main tool for negotiation is language, but the necessity of completing millions of seemingly standardised transactions on a daily basis creates the illusion of a "market" in which exchange values and prices appear to be determined, as if by a self-governing mechanism of market forces, a delusion.

This process eschews language and action in favour of symbols and the process of quantification enables sophisticated propositions to be made and incorporated within functioning algorithms, obscuring the basic character of transactions as negotiated events. There is no such thing as a free market, just as there is no such thing as a negotiation without advantage and disadvantage.

There is however, a perceived market, or rather a series of markets, in which actual transactions are conducted on a generalised basis, both as direct decisions to acquire, or dispose of goods and as indirect decisions to buy and sell to achieve a material advantage within the perceived framework of the market as a sustainable model. Market perception is a social human activity subject to technological abstraction and subsequent technocratic development. This substantiates the illusion of market coherence. Empty abstractions give rise to material worth.

The profound separation between human society and the natural world is such that the majority of human beings are ignorant of the most basic requirements for their individual survival, though they seek to inhabit inhospitable environments in which their basic needs could never be fulfilled without a complete dependence on goods and services from outside. Indeed most human beings would not know whether a particular location could fulfil the fundamental habitat requirements of access to food, water, shelter and clothing.

Left alone on a tropical island, a typical human has less affinity with their surroundings than a polyp on the coral reef that surrounds it. Traditional knowledge, for example, the understanding of medicinal properties of plants, has been almost completely lost among all those who are unfamiliar with pharmaceuticals. Humanity has prioritised the specialisation of individual skills and created an extraordinary dependence on the production, distribution and consumption of goods and services within systems of payment and exchange defined within the perceived market. Most individuals would only approach a tropical island having purchased services within a well defined system of transport and accommodation catering both for their basic needs and illusory whims.

The algorithmic nature of the perceived market ensures that patterns of advantage and disadvantage may be deeply embedded and obscured from view. The majority of actual transactions are denuded of any negotiating factors with respect to price and none with respect to availability. There is no guarantee of supply, or access to available stocks of goods, whatever the world's leaders might proclaim.

Arbitrary intervention to redefine the parameters of the market algorithmic are extremely common and straightforward to implement. Untoward events may interrupt trade, or undermine the valuation of a business. Taxes may be imposed without prior warning. These are a normal part of everyday business processes.

Less often, a new concept is accepted into the framework for trade and business development, which will allow certain decisions to be explained and action taken. Such market concepts are key elements enabling and legitimising arbitrary interventions. A decision to float exchange rates, or maintain fixed parity between currencies needs underpinning by a series of propositions that the financial community will accept. Practices such as slavery may be deemed illegal. Practices such as charging interest on loans may be forbidden, or permitted. The threat of fines, or imprisonment, for ignoring or evading such provisions ensures a degree of compliance. In all such cases, economic theory is called upon to justify change and to overcome the reticence of those with entrenched interests. That is, to effect change in order to overcome a failure in the compressed processes of negotiation. (see: "Off with His Head – Reforming Monarchs in Medieval Europe", Tewkesbury, PhD Thesis, 1982, St. Albans Poly)

Economic Theory is therefore a theory of nothing, yet a powerful tool by which to move intransigent market functionaries and to effect a change in the algorithmic character of the perceived market behaviour, theory as marketing, no more and no less. Economic Theory is a persuasive tool, with no claim to scientific authority. Economics is a misnomer for marketing. The "economic" domain arises only when the boundary of self-sufficiency has been surpassed. Therefore for any individual, or organisation which defines itself as a business within the framework of the market, self-sufficient individuals are uneconomic. (see: "Lionising Liars – A History of the Nobel Prize for Economics and its Prize Winners" Tewkesbury 2024, & Confessions of an Imposing Imposter, Tewkesbury, 2031).

For a contrary opinion see, J.K. Maidsley's "Blithering Idiot – the Blatherings of an Erudite Con-man", (2040) The Nixon Press, Old Shrubbery, Texas.

A summary of the debate can be found in Chapter 17 of Maidley's memoir "From Distinguished to Extinguished – Barbara Happle in life and death." (2054) Clinton Press, Old Shrubbery, New Mexico.

JOHN CLARK

Appendix B

The Criminality of Eric Selby.
from "SELBY – A Traitor in Our Midst" Robinson, Ann W., Tyburne Verlag, Dordrecht, 2085.

„Four men on horseback burst into the fashion show and took out Hamish O'Kelly, Sir Julian Malpas, Anne-Marie de la Tour and fifty other guests and members of Balkin's entourage. The carnage was over in half a minute. Many of the models busy preening themselves on the catwalk assumed the attack was a pre-planned stunt by designer Molly Balkin and failed to take cover as the bullets began to fly. Some even stepped into the line of fire, hoping to be featured in the ensuing marketing campaign. Hence the very high proportion of casualties. Balkin herself escaped serious injury, but was then badly scarred in the fire that consumed the building.

Eric Selby was identified as one of the horsemen from the security camera recordings, which were used to assemble a 3-D re-enactment of the atrocity. London Reinsure put a price on his head, but none of the registered bounty hunters were willing to take up the challenge and he remained on his island home and repeatedly denied any involvement in the attack.

The coup was financed by a Brussels based business consortium, ContraMode, who claimed Balkin's associates were running a large scale protection racket in the fashion industry worldwide.

Designers had been forced to pay large sums to ensure their concepts were not hacked and sold to counterfeiters. Even larger sums were said to have been paid to safeguard the stocks of clothes shipped in containers around the world on their way to shops and clothing stores. As the owner of thousands of shipping containers, Sir Julian Malpas was discovered to have promoted protection rackets in dozens of industries from electronics to cigarettes, hitting on companies who used his containers to move their products to market.

Selby and his three fellow horsemen are thought to have been paid $250million each for the attack, though it failed in its primary goal of squashing the protection rackets, which were soon being operated by copycat criminal gangs. The OECD estimated that within three years of the attack, protection rackets were siphoning off approximately 3% of global trade by value. Only the iron ore industry seemed to be immune. The Prosecutors tried as they might to build a case against Selby, but it failed on grounds of lack of evidence and his seemingly foolproof alibi that he was attending a première at the Film Festival in Cannes on the day of the attack.

Within three years Eric Selby bought Malpas' container business and 'took it private', delisting the shares from the London Stock Exchange. This acquisition was rumoured to have been financed with the proceeds of the 'one dollar per child' internet charity scandal.[121]

That same year[122] Selby made a bold attempt to persuade James H. Tewkesbury, Government Advisor and Nobel Prize Winner to work as a consultant for his corporate shell, 'New Money' and its subsidiaries 'Fresh Cash' and the cruise ship 'MS Dosh'. The European Archive of Intercepts and Document Co-ordination Centre confirmed that Tewkesbury rebuffed his approaches, but

---

121 Promoted as a charitable effort by a group of popular musicians, who promised donors to send $1 for relief work per child in developing countries. In practise, the donors, many of them school-children, gave more than $1 and the difference of $780m was pocketed by the organisers in addition to the income from their telephone "hot-line", which was estimated at $480m. The organisers were subsequently banned from administering Charities, but no steps were successful in recovering the funds and no prosecutions were brought.

122 2041 (ed)

rumours remain of a meeting on the Channel Island of Sark that the two men met and agreed to create Semint, or the "Semantic League of Interaction", as it was originally known. The rather murky origins of this pivotal organisation in world affairs has been the subject of intensive research, but nothing has been discovered to suggest that Selby and Tewkesbury were in any way colluding when the League was established. As the myth implies, Tewkesbury worked alone. As its Inspirational Founder, James Tewkesbury had lobbied for a decade to win the support of governments and businesses. Eric Selby was no more than an ordinary subscribing member and the Membership Records confirm he joined at the suggestion of his banker, Janet Mulgrave, from the Union Bank of Savoie (UboS). Her links to Selby's sponsors Braunovsky and Smithovitch have been traced through transactions in Austria relating to consignments of humanitarian aid to Japan on behalf of the United Nations in Vienna, following the Tokyo Bay earthquake, which destroyed much of the city's infrastructure and disrupted communications for more than a year. Selby himself is thought to have taken a standard fee of 5% from the deals, which were all fully reported to the European Banking Authorities. Full Austrian windfall tax (€0,00) was paid on all sums.

The UNO Committee looking into the Japanese Recovery Programmes estimated that over thirty percent of original donations were delivered to the Japanese, an unusually high proportion, compared with the usual donor/beneficiary ratio of 17.5%. Selby's claim that B&S Austria were a more reliable delivery agency than the UNO Bureaucracy led to demands that international aid be privatised.

Ten years passed before 'New Money' was awarded the contract to provide serviced office space and network resources for Semint and by this date Eric Selby is no longer listed as a major shareholder. The only direct connection between Selby and

Tewkesbury at this stage in their careers was an annual conference, to which they both contributed, in the Vatican City. (Ed: The rest of this chapter is devoted to Piracy and the Channel Islands War against the Dutch. It is official policy not to comment on these sad events and the destruction of Jersey – all speculation as to Selby's role is unfounded .)

Oil – Created in 2054, the oil for food programme was set up to barter food from non-oil producing countries in return for supplies of petroleum and diesel. As Chairman, Eric Selby set up the system whereby 48% of the value of the trade was swallowed in administrative costs and a variety surcharges. This became the main source of Selby's ever increasing private wealth, until he relinquished business activities shortly before the Tewkesbury assassination.

Selby-Tewkesbury
"There have been innumerable explanations for the seemingly imprudent relationship James Tewkesbury enjoyed with Eric Selby. None of them are more convincing than the others and my conclusion is simply that the two of them had a strong affinity for one another, which ended in tears, or to be more precise – a splash."
from "SELBY – A Traitor in Our Midst" Robinson, Ann W., Tyburne Verlag, Dordrecht, 2085.

Appendix C

SELBY

With hindsight it was easy to understand why Selby had turned to crime. Born in 1990, he graduated from the Cambridge Institute of Fiscal Prudence only three months before the Swoop became official policy and the unhappy young man saw his career opportunities disintegrate in a matter of weeks.

His grandfather, George Selby, escaped the worst of the Swoop, having sold a comfortable five bedroomed detached house to cash in the equity he had accumulated over a thirty five year career as a bank manager in Ilkley. This Selby patriarch had been born in February 1947 and retired six months before the Swoop began to bite.

The early waves of retirees showed little, or no concern as the collapse in house prices began to avalanche. Of course, George's family home had been worth twenty percent more the previous month, but cash was acquiring a new caché, so he paid off every one of his credit cards and walked away with half a million in folding money. Then he moved to the bungalow in Devon, where he and Desiré had spent their holidays for the previous ten years and had long planned as a base to enjoy their retirement. As prices generally were falling, they were pleasantly surprised that their standard of living improved, rather than diminished as the Swoop began to bite. After George succumbed to a heart attack in the summer of 2012, Desiré found herself enjoying life more than ever. Their first home on the outskirts of Leeds had been bought in 1969 for the princely sum of three thousand pounds with a 50% mortgage and a down payment provided jointly by Desiré's father, a family butcher with three shops in Dewsbury, Wakefield and Goole, and George's father Harry, who had worked for the newly nationalised steel industry as a "Work Study" manager in Rotherham. Never having had reason to doubt their wisdom, the two old men had believed in the value of 'bricks and mortar' to the end of their days.

For George, 'bricks and mortar' had meant a life of dull security. But for his son, Eric's father, Tom, a lifelong Tory, it brought his personal sword of Damocles and Britain's least favourite four letter word, 'debt".

He had climbed on the property bandwagon in the early nineteen eighties and was paying off the last and biggest hike in his mortgage debt and piling on the credit cards when the Swoop bit in. It had been expensive paying to get their children through University.

So, Eric Selby was a child raised on the comfortable brink of personal financial catastrophe and a naive, but sadly mistaken conviction that everything would be alright in the end. The deluge cascaded half of Britain towards insolvency, as a combination of rising interest rates and falling property values brutally reversed their financial standing.

Once the interest rates began to rise, Eric's father Tom was lucky to sell the family home in time to trade down. It was a bitter change in lifestyle, but he still had a job and they had a modest roof over their head. His only cause for celebration was that his much disliked boss was actually forced to flee the country to escape his creditors. Cheerful and benign, Tom Selby set about getting the small garden into some kind of order and found himself a new pub to settle into as a three-pints-of-beer a night 'regular'. His wife Fiona took up knitting and tried to avoid complaining in her long and dreary letters to Eric and his elder sister, Jessica......", from "SELBY – A Traitor in Our Midst" Robinson, Ann W., Tyburne Verlag, Dordrecht, 2085

see also: "Fundamentalist Economics", Schroeder-Schaeuble, Angela & Voularkis, Wladimir, SwabenVerlag, Aachen, 2099.
and
  "Killing for profit, or Killing for Pleasure" - Pope Pauline 2, Vatican Encyclicals, 2100.
or,
"Searching for SemInt – the key to 'All Known History' and the Creation Myths of Miasmatics" - Vol 23: Humanity Net and Infinities, Godhead Data, Online Everywhere – Forever.

Afterword.

'The Swoop' is set three hundred years in the future, though it might as well be three thousand years, or thirty thousand, depending on the pace of tech development, yet it returns to the issues of authenticity and identity arising in the first two volumes of the Moses Hoffman Trilogy from quite a different perspective, that of the historian and a brand of historian who have yet to be defined - the Reconstructionists, who base their research on advanced forms of data mining and virtual experience.

Perhaps the most unusual aspect of this work is not the extremes of climate change, or the genetic changes that form an important aspect of the narrative, but the absence of the main character, who is represented only as a passive source for a massive data set in a memorial library that bears his name, as proposed in the final scene of 'Animal Self'.

One of the greatest weaknesses of fiction is to anticipate short term technical change. Having grown up in the nineteen fifties and sixties, I had fully expected by the year 2020 that there would be super-efficient means of very fast clean transportation that would take people anywhere they wanted to go in the world and we would live in a global society where basic needs such as housing, food and clothing would no longer be an issue and money a redundant and outmoded measure of primitive greed. Well, I was wrong and would expect to be wrong about the changes to expect between 2020 and 2030, but less so about general expectations for the very long term.

When it came to writing 'The Swoop', I was therefore prepared to swap short term expectations for long term assumptions.

With respect to virtual reality, for example, a general virtual space supporting interaction of all kinds is referred to as the Miasma. There's an interesting contrast between 'Interactivity' as a technical characteristic of a system and the actual 'Interaction' involved as people and systems 'interact'. The term interaction has a surprisingly short history, having first been coined by Ed Berman, a US theatre director, whose co-operative 'Inter-action' developed notions of interactivity as social activism with projects like the 'Free Art Bus', 'Almost Free Theatre' leading to the notion of 'social enterprises' and initiatives such as the first 'city farms'.

Had anyone asked me about the development of the internet in the year 2000, I would have pointed optimistically towards projects akin to Berman's social interactivity, rather than the slough of pornography and nurseries of fascist intolerance, online criminality and trafficking experienced over the last decade. I still wonder how much the gaming industry has been responsible for that contrast and the shift towards thinking of interactivity as a measure of agility between user and system.

The odd and often implausible mechanisms leading to massive rewards for individuals rising to prominence through technology had already begin to emerge as I started writing 'The Swoop', whether people like Elon Musk, Kim Dotcom and Mark Zuckerburg, the Google guys, Gates and Jobs,   or business opportunists like UK entrepreneur Richard Branson, the majority were men.

The economic crisis of 2008 had different symptoms to those I had anticipated in my scenario, which was largely based on overinflated asset prices rather than hollow derivatives that actually undermined the world economy.

Jumping ahead several centuries, however, some things seem unlikely to have changed - greed and egoism,   opportunist exploitation and corruption. Presumably the gender imbalance will be resolved. Regrettably the sense that otherwise decent people will be trapped into unethical collaboration seems unavoidable and there is always an uneasy suspicion that many victims unwittingly collaborate in their own downfall.

The intense complexity of social technologies points to one abiding dilemma of good government, the contradiction between competent management of existing arrangements and the need for, or resistance to substantial change. Faced with that kind of challenge traditional notions of representative democracy seem inadequate, yet faith in market mechanisms is blindingly naive. This led to the notion I present of 'indirect democracy' involved 'characters' supposedly representing particular cohorts in society. Have I been surprised by the Snowden revelations, or the emerging surveillance state? Quite frankly, no.

Having seen how technical developments can be planned decades into the future before any public awareness of their implications begins to form, I began to ask myself about the place of elites in societies based on the new technologies and the semblence of representation in a new space defined largely by data mining and analysis resembling the techniques of market research.

Fishing around for a way of assembling a mass of data sufficient to power a system that could sustain a whole society, the easiest cheat seemed to be to decant an existing mind to use as a template for future enhancement and development as part of a general framework of artificial intelligence, so the notion of picking out Moses Hoffman as a potential 'Ur' donor was immediately attractive. Who could be better? His loose relationship with notions of truth and authenticity during his lifetime made him a potent potential source for controversy and confusion among future historians. Yet he is also, supposedly, one of that generation who bridged the era from Cold War to the digital brave new world.

Will Mo get his people to the promised land?

The little group of historians in 'The Swoop' face exactly the same kinds of problems historians of our own period already have to encounter. How reliable are their sources? Is the archive of documentation and information corrupted? Are commonly held assumptions about past events credible? Can people's memories be relied upon? Is there pressure for historic events to be presented and packaged according to certain preferences? The events of 1989 and the collapse of communism have already been mythologised, with preferred accounts embedded as symbolic descriptions of what happened. Our links to those quite recent events are already diminishing as people die, records are lost and memories fail. Is their history a kind of fiction? It is for the reader to conclude which version of events they prefer to take on board.

Following the Moses Hoffman Trilogy, my next projects were less general. 'Ciao Charlie' plays with 'online dating' and opportunistic networking in Trieste, while 'Urban Weather' takes a look at the distant death and destruction business from the perspective of an assassin who turns her skills to weather forecasting from a base in Brussels.

'Gaming with Attitudes' is a Berlin tale, where everyday deceptions and betrayals leave tangled trails of suspicion and mistrust as the unexpected death of a mildly disparaged husband seem to unravel all kinds of bonds exposing fragile webs of friendship and business arrangements that depend on everyone looking the other way, without revealing just how nasty things can get in a world of fragmented online experience.

'The People that Nobody wants to Meet', a new novel for 2020, concerns the way government runs in an era of 'predictive analytics' and the implicit question whether this is really the way people want things to go? Maybe so.

THE SWOOP

Publishing History.

'The Moses Hoffman Trilogy' was originally available in three parts. An earlier version of 'Lone Hunter' was published by the AVINUS Verlag in 2004 as an English edition for German. Early drafts of ANIMAL SELF and The SWOOP were available online at our websites.

Volumes 1 & 2 of The Moses Hoffman Trilogy, 'Lone Hunter' and 'Animal Self' are published with minor revisions and new afterwords as companion volumes to this edition of 'The Swoop' and are available at bookshops and via bod.de/buchshop

Other Works by John Clark

Novels

CIAO CHARLIE (2015)

URBAN WEATHER (2016)

GAMING WITH ATTITUDES (2018)

THE PEOPLE THAT NOBODY WANTS TO MEET (2020)

MOVIE
"WRITERS BLOCK" (2013)

berlinpicturecompany.com

JOHN CLARK

THE AUTHOR

John Clark is a British born writer based in Berlin.